After working mainly for Pearson and Oxford University Press, Keith Mansfield is now a freelance writer and publisher. He has scripted light entertainment shows for TV and also contributed to *The Science of Spying* exhibition at London's Science Museum.

Based on childhood daydreams of being captured by aliens and escaping to see the wonders of the galaxy, this is his first novel. In reality, Keith lives in Spitalfields in the East End of London. Every window of his home looks out onto Norman Foster's beautiful Gherkin . . . or is it the *Spirit of London*?

KEITH MANSFIELD

Quercus

First published in Great Britain in 2008
This paperback edition first published in 2009 by

Quercus
21 Bloomsbury Square
London
WC1A 2NS

A CIP catalogue reference for this book is available
from the British Library.

ISBN 978 1 84724 774 2

10 9 8 7 6 5 4 3 2 1

Designed and typeset by Rook Books, London
Printed and bound in Great Britain by Clays Ltd, St Ives plc

For Luke and Ross, hoping the stars call you both ✰ ✦

Kovac Finds a Signal ✧ ✦

The twenty-third of April was a very special day in the life of Johnny Mackintosh – it was his thirteenth birthday, although he hadn't told anybody. The last thing he wanted was to be given the bumps by Spencer Mitchell and the rest. And Johnny was even happier than most boys would be on becoming a teenager, having just helped his football team to victory in the semifinals of the Essex Schools Cup. In fact, today was also another anniversary, but one that he'd forgotten – it was exactly eleven years to the day since he'd come to live at Halader House, a children's home located at 33 Barnard Way, Castle Dudbury New Town. But it was none of these things that made the twenty-third of April really special – that was because of the flashing green light leaking out from underneath the ill-fitting door to the computer room of Halader House.

As chance would have it, Johnny Mackintosh, carrying a red sports bag over his left shoulder, was walking along a windowless corridor towards this very room. He was covered head to toe in mud, from beneath his pale blond hair, around his dark green eyes (with striking silver flecks), across his once-white football shirt, spattering his black shorts and almost totally obscuring his white socks. Any bits of skin not concealed by mud, which were very few, were so pale they looked almost blue. Lolloping along beside him, leaving muddy paw prints on the beige carpet, was a particularly shaggy grey and white Old

English sheepdog with a long fringe completely masking his eyes.

Johnny walked past the door in question and continued on his way to the shower room. The sheepdog, however, stopped and began sniffing around its base. Then he lifted his head, turned towards Johnny and barked.

'Bentley – shhhhhh!' hissed Johnny. 'Come on – before someone sees you inside.'

The dog's only response was to turn his head and point his little black nose towards the gap at the foot of the door and bark again.

'Bents – we haven't got time for this.' Johnny shook his head in a manner that suggested he was used to Bentley disobeying his instructions. He stomped back up the corridor towards the dog, knelt down and lifted Bentley's fringe so he could stare straight into the dog's one brown and one blue eye. 'Listen, Bents. If you get caught inside again I'm for it.' Bentley didn't want to listen. Instead, he pulled his head away and barked at the door. Only then did Johnny notice the green glow coming from underneath it. He straightened up and tried turning the handle, but the door was locked. By the side of the handle was a reader for magnetic swipe cards. Johnny banged it with frustration and, to his surprise, there was a soft click. He tried the handle again and the door opened. Bentley scampered inside and Johnny followed.

The reason for the green glow was immediately apparent. On each of the eight computer screens positioned around a large central table were the same two words, displayed in blinking green text against a black background. They read:

SIGNAL DETECTED

Johnny sat down at one of the terminals and entered a sequence of numbers and letters. Bentley placed his front legs on the table, covering the surface in muddy paw prints, and lifted his face up so he, too, could stare at the screen. The display changed. The text was replaced by two green wireframe globes, one of which had the outlines of the continents superimposed on top of it. 'It can't be,' Johnny muttered to himself as he stared open-mouthed at the image in front of him. 'Kovac,' he said, but before he could continue there was a sharp pain in his left ear as a thumb and forefinger closed around it and he was yanked upwards out of the chair.

'Gotcha!'

As a reflex action, Johnny hit the escape button on the keyboard, and the displays of all eight of the computers on the table transformed so that a drawing of a very large, bearded man, wearing a puffed-up white hat, began bouncing around like a rubber ball. To make matters worse, the cartoon face of an Old English sheepdog appeared right in the middle of each screen and opened its mouth. Instead of a bark, out popped a speech bubble with the words 'Mr Wilkins stinks.' At the time it had seemed a laugh to make this the default screensaver on each of the Halader House computers. Now Mr Wilkins, the bearded Halader House cook, was holding Johnny by his increasingly reddening earlobe, it didn't seem quite so funny. Johnny tried to wriggle free, but only succeeded in burying his face in the folds of the cook's flabby stomach. Mr Wilkins's tiny, beetle-like eyes were staring at the nearest screen from beneath his curly black hair and his round face was becoming redder and redder, as though about to explode.

'That's the last straw, sonny,' said the cook, thrusting his curly beard right into Johnny's face so it tickled. 'We're going to see the Manager. This time she's got to see sense. Oh yes.' The huge man attempted to march Johnny out of the room, but Bentley took hold of the hem of Mr Wilkins's elasticated blue trousers with his teeth. The Old English sheepdog was dragged along the carpet behind them towards the door. Mr Wilkins kicked out his leg, swinging Bentley's head to and fro as the dog growled and something ripped. Both Bentley and a piece of Mr Wilkins's trousers had become detached. Finally outside, Mr Wilkins began pushing Johnny down the corridor, keeping a very tight hold on his ear.

With Bentley barking right behind them, Mr Wilkins stopped, rolled up his trouser leg to reveal a chunky calf and said, 'Come on, you filthy horrible little dog.' Johnny knew exactly what the cook was trying to do. Mr Wilkins had been at Halader House for as long as Johnny could remember and, throughout that time, seemed set on a one-man mission to have Bentley permanently removed from the establishment – without, or preferably with, Johnny. The cook was always reminding Johnny that the special permission to let him keep the dog could be cancelled at any moment. And it was sure to be the moment Bentley sank his teeth into Mr Wilkins's exposed skin.

Luckily, Bentley seemed to sense Johnny's desperation and backed off. He followed, growling, as Mr Wilkins forced Johnny past the kitchens, up a flight of stairs and all the way along another corridor to a dark wooden door with a brass doorknob and matching brass plate, on which were written the words 'Manager's Office.'

The cook rapped excitedly on the door and a woman's voice shouted, 'Come in.' As Johnny opened the door, Mr Wilkins released his earlobe and pushed him inside, closing the door quickly behind them to keep Bentley on the other side. Johnny stumbled forward into the spotless office, showering some dried mud onto the wooden floor. Johnny hated this room. It was where you were sent if you were in trouble and with Johnny that was pretty much all the time. He couldn't help it – things always seemed to happen around him.

The room was large, lit by a window taking up the entire far wall and which looked out across a grey tarmac carpark to Castle Dudbury railway station. Near the door stood a little round wood-effect table and four chairs. Around the walls were several framed black and white photographs of scruffy children playing barefoot in run-down terraced streets. In front of the window was a large wood-effect desk, either side of which stood floor-to-ceiling bookshelves jam-packed with large tomes in dusty thick black covers. And behind the desk sat a woman with pointy silver glasses and black and grey streaky hair. She wore an ancient tiger-striped dress, with a pearl necklace and matching earrings, and followed Johnny's progress into the room with round owl-like eyes.

'Mr Wilkins, to what do I owe the pleasure?' she asked in a clipped Scottish accent, hardly moving her narrow lips.

'Mrs Irvine, it's the boy,' said the cook, shifting his enormous bulk from foot to foot with excitement.

'So I see, Mr Wilkins. But why, as you put it, is "the boy" in my office? And so dirty . . .' Mrs Irvine looked Johnny up and down with a disapproving stare. He looked down at his socks and concentrated very hard on not spreading any more mud than he could help on the floor.

'Broke into the computer room, didn't he? I came back from the butcher's and followed his filthy mutt's paw prints all the way from main reception.' Johnny knew he shouldn't have let Bentley come inside with him. So that was how he'd been found so quickly. 'And then the dog bit me,' continued Mr Wilkins, holding up his tattered trouser leg.

'That's not true,' shouted Johnny. 'Bentley's never bitten anyone.'

Mrs Irvine turned her large round eyes back to Mr Wilkins. 'Is it true?' she asked.

'Well – he nearly bit me,' said the cook, his face turning red again. 'I'm telling you – that mutt's got to go. It's not hygienic.'

5

'Come, Mr Wilkins,' said the Manager. 'Surely, after all this time, we all have a soft spot for Bentley?'

Johnny let out a long deep breath – Bentley was going to be OK.

'Well the boy should be punished. Breaking in like that.'

Mrs Irvine leant forward, staring at Johnny, but then her gaze wandered to the mud on the floor. Johnny couldn't help thinking she seemed more bothered by the dirt than the computer room. After a few seconds, she turned to the cook and asked, 'What would you suggest?'

Johnny could picture himself peeling potatoes for the next month. Mr Wilkins stepped closer to the desk. 'No trip for him tomorrow. Let him stay here. My oven could do with a scrub down.'

Tomorrow was the annual Halader House outing. Everyone was going on the train to visit the Tower of London. Johnny had really been looking forward to it.

'Hmmm.' Mrs Irvine sat back in her chair and sucked her lips together, contemplating Johnny's fate. Then she looked at him and said, 'All right – I'm afraid there'll be no visit to the Tower. Jonathan – I expected better of you than using the computer room without permission.' Johnny felt about a foot tall. He hated being told off. 'But I can't have you staying here on your own. I had a journalist on the phone this morning sniffing around for another salacious story. Naturally, I got rid of him, but it's started me thinking. When did you last visit your mother?'

'What?' asked Johnny, caught off guard by the question.

'Your mother,' repeated Mrs Irvine. 'Your care plan says you should see her at least twice a year.'

'It's OK,' said Johnny. 'I can stay here. I don't mind cleaning the oven.' Although he couldn't go to the Tower, with the others away, at least he'd be able to spend some time in the computer room undisturbed. He hadn't seen his mum for at least a year now – visiting her had become unbearable. Anything was better than another trip to St Catharine's Hospital for the Criminally Insane, where she was only kept alive by a collection of high-tech machines around her bedside.

'Good idea, Miss. Why don't I take him?' said Mr Wilkins, his bushy beard twitching with anticipation. 'Can't go on his own can he?' Mr Wilkins never missed an opportunity to inflict misery on the children, but Johnny was his special favourite.

There was a knock on the door and, before anyone could speak, in walked a young woman only a little taller than Johnny. She was slightly out of breath, with red hair cut into a bob and wearing jeans and a T-shirt. She stepped between Johnny and Mr Wilkins, walked right up to the desk and asked, in an American accent, 'Is everything OK, Mrs Irvine?'

'Miss Harutunian,' replied the Manager. 'I am aware that you're new to Ben Halader House and people behave differently where you come from. I, however, am accustomed to members of staff waiting outside my door until I invite them to enter. For your information, everything is fine.' Mrs Irvine was the only person Johnny knew who used the building's full title. She leaned forward towards Miss Harutunian, who didn't look the least bit embarrassed. 'Because Jonathan broke into the computer room earlier, he won't be coming with us to the Tower tomorrow. Instead, Mr Wilkins has kindly volunteered to take him to see his mother in hospital.'

'But that's awful,' said Miss Harutunian, turning to the cook. 'You were busy all afternoon making those packed lunches – you can't *not* go. I'll take Johnny instead.' Johnny could have sworn Miss Harutunian gave him a little wink. She'd only been at Halader House a couple of weeks but already she was his favourite social worker.

'I'm not sure that's such a good idea, missy. You don't know what he's capable of. Like father like son – that's what I say.' As he spat the words out Mr Wilkins thrust his beard forward towards Johnny, who felt its bristles brush the top of his head.

Miss Harutunian folded her arms. 'Where I come from we judge children by their own actions – not those of their parents.'

'His mum was in on it too – I say it's bad genes.'

'Mr Wilkins,' said Mrs Irvine, rising from her chair and walking around the desk. 'Miss Harutunian is quite right. And it makes perfect sense for her to accompany Jonathan tomorrow – far better to see for herself than simply read a case file.' The cook looked as though Christmas had just been cancelled. 'Now if you all don't mind I do have work to be getting on with.' She ushered all three of them out of the office, half closed the door, and then opened it again to add, 'Jonathan – if any more journalists start asking questions about your family, I want you to come and tell me at once. Is that clear?'

Johnny nodded. Bentley was waiting for him outside, wagging his tail. Mr Wilkins pulled Johnny close and whispered in his ear, 'I'm short of meat this month, sonny. I'd keep a close eye on that dog if I were you.' Then he pushed Johnny away and stomped off down the corridor.

Miss Harutunian was kneeling down, stroking the sheepdog. 'You get yourself cleaned up,' she said to Johnny, 'and I'll take Bentley outside before he gets into any more trouble.'

'OK,' said Johnny. 'And thanks.' He gave Bentley a pat on the head and ran off towards the shower room, his bag swinging behind him.

☆   ☆   ☆
☆   ☆

Relatively clean, wearing jeans and a black T-shirt with a faded NASA logo, Johnny entered the common room. He walked straight over to the television, fixed to a bracket on the wall. A music video was playing, while a few children and adults were scattered around, chatting on the various battered sofas different people had donated to the home. Making sure no one was looking, Johnny took a little box from out of his jeans pocket and quickly hid it behind the old satellite decoder underneath the television. He'd built the box himself – although the satellite subscription had long since lapsed, it caused the picture to change into the buildup for a big football match. At the same time, a blue spark leapt unexpectedly from the decoder and Johnny cried out. Quite a few people looked round and, seeing the football, stayed watching as Johnny moved away from the screen, rubbing his hand. The oldest boy in the room, wearing a hooded top and combat trousers, got up and joined Johnny near the TV. 'How'd you do that, Mackintosh?' he asked. 'Didn't think we could get the footie.'

'It's easy,' Johnny replied. 'They scramble the signal with fractal algorithms. I'll show you some time, Spencer.'

'Nice one,' said Spencer. 'You win today?'

'Yeah – three–one,' Johnny replied. 'It was one–all most of the game. Then Dave Spedding got a header from my free kick. We scored the last on the break at the end.'

'Nice one,' said Spencer again. He nodded at Johnny and went back to his gang on the settee.

England were playing tonight. And, best of all, Johnny saw Mr Wilkins was already sitting up, filling one of the sofas on his own and giving the buildup to the match his full attention.

'Over here, Mackintosh,' said Spencer, pushing a ripped leather sofa with lots of foam oozing from its insides, right in front of the television.

'In a minute,' said Johnny. 'Just got to get something.' Johnny hated the thought of missing the match – it was a really important game. But it wasn't as important as what he'd seen on the computer screen earlier. The television was getting its signal from a satellite up in space; what Johnny had programmed the Halader House computers to do was also to search for signals from space – but much further out. They weren't looking for satellite signals – they were after messages from extraterrestrials. He'd hacked into a network of radio telescopes and was busy searching for messages in the background noise while the telescopes themselves scanned the heavens for other things. It seemed he'd found something and he could hardly wait to go and investigate.

All his life Johnny had loved the stars. On some nights when he lay gazing up at them it almost felt as if they were calling out to him, whispering his name across the vastness of space. He knew loads of their names and could easily point to Shedir, Procyon or Betelgeuse, or any of the constellations they helped make up – in their case Cassiopeia, Canis Minor and Orion. He knew how stars evolved, and how they sometimes died. One of the things he loved was that he, like everyone, was made of starstuff. The only place in the universe where heavy atoms could be made was at the centre of a star, and only when that star died and then exploded, going nova – sometimes supernova – could those atoms travel across space. Five billion years ago some of that starstuff had come together and formed the Earth. Five billion years later it had come together to form Johnny. And for as long as he could remember Johnny knew he wanted to return to the stars from where he came.

Johnny turned into the computer room corridor and saw someone was already waiting outside the door. It was Bentley. The dog got to his feet and barked the moment Johnny came round the corner. Johnny's legs were now really stiff after the semifinal earlier, but he quickened his stride until he reached his friend. 'How did you get back here?' he said to the dog, who barked again. Johnny put a finger to his lips and, this time, the dog fell silent. The card reader must be faulty – it had opened before. Johnny placed his thumb and forefinger either side, but pulled them sharply away as he felt an electric shock. Still, at least the lock had clicked open. Gingerly, he turned the handle. Bentley shot straight inside and Johnny followed, closing the door quietly. He decided against turning on the lights, walked over to the master computer terminal and sat down.

What happened next would have amazed anyone from Halader House who regularly used the computer room. Instead of the terminal booting up in the normal way, Johnny deftly diverted it into a separate operating system he'd written for it himself that was much more efficient. And a lot more fun.

'Good evening, Johnny,' came a slightly flat mechanical voice from out of the computer's speakers.

'Kovac – volume minimal,' Johnny replied, as though a talking computer was the most normal thing in the world. Kovac was Johnny's special invention and stood for Keyboard Or Voice-Activated Computer, as well as sounding like a Russian footballer which Johnny thought was cool – especially because underneath his bed Johnny kept a box with a few bits and pieces that had belonged to his parents. One was his dad's journal about a trip he'd taken to somewhere in Russia. 'Kovac – signal detection reported. Show findings.'

'Data incomplete – partial location vector available,' said Kovac, projecting some complex graphics onto the screen with a stylized Earth at the centre.

'Partial? No!' Johnny banged the table in frustration. If there was a signal, maybe even a message, he couldn't pinpoint it properly without more data. He looked at the screen for a little while, thinking. Where could he try?

'Kovac – activate Very Large Array, New Mexico.'

'Unable to comply,' was the computer's response.

'What?' Johnny exclaimed. 'Kovac – define "unable to comply".'

'Security codes overridden,' said Kovac.

That had never happened before. Johnny tried again. 'Kovac – activate Very Large Array, New Mexico. Full security override.'

'Unable to comply,' said Kovac again.

'Why not?' Johnny said, becoming impatient.

'Warning . . . warning.' Kovac's screen had switched to a two-dimensional map of the Earth that had a fine red line growing out of New Mexico and heading east across the United States. 'Backwards trace initiated,' said the computer.

'Kovac – run trace decoy program,' said Johnny quickly, glad he'd coded such a thing without ever expecting to use it. The red line on the computer screen turned north towards Canada and stopped somewhere near Montreal.

He decided not to try again straight away. Someone was apparently onto him and Johnny suspected Mrs Irvine would be far from happy if a member of the CIA came knocking on the door of Halader House in deepest Essex.

'Kovac – display signal detection results,' he said and the screen returned to the earlier visual. Johnny looked at it, studying the criss-crossing lines radiating from points representing telescopes on Earth and cross-checking it with data scrolling down the side of the display. This was certainly odd, and not at all what he expected. In fact this was much better. Since Johnny had programmed Kovac to check for signals from space there had been a few interesting results – things that Johnny couldn't explain. But all of them were pretty much as he'd expected in that they were from a long way away – a spike or two in the background signal from the direction of the galactic centre, or out on a spiral arm somewhere. Why Kovac hadn't been able to get a fix in this case was that it was all so near to home. The signal had moved across the sky so quickly it had to be somewhere within the Earth–Moon orbit, or travelling faster than light, and Johnny knew enough about physics to know that wasn't possible.

Bentley licked Johnny's ear. It broke Johnny's concentration but alerted him to footsteps coming along the corridor. He whispered, 'Kovac – camouflage mode,' and instantly the screen went blank. Whoever it was had stopped right outside the computer room door. Johnny grabbed hold of Bentley's collar and dragged the dog across the floor to just beside the door. He only just got there in time as it was flung open, but he managed to grab the handle to stop it swinging back behind whoever had come in. The lights flickered on and heavy footsteps walked over to the computer table.

'I've got him this time,' somebody muttered – it was Mr Wilkins. It sounded as though he'd pulled the chairs away and crawled underneath the table, which was weird, but Johnny didn't dare put his head round the door to check. Instead, he just held the door handle as tightly as his breath and prayed Bentley wouldn't make any noise. The Old English sheepdog seemed to understand how important it was. The sound of Johnny's heart pounding away in his chest, which was almost deafening, became his next worry. Luckily, Mr Wilkins was really clunking around and wheezing loudly. 'That should do it,' said the cook to himself. 'Now we'll know exactly what you're up to, sonny.' There was the sound of chairs being pushed back under the table and footsteps coming towards the door. Johnny let go of the handle as he felt Mr Wilkins take hold of it from the other side. The lights went out and the door clunked shut.

Johnny slid down the wall until he was sitting on the floor next to Bentley, who slathered a long wet tongue over Johnny's face. Tiredness was really beginning to set in now. Johnny crawled along the floor and under the table to see if he could discover what Mr Wilkins had been up to. It was hard finding anything in the dark. He took a handheld games console from out of his pocket and switched it on so the blue screen lit up the underside of the table. He saw it almost at once – a shiny new keylogger was plugged into the back of the master machine. Johnny was almost impressed – every keystroke he typed at the terminal would be recorded on this. It was just a shame for Mr Wilkins that Johnny was using a voice-activated interface.

He clambered out from under the table and went over to the door. Pressing one ear against it, he heard nothing from outside. Silently, he turned the handle and slipped out into the corridor with Bentley. They walked along, up a flight of stairs and turned left down another corridor, then round another corner until they came to a narrow spiral staircase leading up to the white ceiling, where there was a trapdoor with a red 'no entry' sign screwed onto it. Johnny climbed the staircase a little more easily than Bentley, pulled down the door and carried on through into a small room built into the roof space, every square centimetre of its sloping walls covered with posters of space scenes. There was a huge picture of Saturn, one of the International Space Station and another showing all the planets in the solar system together. Once Bentley was inside Johnny pulled on a rope and the door closed shut behind them.

This was Johnny's room. Opposite the trapdoor was a large square window built out of the roof to form a box shape. In front of the window was an old-fashioned chunky radiator. Right in front of the radiator was Johnny's bed, with a box and his red sports bag underneath. Bentley made a beeline for under the bed and curled up in the warmth of the radiator. Against the wall on the left-hand side of the room was a battered chest of drawers with some dirty clothes piled on top.

Johnny heard footsteps on the staircase outside, there was a knock on the trapdoor, it opened and up came Miss Harutunian carrying a steaming mug of hot chocolate. 'Hi Johnny – why weren't you watching the soccer game? Everyone else was there.'

'I'm dead tired,' Johnny replied, yawning for extra effect. 'We had a big match this afternoon.'

'OK. Well I just wanted to tell you we're going into London with the others tomorrow so it's half-seven for breakfast in the dining room. Oh, and I thought I'd bring you this – help you sleep.' Miss Harutunian handed over the hot chocolate. Johnny took the mug and had a sip. 'And please stay out of the basement from now on, Johnny. We don't want you getting into any more trouble.' Johnny nodded. His social worker must have recognized the 'no entry' sign Johnny had unscrewed from a locked door in the bowels of Halader House for a dare. Miss Harutunian fixed Johnny with a firm stare before leaving the room. At least it didn't seem she'd spotted Bentley underneath the bed. The Old English sheepdog was meant to sleep in a little kennel in the yard behind Halader House, but he hardly ever ended up doing that.

Johnny changed into his pyjamas and sat down on the bed, sipping his hot chocolate. He always left the curtains open so he could lie on his bed and look out. There was a streetlight down below outside, but it had stopped working a couple of days after he'd moved into this room, so he could gaze at the stars all he wanted. Cassiopeia was clearly visible, dominating the heavens. Johnny smiled. Unusually for a boy of his age, particularly such a fair one, he didn't have any freckles to speak of except on his left arm, just below his elbow, where five little brown dots mirrored the wonky 'W' he was now looking at. He always liked looking at Cassiopeia. He yawned – this time it was for real. He was really tired and hated the thought of getting up so early on a Saturday morning. Even so, he tried to think about the signal and what it might mean. Would he ever find it again and, if he did, how could he get a proper fix next time? He pictured himself in New York being presented with a medal by the Secretary General of the United Nations – the first person on

Earth to find clear evidence of extraterrestrial life.

The thoughts eventually switched to his mum and the trip to St Catharine's tomorrow. He didn't know what he'd say to her, but as she never reacted it probably didn't matter. Bentley barked and Johnny came to with a start, nearly spilling the drink which was now cold. The Old English sheepdog had climbed onto the bed and was staring out of the window into the blackness. Johnny put his face to the cold glass and peered outside. And then he saw it – or did he? An insect's head bigger than his own, staring back at him. Before he could really be sure, the window had fogged up with his hot breath on the glass. Frantically he wiped it dry with the sleeve of his pyjama top, but when he looked again there was nothing there.

Johnny looked at the alarm clock by his bed – it was much later than he'd thought. Just then the Moon emerged from behind a cloud, before another obscured it a few seconds later, the eerie silhouette backlit by a silvery glow. That must have been it. He'd been half asleep and had seen a strangely shaped cloud outside the window. It was a trick of the light – his mind had put two and two together and made lots. He got into bed properly, with Bentley's heavy frame on top of the duvet. Johnny put his head onto the pillow and closed his eyes, but it was a very long time before he went off to sleep.

2

ST CATHARINE'S HOSPITAL FOR THE CRIMINALLY INSANE

Breakfast hadn't been good. Johnny hated getting up in the morning, especially so early, and arrived late in the Halader House dining room on the ground floor. By the time he was there all the bacon sandwiches had gone, leaving him to go without or accept the thick, cold porridge a sneering Mr Wilkins had slopped into his bowl. Now, as he sat on the 08.33 from Castle Dudbury to London Liverpool Street station, it felt as though the porridge had turned to concrete in his stomach.

Johnny had partly got his own back – Mr Wilkins was most unhappy that Bentley had been allowed onto the train. In fact, the cook had asked several members of the railway company staff to see if any of them had heard of rules to prevent dogs travelling but, much to his disappointment, there were none. Everyone from Halader House seemed to be on board with Mrs Irvine, resplendent in a tartan coat, leading the outing. They'd taken over one entire carriage and from the chatter it sounded as though Johnny would be missing a great day out.

He was sitting with his forehead pressed against the window, watching the fields flying past outside, with Bentley lying at his feet. Miss Harutunian was next to him on his right, reading a magazine and wearing a navy, what she'd called, 'pant suit', which Johnny found very funny. He knew he should look his best for his mum, so had on his own brown suit. The sleeves and legs were too short as Mrs Irvine had bought it for him a couple of years before. Mr Wilkins was sitting opposite, taking up both seats and pretending to read the paper, but holding it at an angle so he could keep an eye on Johnny. The shoulders of his faded grey jacket were now covered with white flakes of dandruff that he kept trying to brush off every few minutes, hoping no one noticed.

Normally, Johnny would have thought that any day away from Castle Dudbury had to be a day well spent – it was surely the dullest place anyone had ever imagined. Today, though, was a double whammy. On the one hand he couldn't be where he desperately wanted to be – in the Halader House computer room analysing the signal that Kovac had intercepted the day before. Then, to make matters even worse, he had to go on the soul-destroying trip to St Catharine's to sit in a room with a mum who didn't even know he was there. Life was really unfair.

Mr Wilkins lowered his newspaper and started talking to Miss Harutunian. 'Most of the staff think Mrs Irvine's mad to let the boy visit his mother.'

Johnny hated it when people talked as though he was invisible. Miss Harutunian ignored the cook and turned the page of her magazine. Mr Wilkins continued, 'You know his father's in prison – maximum security somewhere. If you ask me, it'd be far better in the long run if he just forgot about them both.'

Slowly, Miss Harutunian closed her magazine and looked across at Mr Wilkins. 'Exactly how do you figure that?' she asked in a steely voice.

'Just look at the boy – he's practically a delinquent. But can you blame him? They were hardly good role models. That's what you social worker types say they need, isn't it?'

Johnny's fingernails were digging into his hands. He was still facing out of the window – next to him he could see his own reflection becoming redder, while further away he watched Mr Wilkins shoving his bushy beard forward towards Miss Harutunian. Johnny felt a calming hand from her on his shoulder. She said, 'We social workers believe there's nothing more important for a child than maintaining a close family bond.'

'Don't you know what they did?' asked the cook. 'Both of them? They killed his older brother – in cold blood. Micky.'

'Nicky!' snapped Johnny, turning round. 'His name was Nicky.'

Johnny stared defiantly at Mr Wilkins, who lifted the newspaper in front of his face and hid behind a headline that read 'YARNTON HILL HORROR!' Johnny sensed Miss Harutunian looking at him, but he turned away and stared out of the window again. He missed his family more than anything, but didn't want to talk about them. He hadn't seen his dad since he was a little boy and he didn't want to see his mum like this. He wanted his real mum, the walking, talking, fun one he'd loved as a little boy. But, as he knew that would never happen now, he just wanted to go to the Tower of London with everyone else. Outside, the fields had given way to tower blocks. A giant mural had been painted on the side of one, showing children, several metres tall, playing. Calming down a little he wondered if you were born on Mars, might you actually grow to be that tall because of the low gravity? Soon an announcement came over the tannoy: 'We will shortly be arriving at London Liverpool Street where this train terminates. Passengers are reminded to take all their . . .'

'Here we are then,' Mr Wilkins said, struggling out of his seat and dusting more dandruff off his lapels. As soon as the cook walked over towards the doors, Bentley climbed up onto his empty seat and watched the station come into view. Miss Harutunian gave the dog a friendly pat, before standing up. The doors opened and everyone started spilling out onto the platform. Reluctantly, Johnny got to his feet and gave a gentle tug on Bentley's lead. The dog jumped down and joined him in the middle of the carriage. Johnny gave him a little rub under his collar and followed the others through the doors, keeping a tight hold of the lead.

Johnny had no idea a train station could be *this* busy. Mrs Irvine lifted a large tartan umbrella above her head and shouted, 'Follow me,' above the noise of the public address system. The crowds of morning commuters parted before her and a long line of children snaked towards a set of escalators leading up to street level.

Johnny looked round and found Miss Harutunian immediately behind him. 'Can't we go on the Underground?' he asked. It was the one part of the day he'd been looking forward to. The few times he'd been to London before, he'd travelled by Tube, going in at one end and popping out the other in no time at all.

'The Manager says it's "not natural" travelling through all those tunnels,' said Miss Harutunian, grinning broadly. 'We'll walk part way with the others – then it's a . . . number 8 bus,' she added, checking the printout she was holding.

Mrs Irvine gathered everyone together for a roll-call at the top of the escalators, and then stepped into the street, holding out her arm to stop the oncoming traffic. The long line of inhabitants of 33 Barnard Way set off in pursuit.

Johnny, though, stopped in the middle of the road and stared open-mouthed at an incredible sight. 'What's that?' he asked, pointing up at the sky.

'What?' Miss Harutunian asked, trying to follow his arm.

'That,' said Johnny. 'That building. It's amazing.'

Johnny was staring at an enormous curved, cylindrical tower of gleaming glass and metal rising above the shops in front of the station. It was one of the most beautiful things he'd ever seen.

'Oh. You mean the Gherkin,' Miss Harutunian said.

'Actually it's called 30 St Mary Axe,' said Mr Wilkins, who'd come back to hurry them up.

'Wow,' said Johnny.

'Don't care for it myself' said Mr Wilkins. 'Huge waste of money. Why they had to go and build this monstrosity when there's plenty of perfectly good office space around London. Or in Castle Dudbury for that matter.'

'But it's beautiful,' said Johnny. 'I've never seen anything like it.'

'The boy's got no taste,' the cook said to Miss Harutunian. 'Same with his food. Won't eat his liver and onions – oh no. Only likes fancy stuff – like pizza. You've got to watch him – we don't want him lagging behind and running off.' Mr Wilkins's little black eyes narrowed on Johnny before he turned and walked away to rejoin the others.

'If you like this, you should come to New York,' said Miss Harutunian. 'We've got hundreds. The Chrysler Building's much prettier.'

A car honked its horn and Johnny, Miss Harutunian and even Bentley jumped. Quickly, they scurried across the road and joined the back of the straggling group that Mrs Irvine, umbrella still aloft, was guiding south towards the Tower of London. Johnny kept almost bumping into things as he stared upwards at the Gherkin. One of these turned out to be the shelter for the number 8 bus, which was going to take them all the way to Victoria station. A display told them a bus was due and, sure enough, a bright red double-decker soon pulled up at the stop. Miss Harutunian, Johnny and Bentley stepped on board.

'Can we go upstairs?' Johnny asked.

'Oh go on then,' Miss Harutunian replied, looking slightly anxious. 'You promise it won't topple over?'

'It doesn't happen too often,' said Johnny, smiling innocently. Miss Harutunian returned the smile weakly. 'Come on, boy.' Johnny half ran up the stairs with Bentley following enthusiastically behind. All the front seats were free so they sat down there with Miss Harutunian making her way over rather gingerly to join them.

The number 8 bus jerked away from the stop, with the social worker holding on tightly to the railings in front of her while Johnny craned his neck to watch the smooth criss-crossing curves and reflections of the Gherkin for as long as possible.

☼   ☼   ☼
☼   ☼

St Catharine's Hospital for the Criminally Insane was as unwelcoming as the name suggested. The walk from nearby Wittonbury station was exposed, and it was drizzling and horribly windy. Johnny had bought some brightly coloured flowers – gerberas Miss Harutunian had called them – from a florist at Victoria station, but already they were beginning to look very sorry for themselves. Bentley, however, did seem in good spirits and pulled Johnny along on the lead. The red-haired American struggled to keep up, but it meant they soon reached the stone bridge over the choppy little brook that marked the edge of the hospital grounds. Miss Harutunian's eyes narrowed when she found no one in the booth beside the long white barrier. 'This country,' she said to Johnny. 'Anyone could simply walk in or out of here and they'd never know.'

Johnny thought 'anyone' clearly didn't include his mum. As soon as they passed the empty booth he felt really sick, wondering what he'd find inside the hospital. There was no one at all to be seen outdoors. He wasn't surprised – the grounds at St Catharine's looked bleaker than his school's playing fields. They were only broken up by a redbrick, cylindrical incinerator tower, close to the gate, that was emitting a low hum. Bentley led the way to the main reception where Miss Harutunian pulled open a pair of huge oak doors. Johnny and the sheepdog entered behind her.

A large, miserable woman, wearing a blue security uniform, was sitting behind a desk on the right. She looked up and said, 'No dogs.'

Johnny had been expecting this. 'But he's always been allowed in before,' he lied, trying not to turn red.

'No dogs or no visits,' said the woman. 'Them's the rules.'

'Please – it'll really cheer my mum up.'

'No dogs,' the guard said again. 'Patients might catch summin'.'

'It's OK, Johnny.' said Miss Harutunian, crouching down to stroke Bentley who tried to lick her in return. 'I can stay here and look after him.'

'No, don't worry,' said Johnny. 'I can tie him to something out there.' Johnny tugged at Bentley's lead and pulled him through the oak doors and back outside. Between Johnny and the sheepdog this used to be a well-worked routine and he hoped Bentley would remember. Try as he might, Johnny had always failed to persuade whoever was behind that desk to let Bentley through, but he did have a plan B. Once they were outside, Johnny held his friend's fringe out of his eyes – how the sheepdog actually saw normally he never knew. 'Bents,' he said. 'Remember Mum's room. Wait outside . . . very quiet . . . OK?' He let go of the lead and Bentley scampered off around the corner of the building. Johnny went back inside.

Miss Harutunian had signed them in and said they had to go to a Dr Carrington's office. Johnny remembered it well enough. The guard pressed a button behind the desk and a glass door in front of Johnny and Miss Harutunian buzzed. Johnny pushed it open and led the way through into the long corridor that ran along the length of the hospital and smelled of disinfectant. He had made this journey many times when he was younger and dimly registered the same tired artwork on the walls. He crossed over one corridor and at the next one he turned left – the route was still second nature. Then he took a staircase on the right and went up one floor.

'It's room 118. That's this floor isn't it?' Miss Harutunian was whispering as it seemed wrong to speak normally. The only other sound was of their feet echoing along the empty corridors. Johnny grunted assent as he walked along counting down the room numbers: 124, 122, 120. He stopped outside the next door. The number had fallen off but he knew it was the right one.

'Is this it?' Miss Harutunian asked.

Johnny nodded, took a deep breath and knocked on the door.

'Come in, come in,' came a voice from inside. Johnny opened the door and they both stepped through.

'Ah yes. Jonathan Mackintosh and er . . . Katherine Harutunian,' said a white-coated figure from behind a desk in front of a sash window. Despite an attempt to comb what little hair remained across his scalp, Dr Carrington was very nearly bald. There was a bulky computer on his desk, but he was reading from a manila file in front of him, through round steel-framed glasses. He looked up to reveal enormous purple bags underneath his eyes. 'Sit down, sit down.' He gestured to two chairs in front of the desk.

'Good to meet you, Dr Carrington,' said Miss Harutunian, walking straight over to the desk and stretching out her hand.

Dr Carrington stood up – he towered above the social worker but looked as though the slightest push would knock him over. He shook hands and smiled. 'So you're American? American . . . of course . . . yes.' Everyone sat down. Johnny gripped the bedraggled flowers tightly. Dr Carrington turned to him. 'I'm sorry to report there's been no change in your mother's condition, Jonathan. No, no change.' Johnny wasn't expecting to hear anything else. He looked down at the floor and nodded, bracing himself for the worst. Dr Carrington continued. 'She is breathing unaided, and basic bodily functions are working normally. Our tests on higher brainwave functions are still inconclusive. I might as well take you straight down there.' Dr Carrington stood up, so Johnny and his social worker followed suit. Miss Harutunian gave Johnny's free hand a squeeze. Dr Carrington led them out of the office, turning right down the corridor and left down a staircase back onto the ground floor.

'Is there any chance she can get better?' asked the social worker.

'There's always a chance . . . always,' said Dr Carrington. 'Jonathan's mother's illness isn't physical. It's a form of post traumatic stress disorder. But it's been a few years now, a few years, and the longer without a response to her treatment the less likely a recovery becomes.'

Miss Harutunian squeezed Johnny's hand again but he quickly let go. They were close to the room where Johnny's mother was normally kept, but something wasn't normal. A very tall, thick-set man in a black suit was standing outside the door, watching Johnny approach.

'Who's that man?' Johnny asked.

'What? Oh yes,' said Dr Carrington. 'That's Stevens. Might not have been here last time you came. No, probably not. Extra security . . . Home Office regulations . . . more protection. Yes that's right – more protection.'

'Protection from who?' Johnny asked, but they'd already reached the door.

'Two people to see the er . . . to see the patient,' said Dr Carrington.

Stevens looked quickly at Miss Harutunian before turning his attention to Johnny, who stared back. Stevens studied him through cruel grey eyes, slowly looking up and down before nodding and stepping to the side of the door. He keyed a four digit number into a panel on the wall. There was a click, allowing Dr Carrington to enter the room followed by Miss Harutunian and then Johnny, with Stevens behind.

Considering it contained only one patient, the room was large. It had to be to accommodate the various machines ranged around the single bed protruding from the middle of the left-hand wall. Either side of the bed was a wooden chair – next to the nearest of these, pushed against the wall, was a stand holding a drip taking fluid down and into the arm of a middle-aged woman. She was lying motionless on the bed, with her limp blonde hair falling over a flat pillow. Her pale blue eyes were open, staring up at the ceiling.

'I'll have those, shall I?' Miss Harutunian said to Johnny, taking the flowers from his grip and walking over to a sink in the far corner. She started opening the surrounding cupboards, looking for something to put them in. Dr Carrington picked up a clipboard hanging from the end of the bed and gave it a quick look over.

'As I was saying . . . yes . . . no change really . . . probable PVS.'

'What's PVS?' Miss Harutuian asked from the corner of the room.

'PVS? Oh yes. Persistent vegetative state. This machine here's an EEG,' said Dr Carrington, pointing to one of the older-looking pieces of equipment. 'It's measuring brainwave activity. Sadly we don't believe she's . . . she's not really thinking anymore. The coma's deep . . . very deep.' On a large display screen, four coloured lines were being traced out, slowly rising and falling but never rising very far. A wire from the front of the machine split into four when it reached Johnny's mum, with each end connected to an electrode fixed onto her scalp.

'There you are – best I could do,' said Miss Harutunian. The gerberas were in a clear plastic jug half full of water that she brought over and placed on a trolley near the bed.

'Thanks,' muttered Johnny. 'Can I talk to my mum on my own, please?'

He could feel Stevens's eyes boring into him, but looked between his social worker and Dr Carrington. The doctor seemed reluctant, but Miss Harutunian took charge. 'Of course you can. I'm sure we can leave you alone for a few minutes can't we?' she said, putting a hand on Dr Carrington's and Stevens's elbows and steering them towards the door.

Once all three of them had left the room, Johnny walked over to the bed, but instead of sitting down he picked up one of the chairs and carried it to the door, wedging it under the handle. He really didn't want to be disturbed. Then he walked over to the window and, after some delicate prodding and pushing, was able to open it. He poked his head outside and whistled. A few seconds later a large white head appeared beneath him and, with Johnny's help, Bentley scrambled up into the room, wagging his tail.

'Good boy . . . good boy,' said Johnny, as the dog bounded over towards Johnny's mum. He turned back to Johnny and whimpered.

'It's OK, Bents,' Johnny said, rubbing Bentley underneath his collar. He leant over his mum and looked down into her eyes. They were so empty, not registering anything at all and simply stared straight through Johnny up to the ceiling. He kissed her on the forehead and sat down in the one remaining chair, taking her hand. Johnny had read about people in hospital suddenly waking up after many years in a coma. They said they were able to remember things people had said to them when supposedly unconscious, so he started to talk.

'Hi, Mum. It's me . . . Johnny. I'm sorry it's been so long. I'm still living at Halader House – out in Essex. Mr Wilkins – the cook – he's horrid as ever. Hate to think what he puts in the food. Mrs Irvine's still there too. And I've got a new social worker. She's American – really nice. She came on the train with me. Bentley's here too. I know he misses you. On the train, Mr Wilkins was saying I should forget you. But I miss you, Mum . . . and Dad. I wish you'd get better so I didn't have to live there any more. You know I don't believe any of those things they said you and Dad did.'

He hadn't meant to say all that, but once he'd started it just poured out – he didn't have anyone else he could say this sort of stuff to. As he talked he half noticed the lines on the EEG spike, just for a second. He'd probably imagined it. He tried to compose himself and started again.

'I've built a cool computer there. It talks and I've called it Kovac. I'm getting really good at computers. Wish you could come to a parent's evening. You'd be dead proud – honest. And I'm in the football team. We're in the county final – we won the semi yesterday . . . three–one. And when I came back Kovac was saying there was a signal. I've got him set up doing a kind of special SETI thing. That's the Search for Extraterrestrial Intelligence. You know – looking for aliens. They've got to be out there and I'm going to find them and make you really proud and I'll be famous, and maybe rich, and I'll be able to get you out of here and looked after by some proper doctors – not like Dr Carrington – and they'll make you better . . . promise. So when I get back tonight I'll do some more work and try and find out what it was and where it came from. It seemed really close.'

There it was again. He was sure there'd been a spike this time. Maybe he should go and fetch Dr Carrington? And then it was as though a wind was blowing around the room. Johnny felt his hand getting warmer and warmer, but he couldn't seem to let go of his mother's. It was like when he was dreaming he had to run away from something, but however quickly his legs moved he stayed rooted to the spot. He wasn't afraid – it didn't feel like a bad dream. Now his hand was hot, or rather something hot was in his hand. But it wasn't burning him – it was as if the warmth was flowing up his arm and energizing his whole body. The EEG was now off the scale. His mother's eyes looked suddenly silvery bright, and it wasn't just her eyes. A light was emanating from her. Her body twitched and the light went out. The plastic jug flew off the trolley, scattering the gerberas across the floor, the window slammed shut and the room was suddenly still.

Johnny let go of his mother's hand and something fell to the floor. It was a sort of pendant on a chain. He picked it up but didn't have time to look at it. The door burst open, sending the wedged chair flying across the room and in came the man in the suit, followed by Dr Carrington and Miss Harutunian. Instinctively, Johnny slipped the pendant into his trouser pocket.

'What's going on?' asked Stevens. 'What happened? What was that noise?' As he spoke Bentley bared his teeth and growled.

'She moved,' said Johnny. 'She moved and those lines starting going funny on the screen over there.' He was pointing at the EEG.

'Impossible,' said Dr Carrington, coming over to the bedside. He looked at Johnny's mother and checked the machines, which by now had returned to normal.

'Oh, Johnny,' said Miss Harutunian. 'And just look at your flowers.' She put a hand on his chin and took out a tissue to wipe his face. Johnny hadn't noticed he'd been crying.

'No. There's no record of anything here,' said Dr Carrington. 'Johnny must be imagining it. Either that or it was a reflex. A reflex . . . yes.' He looked at the machines and then to Miss Harutunian, as though for confirmation.

'Yeah – it's classic wish fulfilment,' the American replied.

'Of course nothing happened.'

'But she did . . .' said Johnny, annoyed at feeling invisible again. But then he caught sight of Stevens and stopped. He realized he didn't want to say any more.

'What's that *thing* doing in here?' Stevens was looking at Bentley. He moved towards the dog while taking out some sort of weapon from a holster inside his jacket. It was probably a taser gun – Johnny hadn't seen anything like it before. Bentley growled again.

Johnny got up. 'Leave him alone,' he said.

Stevens looked at Johnny, who felt a chill pass through him for a moment. The man's eyes were ice cold.

'No dogs in the facility,' said Stevens. 'If you don't get it out of here in ten seconds it'll never leave.' He pointed the weapon at Bentley.

'No!' said Johnny, stepping between the man and the dog.

'Nine, eight, seven . . .' Stevens counted down.

Bentley was facing Stevens as though about to pounce. Johnny had never seen him like this before.

'How dare you talk to Johnny like that,' said Miss Harutunian, also stepping between Stevens and the sheepdog. The man kept the gun where it was, now pointing directly at the social worker. Dr Carrington looked frantically from one to the other.

'Four . . . three . . .'

Johnny took Bentley's lead and yanked it with all his strength, dragging the dog along the floor towards the door.

'Two . . . one . . .'

They were out of the door. Looking back he saw Stevens turn to Dr Carrington. 'Get them out of here now,' he said.

'Yes, of course, yes,' Dr Carrington mumbled.

'Don't think you've heard the last of this,' Miss Harutunian shouted at Stevens, as Dr Carrington shepherded her towards the door. Johnny was fighting to stop Bentley from going back inside. He could see Stevens pointing the weapon at his mother and cautiously approaching the bed.

'Leave her alone,' Johnny shouted, as Dr Carrington closed the door behind them.

'What's going on? Who was that man?' Miss Harutunian demanded.

Dr Carrington shook his head. 'You've got to leave . . . now,' he said, spreading his long arms and herding Johnny and Miss Harutunian down the corridor at speed. Bentley followed very reluctantly, looking back over his shoulder and whimpering every so often. In no time at all they were back at the main reception. Dr Carrington's hands were shaking but he managed to enter a code number into a box on the wall and opened the clear glass exit door. 'I don't think you should come and see your mother again, Jonathan.'

'Not see his mother?' The social worker looked apoplectic. 'Johnny has every right . . .'

'Please, Miss Harutunian,' pleaded Dr Carrington. 'I'll sign you out. Trust me.' He took the social worker's hand and shook it goodbye. 'Go.'

Miss Harutunian seemed to calm down. 'Come on, Johnny. Let's go then,' she said. The American led Johnny and Bentley through the oak doors and out into a swirling wind. The incinerator tower was silhouetted against a dark sky, far angrier than when they'd set out that morning. Heads down, neither spoke as they crossed the hospital grounds and reached the little stone bridge that marked the path back to Wittonbury station. As they crossed it began to pour with rain and soon Johnny was soaked through. He hoped they wouldn't have to wait too long for a train.

✧   ✧   ✧
✧   ✧

The bedraggled figures of Johnny, Bentley and Miss

Harutunian trudged across the bleak carpark between Castle Dudbury railway station and the children's home, only to find the rear entrance locked. Fed up, they walked round the building and turned the corner into Barnard Way just in time to see the last of the other children being ushered through the main doors to Halader House by Mrs Irvine. 'Come along, you two,' she shouted, holding a door open for them. 'You're both soaked.' Gratefully, they all went inside, where they were greeted by a blast of warm air from the heaters in the entrance hall. 'Jonathan – go and get yourself cleaned up. Dinner's at seven tonight. Miss Harutunian – I want to hear all about your visit. We'll go to my office.'

Johnny took Bentley straight up the stairs before anyone could tell him not to and followed the corridor round till he reached the spiral staircase to his room. He climbed the stairs and collapsed on top of his bed. He couldn't believe he'd resisted looking at the pendant for the entire train journey home, but for some reason he hadn't wanted to show it to Miss Harutunian. Now he took it out of his pocket and turned it over in his hand. It was heavy – he guessed it might even be gold. He couldn't work out where it had come from. He was bound to have noticed something in his mum's hand before. Maybe a nurse had left it in the room by accident. An inscription reading simply '*for love*' had been engraved on the back. A line of five crystals ran down the front with a further one on either side, all surrounded by blue diamond-shaped markings. He ran his finger over one of the crystals and the pendant suddenly sprang open. Something fell out. Panicking he searched the duvet before finding a lock of black hair, even including the roots, all held together by a very fine blue ribbon on which the name 'Nicholas' was written in beautiful, minute handwriting. It was a locket, not a pendant, and inside were two more locks of hair, both blond, one bound with a golden ribbon with the name 'Jonathan' written on it and the other, in a lilac ribbon, that read 'Clara'.

The inside of the locket held two photos, one in each half. There was a dark-haired man, a blonde woman and an Old English sheepdog in one side. He looked closer – the picture was small but it did look like Bentley. He'd seen photos of his father, Michael Mackintosh, once before in some old newspapers, and he recognized his mum. The couple were beaming huge smiles at the camera. Johnny's heart was beating off the scale – he didn't have any pictures of his parents. But what was even stranger were the three faces in the other half of the locket. The image made no sense. Johnny was sure he'd seen a magnifying glass somewhere. He rummaged around in the box underneath his bed until he found it – it must have belonged to his dad at some point. He picked up the locket and held it underneath the lampshade in the middle of the room, peering through the lens. There was no question. The middle face was him, Johnny, but it wasn't a picture of him as a baby. It was him now. He could clearly see the lapels of his suit jacket that he'd thrown onto the bed when he came in. But how? And was that his brother Nicky on one side of him? If it was, he was wearing weird clothes and looking as though he was nearly twenty when in fact he'd died eleven years earlier. It was hard to say as half the person's face was in shadow. And on the other side was a blonde girl who looked two or three years younger than Johnny. Was this Clara? *Who* was Clara?

He changed out of his wet clothes, said goodbye to Bentley who was drying out underneath the bed by the radiator, and opened the trapdoor. Down two sets of stairs and back on the ground floor, he tiptoed past the dining room where the hubbub suggested everyone was already eating. He hurried along the corridor past the kitchens and soon came to the door of the computer room. This time Johnny was confident – he knew he could open it and, almost before he stretched out his hand, he heard the soft click of the electronic mechanism unlocking. He turned the door handle, walked across to the table and switched the master computer on.

'Good evening, Johnny,' said Kovac.

'Kovac – scan images – maximum resolution,' Johnny replied. He walked over to the far wall where he placed the opened locket face down on top of a flatbed scanner.

'Scan complete,' Kovac said after a few seconds. 'Displaying results.'

Johnny sat down in front of the computer. 'Kovac – overlay grid – 20 by 10 squares,' he said, studying the screen on which gridlines instantly appeared. Clara was on the far right.

'Kovac – enhance P to S, 4 to 9,' said Johnny and as he did so the girl's face was magnified while a new grid was superimposed across it.

'Kovac – copy and save as Clara one.'

Johnny leaned back in the chair and wondered how best to begin a search for this mysterious Clara. Looking for patterns was something he'd designed Kovac specifically for, but this was still a very complex problem. The web was the obvious choice so he asked the computer to compare his file with all internet images.

An hour later and Johnny was getting nowhere. He'd examined lots of Kovac's 'possibles' but there were no matches he'd describe as 'probables'. He wasn't too surprised. He needed another way.

'Kovac – print Clara one.'

The sound of the printer whirring into life was nearly drowned out by Johnny's stomach rumbling. He suddenly realized how hungry he was. 'Kovac – shut down – maintain background functions,' he instructed. Then he got up, took the photo from the printer and the locket from the scanner and went out of the computer room door. He ran through the Halader House corridors till he was back in his bedroom, where

34

he put both the printout and the locket under his pillow. He turned to leave the room and was halfway to the trapdoor when he stopped. He walked back over to the bed, picked up the chain and slipped it over his head, tucking the locket inside his T-shirt. Then he headed out of the room and down his private staircase, desperately hoping he could sneak out for some chips without anyone noticing.

3

THE GIRL FROM THE INSTITUTE ✩ ✩

Three girls walked down the steps in the late afternoon
sunshine with a boy in tow. Each of the girls wore the same
uniform – a pink knee-length gingham checked dress and a
panama hat with blue edging. The boy wore tailored shorts, a
white shirt with striped tie and a straw boater. The particular
girl Johnny was watching had long blonde hair, tied into
bunches either side of her face by blue ribbons. She was
clutching a leather satchel to her chest. All four children sat
down towards the bottom of the steps near a statue of a man in
a helmet pointing upwards towards the skies. It looked like a
war memorial. They were talking, but there was no sound with
the picture.

'Kovac – zoom out slowly,' said Johnny.

After several days of searching, the computer said it was a
99.9997% match and Johnny agreed this must be Clara. He
still wasn't sure who Clara was, but he was working on that too.
At least now he should be able to find out where she was. The
picture from the CCTV camera he'd hacked was slowly
becoming wider and wider, until Clara and her friends were
just dots in the middle. Finally, on the left edge, he saw a set of
gates with a sign beside them.

'Kovac – stop – pan left – stop – zoom in and centre.'

'Kovac – capture image – save as Clara school sign.'

The image froze on the display and Johnny took in the

details. In large ornate white letters painted on a black background were the words 'Proteus Institute for the Gifted'. Beneath in smaller plainer type it read 'Strictly No Admittance Without Appointment'. Was it too much to ask them to write an address somewhere? Or a URL? Johnny rolled over onto his back. Most of the school team had come out to the park for a last kickaround before the cup final. They'd finished nearly an hour earlier and it was beginning to get dark. Johnny had hoped one of the other boys would ask him back for tea, but nobody did and even if he'd been allowed visitors he didn't think they'd fancy Mr Wilkins's cooking. So the other boys had all gone off leaving him lying underneath his favourite conker tree with Bentley beside him.

Almost every time Johnny had been anywhere near the computer room that week he'd found himself face to face with Mr Wilkins who 'just happened' to be coming out of the kitchen. It looked as though it would be impossible to find out more about Clara or the signal – but then he'd had a brainwave. He'd converted his handheld games console into a mobile terminal that linked to Kovac remotely. He didn't know why he hadn't done it earlier. A boy holding one of those and sometimes talking to it was far less likely to be noticed than a boy who spent so much time pretending to do homework on a PC. Besides, grownups didn't seem to know the first thing about computer games and whether or not you sometimes had to speak to play them.

Johnny balanced the screen on the grass while doing various web searches for 'Proteus Institute,' but nothing came up that looked at all promising. Finally giving up, he switched the tiny display back to the CCTV feed. Now there were only the two girls on the steps and a large off-road car with tinted windows was parked in front of them. A man in a black suit was shutting the passenger door. Johnny couldn't see if Clara was inside and wished now he'd watched the footage more closely. The man walked round the car to the driver's door and opened it. He was about to get inside when something distracted him. He touched his ear, stopped and looked around. For a second it was as though he was staring straight out of the screen, but before Johnny could get a good look at him the display dissolved into static.

'Kovac – restore picture,' he yelled at the games console.

'Camera malfunction,' replied the computer. 'Picture unavailable.'

'Kovac – switch to nearest alternative camera feed,' said Johnny. He might be able to pick up the car on a nearby CCTV camera.

'No alternative available. All cameras within grid 35151385 malfunctioning,' said Kovac with no emotion whatsoever, as though this was an everyday occurrence.

'All of them? No!' Why now of all times? 'Kovac – display grid reference,' he said to the console and then sat bolt upright as he found himself looking at a map of the southwest of England. 'No way!' gasped Johnny, while Bentley growled beside him.

☼   ☼   ☼
☼   ☼

It had been a week since Johnny's visit to St Catharine's and, incredibly, in that time Kovac had found two more possible extraterrestrial signals. The first happened during football practice after school on Tuesday. He'd come back into the changing rooms to find the handheld flashing in his sports bag. He presumed it was a false alarm as he'd only just made the mobile link, but that evening Spencer Mitchell created a series of diversions around Halader House so Johnny had at least an hour and a half to debug his program and check the connection properly. He'd crept into the computer room, turned Kovac on and what he saw had astonished him. There was another genuine signal – it seemed to come to a halt in earth orbit, which of course meant it could be human, but the original vector implied it came from behind the moon. Again it was all so fast that he couldn't get an exact fix, but something very strange seemed to be happening.

That was confirmed when the alarm went off during double biology on Thursday morning. Mr Jennings was telling the class about Mendel breeding peas and wasn't at all happy to be interrupted by the beeping from Johnny's schoolbag. The words, 'Mackintosh – see me after school,' were the last thing Johnny wanted to hear when he was desperate to get back to Barnard Way to study this third signal, but as the rest of the lesson unfolded he concocted a plan. When it came to half-past three and the dreaded summons – Dave Spedding was sure he'd get detention – what Johnny actually came away with was a whole lot of equipment and instructions for an experiment he could perform at the children's home.

Johnny didn't want to get into any more trouble so he'd asked Mrs Irvine for permission to use the room next to her office to set everything up. The manager claimed she used to be a bit of a scientist herself, and had been only too happy to help. They put all the apparatus together, before Mrs Irvine called a halt because of a meeting with Mr Wilkins. It was the chance Johnny wanted – with the cook out of the way he snuck into the computer room to make use of the full-sized screen. Again Kovac could offer only a partial answer. Frustrated, Johnny had gone downstairs into the common room. Some of the older kids were watching a really dull film about a pirate radio station. Johnny was about to leave to take Bentley out for a walk when something he saw gave him the inspiration he needed – 'triangulation.' He now had three partial signals. By combining them he might get a proper fix. He ran back down the corridor and had to stifle a yell of excitement as the results came together. The signals combined at a point about 36,000 km above the Earth. Johnny knew 36,000 km was a special distance – it was called 'geocentric orbit' – where weather or communications satellites were positioned because from there they could stay over the same point on the Earth's surface all of the time. Incredibly the point on the Earth's surface directly below where Johnny's signal was coming from was exactly the same point on the map that he was staring at now as he lay in the grass. It was directly above Clara's school.

✿ ✿ ✿
✿ ✿

Something flashed in Johnny's eye, breaking his concentration. He looked around, but the park was deserted apart from some dog walkers with a couple of terriers in the far corner. Bentley growled again. Johnny looked back at the map on the screen of his handheld. He noted a small town called Yarnton Hill was closest to its centre. There it was again – another flash. A black four-by-four was parked over by the main gates, and the light seemed to have come from there. Was someone watching him through binoculars? It seemed stupid, but Mrs Irvine did say a journalist had been on the phone. Johnny pretended to look back at his console, but was watching when it happened a third time. There was no mistaking it – why couldn't they leave him alone? He got up and tucked the locket swinging from his neck back inside his T-shirt. 'Come on, Bents,' he said to his dog who was already on his feet, facing towards the park gates. 'Let's get out of here.' Instead of walking the main entrance where they'd come in, Johnny pulled Bentley around and marched in the opposite direction, to the little cut-through that ran along the side of some new houses on the edge of the park. When they reached the alleyway a man was standing halfway along, reading a newspaper. Johnny hesitated but then carried on. He didn't want to go back past the black car and he did have Bentley with him after all. But that didn't stop his heart beating a little faster. He carried on into the cut-through and as he drew close the man lowered his newspaper.

'Hello, Johnny,' he said.

Johnny stopped. 'Who are you? What do you want?'

'Call me a friend of the family,' the man replied. 'Your *real* family. I used to know your father.' He held out his right hand to Johnny who took it warily. Johnny was desperate to find out more about his dad, but he knew to be careful. Though his childhood memories were all good, his dad was still a convicted murderer. If this man really was his father's friend, he could be dangerous. No sooner had they started shaking when the man pulled Johnny towards him, spinning him round in an armlock and grabbing hold of his hair. Johnny felt a sharp pain, but then the man screamed and let go. As Johnny stumbled away, he turned to see the man holding a tuft of Johnny's hair, as he fell backwards with Bentley's teeth clamped to his leg.

'Get him off. Get him off me,' pleaded the man on the tarmac. Shaken, Johnny picked up the end of Bentley's lead. 'He's hurting me,' moaned the man.

'Bentley, let go,' said Johnny slowly, holding the lead taut. 'Guard.' Reluctantly, Bentley released the man's leg from his jaws. 'If I give the code word he'll kill you,' said Johnny, knowing there was no such word and Bentley would do nothing of the sort anyway. He hadn't realized, though, that the Old English sheepdog could look quite so fierce, and was glad that he did. Bentley growled above the man as if to make the point.

The man's wallet had fallen onto the tarmac when Bentley knocked him over. Johnny picked it up and opened it.

'G . . . give that here,' stammered the man.

Johnny took out a business card and read aloud. 'Colin Watchorn, Journalist, *Evening Post*.'

'Why can't you people leave me alone?' Johnny asked, as he threw the wallet back to him.

'Bet you'd like that wouldn't you? Just forget what you're capable of. Only I know who you are – I know what you are,' said the man, as he edged slowly away from Bentley and raised himself into a sitting position against the wall of the alley.

'What do you mean?' said Johnny. 'I was a baby. It's not my fault what happened.'

'You could say "like father, like son",' said the man, gingerly getting to his feet while watching Bentley very carefully. 'But in your case I expect you're more like your mother, and that frightens me, Johnny.'

'Why? What about her? What about me?' Johnny said uncertainly. When it came to it he knew very little about his family.

'You really don't know, do you?' said the man. 'You don't know who you are.' He sounded genuinely surprised.

'So why don't you tell me?' said Johnny, confident of Bentley's protection but nervous about the way the conversation was going.

'Why don't you take a DNA test, little boy?' said the man. 'That's what I'm going to do with this.' Triumphantly he held up his closed fist that contained the tuft of Johnny's blond hair. 'Then I can prove it. Everyone will know.'

The man turned and made a run for it down the alley into the park. Bentley would have followed but Johnny held on to the lead. 'It's OK, boy,' he said. 'Let him go. Let's get home.' Johnny had a very good reason to get home. He had no idea what the reporter was talking about, but for the last three days the office next door to Mrs Irvine's had become his new laboratory. While he'd pretended it was something to do with his biology homework, in fact the equipment he'd borrowed from school was already doing a DNA test.

Mr Jennings had confirmed that hair was meant to be a good

source of DNA (so long as it had the roots). Johnny had taken some from inside the 'Clara' ribbon in the locket and also pulled out a few of his own. He wanted to compare the two but he needed to do it properly so he'd asked Mrs Irvine for a few of hers. These long grey follicles were his control sample. He looked at the timer counting down on his games console. It had seemed a long process but in three hours' time he should be able to take a first look at the results. He started running, Bentley struggling alongside to keep up.

☆   ☆   ☆
☆   ☆

Johnny was impatient for the results and arrived outside the Manager's office long before the countdown was over. For ten minutes he and Mrs Irvine stared at the complicated array of glassware, sensors and DVD writer, with no indication of anything happening, while she quizzed him about the visit to St Catharine's the week before. Johnny was desperate to change the subject, and the parting words of the journalist were still ringing in his ears. Besides, Mrs Irvine had said a reporter was asking questions – maybe it was the same one? He needed to find out, so he told her an edited version of what had happened earlier that evening. Quickly he realized it was a mistake.

'Waiting for you in an alley?' Mrs Irvine exploded. 'I don't believe it. That's harassment, that is. It's my duty to protect you and I will not stand for this any longer.'

'It's all right,' Johnny said. 'I just wondered if it was the same person. And if he said anything in particular. That's all.'

'It most certainly is not all right,' said Mrs Irvine. She picked up the business card that Johnny had shown her. 'I want you in my office at eight-thirty tomorrow morning. I shall be calling the newspaper first thing and will make quite sure neither this Mr Watchorn nor his associates bother you again.'

Johnny thought the way Mr Watchorn had acted suggested

he wasn't going to be deterred by a phone call, even if Mrs Irvine could be rather scary sometimes. He wished he knew what the journalist had been talking about. He stole a glance at the handheld – five minutes to go. Johnny walked over to the window. A train whizzed through Castle Dudbury station without stopping. Behind him, Mrs Irvine had calmed down a little and fell silent. A couple of black London taxis were waiting hopefully outside the station entrance, but there was no one going in or out. This was taking forever, and now it was quiet it seemed even worse than when Mrs Irvine was asking questions. Finally, Johnny allowed himself another look at his little screen – there were ten seconds to go. Silently he counted them down. The alarm on his games console started beeping. Time was up. The experiment was complete. He could take a look at the results.

Johnny took the DVD from the writer and followed Mrs Irvine out of the office, down a flight of stairs onto the ground floor and into the computer room corridor. At that moment, Mr Wilkins emerged from the kitchens and began walking towards them, whistling as he came nearer. Mrs Irvine took a little card from out of her handbag, swiped it through the reader beside the door and turned the handle. The whistling stopped and the cook quickened his step, hurrying over.

'Can I help you, Mr Wilkins?' asked the Manager.

Underneath his bushy beard the cook's face was turning pink. 'Excuse me, ma'am, but you can't . . . you can't let the boy in there. He's up to something. I know it.'

'Mr Wilkins – Ben Halader is a happy house and I intend it to remain so. That will only happen if we trust all the charges in our care.' She turned to Johnny and said 'Jonathan, in you go. You may do your homework on your own.' Johnny didn't need telling twice. 'Mr Wilkins, come with me. Next door to my office there's some equipment for your dishwasher.' Mrs

Irvine did an about turn and walked away, leaving the cook no choice but to follow. Johnny couldn't believe his luck. He walked over to the computer table and inserted the DVD into the drive. The gene sequences were so large it took a full two minutes for Kovac to copy them into its memory core. It seemed like an eternity. Finally the results started to scroll across the screen, long streams of the letters

```
GATCCATAGGCAAATTTCCACTGACTACAAAATCGGAT
ACTTATTCTAGGCATCTTAGCGATTGAGGGTAATCCAG
GGCTTTACTATTCCGTGTCATCGAATGTTACGCGCGCG
ATTAGGCATCTTAGCACTATTCCGACTATTCCGCTAGG
```

going on seemingly for ever. Mrs Irvine's DNA was the first to be displayed. Johnny wasn't interested in the letters themselves – he'd programmed Kovac to look at sixteen specific points on each of the genomes and compare them. They were places between genes where the DNA was meant to be more variable. He didn't understand how he and Clara could be brother and sister as the locket suggested but, if they were, then almost all sixteen of the points should match.

'Kovac – display DNA results for test sample Clara,' Johnny said.

'Results anomalous,' said the computer. 'Regenerating DNA profile. Estimated time to completion 97 seconds.'

At least it wasn't long thought Johnny, though he didn't understand what might be wrong. He'd set up the experiment very carefully and did hope Mrs Irvine hadn't interfered with the sample containers when he wasn't there. In the meantime he might as well take a look at his own. 'Kovac – display DNA results for test sample Johnny,' he told the computer.

'Results anomalous,' said the computer. 'Regenerating DNA profile. Estimated time to completion 62 seconds.' Kovac must have already been working on the problem.

After a short time the computer spoke again. 'Anomaly confirmed. Displaying DNA results for test sample Clara.' Another string of letters started scrolling across the screen, but something didn't look quite right:

```
GT  C  AA  TG  C  ATGG  C  AT  GTT  CA
TGC  AAA  GT  C  CT  AGGCC  ATTATC  GC
ATAG  C  GCCCT  AA  ATC  TC  AGACA  TA
CAT  GCTAT  GC  GT  C  AA  TG  C  AGAC
```

There were gaps. Somehow Kovac hadn't been able to read the DNA properly. And not just little bits – about half of it. The test was a failure.

'Anomaly confirmed. Displaying DNA results for test sample Johnny,' said Kovac and more letters started to scroll across the screen:

```
GT  C  AA  TG  C  ATGG  C  AT  GTT  CA
TGC  AAA  GT  C  CT  AAGCC  ATTATC  GC
ATAG  C  GCCGT  AA  ATC  TC  AGACA  TA
CAT  GCTAT  GC  GT  C  AA  TG  C  AGAC
```

'Calculating DNA correlation for subjects,' said Kovac in full flow.

Johnny stared at the screen. The match between the Clara and Johnny samples was over 97%. All sixteen sites examined revealed practically the same sequence, including blanks. None of the sites matched Mrs Irvine's DNA, but again that must be because of the gaps. What did it mean? It looked as though he'd found himself a sister, but he couldn't be sure and had no idea how it was possible. He was only two years old when his parents first went to prison, but he was sure he'd remember having a sister. Frustrated, Johnny shut Kovac down, thought about going off to the common room but remembered his stupidly early start the next day and decided to turn in.

☆   ☆   ☆
☆   ☆

Johnny was being chased by a T. Rex as he ran along a clifftop towards the London Gherkin. He wasn't going to make it. The roars of the dinosaur were almost deafening – right next to his left ear – louder and louder. Finally, Johnny woke up. He'd set his alarm to the deep growl he used when he really needed to get up – the radio would never have woken him so early on a Sunday. It was already half-past eight. The noise must have been going on for ten minutes. Johnny threw on his jeans and the T-shirt from the night before, checked under the bed to find Bentley snoring quietly, and made his way through the sleepy corridors of Halader House towards the Manager's office. He wasn't looking forward to this at all. He knocked quietly on the wooden door with the plaque. Maybe Mrs Irvine had overslept too and wouldn't be there?

'Come in,' came a wide-awake sounding voice from inside. 'So tell me, Jonathan – how was the experiment?'

Johnny wondered how Mrs Irvine could seem quite so alert first thing in the morning. 'I'm not sure,' he mumbled. 'It wasn't what I expected.'

'No? Why was that?' Mrs Irvine pointed for Johnny to sit down in the chair in front of the desk.

'It was sort of incomplete. You didn't touch anything did you?'

'Heavens no. I didn't dare go anywhere near it.' Mrs Irvine pursed her lips together and stared into space for a second as though thinking something over. 'Well that's a shame. And now Mr Wilkins has cleared everything away. But of course that's not why we're here.' Johnny's heart sank. He should have known it was stupid to mention the journalist to anyone else. 'I'm going to put a stop to this nonsense right now,' Mrs Irvine continued. 'They should leave you alone to get on with your life.'

Johnny nodded and sank lower into the chair, wishing he was

back in his bed. Mrs Irvine began to dial the number and Johnny closed his eyes. He could picture the look of triumph in the journalist's face as he'd told Johnny that soon 'everyone will know.' Everyone will know what? It was clearly important to the man – it was as though he was disappointed when Johnny hadn't responded. Of course he might have got the wrong boy. Johnny thought he would know if something about him mattered that much to someone else.

Mrs Irvine was asking to speak with Mr Watchorn. Then she was demanding to speak with Mr Watchorn's superior. Then she fell silent while she listened to a voice on the line for a while. Finally, she said, 'I'm so sorry,' and replaced the receiver.

'What did they say?' Johnny asked, bracing himself for the news.

Mrs Irvine took a deep breath. 'That journalist . . . Mr Watchorn . . . he's . . .'

'He's what?' Johnny prompted.

'He's dead.' Mrs Irvine's face had turned white.

Johnny could feel the blood draining from his own face and was glad he was sitting down. He was shocked but he was also trying to think. The journalist had run into the park. Presumably he'd gone up to the main gates. That was where the black car had been, the reason he'd gone into the alley in the first place.

'Mrs Irvine?' Johnny asked.

'Yes, Jonathan?' A tear was rolling down the Manager's cheek.

'Did they say how it happened?'

'They just said a hit-and-run accident outside the park gates. The car that hit him didn't even stop.' Mrs Irvine looked as if she might start sobbing at any moment.

Johnny was wide awake now. Those people in the car were probably after him. If they'd killed the journalist they weren't going to mind doing it again. Who were they? He couldn't stay here just waiting for the next terrible thing to happen. He had to take control and find out what was going on. He would run away. He would find Clara.

✿　✿　✿
✿　✿

Johnny was up in his attic bedroom. He hadn't felt hungry – he rarely did with Mr Wilkins's cooking – but he'd still eaten the enormous Sunday roast that was a weekly event at Halader House. He wasn't sure where his next big meal would come from. He'd left his sports bag in the backyard with Bentley, packed full of all the things he thought he'd need – the games console, his sleeping bag, a spare pair of jeans and some T-shirts, his washbag, parka and some socks and pants. He'd looked up the train timetables for Yarnton Hill online. Now he'd just finished going round all the hiding places in the room and had cobbled together thirty-one pounds and sixteen pence. It was less than he'd hoped. And he hated not taking the box of his parents' things with him. He'd have to sneak back and get it one day. Halfway through the trapdoor he stopped and took a last look at his room, with all its fabulous posters clinging to the sloping walls. Then he pushed the door shut above his head and went downstairs towards the back entrance. Miss Harutunian was coming out of the common room.

'Hi, Johnny. I was just coming to see you. Are you OK?'

'Yeah – just taking Bentley for a walk,' Johnny replied.

'Mrs Irvine told me what happened. You want me to come along – keep you company?' Miss Harutunian started walking alongside Johnny towards the back door.

'No it's OK,' said Johnny, stopping still for a moment. 'I think I'd rather be alone. Goodbye.' He said it as forcefully as he could, but trying not to look rude.

'Hey – don't say "goodbye". That means you're going for ever. You say "so long".'

'Sorry – so long,' said Johnny.

'So long, Johnny,' Miss Harutunian replied. She ruffled Johnny's blond hair, turned and walked away.

Johnny opened the back door, put the lead around Bentley's neck, picked up the football bag and, with his dog by his side, walked across the yard and out of the back gate. He closed it behind him, took a last look at Halader House and started jogging across the tarmac towards the railway station.

☼   ☼   ☼
☼   ☼

Johnny had decided on a way of travelling that would make his path harder to follow. At Castle Dudbury Station he just bought a single ticket into London and came out of Liverpool Street to stare at the Gherkin for as long as he felt was safe, which wasn't very long at all. He walked all the way round it. It was built so it curved away as you looked up; close to, you couldn't see the very top – just swirling patterns of glass and steel reflecting the clear blue sky around it. There was only one way in, a giant entrance that looked like a letter 'M' on top with a matching 'W' beneath. He'd have loved to walk through it – inside was a shiny silver statue that looked like an alien, but a security guard started paying him too much attention and he knew it was time to go. With Bentley beside him he was too conspicuous. Johnny retraced his steps back to Liverpool Street station, pausing outside an electrical store to watch a bit of the title decider on a TV in the shop window. It was Arsenal versus Manchester United. But he had a train to catch. He tore himself away, caught the tube to Waterloo and from there he bought a single ticket to Wexenham, the last stop on the line, rather than to Yarnton Hill itself.

It was hard staying out of sight with a large Old English

sheepdog by your side, but Johnny thought he'd made a reasonable job of it and, as night fell, he slipped out of Yarnton Hill station, away from the small town centre and out into some nearby fields. There weren't many streetlights in Yarnton Hill, but had someone been watching they would have been surprised to see what few there were go out as a young boy and his shaggy dog walked underneath them, only to turn back on once the distinctive pair had passed. Johnny was too wrapped up in his own thoughts to notice this happening. It had started to rain and he was feeling miserable. He was cold, wet, alone, frightened and missing the final of the Essex Under Thirteens Schools Cup which would take place the following day.

¤   ¤   ¤
¤   ¤

The next morning Johnny woke up to beeps coming from his sports bag and Bentley licking his face. He looked at his watch – it was 08.34 and his neck hurt. For a moment he thought his alarm clock must have gone off, but his bed was never this uncomfortable. He took in the rural scene around him and sussed that the beeping must be from the games console because the signal search was still running. 'Kovac,' he said sleepily. 'Show results.' The screen on his console transformed into the graphic of the Earth with a pulsating dot above it.

'Results confirmed,' came Kovac's tinny voice through the little speakers. 'Signal coordinates identified. Signal frequency identified.' This time the signal position was verifiable on its own.

'Kovac,' said Johnny, now properly awake. 'Project signal position onto global map.' The screen switched to an Ordnance Survey map with a red dot flashing in the centre.

'Kovac – identify current location of mobile terminal.'

There could be no doubt. A blue dot was now flashing less than two miles from the red one. Whatever was going on, it was going on almost right above Johnny's head. Looking upwards, there was nothing to see except a clear blue sky with occasional wisps of cloud. It was going to be a lovely day – perfect for a cup final.

He wriggled out of his sleeping bag, rolled it up and packed it away, and then looked around in the early morning light. The night before he'd found a grassy field with a few trees round the edge, one of which he'd slept under next to a hedgerow border. He was hungry but knew he didn't have much money left. A confirmed signal and exact position was just the break he needed – he decided to go straight to the spot where the red dot was flashing. He rummaged around in his bag and found a partly eaten chocolate bar from the train journey. He broke the remainder in half, gave one of the pieces to Bentley and ate the other himself. Then he rolled his neck slowly round a few times till the stiffness went, picked up the bag, and started to walk up a little hill with the shaggy sheepdog, wide awake and trotting alongside him. They reached the end of the field and he climbed a gate into the next one with Bentley just squeezing through a large gap between the bars.

Although it was early, there was a tall girl in the next field. She looked a bit older than Johnny and was walking a red setter. She had brown straggly hair and wore a green jacket with matching green wellington boots. She'd clearly already seen him climbing the gate so he couldn't very well go back. Besides, it was grownups he really had to avoid – not kids. Adults watched the news, or at least some of them did. A boy on his own with an Old English sheepdog would be hard to miss if people knew to be looking for him, but he hoped that to her he was just another kid with another dog. The setter was racing over towards Bentley.

'Rusty!' the girl shouted, but her dog wasn't paying her any attention. Bentley skipped away from Johnny and met the other dog halfway. By the time their owners caught up with them, the dogs already seemed best of friends.

'He's lovely – what's his name?' the girl asked Johnny. Close up she had lots of freckles, which matched the brown collar of her jacket.

'Bentley – and I'm Johnny,' Johnny replied before he realized he should probably have given a false name.

'Louise . . . and she's Rusty,' said the girl, patting the setter on the head. 'What you doing here then?'

'I'm staying with my aunt and uncle,' Johnny replied. He could feel his face turning red and willed it to stop.

'Oh. Where do they live?' Louise asked.

'The main road . . . er . . . down near the station,' Johnny said, not having noticed any street names last night.

'Oh, Bert and Josie Peterson? They said their nephew was coming to visit.'

'Yeah – that's them,' Johnny replied.

'I made them up,' said the girl, looking down her upturned nose at Johnny. 'You slept out in the field last night.' Johnny looked sheepish – he'd been rumbled easily and there didn't seem any point denying it. Louise continued, 'I saw you when I started walking Rusty. Didn't want to wake sleeping beauty, so I ended up out here.'

'I'm running away,' said Johnny simply.

'And you ran away to Yarnton Hill?' Louise said, laughing. 'That's not very bright is it?'

'Why's that?' Johnny asked, looking beyond the girl and towards the village. 'It seems OK here.'

'OK? Are you stupid? Kids run away *from* here. If they don't the pigs take them,' Louise said. 'And if you hadn't met me you were heading right for them.'

'The pigs?' Johnny didn't understand and he hated being called stupid.

'I don't know. That's what we call them. Pigs in suits.'

'Pigs in suits?' Johnny asked, wishing the girl would make it a bit clearer.

'S'pose it's from the name,' Louise said. 'Proteus Institute for the Gifted – for the unlucky more like.'

The penny dropped. 'That's where I'm going,' Johnny said. 'My sister's there.'

'How do you know? No one knows what goes on there,' said Louise through a very narrow mouth.

'Trust me, I know,' Johnny said. 'And I've got to find her.' Johnny hitched his bag back over his shoulder, about to set off.

'You mustn't – it's dangerous,' Louise said. 'We're already too far out. I'm going back to town.'

'Go if you're scared,' said Johnny. In his experience no one was prepared to admit to that and he could do with a local guide.

'I am scared and you should be too. Come on, Rusty,' Louise said. She turned and started walking down the hill, with the setter at her side.

'What are we going to do now, Bents?' said Johnny and to his surprise Bentley turned and started barking in the direction of Rusty. Even more to his surprise, Rusty stopped in her tracks and turned and sprinted back up the hill to Johnny and Bentley. 'Nice one, Bents,' Johnny said to his sheepdog. 'Come on then.' Johnny started walking up the hill, now with two dogs in tow.

'Rusty!' Louise was clearly desperate, but the setter ignored her as she pattered alongside Bentley. 'Rusty! Heel!' Louise tried again, but Rusty just kept skipping away from her. Johnny heard footsteps coming up behind but didn't turn round. Louise caught him up.

'Your dog's braver than you,' Johnny said to Louise, who looked terrified.

'I can't leave her,' she replied. 'Pigs don't like dogs, but

54

they'll take me if I'm not with her. It happened to Peter.'

'Who's Peter?' Johnny asked.

'My neighbour. He disappeared last month. He was stupid and went out without his dog – I told him not to.'

'Well I'll find Clara and you can find Peter,' said Johnny. 'At least let's have a look.'

'You don't understand,' Louise said. 'This isn't some silly boy's game. At least let's get under some cover – I'll be amazed if they've not seen us already.'

The foursome – two children and two dogs – moved to the edge of the field and underneath the protection of some trees. They walked along one of the hedgerows and up to the brow of the hill. As they neared the very top Louise pulled Johnny down and they crawled the final few feet on all fours, mirroring the dogs beside them. From the summit they peered down into the valley below. Johnny had seen this sight before, albeit from the vantage point of the main road running beneath them, empty now apart from a black taxi parked in a lay-by.

The Proteus Institute for the Gifted stood impressively in manicured grounds. It was a four-storey, red-brick Victorian building with a large square central tower, all set above some weathered steps cut into the hillside on the opposite side of the valley. There were greenhouses to the left of the main school buildings, around which were patches of vibrant reds and blues from flowers in bloom. A tree-lined drive ran from the foot of the steps, by the war memorial, and out to the main road. Apart from the drive there was a tall wire perimeter fence that seemed to run for miles without a break around the grounds. On the inside of the fence was a continuous band of lawn, except in the right-hand corner where a maze, built from hedges, almost touched it. On the far side of the building, overshadowed by the hill, were a couple of sports fields with rugby posts and a pavilion. Although early, it was turning into a lovely sunny day and already Johnny saw a handful of children running though the maze, while others played a game hitting balls through hoops with giant hammers. It was too far away to see if any of them was Clara.

'You've seen it now. OK? Let's go,' hissed Louise in Johnny's ear. Louise seemed very scared of what just looked like a posh school. It didn't make any sense and Johnny wasn't about to turn around and hop on a train to Castle Dudbury.

'I can't go back now,' he whispered. 'This is what I came for. I've got to find Clara.'

'You're mad,' said Louise, who'd turned white and was trembling. 'You'll never get in there. And if you do you'll never get out.'

Johnny put his hand on her arm to steady her. 'Yes I will. And if you tell me what Peter looks like I'll find him too.' He looked her square in the eye and hoped he sounded braver than he felt.

Louise buried her face in the grass, steeling herself. Then she spoke, slowly and controlled. 'You can't go on your own – you don't know what you're getting into. And if we're going down there you'd better dump that bag and make sure your dog stays quiet.'

'You're coming too?' Johnny asked, surprised.

'Looks like I've no choice,' said Louise, nodding towards Bentley who was already leading Rusty along the hedgerow and down the hill towards the institute.

Johnny took the little console out of his sports bag and slipped it into the back pocket of his jeans – he didn't know when he might need Kovac's help. Then he pushed the bag out of sight underneath the hedgerow and ran after Louise, who'd nearly caught up with the dogs a little further ahead.

They reached the main road – there was a wide ditch on the far side from the Proteus Institute so they made their way along it, hoping to keep out of sight while heading for the part of the fence closest to the maze. Climb the fence anywhere else and they were bound to be spotted; next to the maze they had a chance of sneaking into the grounds unseen. As they reached the lay-by with the black cab, two cars rounded a bend and came into view. The children and dogs hid behind the empty taxi. From a brief glimpse, Johnny thought either of the passing cars could have been the one he'd seen outside the park gates a few days before. Of course he couldn't be sure, but a shiver still went down his spine as they drove by. Once the cars were safely out of sight, Johnny led the way forward until they reached the right part of the fence.

'What now?' Johnny asked.

'You're the one who wants to go inside,' said Louise. 'I guess we climb it.'

'But what about the dogs? I can't leave Bentley here.' The sheepdog was looking up at Johnny, panting with his tongue hanging out.

'Can he climb a ten foot fence?' Louise asked.

Johnny looked at the fence and wasn't sure he could climb it either. And even if he did there was some very vicious barbed wire running along the top. And once he got over that he didn't know how he'd go about looking for Clara. Maybe he was being stupid, but he couldn't go back now. He knelt down beside his faithful friend. 'Sorry Bents – stay here out of sight. OK? I'll be back.' Johnny held Bentley for a few seconds while the sheepdog met his gaze as though he understood.

'You need a leg up?' Johnny asked Louise.

'I'm not a useless girl, you know. I can climb it. I'm not sure you can though.'

'Both together then,' said Johnny. There was no traffic. Louise said her goodbyes to Rusty and the pair sprinted across the road and jumped up onto the fence. Johnny was a good climber and Louise proved to be too – they reached the top together, which

57

was a mistake. The fence gave way and they fell forward, landing with a thud right on top of the outermost hedge of the maze, just thick enough to hold them for a second, before they tumbled forward inside. Louise was bleeding from the barbed wire.

'You OK?' Johnny asked.

'Fine,' Louise said, clutching her stomach which most definitely did not look fine. Her jacket had been undone and the white T-shirt underneath was quickly turning red. 'There's worse stuff in here – believe me,' she added. 'For a start how do we get out of here?' The hedges making up the maze were a lot higher than they'd looked from the hillside. Even jumping, Johnny couldn't see over them. As she was taller, Louise tried doing the same, but only the once. Johnny could see it had hurt, even if she didn't make a noise.

'I wrote a program to solve a maze in homework last year,' Johnny said. 'Just follow the right or left wall and we'll get through it.'

'You're funny,' Louise said. 'You don't look like a nerd. It's really that simple?'

'Yeah,' said Johnny. 'It can take a while though. Your choice – left or right?'

Louise chose the right wall and they set off. They could hear children's voices wafting over the hedges, but were careful not to make any noise themselves. Normally exploring a maze would have been great fun, but with Louise gripping Johnny's arm as though her life depended on it, everything felt deadly serious. They walked slowly and carefully for five or ten minutes, taking every right turn they found between the thick hedges. Finally Louise stopped, holding her stomach, and said 'Are you sure this is working? We're just going round in circles.'

Johnny hissed, 'Trust me.' He turned a corner a little carelessly and bumped into two girls in pink gingham checked dresses. They took one look at Johnny and Louise, another at

Louise's bloodstained T-shirt, and turned and ran screaming. 'Quick,' said Johnny. 'Don't let them get away,' and he sprinted after them with Louise following. He was gaining but it was hard to follow the schoolgirls as they darted quickly round the different corners. Johnny had almost caught them up when they turned left and the maze opened up into a central clearing with a sundial in the middle and a few other girls sitting on the grass.

One of the girls he'd been chasing shouted, 'Strangers – run!' as she careered past the sundial and out the other side. All the other schoolgirls leapt up and followed – all of them except one.

A fair-skinned, blonde haired girl jumped to her feet with the others but as they ran off she stopped and turned to Johnny who also halted. Louise staggered into the clearing clutching her stomach. Johnny, all out of breath, managed to say 'Clara?'

The girl in front of him replied, 'It's you.'

Of all the things she might have said that wasn't what Johnny was expecting. 'You know me?' he asked. 'How?'

Clara took hold of a golden chain around her neck and, from beneath her uniform, pulled out a locket, with swirls of green delicately covering a golden base dotted with crystals. 'Your photo's in my locket,' she said. 'Who are you?'

Still breathing heavily, Johnny managed to say, 'I'm your brother . . . Johnny . . . here to rescue you.'

'Rescue me? What from?' asked Clara and then, looking at Louise, 'Who's she? Is she OK?'

Louise didn't look OK. She was holding onto the sundial for support and her face had become as pale as Johnny's and Clara's. 'I'm looking for Peter . . . Peter Dalrymple,' she said. 'They took him a month ago.'

Clara scrunched up her face, concentrating hard. 'Short, brown hair – posh boy?' she said. Louise nodded. 'Yeah – he was here,' Clara continued. 'He didn't last long.'

'They killed him?' Johnny and Louise asked together.

Clara put her hands on her hips. 'What is it with you two? Don't be silly – he wasn't good enough.' Johnny and Louise exchanged dark glances. 'Look,' said Clara, 'it's very competitive at Proteus: "fitter than the fittest". I've lasted longer than anyone. He'll have gone off to Triton.' When neither Johnny nor Louise showed any sign of understanding her, Clara added, 'It's another school – I think it's in Wales.'

Louise didn't look convinced. She turned to Johnny. 'Peter's gone – you've found her. C'mon let's go, before the pigs find us.'

'Who are the pigs?' Clara asked.

'Pigs in suits,' Louise said urgently. 'They take kids and bring them here.'

'I rather think she means us.' The voice belonged to a tall man in a black suit who'd just walked into the central clearing.

'Stevens!' Johnny recognized the man from his mum's hospital.

Stevens smiled coldly at him. 'Johnny Mackintosh flies straight into our spider's web,' he said, before sticking a finger in his ear and adding 'both children are secure . . . with an unwanted stray from the village. Request permission to terminate . . . thank you.' Stevens turned towards Louise and pulled a weapon out from a holster inside his suit. 'You know you're not meant to come here, silly girl.'

'No!' Clara shouted. Louise was rooted to the spot by the sundial, but Clara ran between her and Stevens and shouted, 'What on earth are you doing?'

'If only you knew, Miss Clara,' Stevens said coldly. 'Out of the way.'

'I won't,' Clara said, stubbornly refusing to move. 'Don't hurt her.'

'She doesn't concern you. Now your brother's decided to

come and visit us you're going on a little journey. People in high places are very interested in him. And you'll be the icing on the cake.' Clara didn't budge; Stevens squeezed the trigger of his weapon and a beam of green light shot past her shoulder, just missing Louise and setting fire to a hedge behind. Before the man could take aim again, a grey and white missile hurtled at him from behind, knocking him to the ground.

'Bentley!' shouted Johnny. The sheepdog wrestled with Stevens, shaking his head from side to side. Stevens, his suit being torn to shreds, managed to get both hands around Bentley's neck and began to throttle the dog while lifting him away. Then Rusty appeared, clamping her jaws onto Stevens's arm. There was a horrible sound – a sharp snap from beneath the blur of canine limbs – that echoed along the valley. Rusty jumped away and ran from the clearing, while Bentley stood over the motionless figure.

'Quick – we've got to get out of here,' said Louise. 'They'll all be coming now.'

'I'm not going anywhere till you tell me what's going on,' said Clara, looking anxiously at Stevens's limp body. 'You might have killed a Protector. I've never met you before, you breeze into my school giving orders . . .' She looked at Louise, '. . . bleeding.'

'We're wasting time,' said Johnny. 'Come on, Clara.' He reached into his T-shirt and pulled out his locket. 'Trust me – how else would we both have one of these?' Johnny felt the locket turn warm in his hands and looked down. The crystals had started to glow – so had the ones on Clara's. Then it became light in his hand – he let go and it lifted up into the air, pointing straight at Clara's locket which was behaving in just the same way.

'Wow,' said Clara, open-mouthed. 'OK, I believe you.' The spell somehow broken, both lockets fell back to hang normally.

'In here.' She moved to the sundial by Louise and was soon turning the fittings like an expert safe-cracker. The sundial slid across the grass to reveal a hidden entrance with steps leading downwards into the earth. 'No one knows about this – get in.' Louise didn't need asking twice. She started down the steps, wincing and holding her stomach, followed by Clara.

'Come on, Bents,' shouted Johnny. 'In here, boy.' The dog turned to follow the children into the opening, but at that moment Stevens lifted his right arm and fired a shot. With a whimper Bentley collapsed to the ground.

'No!' Johnny shouted, running over to Bentley and cradling the dog in his arms.

'Leave him,' shouted Clara from halfway down the steps. 'It's closing.' She was right – the sundial was slowly sliding back across the grass to return to its original position. Without thinking Johnny picked up Bentley and ran, stumbling towards Clara and down the stairs just before the sundial closed the opening above him. Johnny was covered in blood, but it wasn't his. The three children reached the foot of the stairs, where their way was blocked by piles of discarded boxes and wooden crates. Johnny lay Bentley gently down and he and Clara set to work on clearing a path. Finally, they were all able to squeeze through into a very long corridor, criss-crossed by many others. They started running along it. Johnny was doing his best but carrying Bentley meant he couldn't keep up with the two girls.

'You've got to leave him, Johnny,' said Louise. 'I'm sorry. He's no good to us now. If we're not quick they're bound to catch us.'

'I'm not leaving Bentley,' Johnny replied, almost out of breath. 'You go on.'

'She's right,' said Clara. 'The Protectors will be everywhere in a minute. He's only a dog.'

'Only a dog?' said Johnny, outraged, but just then they heard a bang and turned to see a shower of splintered crates fly into the main corridor they'd just joined.

'Quickly – this way,' Clara shouted. She led them into another corridor at right angles to the first. 'Look – if he's that important I'll come back for him later. OK?'

Johnny's arms were aching so much he knew he couldn't carry Bentley another metre anyway. Very reluctantly he said 'OK – in here,' pointing into a storeroom off to the side. They all piled in and he lowered Bentley carefully to the floor in front of some cardboard cartons. 'Listen, Bents,' he said, stroking the dog's blood-matted fur. 'We're gonna come back for you – I promise.' He stood up and followed the two girls to the doorway. Bentley whimpered. Johnny turned and stopped, seeing the pleading look in the sheepdog's different-coloured eyes.

'Come on,' said Louise, grabbing his arm and tugging him out of the storeroom.

There were voices and footsteps coming from nearby. The three children ran as fast as they could in the other direction, Louise trying not to drip blood on the floor, turning this way and that as they attempted to lose their pursuers.

They passed a half-glass, half-wooden door on the left and Johnny stopped. 'Let's hide in here till they've gone.' He knew Louise needed to rest. Her bleeding was getting much worse. They couldn't outrun the men chasing them, but maybe they could lie low for a little while, double back, pick up Bentley and make a run for the fence. He turned the handle, but the door didn't budge – only then did he notice the electronic keypad beside the lock. The footsteps behind were quite loud now. He pressed his hand onto the keypad, pushing numbers frantically at random, thinking 'please open,' and by some miracle there was an electronic click.

The three of them burst into the darkened room and ran the

length of it, bashing into unseen pieces of furniture as they made their way through the blackness. Finally they reached the far end and slid to the floor, resting their backs against a large glass tank while breathing heavily. They could hear shouting from the corridor; footsteps stopped outside the door. Johnny peered around the corner of the tank – through the clear panel halfway up the door he could see three silhouettes. He shushed the others, and they all held their breath, but then the footsteps disappeared and there was silence. Johnny looked at his watch. It was 11.16. They'd wait five minutes and then make a run for it.

'Where are we?' whispered Louise. 'What is this place?'

'I don't know,' said Clara. 'I've never been down this corridor.'

Despite Johnny's shushing, Louise stood up. 'What are you doing?' Johnny said. 'Stay still.'

'Don't tell me what to do,' Louise whispered back. 'You're the one who got us into this mess. There's evil here – this place stinks of it. I want to see for myself.' Louise was feeling along the wall for a light switch. She found it and there was a flickering of fluorescent tubes before the room was bathed in dingy light.

'No!' Johnny hissed, but then his jaw dropped. There wasn't just one tank in the room – there were dozens, in rows, leading all the way back to the far wall. And in each, suspended in the murky water within, was the body of a different boy or girl. Johnny looked at the tank beside them, containing a boy floating face down in water, arms and legs splayed either side of him. He'd been left there so long his skin was turning green. He must have drowned.

'It's not Peter, is it?' Johnny asked. Louise and Clara shook their heads. Nobody moved – they simply stood there, transfixed by the terrible sight. Then the boy in the tank opened his eyes. Clara screamed and ran. She reached the door, opened it and was out in the corridor before Johnny could stop her. Louise was frozen to the spot as the boy pressed his face against the glass walls, smiling manically at her and breathing happily from underneath the water. Johnny had to make a choice.

'Stay here,' he said to Louise, who clearly wasn't going anywhere. 'I'll be back,' and with that he ran through the door after Clara. As he looked one way then the other he saw her feet disappearing up some metal steps further along. He ran as fast as he could and started climbing the stairs. 'Clara, wait,' he shouted, but his sister was already through the door and out. Johnny followed. He pushed the door open to find her standing right in front of him. They'd emerged into the main building at the T-shaped junction of two corridors. Several thick-set men in suits were calmly walking towards them from both the left and the right – there was only way to go. 'Come on,' said Johnny, grabbing Clara's hand and dragging her forward, running towards a lift at the far end. Perhaps if they got there in time they could lose their pursuers on the upper floors.

Clara was shaking her head from side to side. 'I don't understand,' she said. 'I thought they were my friends.'

'Well they're not anymore,' said Johnny. They reached the lift and he pushed the call button over and over again. He turned to see two of the men in suits with their weapons out, walking together towards them. A bell chimed and the lift doors opened. Johnny and Clara backed inside.

'We're not supposed to go in the lift,' Clara muttered, more to herself than Johnny. 'Use of the tower lift will lead to automatic expulsion.' She seemed to be mimicking an announcement she must have heard many times before.

'That's the least of our problems,' said Johnny, now frantically pushing the only button in sight, hoping the lift doors would close before they were caught. But they were staying resolutely open and the men in suits were now only five metres away. Unexpectedly, the men stopped. One of them pointed his weapon at Johnny and made a pretend shooting movement. Then he lowered it and, as the lift doors finally closed, Johnny could see him laughing on the other side. The truth dawned on him. They had been directed here. It was a trap. He'd walked right into it and brought his new-found sister with him.

The lift started going up – and quickly. The odd thing was it didn't show any sign of stopping. Its walls began glowing electric blue. They were still going up. Johnny braced himself – they were bound to smash into the roof at any moment. The tower was tall but it couldn't be *that* tall. Gradually, though, the lift walls were becoming transparent as they moved faster and faster upwards.

'What's happening?' Clara asked.

Outside, Johnny could now see fields disappearing beneath wispy clouds and still they went upwards. 'No way,' Johnny said, more to himself than to Clara. The roof of the institute was far below them and the sky turning from blue to black before he finally understood what was going on. He'd read about these things, but they weren't meant to exist. Incredible as it seemed, someone had built a space elevator. The lift only had one button because they were only going to one place. That place was exactly 36,000 kilometres above the tower of the Proteus Institute – the place from where Kovac had identified the signal.

'I'm scared,' said Clara, squeezing Johnny's hand tightly.

'It's OK,' he told her, thinking it was definitely not OK. 'We're going to be fine.'

'It's not that,' said Clara, looking up at Johnny. He saw that her eyes, although pale blue, had the same silver flecks as his own. 'I just really hate heights.'

Johnny started to laugh, but that turned to choking as gas

66

began pouring into the lift from above their heads. Johnny could feel it burrowing into every corner of his lungs – his legs buckled and he had to struggle to stay standing. 'Close your eyes, Clara,' he said. 'Go to sleep. We'll wake up in a nice place.' He tried to squeeze her hand but his body went into spasm and he found himself on the floor of the lift, looking down at the curvature of the Earth beneath him. All his life he'd wanted to witness that view, to be entering space. He closed his own eyes hoping he'd wake up to see it properly.

4 ✮ ✩

Learning to Speak ✮ ✩

Johnny's head really hurt. He didn't want to open his eyes in case he was being watched so he lay there, wherever 'there' was (it felt very strange) and tried to get a sense of his surroundings. The stench was awful – a cross between a toilet and a barrel of rotting vegetables, mainly cabbage. He had to steel himself not to be sick and tried holding his breath so he wouldn't have to smell it. He could hear faraway sounds like a rickety building creaking in the wind. And as he slowly moved his right hand, it disappeared into something wet – which started crawling up his arm. 'Uggggh!' Johnny opened his eyes to see his fingers covered in dirty orange slime. He tried to roll away, but there was only air to push against. He was floating . . . in a vast, gloomy chamber . . . in mid-air. And, having pushed against it, he was now moving ever so slowly away from the goo beside him, which was contained within a square, about twice his height, cut into the wall or floor or ceiling or whatever it was. Wherever he was it had to be a spaceship, but it didn't look at all how any spaceship Johnny had imagined would look. It wasn't gleaming metal or plastic or supermaterials he couldn't even dream about. Instead, it looked almost alive, like the leaves of a giant blue-grey vegetable, but covered on every surface with mushroom-shaped nodules. Looking up, he could just about see a dark floating figure silhouetted against the ceiling, beside the next patch of the orange slime. There were squares of the goo regularly spaced all along the wall, and a collection of weird and wonderfully shaped things tethered to the ceiling by giant tendrils with octopus-like suckers along their length.

As he squinted, getting used to the darkness, he could make out the checked pattern of Clara's school uniform on the figure above. Johnny looked around the chamber – there was no sign of anyone else.

'Clara,' he whispered. There was no reply. He tried again a little louder, but again nothing. She must still be asleep and he was slowly drifting further away from her and into the middle of the chamber . . . with no way to stop himself. It was as if he was floating in a swimming pool but with no water. He shouted Clara's name and this time she stirred. Johnny had to get back to her. He felt inside his jeans pockets – the only thing he found was the games console. He knew he didn't need it any more, but even so . . . He flung it as hard as he could in the opposite direction to Clara. It worked. Johnny changed direction and began to float towards his sister.

'Johnny?' Clara asked sleepily. 'Where are we? What's going on?'

'I think we're in a spaceship,' Johnny replied. 'We're in zero G.'

'Zero what?' Clara asked.

'Zero G. Zero gravity. That's why everything's floating,' Johnny said.

'But what's happening behind you? The walls . . . the space . . .'

Johnny didn't need to look back – he could see it in front of him. The blue-grey walls were collapsing and coming closer. His insides were being scrunched up too. He felt really sick. Clara was suddenly right on top of him. They were going to collide . . . hard. As Clara was about to bash into him he heard her say, 'It's so beautiful,' only she didn't hit him – they seemed to pass right through each other. And then the wall was going to hit him but again he passed through it, or it through him. Was that ringed planet off to one side Saturn? It looked like it, but before he could check he was pulled upwards at ever increasing speed and found himself rushing towards what could only be a star. Then, just as suddenly, he was jerked ninety degrees in another direction. He thought he could hear screams. Hundreds of stars rushed by – becoming lines rather than points of light. He changed direction again and then, without warning, he stopped dead. The walls of the ship flew through him and beyond and then stopped in their original position. Clara did the same. Johnny couldn't hold it in anymore and was violently sick. Without gravity, a ball of vomit flew out of his mouth and wobbled towards Clara, only just missing her. As a result, Johnny's momentum changed, sending him floating slowly away from his sister towards a nearby wall.

'Wow! That was unbelievable – didn't you think?' Clara said, breathlessly. 'Wasn't it just amazing? I've never felt anything like it. It was like being part of everything . . . of the whole universe. It was incredible.'

Johnny moaned.

'Are you OK?' Clara asked, now noticing he might not be.

'I'm not sure,' replied Johnny, who was actually very sure he'd be sick again at any moment.

'What was that?' Clara asked. 'I didn't know anything could be like that.'

A noise from above interrupted her – the tethered pieces of space junk were being pulled upwards onto the ceiling. A moment later, Clara screamed and started falling upwards towards the ceiling, only now it had become the floor. Someone had turned on a gravity field and it was moving closer. Johnny stretched out his arms as far as he could and just touched one of the mushroom-shaped growths on the wall. He felt his body start to become heavy, but he didn't fall. The wall was sticky and he pulled himself forward so his hands and trainers were glued tightly onto it. But his body was getting heavier. He looked down – Clara seemed OK, but there were two people walking towards her. Before Johnny had time to shout out his hands peeled away from the wall and, with his trainers still attached, he fell backwards till he was hanging upside down facing outwards. He stayed that way for about half a second, but then his feet peeled away and he fell again, finishing upright facing the wall. Almost at once he was on the move again . . . and again, somersaulting ever faster down the wall until he finished dizzily in a crumpled heap on the floor of the chamber. Lifting his head from the smelly blue-grey surface he found himself staring into a shiny black pair of shoes. On all fours, Johnny looked upwards.

'Nice of you to join us,' said Stevens. 'Come.' The man who'd pretended to shoot Johnny outside the space elevator was leading Clara across the floor of the chamber, weaving between giant tentacles and mysterious objects littered everywhere. Johnny had no choice but to follow in silence, with Stevens behind, pushing him in the back.

Nearing the far wall, Johnny saw his little games console, poking out from a puddle that smelled of vomit on the floor. If it was sick he really hoped it was his, as he pretended to trip up, getting close enough to pick up the handheld in one slick movement. Stevens muttered, 'Disgusting species – filthy little humans.'

Ahead of them, Clara stopped and turned round. 'Well I don't think much of your dirty stinking spaceship.'

'I suppose you could do better? You are nothing – we are the krun. We are perfection.' He pointed to the man beside her and said, 'Show her perfection. Show her our true form. Then release the hundra.'

The man nodded and stepped into a clear cubicle nearby.

Once inside, he turned to face Johnny and Clara and smiled as dense white bubbles began to fall on him from above. He began to change – thick black hairs sprouted across his face, his eyes ballooned out like pudding bowls and his nose grew to become a snout. As the foam filled the chamber, it became harder to see what was going on, but it didn't stop Johnny staring, fascinated. The bubbles reminded him of the stuff he'd extracted from his own hair back in Halader House – this was some sort of DNA shower. The door to the cubicle opened and out stepped something totally different from the man who had entered. It had two legs, four very long arms and a short stubby neck on which sat a giant, fly-like face. From beside him Johnny dimly heard Clara say, 'That's disgusting.' He was too shocked to say anything. He'd seen a creature just like this only a week before, in the moonlight outside his bedroom window.

The krun, saliva dripping from its snout, waddled towards a container that opened automatically. In two of its four hands, each with a thumb and three long fingers, it took hold of coiled whips which crackled with electric red sparks as it unleashed them. Satisfied, it walked over to a cube the size of a big car and inserted one of its free hands into a hole in the side. The walls fell away to reveal a giant brown floating ball, with leathery skin like an elephant's, chained to the floor. The krun took hold of the chains and whipped the ball, fleetingly turning its surface red.

Meanwhile Stevens walked over to the wall and touched it beside one of the squares of orange goo. Slime began to ooze out onto the floor. 'My turn,' he said, now walking into the same DNA shower that the other 'man' had entered. There was so much going on, Johnny didn't know where to look. Stevens began to transform before them, while the chained giant ball floated towards the wall, but Johnny's eyes were drawn away from them both. Instead he stared at the inside of the cavity that was appearing as the slime emptied out from it and a strange sight began to emerge.

In the centre, nearly three metres tall and dressed, if that was the right word, in shimmering metallic robes with the most vivid colours that reminded Johnny of dragonfly wings, was a bottle green alien with a long thin head – almost a metre long – with two antenna sprouting from the top, only to droop feebly down the side of the thing's face. Any arms or legs were covered by the robes. At its feet was a little brown creature, very much smaller, that waddled around its larger companion on four bowed legs, like those of a piano stool. It was attempting to remove clumps of dirty orange goo from the bigger alien, while straightening out its robes with two spindly arms.

The two creatures completely ignored Johnny, who felt a push in the back sending him towards the wall. Clara was thrust forwards too, as the krun that had been Stevens shoved them with two of his arms. A circular hole widened in front of them, like a camera shutter, and their momentum carried Johnny and Clara through. Clara froze. They were now standing on the beginning of a very narrow walkway, stretching across to a distant wall like a giant ligament and so high above the floor of an enormous cavern that machines were flying around beneath them. There were no railings on either side and a very long drop, but another push from Stevens saw them forced out onto it. Clara stared resolutely ahead, but Johnny turned round to look behind. Both krun, the floating ball and the other two aliens had followed them through the opening and were walking behind, causing the walkway to bounce alarmingly. The creature that had been Stevens began making strange clicks using two arms and his snout and the other krun started whipping the leathery ball, turning its surface a vibrant red. A voice, Stevens's voice

73

speaking in English, boomed out, 'We are the krun – you are our prisoners. You will make your way to the transit tube and transfer to an Andromedan vessel.'

'Transit tube? They simply cannot be serious,' squeaked a voice from the tall alien. 'Just how primitive is this ship? I, the Dauphin taking . . .'

As the surface of the ball returned to its original colouring, the voice was replaced by chirping sounds. Clara had managed to turn round by holding onto Johnny, but was determinedly not looking down. The krun began the whipping again. With every lash Clara's fingernails dug deeper into Johnny's arm.

' . . . the indignity of it all. I will not transfer through a transit tube. I will not be treated the same as these primitives.' The voice was still coming from the tall creature who seemed to be gesturing towards Johnny and Clara. 'I am the Dauphin of . . .'

'Silence!' boomed Stevens, as the other krun whipped the leather ball again, this time far more violently than before. 'I don't care if you're the Emperor himself. You will do exactly as you are told. Do you understand or do you want to die?' As he said this, the other krun started whipping the leather ball constantly, turning it red all over.

'Stop!' Clara cried. 'You're hurting it.'

Stevens looked at Clara. 'For years I've had to put up with your do-gooder nonsense. Not any more.' He laughed, took hold of one of the whips and started lashing the ball so hard the whip was now piercing the outer hide.

'No!' Johnny heard himself say. He didn't know what, but he had to do something. Trying to run towards Stevens he misjudged the low gravity and crashed straight into the floating gas bag. Instead of bouncing off he found he'd stuck to it. Somewhere in the distance he thought he heard a scream of pain as the whip lashed into the back of his skull over again, forcing his head into one of the lesions that had opened up in the ball's side. He squeezed his eyes tightly shut for a moment and everything went quiet.

The silence was broken by a rich, deep voice that seemed to be inside Johnny's head. It said, 'Hello . . . that was rather unexpected.'

Johnny opened his eyes again. His face was somehow inside the huge ball, which was hollow. From his new vantage point the outer hide was translucent, a battered brown membrane on which red streaks were appearing and disappearing from the continuing, but now silent, cracks of the whip. The ball's insides were illuminated by a swirling, glowing golden pattern of light at its very centre. Somehow Johnny knew that this was where the voice he'd heard had come from.

'Hello,' Johnny said back. He couldn't actually tell if he'd simply thought the words or had spoken them out loud. 'Where am I? What are you?' He'd tried to hold this final question back as it did seem rather rude, but he'd simply thought it and out it came.

'I,' said the voice, 'am a hundra. And you,' it continued, 'do not appear to be dead.'

'No, I don't think I am,' said Johnny. The atmosphere inside the hundra was old, stale and very thick – it was like being under the surface of a swimming pool where the water hadn't been changed for months. Yet he could breathe.

'How very curious,' said the hundra.

'Are you OK?' Johnny asked. 'They seemed to be hurting you.' As the red weals appeared on the brown membrane, he could dimly hear Clara calling his name in the distance.

'Regrettably, I shall live,' said the hundra. 'Tell me, what race are you?'

'I'm human,' Johnny replied. 'My name's Johnny – Johnny Mackintosh.'

'I have lived many years and witnessed many things,' boomed the hundra. 'But never have I seen a human, Johnny – Johnny Mackintosh. It is thought no race can touch the hundra, without suffering an instant and most horrible death. Not since the ancients – the ones who gave us our gift.'

'I don't understand,' said Johnny. 'What gift? And how could I touch you?'

'We, the hundra,' said the creature, 'are the galaxy's translators. We feed on language. We ingest words from one people and emit brainwaves in the language of others. As to how you come to be bonded to me, and how you lived, I do not know. Stay with me a while, Johnny – Johnny Mackintosh. I would welcome a companion with whom to enter discourse.'

'I can't,' said Johnny. 'There's loads I need to ask, but my sister's out there. I can't leave her. Is there any way you can send me back?'

'If that is your wish,' said the hundra sadly, all the time its golden lights swirling. 'I fear after all these years my conversation may have been lacking anyway. You show courage, human. And kindness for trying to help me. Such qualities are rare in these modern times.' Johnny felt the word 'modern' was meant to sound insulting. 'Before I expel you, will you do me one favour?'

'Of course,' said Johnny. 'Whatever I can.'

'I have grown stale, for too long a victim of these vicious krun. I fear I shall die here, forsaken in this dark place, never again seeing the light this galaxy offers.' Johnny made to interrupt, but the hundra silenced him. 'There is a quality of the ancients that, when the need is great, we can divide ourselves, cleaving our souls apart. You cannot save me Johnny – Johnny Mackintosh but, should you accept, you may take with you a fragment of my being. Through you a little light may fall on me again, before the darkness closes in.'

Johnny wasn't at all sure he liked the sound of this, but he had practically promised. 'OK, I guess,' he said focusing as best he could on the glittering gold lights.

'My gratitude will go with you always, most noble human,' said the voice inside Johnny's head and, as he watched, a single speck of light separated itself from the swirling mass and floated towards him, sparkling all the way up his left nostril. Happily, Johnny decided he didn't feel any different at all.

'It is a great gift,' boomed the hundra, 'unique in all the galaxy. Use it well.'

Before he could say thank you, though he wasn't really sure what for, Johnny found his face separating from the wall of the creature and he was thrown out onto a ledge. While he had been inside the hundra the party had crossed the walkway.

'Johnny!' shouted Clara.

The whip bounced off the hundra's hide and Johnny rolled out of the way just in time as it crashed onto the floor next to him. He got to his feet and ran over to her.

'It lives, sire,' clicked the little brown alien to the tall Dauphin. 'What thing can touch the hundra and live?'

'Silence!' boomed the Dauphin. 'How dare you address me without being spoken to.'

'Your Highness. Please forgive me. I, your humble servant, prostrate myself,' said the creature, collapsing all four legs and falling in front of the Dauphin.

'You will proceed to the transit tunnel . . . now,' said Stevens, and he pointed with a long finger to an opening in the wall.

'Very well,' said the Dauphin, striding quickly towards the opening. The little brown servant scuttled behind.

'Come on,' said Johnny to Clara, taking her hand and following the two aliens. 'Anywhere's better than this.' Clara didn't look very sure about that. Through the opening they found themselves in a small chamber facing a sealed hatch. The doorway closed behind them, leaving Stevens, the other krun and the hundra on the far side. There was a hiss, as though some air was escaping. Then the hatch in front opened, revealing a tunnel with corrugated translucent walls. 'It's an airlock,' said Johnny. 'We must be transferring to another ship.'

The Dauphin looked at him strangely, before ushering the little brown creature in front of it and into the tunnel. As soon as it crossed the opening it started floating, arms and legs flailing everywhere. However the gravity was being generated, it didn't seem to extend beyond the ship.

'It doesn't look very long,' Johnny said.

Clara took Johnny's hand and squeezed. 'Let's go together,' she said, and they both pushed off, following the Dauphin into the zero G tunnel.

The hatch behind them closed automatically as they floated through the corrugated corridor. It looked as though it was made of skin, covered with dark veins and spots, with little flaps of extra tissue hanging off in places. They'd set out rather too quickly and were catching the Dauphin and its servant. A light appeared at the end they were floating towards, suggesting the airlock there must be opening. Johnny squinted to see if he could make out anything. If the krun on the ship they were leaving were scary, they were nothing compared to the monstrous shapes Johnny thought he could make out before he smacked straight into the back of the Dauphin, sending them both spinning out of control. He was rotating so now he could see where they'd come from and where they were going every couple of seconds, and something unexpected was happening. The light they'd been heading towards had gone out. The tube, in both directions, seemed to be closing together as if it were being pinched tight. He could understand them closing the route off behind them, but not in front. He really hoped they hadn't been too slow – that they weren't going to be stuck in this little organic tube in space until the air ran out. He kicked out, but it didn't stop his rotating motion. The Dauphin was shouting at him for his clumsiness. And then the tunnel itself jerked in one direction and all four of them inside it were flung violently against a wall by the acceleration.

What followed was a rollercoaster ride, but without seatbelts and not seeing where you were going. Inside the tunnel was like being in a washing machine, as they all crashed into each other and the walls, which at least were a little elastic, for what seemed like for ever. And then it stopped as suddenly as it had begun. They had gravity. The bow-legged brown alien had rolled itself into a little ball, revealing a set of porcupine-style quills along its back. Clara had banged her forehead and a lump was already beginning to swell up. Johnny was impressed. He'd only met his sister a little while before but she was clearly made of stern stuff. He'd expected her to start crying but she just turned to him in her battered school uniform and said, 'What now, do you think?'

Johnny shrugged and looked in the direction of the Dauphin who had got to its feet – it looked like it only had two – and was dusting itself off, while the little bow-legged servant unfurled and started to fuss around it, straightening out the metallic robes.

'Er, excuse me,' said Clara. There was no reply.

'Excuse me, Your Highness,' Johnny tried, hoping that might get a response.

The brown alien looked around. 'How dare you address the Dauphin directly? And you a barbarian. Just because you speak Universal does not give you the right. You will speak when you are spoken to and not before.'

'I'm sorry,' said Johnny. 'But what's Universal? And do you know what's happening – where we are?'

'Speak when you are spoken to. Didn't you hear me?' said the four-legged creature.

'Johnny,' said Clara. 'What did it say? How can you understand it?'

'It was that thing – the big floating ball. It did something to me,' said Johnny, but before he could finish a flap in the skin of the tunnel opened above their heads and a triangular white face peered in through the gap. 'Captain – I'm in,' it shouted over its shoulder.

A second face appeared. It looked humanoid – and male – with very dark brown and weathered skin, and a patch covering its right eye, next to a deep scar that ran from top to bottom down his face. He scanned the tunnel and his eyes fell upon the tall alien. 'Your Highness,' he said. 'We picked up the imperial distress beacon, but I had no idea it was from you.'

'Captain Valdour,' replied the Dauphin. 'Of all the blundering buffoons charging to my rescue it would have to be you.'

'Your Highness?' asked Valdour.

The Dauphin's robes had changed colour to a bright scarlet. 'There was no distress signal. I was on my way to tell that upstart Nymac that his war is futile and he had better retreat before I blast him and his ships all the way back to Andromeda.'

There was a loud crash and the tunnel vibrated backwards and forwards, throwing its inhabitants off their various feet.

'Get me out of here NOW,' ordered the Dauphin, with what Johnny thought was an unfortunately high-pitched squeak. Everyone stood up nervously.

'Of course, Your Highness – if you would care to climb this,' said Captain Valdour, lowering what looked unmistakably like a stepladder down towards them.

'I would care to do no such thing,' said the Dauphin. 'Send a gravity assist immediately, before I have your head.'

Another bang sounded above them and the four occupants of the tunnel were again flung to the floor. Valdour, still peering through the hole, said, 'You may not have noticed but we are experiencing some difficulties. It is not possible to communicate with my ship's brain at this time. Your Highness has the option of staying there or climbing out and walking to the bridge.'

'The indignity of it,' chuntered the Dauphin, starting to climb the stepladder. The others followed suit, emerging onto the outer wall of the tunnel and sliding down into the heart of what looked like a very chaotic junkyard, about the size of a school gym. Johnny wondered if he was ever going to see the type of gleaming hi-tech spaceship he'd always imagined. A tiny hundra, only a few centimetres wide, was floating close to him.

'Follow me,' said Valdour, turning on his heels and leading them forward. 'We must re-establish communications or we cannot fold and the ship will be destroyed.'

Johnny squeezed Clara's hand. He didn't know what 'fold' meant but it didn't sound like good news.

'We cannot fold?' asked the Dauphin. 'Then we must surrender.'

'Your Highness,' replied Valdour. 'This ship was born to fight. She has lived her life well. I will not disgrace her by surrendering now.'

'Are you mad?' said the Dauphin. 'I order you to surrender the ship . . . at once.'

'We can argue over the chain of command on my ship, Your Highness,' said Valdour, 'but as you see the point is moot.' They had just arrived in a circular chamber that was unmistakably the bridge. The doors weren't designed for anyone much taller than a human and the Dauphin had to stoop to get inside. Valdour was pointing to a wrecked console in front of them. 'Our link to the brain has been destroyed – she has shut down. Without entering a command code we can neither free my plican nor fight back.' As he said the word 'plican,' Captain Valdour pointed towards something that was shaped like a hot-air balloon at the top of a cylindrical floor-to-ceiling tank in the very centre of the room. 'My crew are trying their best,' he continued, indicating two more white triangular-faced aliens busy in front of some instruments, 'but for now we are becalmed and at the Andromedans' mercy.'

'Well order them to try harder,' squeaked the Dauphin.

'As I said,' replied Valdour, 'they are doing their best.'

No one was paying them any attention so Johnny let go of Clara's hand and began to wander around the bridge – it looked badly damaged. Steam was rising through vents in the floor and almost all the control stations were blackened from electrical fires. The only thing that appeared to be working was a giant viewscreen at the front, on which an enormous and sinister-looking vessel, jet black, was approaching. Against the background of deep space it was difficult to make out its exact shape, but Johnny would have bet all the money he had left that it was bristling with weapons. The little alien had curled back into a ball. Clara walked forward to the tank in the centre and peered up at the strange balloon-like creature inside. Johnny took out the battered games console from his pocket – it was worth a try. After all, he'd designed it to communicate with a computer, which was a type of brain, but when he tried to switch it on nothing happened – it wouldn't be surprising if it had broken when he'd thrown it. 'Please work,' he muttered to the little handheld console. He pressed the on button again and this time it sprang into life. Deftly Johnny's fingers programmed the handset to do what he'd had lots of practice getting it to do – to search for a signal.

' . . . I must insist that you surrender the ship,' said the Dauphin in the background.

Text appeared on the screen in front of Johnny. He read it three times before it sank in. It spelt out, 'I am Cheybora.'

Holding out the handset he approached the captain and the Dauphin, who were still arguing as the little hundra circled them excitedly. 'Who's Cheybora?' Johnny asked, hoping to get the attention of one of them.

'. . . Your Highness. Even if I could I would never give such a dishonourable order,' said Valdour. 'Better to die in glory on the battlefield than in an Andromedan slave mine.'

'How dare you disobey me,' squeaked the Dauphin. 'Treason!'

The ship lurched as it was hit again, flinging everyone to the floor. Johnny was first to his feet and said, with lots more urgency this time, 'Excuse me but who's Cheybora?'

'Silence, barbarian,' said the Dauphin.

'Be quiet,' snapped Valdour.

'Thank you,' said the Dauphin.

'I meant you, Your Highness,' Valdour said to the Dauphin though gritted teeth. Looking straight at Johnny, he asked, 'What did you say, child?'

'Er . . . who's Cheybora?' repeated Johnny quietly. Captain Valdour looked very frightening when he stared at you.

'Cheybora's my ship – that's her name.' said the captain. 'How would you know that?'

'I can talk to her on my console,' said Johnny, holding up his little device. 'What should I say?'

To Johnny's relief, Valdour seemed to understand. 'Tell her we need to fold,' said Valdour. 'At once. Can you do that?' Johnny nodded and started inputting the message. Valdour continued, 'They'd have destroyed us by now if they'd wanted to. They must be about to board.'

Johnny typed in 'must fold now,' although he had no idea what it meant.

'Really?' was the reply that scrolled across his screen, followed by, 'I only obey my captain. You'll need a command code.'

'What's the command code?' Johnny asked Valdour.

'3 1 4 1 5 9 authorization Emperor BK1,' shouted Valdour as metallic clunks rang out from the hull above their heads. 'Quickly, they'll be aboard any minute.'

Johnny frantically typed it in, hoping he'd not made any mistakes. The viewscreen was completely filled by the other ship now. As he keyed in the final character the tank next to Clara in the middle of the bridge started pulsating with blue light. An invisible barrier that had been holding the creature in the uppermost section was removed and it dropped through, opening out to reveal eight tentacles. It was like an octopus that had been scrunched up before. All of a sudden they were rushing straight for the other ship, only they passed through it. A sharp turn and stars flashed before Johnny's eyes. He dimly heard someone gasp in wonder before his world went black and he collapsed onto the floor of the bridge.

✰   ✰   ✰
✰   ✰

'Wake up, Johnny, please wake up.' Clara's voice gradually became louder and clearer. Johnny tried to lift his head, but was sick. 'Johnny,' pleaded Clara again. Though he felt terrible he tried opening his eyes – the bridge was bathed in an intense blue light. To his surprise everyone else who'd been on the bridge seemed to be unconscious apart from Clara. The little hundra looked somewhat deflated, and had settled on top of a smoking, battered terminal, while the octopus-like creature Valdour had called a plican was curled up like a hot-air balloon again, with its tentacles retracted.

Johnny opened his mouth to speak, but just retched instead. There was nothing left to come out. 'The captain,' he just managed to say, pointing in Valdour's direction. Clara understood and moved over to Captain Valdour, gingerly tapping him on the shoulder.

A hand darted out and grabbed Clara's arm and Valdour leapt to his feet, knocking her over. With all his strength, Johnny forced himself off the floor as Valdour hovered menacingly over Clara, but instead of striking her he picked her up in his muscly arms, looked into her eyes and said, 'Forgive me, little one. It was the fold. I am deeply sorry if I injured you . . . and ashamed I was not the first to rise. Your recovery belies your stature.'

'Johnny,' Clara said anxiously, not taking her eyes off Captain Valdour's scarred face.

It seemed the tiny hundra wasn't translating. 'It's OK, Clara,' Johnny groaned. 'He's not going to hurt you.'

'Are you sure?' Clara asked, her arms out in front of her so the captain wouldn't get any closer.

Captain Valdour put Clara down and turned to Johnny. 'Does the little one not understand me?' he asked.

'No,' Johnny replied. 'She can't speak your language.'

'Yet I understand when you speak to her,' said Valdour, perplexed.

'It's a long story,' Johnny replied. 'I don't really understand it myself. What's the fold?' he asked, walking across to Valdour and Clara.

'The plican, there in the tank,' said Valdour gesturing across to it, 'can fold space. We have crossed a vast distance instantaneously but, as you surmised, it is not pleasant.'

'My sister – the little one – loved it,' said Johnny. 'And before, when we were on the other spaceship.'

'The little one?' scoffed Clara, but she went quiet. Valdour had turned back to her and was studying her face carefully.

'She is unusual to feel that,' he said, turning towards Johnny. 'Folding is so traumatic it can even be fatal. It is only ever done like that, without protection, in extreme emergency. I fear the Dauphin will be most displeased,' he said, looking at the spindly figure still unconscious on the floor and smiling so that his scarred face looked even more grotesque. 'Normally we would be in protective gel. I must thank you,' Valdour continued. 'I cannot comprehend that device of yours, but you saved us all. I owe you my life and I don't even know your name.'

'It was nothing,' said Johnny, looking awkwardly at the floor. 'This is my sister Clara and I'm Johnny Mackintosh. I've just always been good with computers.'

Valdour laughed a deep hearty laugh: 'A computer, Johnny Mackintosh? Cheybora is hardly some glorified calculator. Yes electricity flows through her circuits, but she is alive.'

'Oh I know about artificial intelligence,' said Johnny.

'You speak strangely,' said Valdour. 'There is nothing "artificial" about this ship. She was grown near the planet Phynon millennia ago. She is as alive as you or I – maybe more so.'

'You grow spaceships?' said Johnny. 'Cool.'

The other figures on the bridge were beginning to stir and Valdour walked across to the terminal on which the hundra had settled, prodding the creature with a piece of twisted metal that had fallen from somewhere. The little brown ball rose unsteadily into the air and began to circle the bridge, just below the ceiling. The two crew members got to their feet first, followed by the Dauphin who kicked the little brown alien until it uncurled onto its four legs.

'This is outrageous,' said the Dauphin, who was ignored by everyone except its servant.

Valdour looked briefly across to them and then turned back to Johnny. 'Can you use your device to ask Cheybora to plot a course for Melania?' he asked. 'Oh and ask her to dim the viewscreen.'

'What is that light?' Johnny asked.

'A star, what else?' asked Valdour. 'It is a blue giant – a young star. Too young for this system to be colonized. No planets can have yet formed.'

Though he wanted to, it was too bright for Johnny to look at the star. He typed in a message for Cheybora who sent back that they could fold again in five minutes. 'I'm not sure I'm ready for it,' Johnny said to Valdour, while holding his stomach.

'Don't worry,' Valdour replied. 'It will take many folds for us to reach Melania, but we shall be protected.'

'Melania? Civilization, thank goodness,' said the Dauphin.

'Yes, Your Highness,' said Valdour to the elongated stick insect. 'We shall go to Melania. I must return you to the capital and Cheybora must be healed – she is badly damaged.'

'You try to curry favour with the Regent,' said the Dauphin dismissively.

'I serve your parent at the Emperor's behest, and in his unhappy absence.' Captain Valdour scowled back.

'My parent rules the galaxy as mightily as the Emperor ever did,' spat the Dauphin. 'And doubtless it will be delighted by my safe return.'

'Your parent?' Johnny asked. 'You mean your mum or dad?'

'Do not address the Dauphin unless spoken to,' piped the bow-legged alien. 'The Regent who now rules us is unity. It is neither male nor female. The same is true for its heir.' As it said this, the servant bowed in the direction of the Dauphin. 'Gender is for the . . . uncivilized.' Johnny thought the look the little creature gave him was probably some sort of sneer.

'You mean it's really an it?' said Clara. 'That's funny.'

'Do not waste time communicating with these primitives,' said the Dauphin to his servant. 'Valdour – if you wish to keep your head when you arrive on Melania you will open the gel pods now. Let us get this tiresome journey over with.'

'Of course, Your Highness,' said Valdour, who led the way to the left-hand side of the viewscreen and pressed a button on the wall. A door lifted upwards, with a hydraulic hiss, revealing a transparent amber gel, like on the last ship but clean and fresh. Valdour pointed inside.

'I take it you are serious,' said the Dauphin, who walked a

87

little reluctantly into the gel and disappeared. A moment later the door to the little chamber closed behind it.

'All of us must do the same before we fold,' said Valdour, circling the bridge and opening hatches along the wall as he went. He pointed for Clara to go inside one of them.

'Will it be the same in there? Will I still feel it?' Clara asked the captain.

'The idea of the gel is to remove as much of the sensation as possible,' said Valdour. 'But if you are truly sure, little one, you may remain outside with the plican.'

'Oh, can I?' asked Clara.

'There'll be no gravity either,' said Valdour.

'I can float too?' said Clara. 'Even better.' She flashed a smile back at his ravaged face.

'For a little one, I expect big things of you,' said the captain, smiling back.

Johnny looked at the tank where the creature was beginning to stretch out its tentacles again. 'You sure you'll be OK out here?' he asked his sister.

'It's wonderful,' said Clara. 'I love it. It's like seeing everything, the whole galaxy, all at once.'

'Well, if you're sure,' Johnny replied.

'Positive,' said Clara, beaming back at him.

Everyone else entered their gel pods, except for Valdour, who insisted on being last in. Johnny looked at the amber gel, and turned uncertainly to the captain. 'Can I breathe in there?' he asked.

Valdour laughed. 'The gel is oxygenated,' he said. 'You must take it inside you to balance the pressure within and without. But before you do, send a message to Cheybora to deactivate the gravity field. It is safer for the plican that way. Just now we came far too close to this star.'

Johnny sent a message from his handheld, and took a deep

breath. 'Here goes then,' he said to himself, trying to sound brave. He closed his eyes and stepped through. It felt as though he was underwater in a warm bath. He opened his eyes and imagined he was wearing orange goggles. Seeing a switch on the inside of the chamber he pressed it and the door closed behind him, shutting out the light. He was holding his breath and his heart was pounding, but he knew he wouldn't be able to hold out for much longer. His chest tightened – it was now or never so he forced himself to open his mouth and the gel flowed inside. It was warm in his throat, as though someone was pouring hot water down it. And the next thing he knew he was blowing up like a balloon. His legs felt really light, and as the sensation moved up his body his hands looked as if they'd been covered by a pair of inflated rubber gloves. After a few moments, breathing the orange gel seemed almost as natural as breathing air.

For the first time in days it felt as though he could rest. He couldn't forget what had happened to Louise and Bentley – he felt terrible for having left them behind, and would do anything to help them if he could. And now he knew he'd never see his mum and dad again. Thinking about them brought a lump to his inflated throat. Earth was a long way away – he'd never be able to get back. But he had a sister – he had found Clara. And he was on a spaceship. And he was heading for the capital of the galaxy.

5 ✩ ✩
An Unexpected Audience ✩ ✩

Johnny opened his eyes and laughed. Something was tickling him. Lying down, he felt rested – he must have slept and, when he thought about it, he'd really needed to. When he lifted his arm he found it was no longer balloon-like and he could move it easily. The amber gel had drained away – or most of it anyway, though the compartment still looked an odd colour. He wiped the orange remains from in front of his eyes and lifted his head. The last of the gel was being hoovered up by something that looked like an elephant's trunk which was currently busy working on his T-shirt and under his arms. It was this that was doing the tickling. He lay still as the trunk moved over his clothes and his face, gently sucking the dregs off him. It nearly sucked his locket up its long grey tube, but Johnny pulled it back and tucked it inside his T-shirt. The trunk retreated into a cavity in the ceiling and Johnny turned onto his side, pressing the switch to open the door to the bridge.

He was bathed in a red glow. Most of the others were already out of their pods and were gathered beneath the hundra and around the plican's tank – where Clara was. Johnny leapt up and ran across the bridge to her. She was sitting cross-legged on the floor with both arms outstretched holding onto the tank, with the plican's tentacles at the same point on the other side of the divide. Her eyes were open and she was grinning from ear to ear, but something wasn't right. She wasn't blinking – she wasn't even moving. He stepped forward to touch her but was pulled back from behind.

'Let me go,' said Johnny.

'Johnny – she's OK,' said Captain Valdour, 'but I don't think we should move her.'

'She's OK is she?' said Johnny. 'What's it doing to her? Let me go. We've got to get her away.'

'As good as dead if you ask me,' said the Dauphin, whose robes were now a dazzling mixture of blue and green.

'I didn't ask you, you jumped-up idiot,' said Johnny.

The servant was about to speak but a spindly arm shot out from under the Dauphin's robes to silence it. 'You may be under Valdour's protection here, but remember, barbarian,' said the Dauphin, 'on Melania such comments are likely to be deemed fatal.'

'Your Highness,' said Valdour. 'It may have escaped your notice, doubtless with your mind on higher things, but without this "barbarian", this Terran, none of us would be returning to Melania.'

'And I,' said the Dauphin, 'would have made peace with the Andromedans and the war would be over.'

'Or General Nymac would have killed you,' replied Valdour, 'leaving the galaxy a doubtless poorer place.'

'He wouldn't dare,' said the Dauphin.

Valdour whispered, 'I think he might have been tempted,' to Johnny, and smiled his ugly smile.

'What's happened to Clara?' Johnny asked again.

'We don't know. The little one's vital signs are normal,' Valdour replied, loosening his grip on Johnny and letting him go.

'Normal? She doesn't look normal,' said Johnny.

'I admit I was, perhaps, a little reckless allowing her to stay here exposed to so many folds,' said Valdour, 'but her ability seemed astonishing.'

'She's my little sister,' said Johnny. 'I should have protected her. I'm all she's got now.'

Captain Valdour turned Johnny round and squatted down in front of him, looking into his eyes. Try as he might it was hard for Johnny not to stare at either the eye–patch or the accompanying scar, which looked really creepy in the red light. 'Listen to me, Johnny,' said Valdour. 'You have protected her. You saved her life and all our lives. And she will be fine. Cheybora says as much and Cheybora is almost always right.'

'Cheybora – your ship?' said Johnny.

'Hello, Johnny,' said a business-like female voice that came from all around him.

'Hi,' Johnny replied, looking round the bridge not sure in which direction he should be saying this.

'You saved us,' Cheybora continued. 'I was deaf, dumb and blind. Without you reaching through to me, all would have been lost.'

'Are you OK now?' Johnny asked.

'I am better, thank you for asking,' replied Cheybora. 'The ship's healer has treated me and I am recovering.'

'What happened?' Johnny asked. What he'd wanted to ask was how come the ship was really alive and needed a healer rather than an engineer to repair it, but that didn't seem very polite so he just went along with it for now.

'I was hit many times as we answered the distress beacon,' said Cheybora. 'I had to lift the transit tube into my hold without harming you, which meant going rather too slowly to be safe. I am ashamed to say the Andromedan weapons overcame me.'

'Thanks for rescuing us,' replied Johnny. 'I know you were dead brave, but . . . but how do you know my sister will be OK?'

'I have monitored all her vital signs and as far as I can tell she is healthy. In fact, I believe she can now be separated from the tank.'

'How can you know what's healthy for her?' Johnny asked.

'My databanks contain specifications for most spacefaring species,' Cheybora replied.

'Spacefaring?' Johnny muttered. 'But we've hardly gone anywhere yet – just to the Moon.'

'There are records of your species,' said Cheybora, 'admittedly dated, but you are a match. Given a little time, your sister will return to full health and awareness.'

Johnny looked at Clara who hadn't moved at all. He went to sit down beside her, put an arm round her waist and tried to prise one of her hands off the tank. It wouldn't budge – it seemed to be stuck there. Captain Valdour came across to help and together they pulled harder, but again nothing happened. Then they heard Cheybora's voice say, 'Allow me,' and the plican was suddenly forced up the tank towards the ceiling – to the position they'd first seen it in – physically separated from the main tank. Clara's hands rose with the creature's tentacles for a little while, lifting her whole body off the floor as she slid up the outside of the tank, but then the bond was broken and with a cry the girl fell back into Johnny's arms. She turned and buried her head in his chest. Johnny held the top of her head close to him, stroking her hair hoping it would make her feel better. In front of him, on the viewscreen, a giant white world was coming into view.

'Behold Melania,' said Captain Valdour from behind him. Johnny stood up where he was, holding onto Clara, but staring at the panorama in front of him. Valdour continued, 'Defender of the weak, guardian of freedom, cradle of life. It has been a long time since I saw the towers of the capital. It's good to be home.'

Johnny gazed at the enormous planet before them. It looked far bigger than Earth, and the view of it from space was very different – there were no mixtures of sea, land and swirling cloud. There were no clouds at all – and no sea either. It appeared to be one continuous city as far as the eye could see. Every inch was built on, in gleaming metal or crystal. Or not quite every inch. 'What's that?' he asked, pointing to a circular area that had just come into view and seemed different from all the rest. It looked perfectly round, probably thousands of miles across, and had the only water and greenery he could see on the entire planet.

'That,' said Valdour, 'is the Imperial Palace. It has seven circles of water and wildlife – the only area of Melania not completely built on. They say the Emperor created it by force of will alone.'

'They say some foolish things at times, don't they?' said the Dauphin. 'I sometimes think tales of the Emperor's abilities are so far-fetched it's no wonder he daren't show himself.'

'You would speak ill of the Emperor?' said Valdour angrily.

It looked to Johnny as though Valdour might actually strike the Dauphin, which he was sure wouldn't be a good idea. For its part the Dauphin, its robes a deep scarlet, was leaning down towards the captain, thrusting its elongated face forward, almost inviting a blow. Perhaps Cheybora thought so too, for the ship interrupted with a subtle, 'Ahem.'

'What?' snapped Valdour and the Dauphin together.

'It appears,' said the ship, 'that quite a welcoming party is being assembled on the surface in both your honour. We dock at Talamine Spaceport in five minutes. May I suggest you prepare yourselves?'

'Five minutes!' the Dauphin exclaimed. 'That's nowhere near enough time.' It turned to its servant and shouted, 'Take us to our quarters now. We must make ready.'

'Of course, Your Highness,' whimpered the servant, 'although, if I may say, Your Highness already looks magnificent.' The odd-looking pair left the bridge, the Dauphin stooping through the doorway.

Johnny looked up at Captain Valdour, expecting him to go and get ready too. Valdour caught sight of him and said, 'What you see is what you get with me, Johnny.'

Johnny smiled. He was still holding onto Clara who didn't seem able to lift her head from his chest, but at least she was now moving a little. 'Your planet's awesome,' he said, followed a moment later by, 'but what's going to happen when we land?'

'If you're lucky,' said Captain Valdour, 'you will see the twin suns of Arros and Deynar setting behind the Great Tower of the Imperial Palace from the Senate Platform. It will be beautiful and Cheybora tells me that it's due in a couple of hours.'

'Really?' said Johnny, excited. He'd always wanted to see a double sunset, ever since there'd been one in *Star Wars*. In real life it was bound to be even better. 'But after that? Where will we go? Will we ever get home?'

'Home?' Valdour asked. 'But you've only just left Terra. There's a whole galaxy out there for you to see. A galaxy that's under threat, Johnny. Join our crew. Cheybora and I would be honoured if you stayed with us.'

'What's Terra?' Johnny asked. 'You called me a Terran before.'

'You don't know?' Valdour asked, sounding surprised. 'But I thought Terra was your homeworld. I researched your kind while we were folding. Don't you call your planet that anymore?'

'It's called Earth,' Johnny replied. 'I've never heard of Terra.'

'Well then,' said Valdour. 'I had better call you an Earthen, I suppose.'

Johnny laughed. 'We say "human",' he told Valdour, 'but I like Terran. I'd like you to call me that.'

'Then Terran it is,' replied Valdour.

'And I'd love it if we could stay on your ship,' said Johnny. 'We would be honoured.'

'Then it is agreed,' said the captain.

'Landing at Talamine Spaceport in two minutes,' Cheybora broadcast across the bridge. 'Gravity normalization commencing.'

'Come,' said Captain Valdour. 'Doubtless the Dauphin is waiting to disembark before the crowds. We can't let it have all the glory.' With that he led them from the bridge and through the ship, back into the chaos of the cargo bay and past the discarded transit tube before reaching an airlock at the far end. As they went Johnny felt himself becoming heavier and heavier.

'Docking complete,' Cheybora broadcast from above the airlock. The Dauphin and its little servant were already waiting.

✿   ✿   ✿
✿   ✿

As the ship's doors opened Johnny couldn't believe his eyes. The crowd disappeared into the distance as far as he could see, made up of the strangest creatures imaginable: there were some like those crewing Cheybora, with their white triangular faces; others had prominent crests on their heads, perhaps made of bone; towering over these and dominating the crowd were furry brown beasts, maybe ten metres tall, and when Johnny stared he could make out little yellow things running up and down inside their mass of hair, as though living in them. In fact, the more he stared, the more he began to see: what had looked like black boxes scattered throughout the crowd proved, on closer inspection, to be living, near-perfect cubes that moved using little jets on each of their faces, and when he looked really closely he could see the outline of more aliens, who were so pale they were almost see-through. Occasionally, drifting above them, he spotted a gas bag hundra. Johnny was glad to see all these deflated footballs were unchained. And above the crowd were flying aliens, some with wings, but many with no obvious sign of support. Music was playing but everything looked so strange that he couldn't tell where it was coming from. There was no way he'd be able to spot the difference between a musical instrument and any other piece of equipment here.

The mass of aliens surged forward and somehow the Dauphin levitated above it. Captain Valdour was mobbed and lifted above the arms of the crowd and onto a plinth atop a crystal column so that he, too, stood above them. He gestured quickly to a flying creature, with four transparent wings, who buzzed down and lifted Johnny, still holding onto Clara, keeping them above the crowd that would have swamped them otherwise. Clara still wasn't speaking, but at least she now moved her bruised head to take a look around.

What she and Johnny saw, coming floating towards them but standing upright, was a carbon copy of the Dauphin only twice the size, with antennae that stuck proudly upwards. Around its feet were swarming a dozen or so of the four-legged servants, each struggling to hold out a portion of the larger creature's crimson robes in a perfect circle, while flying all around were at least a hundred very stocky two-legged creatures in navy blue armour, that looked unmistakably like soldiers. 'The Regent,' Valdour shouted above the noise of the crowd, pointing at it. 'Come to welcome baby home.'

The Regent gestured to what looked like a flying funnel above it, which dropped down until it was hovering just above the long face with its antennae beginning to twitch with anticipation. 'My people,' it began. The sound reverberated across the crowd. Johnny could see the different hundras glow with shimmering electric patterns as the wave of noise spread out from the Regent, and realized it must have summoned some kind of living microphone to address the crowds. 'My people,' the Regent said again. 'This is a day for rejoicing.' The crowd cheered. Johnny couldn't help thinking that, if they hadn't, the Regent's soldier aliens watching them might not have been best pleased. 'As you will know from official Regency newscasts, in an act of great bravery, my offspring and heir sought peace with the Andromedans.' A hush spread across the crowd. 'Sadly, its overtures were refused,' continued the Regent. 'My glorious offspring, and your future ruler,' at this the Dauphin bowed low, 'was to be killed in cold blood by the Andromedan Nymac.' A hubbub began, spreading out over the crowd of aliens, until the Regent gestured with its arms and the noise subsided. 'Until . . . ,' continued the Regent, '. . . until the intervention of this brave captain you see before you.' A hush descended once more as the eyes of the crowd turned towards Valdour, who the Regent was now pointing at, saying, 'Captain Valdour of the Imperial Navy – we salute you.' The crowd cheered. Johnny joined in. 'We award you the Regency Medal for Bravery.' Everyone cheered even louder.

Valdour gestured for the flying microphone to come towards him. 'Thank you, Your Highness,' he said. Then he turned to the vast crowd. 'Citizens of Melania,' he began. 'I am a soldier – not a man of words. I do not have a speech for you, except to say that we live in dark times, so when the light shines, it is all the brighter.' The crowd seemed transfixed and Johnny thought both the Regent and Dauphin looked uncomfortable. 'The Dauphin has been rescued – we should rejoice at that news,' said Valdour. 'We should raise a cheer that will ring in the ears of the Emperor himself,' the captain carried on, and the crowd followed his lead and roared. Johnny thought that for a soldier Captain Valdour was a very good speaker. And when he'd mentioned the Emperor, the Regent looked decidedly awkward. 'It would be wrong, though, for me to take credit where it is not due,' said Valdour. 'Yes I came to the aid of the Dauphin, but the rescue was futile.' Johnny watched as a wave of silence spread outwards from the plinth on which Valdour was standing. 'The hymn of death was ready on my lips.' There was near total silence and stillness now, except for a ripple in the crowd moving towards them from the horizon. Close at hand, the Dauphin was hopping from one foot to the next with violently bright red robes. 'Until the intervention – and the ingenuity – of another who saved us both.' The crowd took a collective intake of breath and Valdour turned towards Johnny, saying, 'People of Melania, I thank – we must all thank – the Terran Johnny Mackintosh.'

The crowd cheered again – Johnny felt his face burning and turning beetroot red and hoped no one could see the change in this unearthly light. He wished the creature holding him and Clara would either drop them into the crowd and out of sight, or fly away so everything would stop staring at him. He looked across at the Dauphin, who could clearly stand it no more and exploded. 'This, Captain Valdour,' it shrieked, 'is an outrage. The savage insulted me. He prevented my mission. He must . . .'

But no one heard what was coming next because the noise from the crowd that had begun some distance away had reached them, building to a crescendo and drowning the Dauphin out. It was clear something unexpected was happening. Johnny could see that the centre of attention had shifted from those around him to something that was passing over the heads of the crowd, coming from the direction of a single glistening tower and making a beeline straight for them. He looked at Valdour who seemed as taken aback as anyone. 'What is it?' Johnny asked the captain. 'What's going on?'

Captain Valdour, more to himself than to Johnny, said, 'It can't be . . . it's the Imperial Guard.'

'Is that bad?' Johnny asked nervously. As they came closer it became clear that the Imperial Guard were definitely heading straight towards him and Clara, rather than any of the others.

'I don't know,' Valdour replied. 'No one's seen them for nearly a hundred years.'

☆   ☆   ☆
☆   ☆

Johnny gulped, and squeezed Clara very tightly. He didn't
think he could keep hold of her for much longer – in the extra
strong gravity of Melania she was really heavy. The Imperial
Guard reached them. Floating in front of him were a dozen
extremely scary-looking aliens in cream uniforms with four
gold stars emblazoned in a diamond across their chests. Each
soldier was around three metres in height, but also so stocky
they seemed half as wide as they were tall, and every centimetre
of it looked like muscle. Hovering in mid-air they made a circle
around Johnny and Clara, with Captain Valdour just outside it.
Johnny thought the four-winged creature holding up him and
Clara was as frightened as he was, as it was beating its wings
furiously while letting out a high-pitched whine. One of the
soldiers broke the circle and moved forward. His eyes were so
close together they almost crossed. They flickered from Johnny
over to Captain Valdour. The soldier turned to the captain and
saluted. Valdour recovered from his open-mouthed shock – he
stood to attention and saluted back. The soldier unrolled a
small scroll and began to read, his voice booming out across the
crowd without need of amplification.

'By order of His Divine Imperial Majesty Bram Khari,
Guardian of the Galaxy, Bringer of Life, Descendent of
Lysentia, Keeper of the Diaquant, Liberator of the Silus Cluster,
Founder of the Freedom Alliance of Zepheron Prime, . . .'

It was quite a long list, thought Johnny. And the scroll had
seemed such a small piece of paper.

' . . . Governor of the Satellite Clouds, Ruler of the Seven
Spheres, Ngog of the . . .'

Maybe it was like an autocue, Johnny thought, with the
words somehow scrolling as the soldier read? He was wishing
the soldier would get to the end, whatever the end was – his

arms were now screaming at him as he struggled to keep hold of Clara. As though sensing this, she moved her arms from his waist to around his neck which helped a little.

'I hereby decree that the Terrans, Johnny and Clara Mackintosh,' said the soldier, looking up, 'be taken forthwith to the Imperial Palace where they will remain at His Divine Imperial Majesty's pleasure.' He looked Johnny straight in the eye and said, 'You will come with me.'

Johnny gulped. He looked across to Captain Vadour, who managed a slight shrug, but that was all. The Dauphin however, was ecstatic. 'I knew it. I knew you would pay the price for your insolence,' it said, skipping from foot to foot, while its servant ran round trying to stop it treading on its robes. 'Didn't I say your insults would be fatal on Melania? Didn't I?'

'Silence!' boomed the Regent at its offspring. 'Let us depart this place with a little dignity.'

The Dauphin, suddenly sheepish, stopped squawking at once and followed its parent and the blue-clad soldiers away. Johnny looked at it, wondering if despite its height it was just a little child.

Up until now everything had happened so quickly he'd not had time to be frightened. Finally it was catching up with him. He looked back to the soldier and nodded. If he'd tried to speak, only a squeak would have come out. Far below the crowd were all whispering and pointing. For a moment they seemed to shift out of focus, and then, high in the air, his feet met solid, but invisible, ground. He, Clara and the soldiers were standing on a perfectly see-through floating platform – like a magic carpet. Johnny's arms gave out in relief now he no longer had to hold Clara. The lead soldier looked up to Johnny and Clara's winged support and said, 'Leave us.' It seemed only too happy to fly away. Then the platform began to move, silently, picking up speed as it went over the heads of the vast assembled crowd.

Johnny thought there must be millions of aliens beneath them. They were heading, straight as an arrow, towards what was unmistakably the Imperial Palace, with the tower that stretched high into the sky in the far distance. Johnny watched as the twin suns Arros and Deynar slipped into the waters behind the palace, turning them blood red and being so much more fantastic than anything he'd ever seen in a film. For the first time since the folds on board Cheybora, Clara turned to Johnny and spoke.

'That's a little what it's like,' she said. 'It's so beautiful.'

Johnny nodded. With his arm around her shoulder and hers around his waist, their silent escort surrounding them, they eventually left the crowds behind and headed towards the sunset.

☆　☆　☆
☆　☆

It was night before they reached the edge of the sprawling mass that was Melania's planet-wide city, and arrived at the waters that marked the border of the Imperial Palace. Johnny told Clara what had been read out before they'd been taken away. The soldiers stood motionless in a circle around them, but facing outward, which he found reassuring. It seemed as if they were protecting Johnny and Clara rather than threatening them. There was plenty of space to see between them too, and nothing blocking the view above or below. Johnny didn't know whether to look down at the wonders beneath him, or up at the sky full of strange new stars. Except it wasn't *all* full of stars. Although the sky was far brighter than any he'd seen on Earth, and included four especially bright stars forming a diamond shape off to one side, directly overhead was a patch of nothing-ness so black it was unlike anything he'd seen before. And at its edge a brilliant jet of light was streaming out, almost touching the closest of the four stars to it.

'I think that's a black hole,' said Johnny, pointing into the darkness for Clara to follow. 'We must be near the centre of the galaxy – they thought there was a really big one here. It's called Sagittarius A*.'

'Have you seen down there?' asked Clara, nodding beneath them. They'd crossed the first ring of water, much larger than it had looked from orbit, and were now directly above the first area of greenery they'd seen on the planet. Johnny watched as a great herd of six-legged animals with horns tried to keep pace with them as they ran below. They managed quite well until reaching a cliff face that the invisible platform effortlessly began to climb. Clusters of little blue creatures, each with suction pads instead of feet, were grouped together, feeding on occasional clumps of vegetation on the rock face.

Then, at the top of the cliff, both of them saw a sight that took their breath away. It was a building, but not like any Johnny had seen before. One moment it looked crystal clear. The next, when it caught a little of the starlight above, it seemed to sparkle with a million colours.

Clara said it was a diamond and Johnny thought she was probably right. Diamond was the hardest and strongest thing there was, as well as being beautiful to look at. And it was fitting for the palaces of the Emperor of the Galaxy. They left the giant diamond behind and reached another band of water. The size of it all amazed Johnny. Next to him, Clara's head began to nod. Johnny realized she couldn't have slept or eaten since the Proteus Institute, at least a day ago. Johnny laid her down on the platform and she curled up and fell asleep next to him.

Johnny didn't want to sleep through the journey, though he didn't want to think too much about what would happen when it finished. He wondered why no one had seen the Emperor for a century and why they had been summoned to him. As they flew with their soldier escort above the decreasing circles, becoming ever grander as they went, he wished Bentley's reassuring presence was there with them. All his life he'd wanted to meet aliens, but he'd feel a lot safer with his faithful companion beside him. And while Johnny was living his dream, his old friend was, at best, lying wounded beneath the Proteus Institute in a storeroom, hiding from the krun. And where was Louise? He didn't want to think of the worst.

The platform began to slow. They were nearing what must be the very centre of the innermost island. The tower stood right at the central point, built almost of blue light, that stretched above them as far as Johnny could see. It might even have gone all the way into space, or it could have been Melania's space elevator. They were heading down rather than up. At the foot of the tower was a diamond-shaped open space, a fire burning with blue flames at its centre. As the platform settled on the ground Johnny spotted a hundra, but clothed, wrapped in the same cream and gold colouring as the soldiers. By the fire was a solitary figure, hooded and robed, who looked to be talking with a levitating head, but before Johnny could focus on the strange sight, whatever it was simply popped out of existence.

Johnny went to shake Clara gently awake, but she was already staring wide-eyed, taking in everything around them. The hundra lifted itself slowly into the air and the circle of soldiers opened, leaving a route out towards the hooded figure. The guard who had read from the scroll gestured for them to move in that direction saying, 'The Emperor Bram Khari.' Johnny expected a long list of titles like they'd heard before, but the soldier didn't continue. Nervously, Johnny and Clara walked towards the figure, exchanging a quick glance and silently agreeing to kneel before the Emperor.

A rich deep voice said, 'Rise.' The hood was removed to reveal an ancient, near-human face, heavily lined, with wild silver hair which (or was Johnny imagining it) radiated light softly out into the square. Although the Emperor looked old his bright blue eyes blazed with energy. 'There is no need for you to kneel before me. The trappings of power are for the weak – the strong have their own protection.' Johnny and Clara got to their feet. 'Leave us,' the Emperor said to the soldiers who, without a sound returned to the clear platform and lifted silently into the air and away. 'I am Bram Khari,' said the figure, a definite twinkling in his eye. 'And I expect, Johnny and Clara Mackintosh, that you are hungry.' Clara smiled and as the Emperor waved an arm a table laden with an enormous feast appeared in front of them, together with huge sofas for each of them to lounge on. 'Come, let us eat,' said the Emperor.

☆ ☆ ☆
☆ ☆

With all the food suddenly in front of him, it seemed to Johnny that he'd never felt so hungry. After a lifetime of Mr Wilkins's cooking this was heaven – he lay on his sofa, like a Roman centurion, tucking in to the most delicious food he'd ever tasted. The Emperor chose mainly blue food that he said came from the magule plant of Naverene, though Johnny noticed he also took a very large helping of mashed potato. Johnny tried the magule but he wasn't keen. Everything else, though, was stunning, and amazingly there was even sticky toffee pudding – his favourite back on Earth. As he scraped the bowl clean the Emperor said to him, 'I thought you'd like that – have some more,' and with a slight swish of the wrist Johnny's bowl was refilled.

'Thank you, Your Majesty,' said Johnny. 'Sorry – is that what I should call you? And what are we doing here, Sir . . . Your Majesty?' He didn't seem able to stop himself – once he'd begun the questions just kept coming out. 'Why did you bring us here? What's going on? Why us?'

The Emperor laughed. 'Slow down, slow down,' he said. 'No

more questions tonight. There's plenty of time for that. You have had a long journey. For now, let us eat and enjoy it. Both of you should try this,' he said, pointing to a ball that proved to be chocolate ice cream on the outside with hot chocolate sauce at its centre. Johnny and Clara both agreed it was delicious.

They finally ate themselves to a standstill. Johnny even thought there was a slight chance he might be sick, which had happened way too much with all this folding recently, but happily he only burped.

'It has been a long time since we were last together,' said Bram.

The pair of them looked quizzically at him. Johnny started, 'Are you sure you've not mixed . . .'

'Uh-uh', said the Emperor, interrupting. 'No questions tonight, remember. That's my rule, and normally when I say something people obey. Now you must sleep – rest yourselves properly. Would one of you care to summon a guide to take you to your quarters?' Bram was pointing behind them, so they turned round and saw that a giant gong had appeared beside the blue fire.

Clara rose first from her sofa, picked up a wooden mallet and brought it crashing into the middle of the dimpled metal. Sound reverberated all around, followed by a whirlwind blur of arms and legs racing towards them at a hundred miles an hour from out of one of the surrounding buildings. It stopped, instantly, just a few metres away, to reveal a figure in a bowler hat and pinstriped suit, looking nearly human. His footsteps clunked the last couple of metres towards them and it was only when he reached the fire that they could see his face properly – it was almost metallic.

'Master Johnny . . . Miss Clara – I am so excited to meet you,' said the creature. 'As you can see, the Emperor told me where we shall be going so I did a bit of research. Do you like it?' The creature lifted the bowler hat for a second, before putting it back on his head.

'Er . . . yes,' said Johnny. 'It's great.' He didn't have a clue what he was being asked, but thought this was probably the right response.

'You think so?' he said. 'Oh I am pleased,' and he started skipping on the spot.

'Alf,' said the Emperor. 'I think that's enough for now. Why don't you take Johnny and Clara to their quarters – without asking them any more questions – I've banned those for the evening.'

'Oh, of course,' Alf replied. 'I am so sorry – you must be exhausted. And you need your rest with everything you have ahead of you . . .'

'Alf,' the Emperor said sternly.

'Of course, Your Majesty', said Alf, again raising the bowler hat off his head.

'Excuse me,' said Johnny.

'What is it Johnny?' Bram asked.

'Can I ask just one question? Then I promise we'll go to bed.'

'Just the one then, if that's what it takes,' said Bram. 'Although I reserve the right not to answer it.'

'It's not actually for you, Sir,' said Johnny. 'It's for Alf.'

'Oh ask away, Master Johnny,' said Alf, excitedly.

'Well,' said Johnny. 'I don't mean to be rude, but . . .'

'Yes,' said Alf, beaming at him.

' . . . but are you a robot?'

'A robot!' Alf exclaimed. 'Well I suppose so but I've never been called *that*.' Alf covered his metallic face with his hands as though devastated.

'I'm sorry,' said Johnny. 'I didn't mean to upset you. Robots . . . especially androids, are cool.' He got up, walked over and stood in front of the creature wondering what to do.

Alf took a neatly ironed, crisp white handkerchief from his

trouser pocket and blew his nose very loudly. 'No harm done,' he said. 'I have always insisted on Artificial Life Form, but I would like to be cool.'

'Oh – that's why you're called Alf,' said Johnny.

'Did you not realize?' said Alf, 'How wonderful. And I would be honoured if you called me an "android". It is not a term I know, but I do like it. Normally, I am . . .'

'Alf! Time for bed,' said the Emperor, leaving absolutely no room for discussion.

'Of course, Your Majesty,' Alf replied. 'You two – follow me. You will just love the rooms we have for you.'

And with that he shepherded Johnny and Clara off, away from the enormous tower, the robed hundra floating silently behind them, leaving Emperor Bram Khari to stare into the blue flames.

☆ ☆ ☆
☆ ☆

Johnny woke to sounds from the next room. He'd been dreaming he was kicking a football with Bentley in the Castle Dudbury park. Or so he thought. He looked around and, unlikely as it seemed, that *had* been the dream and the reality was that he was in an enormous eight-poster sunken octagonal bed filled with an array of the softest and most comfortable duvets and pillows he could ever have imagined, situated in the Imperial Palace on a world at the centre of the galaxy. Reluctantly, Johnny forced himself to climb out of the bed (in the strong gravity getting up was even harder than normal) and, yawning and stretching, walked over to a massive window that was so clear you'd only know it was there by touching it. Only one of either Arros or Deynar was sending out its faint red light into the bedroom. He knew it must be a red giant star – big but old – perhaps near the end of its life. Unlike the Sun you could look directly at it without any problems. But he didn't gaze at it for very long. Something was happening to his feet. He looked down and saw the carpet was massaging them. After a lifetime spent in a children's home this really was the ultimate in luxury. Bentley would have loved it.

'Johnny,' shouted Clara from the next room. 'Come on – breakfast's getting cold.'

'Coming,' he called, putting a white dressing gown over his pyjamas and walking through to where she was sitting on cushions at a low table, looking out of a floor-to-ceiling window that made it seem as though a whole wall was missing. She was tucking into platefuls of bacon and eggs and blueberry pancakes that Alf had apparently brought in a couple of minutes earlier. The robed hundra from the night before was still there, floating near the window which looked out onto a beautiful courtyard. Johnny looked at his watch – they'd slept for a good twelve hours. He sat down on the cushions next to his sister and soon his white robe was covered in purple juice from the blueberries. As he gazed out of the window he saw that a smooth waterfall made up the entire opposite side of the quadrangle, leading at its foot to a circular pool in the very centre of the courtyard. Johnny couldn't help thinking there was something very odd about the view. The harder he looked the more certain he was that the water was flowing out of the pool and up the waterfall, rather than the other way round.

The door opened and Alf entered, still in his suit and bowler hat, carrying a pile of clothes. 'Three sets for each of you,' he said, separating them so there were six outfits hanging by themselves in mid-air. All were white tunics and black trousers, with sleek black boots underneath – but from their sizes it was clear whose belonged to who. What amazed Johnny was that on the front of his clothes were five golden stars exactly matching the shape of Cassiopeia.

'It's got my birthmark,' said Clara, getting up and rushing

over to her outfit. 'Look – it's the Plough.' She lifted her dressing gown to show her calf on which there were seven freckles, arranged just like the seven lilac stars on the front of her top.

'Me too,' said Johnny. He rolled up his sleeve to show Clara the freckled 'W' on his arm.

'I knew you would like them,' said Alf. 'I designed them myself.' The android was skipping on the spot with pride.

'But how did you know?' Johnny asked.

'The Emperor told me, of course,' said Alf, brimming with importance. He bent down and began to clear away the empty plates from the table.

'But how did he know?' Clara asked. 'We didn't even know about each other's.'

'He is the Emperor,' said Alf, as though that explained everything. 'Well then,' he continued, now balancing at least a dozen different-sized plates in one hand. 'What are you waiting for? Go and get changed – we have *so* much to do.'

Johnny and Clara looked at each other for a second and then they each plucked their outfits from the air and rushed into their rooms to try them on.

⁎ ⁎ ⁎
⁎ ⁎

A few minutes later they were dressed and walking with Alf and the hundra across marbled flagstones in the courtyard they could see from their window. It was warm, probably almost forty degrees, thought Johnny, but his loose clothes were doing a very good job of not letting him feel the heat. And he loved the gold stripe down the outside of his trousers, making them look like part of a captain's uniform. In the red light of the day, with both suns now visible in the sky, they could see the wall of the building they'd slept in formed a perfect mirror, reflecting the waterfall which still looked very strange. The other two sides of the square were bounded by ancient white colonnades, their pillars wound with golden and purple blooms. As they headed towards one side, they passed several aliens walking or flying across the square in the other direction. Johnny was very curious, but thought it would be rude to stare, and the aliens seemed to be keeping a discreet distance. That was apart from a very small one, only about a metre high but with a very long tail and nearly see-through, who approached Alf and began to question him about something.

'Over here,' said Johnny to Clara, taking the opportunity to have a closer look at the waterfall. He led her over, as near as they could get without splashing their new outfits.

'Interesting,' said Clara.

'It's more than interesting,' Johnny replied. But as he looked it was as though the waterfall was changing, reverting to how the laws of physics said it should be. The water droplets were slowing down, or rather, slowing up.

'Clara,' said a firm voice behind them. 'Johnny,' it continued. They turned round and the Emperor was standing right behind them. 'If you don't mind I'm ready for you now. Follow me.'

They set off, leaving Alf deep in conversation with the see-through alien, looking almost as though he was talking to himself. Clara wore a broad grin. As they left the square Johnny looked over his shoulder and saw the waterfall had gone back to normal, if an uphill waterfall could ever be called normal.

'Where are we going, Your Majesty?' Johnny asked.

The Emperor turned around. 'Before we continue,' he said, 'there is something I must insist on.'

Johnny thought, 'Oh dear,' as he looked down at his shiny new boots.

'I am old,' said the Emperor. 'I have spent most of my life being bowed to, agreed with, always obeyed. I have many titles – doubtless you heard a few of them when my soldiers came to fetch you yesterday. But you both must always call me "Bram". Nothing else. Understood?'

'Yes Your . . . Bram,' said Johnny. He glanced sideways at Clara who was smiling and not looking nearly as overawed as Johnny felt. It was good that she was adjusting so well.

'Good,' said Bram. 'Then we can begin.' Johnny and Clara both now looked at him expectantly. 'Look above you,' Bram continued. 'Tell me. What do you see?'

'Arros and Deynar,' said Johnny, pleased with himself for remembering both their names.

'There aren't any clouds,' said Clara.

'Good,' said Bram, 'but I was thinking of something a little closer by.'

Johnny looked again. 'You mean the hundra?' he asked, looking over at the floating ball, dressed very similarly to the rest of them.

'Oh is that what it's called?' asked Clara. 'It's translating isn't it?'

'That is indeed what it is called and, yes Clara, it is translating,' said the Emperor. 'I must say you are providing it with a veritable feast – no wonder it has been following you around.'

'Why's that?' Clara asked. 'I don't understand.'

'Tell her, Johnny,' said the Emperor.

Shocked to be asked, Johnny tried to think back to what he'd heard when he was inside the giant hundra earlier. 'Their food is . . . sort of . . . our thoughts,' he said. 'No it's not quite like that – it's our speech.'

'Very good,' said Bram, 'And?'

'And when they eat our words they send out brainwaves that match the language of the other people around them,' Johnny continued, 'so those people hear the words in their own language.'

'Indeed,' said Bram. 'A fine summary.'

Clara continued, 'And I provide the most food because the rest of you here speak the same language.'

'Exactly,' said the Emperor. 'Very perceptive.' Clara smiled.

Johnny wished he'd thought of that as well. The Emperor went on, 'It is a sad day as far as this particular hundra is concerned, because you, Clara, are going to learn Universal – the language of the Imperial Court. And of half the galaxy.'

'In one day?' asked Clara.

'I think you will find your instruction more than adequate,' said the Emperor.

'What about me?' Johnny asked.

'It would appear that you don't need to learn Universal,' said the Emperor. 'When you tried to help the ancient hundra on the krun ship, it gave you a unique gift.'

'How do you know about that?' Johnny asked, not that he was complaining – it was a great excuse not to have to study.

'I know many things,' said Bram, smiling at Johnny. 'And one of them is that you must learn to control your abilities. It won't always do for everyone to understand what you're saying – sometimes you may prefer to be more . . . selective with what you tell them.'

Johnny nodded. It would be nice to be able to tell the Dauphin what he really thought about it without risking execution. Though now he was with the Emperor . . .

'Instead,' Bram continued, 'I'm afraid you will have to spend the day with me.' There was a definite twinkle in his eye. They rounded a corner and came to where they'd first met the night before. The Emperor swished his wrist and the gong that had been there then appeared again out of thin air. 'Your turn, Johnny, I believe,' said the Emperor.

Johnny picked up the mallet and sent it crashing into the metal surface. He felt his whole body vibrate as the sound rebounded around the square.

A blur of movement shot into the quadrangle from the direction they'd just come. Johnny prepared to dive out of the way, but it stopped in an instant and right in front of them stood Alf in his pinstriped suit, twiddling his bowler hat around in his hands. 'So sorry, Your Majesty – I was . . . distracted,' said the android, not even slightly out of breath. 'Miss Clara,' he continued, turning towards her. 'I am so excited to be teaching you – shall we begin?' Alf made a long, sweeping, bowing motion, reaching almost to the ground and pointing in the direction she was meant to take. She giggled nervously, set off with a skipping Alf, and disappeared into a domed building along one side of the square. The hundra drifted upwards and away.

The Emperor turned to Johnny and raised one eyebrow. 'Well, Johnny?'

'Well . . . well what, Your . . . Bram?' asked Johnny, worrying that Bram could see right inside him and may very soon realize he was nothing special at all and had no idea what he was doing here.

'Well surely you have a million questions – maybe more,' said the Emperor, smiling kindly. Johnny nodded. 'Fire away – I shall do my best to answer them all.'

Johnny didn't really know where to start. There was just so much he wanted to know, but he didn't want to look stupid.

'I'll begin then shall I?' said Bram. 'And let us walk while we chat. There is a beautiful park a little way away where the kanefor trees have fruit sweeter than any you have ever tasted. I would like you to try it.' Emperor Khari began to walk, with Johnny by his side. 'I had waited a long time for your arrival here,' Bram continued. 'So long, I wasn't sure I would last, though of course I knew I must. Then, when you appeared so suddenly yesterday, I was taken by surprise – I had become too used to waiting. I'm sorry I wasn't there to meet you.'

'But why?' Johnny asked. 'Surely you weren't expecting me.'

'Oh but I was,' said Bram. 'We have met before. And given the circumstances it was inevitable we would meet again.'

'Are you sure you've not got me mixed up?' Johnny asked. 'I'm just a boy, from planet Earth . . . I mean Terra, who always wanted to go into space, but I never thought I would.'

'I am sure,' said Bram. 'Tell me, how is Earth?'

'You know it?' Johnny asked. Bram nodded. Johnny thought he could see something sparkling, almost like stardust, falling out of the Emperor's hair as he moved his head up and down. Johnny found it hard to believe, but asked, 'You've really been to Earth?'

'I have indeed,' said Bram. 'Several times in fact. It was pivotal in me becoming Emperor.'

'Really?' asked Johnny, amazed. 'But how?'

'Part of me wishes I could tell you,' said the Emperor. 'I remember it so clearly it is incredible to me that you do not.'

'But I wasn't there,' said Johnny. 'It must have been ages ago . . . wasn't it?'

Bram laughed. 'Of course you're right. It was millennia ago – long before you were born. Oh, here we are . . .' He stopped and reached up towards a purple fruit, that looked like a satsuma, hanging on the branch of a tree in front of him. As he did so, the branch moved away. 'One of those days,' said Bram, wearily. 'Lovely fruit but very temperamental trees.' Johnny laughed. 'Why don't you come here and stroke its trunk?' said the Emperor. 'If it likes you I'm sure it will let you have a taste.' Johnny stepped forward a little nervously. He felt a bit silly, but started rubbing his fingers along the bark of the tree trunk. Very soon a branch swayed across to him so that the purple fruit was right next to his face. 'Well done, well done,' said Bram. 'I had a feeling it would take to you. Try it . . . go on.'

Johnny reached up and picked the fruit, which came away easily in his hand. He gave the tree a quick hug and then stood back and took a bite. It tasted like coffee ice cream at exactly the right temperature. It smelled a lot like coffee too, the freshly ground sort, not instant, thought Johnny. 'Lush,' he said to the Emperor. 'It's delicious.'

'It is, isn't it?' said Bram. A branch swayed across to him now. He tapped it gently as a thank you and picked a fruit of his own. 'Now where was I?' asked Bram. 'Yes . . . Earth, of course. What is happening there nowadays?'

6 ✧ ✦

GLOBAL KILLER ✧ ✦

Over the next few days Johnny and Clara fell in love with the Imperial Palace. Alf brought them delicious breakfasts of anything they asked for (Johnny hadn't yet requested fish and chips as even he thought it wasn't really meant for first thing in the morning, but he was certain Alf would prepare it if he did) before leaving them to explore the grounds in the permanent sunshine. The android rejoined them for the afternoons, which were mostly spent on the outer shore of the second circle of the palace. There, beautiful white stone buildings perched on top of a low-lying archipelago, surrounded by dazzling white sandy beaches and crystal clear turquoise waters, made up the Imperial University. It smelt of age, but also of neglect – it had been closed to students for nearly a century, since the Emperor had withdrawn from Melanian life. Even so, it had everything Alf needed to teach Johnny and Clara about the wonders of the galaxy – school had never been so interesting.

Johnny loved the abandoned lecture theatre where Alf took them on their very first day there. It housed a giant revolving model of the Milky Way suspended in mid-air. Alf used different colours, filters and zooms to show them how civilization had evolved, from the initial galactic paradise of Lysentia all the way through to the present. When Johnny pointed out that there couldn't be any such thing as 'the present' because of Einstein's Relativity Theory, Alf became especially excited and went on to show that the galaxy was very much divided between the faster than light or FTL civilizations who could fold, and so travelled *outside* normal space, and others who remained *within* it – for whom the word 'now' didn't really apply.

He told them to imagine the fastest spaceship there was (a Telamine Starfighter) racing a beam of light, say over a hundred metres. However quick the starfighter was, it would always lose if the race was within normal space. The trick was to reduce the distance between the start and finish line so the spaceship had less far to travel. By folding the space between them so small that they were less than a nanometre apart, an FTL spaceship was able to beat the light beam that had to travel the full distance.

By the end of this, Johnny wasn't at all sure he understood and even Clara had become very much more interested in the pictures in her locket than in the lesson, so Alf changed tack and instead told them about the current war with the Andromeda Galaxy. At first no one had bothered much about it because intergalactic distances were thought too vast to cross, even for plicans – it was crazy to think one galaxy could invade another – but with the Emperor passing control to the Regent and the new Andromedan general, Nymac, causing havoc, things had taken a turn for the worse.

Clara's favourite lessons were the unlikely combination of space–time geometry and cosmic cuisine. Johnny much preferred it when Alf brought them their food in the evenings, but Clara sometimes insisted on preparing special treats for them that always ended up a little too blue to be appetizing. It was also in the evenings that Clara would document everything they'd done that day in the diary she'd started keeping, and she and Johnny talked about their growing up, far, far away on Earth. The same picture of their parents was in both of their lockets. Johnny found himself staring at it more and more and he told Clara everything he could remember about them, and also about Nicky who'd died. And how he still found it hard to believe their mum and dad could have murdered him. And he talked about Bentley who had been in the family since before he was born and how he'd give anything not to have left him behind. After that he tried to cheer them both up by making fun of Mr Wilkins's cooking.

Clara's growing up had been the opposite of Halader House. Her earliest memories were of living with the Twyfords, a well-to-do family with a huge house in Mayfair. One day, when she was seven, she'd received a mysterious letter. There was no clue who sent it, but it claimed her real name wasn't Twyford but Mackintosh. Puzzled, she showed it to the people she believed were her parents.

They seemed scared and upset and locked Clara away in her room for two whole days. Through the door she could hear the Twyfords arguing constantly about what to do with her and it became clear they weren't her real mum and dad. On the third day, desperate for food and drink, she'd somehow managed to get outside her bedroom window onto the roof, from where she climbed down and ran away.

She lasted for five days, scavenging food thrown out by the posh hotels and restaurants nearby, and hiding away in the secret places only she knew. She was caught when she travelled further afield to find a place called Somerset House, but got lost on the way.

She'd been sent away to boarding school and didn't see the Twyfords again. As soon as she seemed to make friends she got moved to another school. She'd always done well in class but was also particularly good at tennis and loved a sport called lacrosse that Johnny had never heard of. Then, about a year ago, she'd been sent to the Proteus Institute. It was much tougher than her other schools and sometimes she felt they were studying her rather than letting her study. Only those who passed the monthly tests stayed there, and not many did. She was told the others were sent on to easier schools and she never saw them again. At least that was what the Protectors told them, and she'd believed them until Johnny had come and she'd seen that boy floating in the tank.

Both of them had paid particular attention when Alf had talked about the krun, who lived in colonies like insects and had, academics suspected, something called a 'hive' mind. For the viasynth, the creatures on board Cheybora with triangular white faces, this was seen as a great advantage. Each of them knew instantly what was happening anywhere on the vessel, making them ideal crew members for any spaceship. For the krun it was seen as something terrible. There were relatively few spacefarers from the outer rim of the galaxy which was why not too much was known about them, but everyone agreed they were evil space pirates, abducting creatures from more primitive planets and selling them into slavery, or even to the Andromedans.

But what Johnny found most interesting of all wasn't the actual lessons but the time they spent with the Emperor. On one occasion a 'musician' came to play for them. Instead of sounds, when the hairless creature waved its eight arms over a complicated instrument it generated electric fields that Bram said was the sweetest music in all the galaxy. Clara screwed her face up and concentrated really hard but couldn't sense anything. Johnny, on the other hand, had actually 'heard' it. A little at first, but once he knew what to listen for it all became much clearer. When he closed his eyes and opened his mind, swirls of light and colour and sound had whizzed around inside his head. Bram was right – it was beautiful.

✡   ✡   ✡
✡   ✡

Today had been another of those days with the Emperor. Clara had asked if she could go to the Hall of Plicans in the third circle of the palace as soon as she'd discovered there was such a place. Bram had smiled and agreed, so she'd rushed off excitedly. Johnny had seen the musician approaching them and wondered if that was the real reason Clara wanted to go. The instrument had been set up and the musician performed again for a little while, with Johnny tuning in to the sounds much more easily. Then Johnny and the Emperor had returned to the place where they'd first walked together. The Emperor was trying to get Johnny to work out what language he was actually speaking in. 'English?' said Johnny, guessing again. He was sitting with Bram Khari under a kanefor tree, tickling it intermittently in the hope of being offered one of its wonderfully tasty coffee-flavoured fruits.

'You're guessing, Johnny,' said Bram. 'Listen again.'

Johnny sat on the immaculate lawn trying very hard to concentrate while the Emperor explained about the cornicula worm – his method of instant communication across the galaxy. The worm always spawned in the same place. Take one to Betelgeuse and release it and it would burrow back through the space–time continuum to Melania, leaving an open worm-hole through which a signal could travel. Bram was also switching languages every so often, hoping that Johnny might pick up the nuances and be able to train the tiny speck of the hundra inside him. It wasn't working. Bram reached to his side where there was a doughnut-shaped container. Through the translucent blue shell, Johnny could see a brilliant light, about ten centimetres long, moving around the outside. Encased in the centre of the container were five twinkling circles. Bram handed the blue shell to him.

'One worm for you to release when you're on Earth, so we can always be in contact. Plus some eggs to hatch when you're home so those conrniculae always return there,' said the Emperor.

'I did say I'd go with Captain Valdour,' Johnny told the Emperor. 'He asked me to join his ship, Cheybora.'

'Ah,' said Bram. 'Join the navy – see the galaxy. I'm afraid I've got other plans for you, Johnny. But I think you'll like them.'

'But what if Cheybora leaves?' Johnny asked. 'How would I get to Earth then? I can't contact her on my games console – I've been trying in the evenings. Maybe she already has?'

'Indeed she has,' said the Emperor. 'Cheybora's a good ship and Valdour's a fine captain – one of the best. I had to send them on an urgent mission.'

'But . . .'

'But don't worry, Johnny,' said Bram. 'I'm giving you your own ship.' Johnny stared at the Emperor with his mouth open. 'And I'm not even going to ask you what language I spoke that in,' said the Emperor, laughing.

'Aldebaran,' said Johnny, actually thinking he really had heard a difference this time.

'Very good, Johnny,' said Bram. 'I think you're getting it.'

It was instinct, Johnny thought. He'd been so surprised by what Bram had told him that he hadn't been concentrating. Maybe he'd been trying too hard? 'My own ship?' he repeated to Bram. 'But how will I know what to do?'

'Oh you'll know,' said Bram. 'When the time comes, you'll know.'

'Can I see it?' Johnny asked.

'Why not?' said Bram. 'After all – there's no time like the present.' The Emperor got to his feet, smiling broadly. Johnny jumped up and they started walking. They hadn't gone far before Johnny saw the Dauphin striding on its long legs towards them. Or he thought it was the Dauphin at first, but as it came closer he saw this phasmeer, as Alf had told them they were called, was a good four metres tall. 'Chancellor Gronak,' said Bram to the splindly creature whose robes were a pale cream, in keeping with the surrounding buildings. 'What an unexpected pleasure.' Chancellor Gronack bowed to the Emperor who continued, 'Allow me to introduce Johnny Mackintosh, a Terran.'

'How do you do?' said Johnny. The Chancellor looked at him dismissively before turning back to the Emperor.

'Your Divine Imperial Majesty,' Gronack began, in clipped Universal, Johnny thought. 'There are important matters of state we must discuss. You have become even less visible than normal with the arrival of this,' it turned to Johnny, 'this distraction. The Regent has asked me to insist on an audience to discuss important matters of state.'

'Has it now?' asked the Emperor, smiling at Johnny. 'Tell me, how is the Regent?'

'The Regent is . . . perplexed by your treatment of these . . . *creatures* from the periphery,' Gronack continued. Johnny felt it looked at him as if he was something it would normally wipe off its shoes, which were encrusted with garish pink diamonds. 'There is legislation requiring your approval.'

'Alas,' said Bram, 'we are rather busy at present. Perhaps you could return later, Chancellor?'

'I am sorry Your Divine Imperial Majesty,' said the creature, its robes now showing a hint of pink. 'I must insist on seeing you now.'

'Well then,' said Bram. 'If you must insist, but if I have business with Johnny here, then I see only one solution. You shall have to accompany us.' The Emperor set off, weaving his way through the different colonnades and squares and back towards the rooms where Johnny and Clara slept. The Chancellor, thought Johnny, was clearly not amused.

'I can't wait to see what happens when we get back to Earth,' said Johnny, getting more and more excited as they walked. 'It'll be amazing – I'll land near the UN – The United Nations I told you about. And I'll teach them to build – or grow – more ships. And not to fight – not each other anyway. I'll tell them about the Andromedans . . . and the krun.'

'Slow down, Johnny,' said Bram.

'Am I to understand,' said the Chancellor, 'that you intend to provide this infant with a spaceship? And when resources are so limited right now? Even if they were not it would be wasted on him. His planet would requisition it the moment he landed.'

'The Chancellor is partly right,' said Bram to Johnny. 'Do you think they'd listen to a thirteen-year-old boy? This ship I am giving you will have immense power – your many governments would war over it. In trying to win this prize they could even destroy your world. Besides,' he continued, 'this is my gift to you – not to the Earth. You cannot share this technology. To be valued, such knowledge should not be easily won. It has to be earned. The human race is not yet ready.'

'But what can I do on my own?' Johnny asked.

'You won't be on your own,' said Bram. You'll have Clara – and I'll give you a crew. You can protect the Earth. You can be my eyes and ears there. Perhaps one day you can even show me round – in secret of course.'

'You'd come to Earth again?' Johnny asked.

'Of course I will,' said Bram. 'Though not just Earth. I must say Saturn is one of the most splendid sights in all the galaxy. And as for Titan – there is something there I really must go back for.' Johnny didn't get to hear what it was because the Emperor had stopped suddenly, right in front of the upward-flowing waterfall. 'Prepare yourselves,' he said. 'This won't be pleasant for either of you.' The Chancellor looked nervously across to Johnny. Bram said, 'Follow me,' and stepped smiling into the waterfall.

☆　☆　☆
☆　☆

Johnny woke up feeling really cold. It had never been cold on Melania before. And the light was different, like gloomy twilight back on Earth. Confused, a hand reached down and took hold of his, helping him to his feet. It was easy getting up. All of a sudden he felt much lighter.

'I'm sorry,' said Bram. 'I would have given you more warning if it weren't for our interruption.' He nodded at the slender figure of Chancellor Gronack, unconscious on the ground next to where Johnny had been lying a moment before.

'What happened?' Johnny asked, reaching down to pick up the container holding the cornicula worm. 'Why's it so cold? And dark? Where's the waterfall?' He peered into the thick murky air, where there were some tall plants unlike anything he'd seen around the Imperial Palace.

'If you think everything appears different,' said the Emperor, 'that would be because it is. We have travelled through a wormhole – a portal between worlds. We are no longer on Melania.'

The Emperor pointed into the sky behind Johnny, who turned and looked upwards; dominating the heavens was an enormous planet – a gas giant with broad bands of clouds layering its surface, dotted by occasional spots that he knew must be massive storms bigger than some worlds. 'That's why I passed out?' Johnny asked. 'It was a fold?'

'Exactly,' said the Emperor, 'but only for a few seconds. You are becoming more accustomed to the manipulation of space. Now before we proceed there is something I must do.'

Johnny hadn't seen that look on Bram's face before – it was as though the Emperor was in pain. 'Are you OK?' he asked.

'I will be fine,' said Bram, forcing a smile. 'If I may, can I borrow your locket?'

'Of course,' said Johnny, lifting the chain over his neck and handing it to the Emperor.

'Thank you, Johnny. Excuse me just one moment,' and Bram turned his back on Johnny who watched as, for a second, a brilliant white light silhouetted the Emperor and then was gone. Bram turned round, looking drained, and handed the locket back saying, 'I must ask you not to open this again until you see me on another world. You will know when the time is right.'

Johnny nodded his head slowly. He would miss the times he spent staring at the picture of his mum and dad and Bentley, but he saw how important it seemed to the Emperor. 'What did you put in it?'

'I cannot speak of it, but you will know soon enough,' said Bram. 'Now come quickly – before the Chancellor wakes up. I have something to show you.'

Johnny followed the Emperor through the gloom, fingering his locket, which felt warm, unlike their surroundings. It was raining, stinging his eyes, which slowly became used to the dim light as they walked though a grey wasteland, with diffuse streams of eerie blue mist rising up through the surface at different points on the horizon. 'Where are we?' he asked Bram. 'What is this place?'

'This place,' the Emperor replied, smiling again, 'is my biggest secret. It is my spaceship plantation – where I've been growing your ship. Even by my standards she's very special.' The two were walking along the bottom of a steep cliff. And as they went further, Johnny could see a blue glow up ahead, coming from something around a corner. His heart started to beat faster.

'Is that it?' Johnny asked, pointing towards the light. The Emperor nodded. 'I can't wait to see what it looks like,' said Johnny.

'Well that's really up to you,' said Bram. They turned the corner and Johnny stopped dead and just stared. In front of him, swirling with life, and with power, was a tower of light –

like a two-hundred-metre-high pillar of blue fireflies. It was hard to focus on it. The closer he looked the more it didn't seem to have any form – it was just a blur of energy.

'Your ship,' said the Emperor. 'Or at least she will be.'

'What do you mean?' Johnny asked. 'Isn't it . . . she finished? I can't really tell.'

'Perhaps not, but I know you can sense her power,' said Bram. 'You can hear the music in her.' Johnny nodded. 'That is one of your gifts,' the Emperor continued. 'This moon, where we stand, is almost unique in all the galaxy. Only one other bursts with energy like this – it is alive.' The blueness engulfed Johnny, swirling all around him. He laughed. 'She likes you,' said Bram. 'She's bonding with you . . . drawn to your energy . . . but you must give her form.'

'How?' Johnny asked.

'You must *will* it,' said Bram. 'Focus. Create something beautiful – a shape in your mind for her to take. Perhaps something you have seen on Melania . . . or in your lessons.'

'No,' said Johnny. 'I know what she should be. Something from home . . . from Earth.'

'If you are sure,' said Bram, 'then concentrate. And I will give her some help.' Bram Khari plucked a single silvery hair from his head and blew it gently into the swirling mass of blue light.

'What are you doing?' Johnny asked, catching sight of the Emperor out of the corner of his eye.

'Nanobots,' replied the Emperor, 'the minute organisms that now maintain me. What you see is the soul of your ship – her mind. The nanobots will build a structure for her. The form you have willed her to take.'

Johnny knew how he wanted the ship to look. He tried to hold every last detail he could remember in his mind and, as he watched, the blue lights were echoing his thoughts – and the echoes were growing stronger. He saw the curved shape. He saw the triangular windows and the banded patterns around the outside. He saw two parallel lines encircling the nose cone. And from the bottom, building up, from the entrance with the 'M' above a 'W', the ship was solidifying, all gleaming metal and glass rising upwards from the surface of the strange grey world.

'Good . . . good. Keep your focus, Johnny,' said the Emperor beside him. 'Nearly there now.'

The line of matter rose higher until the blueness disappeared completely inside it. Finally, Johnny sensed it was done. He relaxed and slumped to his knees, exhausted by the effort he'd put into his ship.

'Very impressive,' said Bram. 'I like her Johnny. She is your ship, but because my nanobots built her she bears my mark – the mark of House Khari. It will give you the same protection as if I were on board.'

'What is that monstrosity?' came a voice behind them. Johnny was too drained to turn round but knew at once it was the Chancellor, who he was rapidly beginning to dislike as much as the Dauphin. 'I have never seen such an ugly thing – if this is the ship you're giving this Terran then good riddance to it. No one else would want to fly it.'

'It is not often I say this and mean it,' said Bram, 'but I think her beautiful.'

'Me too,' said Johnny, as he forced himself to his feet, thousands of light years from Earth, in front of a carbon copy of the London Gherkin. For a moment it was almost like being home. And despite all the wonderful things he'd seen on Melania he still thought it was an amazing building. 'Can we go inside?'

'You must go alone,' said the Emperor. 'I shall remain here with the Chancellor until you return. We have things to discuss and you have a friendship to begin.' Johnny looked curiously at the Emperor, who continued, 'You will find it hard to leave, but remember there is always tomorrow. Plus the ship is newborn – you must not wear her out.'

'Your Divine Imperial Majesty,' said the Chancellor. 'I will not stay here another moment. I don't know where we are but I demand I be taken back to the Imperial Palace.'

'I am the Emperor,' said Bram Khari softly, but Johnny could feel the power behind the voice. 'When I say we stay here that is exactly what we will do. We will wait while Johnny makes his acquaintance with the ship.'

Johnny didn't need telling again. He took a deep breath and walked towards the entrance of the Gherkin. The way in through the giant 'W' looked exactly as he remembered it from London – he supposed it was only a few days ago. He hadn't thought about it before, but now it seemed so perfect: 'M' for Mackintosh and 'W' for his symbol, Cassiopeia – it really was his ship. There were four sets of revolving doors. He entered through the ones furthest on the right, walked between two shining pillars, past the reception desk and up to the silver statue facing the lifts. He pressed the 'lift call' button and a set of doors opened in front of him. This, he realized, was where his memory of the Gherkin stopped and where the spaceship design took over, though something didn't seem right. He was peering not into a lift but what looked more like an empty lift shaft. There was no floor and no lift. He looked out to where the Emperor and Chancellor stood together. Bram spotted Johnny and gestured for him to step inside. Johnny felt really stupid – there was no actual lift to step into. He really should have picked a building he knew what the insides of looked like. Now he would have to walk back and face the Emperor without getting beyond the ground floor. Then a booming female voice, like an old teacher, said, 'Enter, Johnny Mackintosh.' It was the ship talking . . . in English. He wanted to say something back, if only to drown the noise of his heart thumping violently in his chest.

'There's no lift,' Johnny said sheepishly, out into the empty space.

'Lift?' the voice came back, only it had changed pitch and this time it was much, much higher. 'Computing . . .'

'It's what you stand in . . . to go up a building,' said Johnny.

'Lifts are inappropriate for antigravity propulsion,' said the sourceless voice, sounding different once again. 'Enter, Johnny Mackintosh.'

Antigravity propulsion? Johnny liked the sound of that. He closed his eyes and stepped forward. Nothing happened. Johnny opened one eye. He was simply floating in mid-air.

'State destination,' said the disembodied voice, now sounding a little like one of the news readers on the BBC.

'Er . . .' it didn't take long for Johnny to think where to go. 'Bridge!' Instantly he was whooshing upwards, very quickly, all the way to the very top of the ship. The 'lift' stopped, leaving Johnny floating again. He stepped gingerly out onto solid ground. It was beautiful. It was the perfect bridge. It was the perfect spaceship.

'Welcome,' said the voice, this time a young woman's, friendly and fun. 'You like that one?' asked the voice. 'I sense it. I will stop there, Johnny Mackintosh.'

'Just call me Johnny,' said Johnny, walking slowly forward, turning round and round as he did to stare at the fascinating instrument panels on the surrounding walls. He was heading towards the very centre of the bridge where, just in front of the empty plican tank, there was a single captain's chair. He thought of Cheybora and wondered what his ship would be called.

'Hello, Johnny,' said the woman's voice. Johnny noticed lights on a large, curved display flash as the words were spoken. 'Thank you,' the voice continued and, as it spoke the two words, two more patterns of light flickered over the screen.

'For what?' Johnny replied. He sat down in the chair, placing the doughnut-shaped container on the floor next to him.

'For giving me form,' said the voice. 'For giving me a part of your soul, to merge with my own. We are bonded for ever.'

Johnny nodded. He knew it was true. The ship was a part of him. It was almost an extension of him. 'What's your name?' he asked.

'I don't know,' said the voice. 'I don't have one yet. Tell me, what am I? I find this structure pleasing – you chose well.'

'You're the Gherkin,' said Johnny, 'in London.'

'Computing . . .' said the voice, as the lights flashed on the curved display next to the main viewscreen before Johnny. 'Gherkin – carnivorous semi-sentient reptile of Procyon Seven; feeling of light-headedness induced by prolonged exposure to the trandetion on Arcturus Prime; vegetable preserved in acid on Sol Three; coming of age ceremony of the Rhanean Kavan. Computing . . .' said the voice again. 'London – art form popular throughout the second epoch of the Varagon Hegemony; high-ranking city of Sol Three. Likelihood 98.7% Thank you, Johnny,' the voice continued. 'I am a preserved vegetable from Sol Three. Is that your homeworld? Is a gherkin your favourite food?'

'No,' said Johnny, feeling himself going red. '*A* gherkin's nothing. You're *the* Gherkin. It's a beautiful building in London – this really big city near where I'm from.

'A beautiful building in London of Sol Three,' came the voice.

'It's called Earth. You'd call it Terra,' said Johnny. 'It's the third planet, so I guess Sol's what you call the Sun?'

'Do you miss Earth, Johnny?' asked the voice, rich and comforting. Johnny nodded. Being in space was great, but he was a long way from home. 'Then I shall always remind you of home,' said the voice. 'I shall take the name "Spirit of

London". The spirit of your people . . . of this city. But you can call me "Sol" for short. The symmetry is pleasing. Do you like it?'

'It's a great name,' said Johnny. 'Pleased to meet you, Sol.'

'And I am pleased to meet you, Johnny,' Sol replied.

Although Johnny felt he could have spent hours with Sol, he left the cornicula worm on board and went back down the anti-grav lift to find Bram and Gronack waiting for him. Bram seemed pleased to be distracted from the Chancellor's affairs of state.

'So how did you like Sol?' Bram asked as Johnny approached them. 'Did you two get along?'

'How do you know her name?' Johnny asked.

'I am Emperor of the Galaxy,' Bram replied. 'I know everything.' Johnny could have sworn Bram had winked at him.

'I don't know how you put up with this questioning child,' said Gronack. 'Your Divine Imperial Majesty. Please can we go now? I will freeze my antennae off if we remain any longer.'

'We wouldn't want that, would we, Johnny?' the Emperor replied, 'though it will be necessary for you to spend a little more time with this "questioning child" yourself. Johnny,' said Bram Khari, turning to him. 'Tomorrow morning I would like you to accompany the Chancellor to the university where you will teach it English. Will that be all right?' Johnny nodded grimly – after the Emperor had given him such a magnificent spaceship he knew he couldn't refuse. Gronack's robes, however, changed colour to such a vivid red it looked as though it might explode. 'Uh-uh,' said Bram to the irate phasmeer. 'No more papers will be signed unless this is done.' With that he turned and started to walk away, retracing his steps towards the portal, his cloak billowing behind him in the wind and the rain.

A little confused by the new task he'd been given, Johnny took one last look at the Spirit of London – he couldn't wait to tell Clara about her – before running to catch the Emperor up. Sulking, the Chancellor hung behind for a while, scrawling furious notes on the unsigned imperial papers.

☆ ☆ ☆
☆ ☆

Later that evening, Johnny was sitting on the cushions at the low table in his quarters, enjoying a kanefor smoothie Alf had been only too happy to make for him when asked. He'd been shattered after coming back through the waterfall, but had managed not to pass out, unlike the Chancellor, who had been carried away while still unconscious by several mannigles (the bow-legged creatures that also looked after the Regent and the Dauphin). Johnny couldn't wait for Clara to return so he'd be able to tell her all about the Spirit of London. He'd already told Alf, but the android was always so excitable it was hard to know whether he was more pleased you'd enjoyed his treacle sponge or had your own spaceship. Finally Clara came bursting through the door, holding out a black drum in front of her.

'Where've you been?' Johnny asked.

'It's been amazing, Johnny,' said Clara. 'You've got to see this.'

'I've got something really exciting to show you too,' Johnny replied. 'Bet it's better that yours.'

'No way,' said Clara, placing the drum on the table. 'This is the best thing ever.'

'My my, Miss Clara,' said Alf, squatting down by the table and peering closely at the object on it. 'Is that what I think it is?' Clara nodded, a massive smile all over her face. 'Well that is as exciting as Johnny's news,' Alf continued.

Johnny was dumbfounded. How could something in a box Clara had brought back be anything like the same as getting your own spaceship? Alf had no sense of proportion. 'OK then,' said Johnny. 'Open it. Let's see what you've got.'

'I can't open it,' said Clara. 'It could fold anywhere.'

'Fold? You mean it's a plican?' Johnny asked.

'I can show you, though,' said Clara, 'if we make it darker – it's sleeping. Blinds down,' she said to the room and the red glow from Arros was shut out as a black line moved down the window in response to Clara's order.

'Lights – dim,' said Johnny, and the three of them found themselves in near pitch black, crouching around the table. Clara leant over to the drum and pressed a combination of little buttons on its side. The black exterior of the drum became transparent, revealing a little white balloon floating in clear fluid inside. 'Wow,' said Johnny.

'Isn't it beautiful?' said Clara.

Johnny stared at the flaps of uneven skin, through which the tentacles were visible, curled up inside the plican's body. Clara had a strange idea of what was and wasn't pretty. 'Why's it white?' he asked.

'The plican lifecycle goes through many colours,' said Alf 'but I have never seen a white one – is it newborn?'

'It's less than three weeks' old,' said Clara. 'It was born the day we arrived.'

'It must be the first new plican for twenty years,' said Alf. 'No offence, Miss Clara, but I am surprised the guardians let you remove it from the hall. You must have asked very nicely.'

'It was really odd,' Clara said. 'I didn't ask anything at all. I just wanted to see it. Then a messenger came from Bram with an Imperial Decree saying I must take it.'

'An Imperial Decree?' said Alf. 'My word – whatever is going on?'

'I told them – the guardians – that I didn't want to take it,' said Clara. 'That they should look after it, but they said I had no choice. It is beautiful isn't it?'

Clara reminded Johnny of how a proud big sister might look when she got to hold her parents' new baby, though he couldn't help thinking the plican looked squashed in. 'Why didn't they give you a bigger tank?' he asked. 'It must be really cramped in there.'

'Of course it's cramped,' said Clara, exasperated. 'I thought you liked spaceship design lessons.'

'I do,' said Johnny. 'I've really been paying attention.'

'Not to the design of the plican tank,' said Clara. 'It has a small separate chamber like this precisely so it can't uncurl its tentacles. If it did we could end up folded anywhere . . . probably dead in deep space.'

Now she mentioned it, Johnny did recall something about that, but he said, 'You can't expect me to remember everything.' Clara rolled her eyes. Johnny continued, 'But I do know why you've got it.'

'Oh of course, Master Johnny,' said Alf. 'You must be right.'

'What?' asked Clara. 'What is it?' She looked from Johnny to Alf and back to Johnny again. It was his turn to smile.

'Because I've got a spaceship,' said Johnny. 'Your plican must be meant to come with us. It's our folder.'

'A spaceship?' gasped Clara.

'And they work best when the ship and plican are both young,' said Johnny, 'so they can mature together – you see I *was* paying attention.'

'That's brilliant,' said Clara. 'Where is it? What's it like? Can I see it?'

'It's a she! Bram's taking us both – and you Alf,' Johnny said, turning to the android. 'Tomorrow afternoon. He made me promise not to tell you where she is. I think he wants it to be a surprise.'

'Oh but this is brilliant,' said Clara. 'We can go back to Earth

– to the Proteus Institute – maybe they'll be OK.'

'We have to try,' said Johnny. 'And then I can take you to see Mum. Maybe we can help her? Sol's bound to have all sorts of medical stuff we can use.'

'Sol?' asked Clara.

'The Spirit of London,' said Johnny. 'She's beautiful. Better than any of the ships we've seen in lessons.'

'What's it . . . what's she like?' Clara asked, and Johnny proceeded to tell Clara everything about the ship.

☆   ☆   ☆
☆   ☆

Johnny was surprised at how well he'd slept. He'd still been so excited when Alf suggested for the umpteenth time that he and Clara should get to bed, that he never thought he'd sleep. But then his exertions had finally caught up with him – two folds and willing a spaceship into existence – not bad for a day's work, he thought. He climbed out of the bed, put on his dressing gown and went through into the next room. The table was empty – Clara had taken the plican with her into her room. Johnny walked over to the window and gazed out at the waterfall, letting the carpet massage his feet. He wondered how long it would be before they could take the Spirit of London back to Earth. He knew they were nowhere near ready, but if they didn't go soon there was no way they could rescue Louise and Bentley. He just hoped it wasn't already too late. Johnny saw Alf, dressed as always in his suit and bowler hat, enter the square in one corner, carrying a silver salver that doubtless contained their breakfast. He went over to Clara's door and tapped gently. 'Alf's coming,' he said. 'Time to get up.' Clara grunted from the other side. Johnny went back to the window. Alf had been waylaid halfway across the square by Chancellor Gronack, nearly twice his size.

The English lesson! He'd forgotten all about it. He went

back and hammered loudly on Clara's door this time. Even paler than usual, with slightly bloodshot eyes, Clara emerged from her room with the plican's tank under her arm. She yawned and grunted at him.

'You OK?' Johnny asked. 'You look exhausted.'

'I'll be fine,' said Clara. 'I was up most of the night with the plican.'

'You're mad,' said Johnny. 'It's not as if it talks or anything.' Clara yawned again and walked sleepily over to the table, plonking herself down on the cushions. Johnny went and sat down next to her. He started to tell her about their morning's teaching duties when they were interrupted by Alf bringing breakfast, followed by an extremely grumpy Chancellor Gronack.

'Is it true?' asked Alf, skipping on the spot as he put the salver down on the table.

'Is what true?' Johnny asked.

'The Chancellor here informs me it is to learn to speak Terran. Please tell me I can come along too? I take it we shall study at the university?'

'First off, Alf, it's English – not Terran,' said Johnny. 'Not everyone back home speaks the same language.'

'Really?' asked Alf, lifting the lid of the salver to reveal smoked salmon and scrambled eggs on toast, with blueberry smoothies. It had been Clara's turn to choose breakfast and she'd picked one of her posh meals that Johnny didn't really like. 'How can they possibly all get along?' Alf asked.

'They don't have to – they're savages,' squeaked the Chancellor, sticking its antennae as high in the air as they could go.

'Chancellor Gronack – how can that be when Johnny and Clara are so delightful and interesting? Their world must be a fascinating place.'

'I sincerely hope I never have to find out,' said Gronack,

before turning to Clara. 'Come, little girl. I have matters of state to deal with – I didn't come here to watch you eat.'

Clara glared at the phasmeer, but didn't have the energy to reply.

'The Chancellor is right, Miss Clara,' said Alf. 'We really should get a move on. It is so good of it to take time out of its schedule – it simply would not do to keep an imperial official waiting.' He started to clear up around Clara as she carried on eating, drawing another glare from her. Soon, however, Johnny and Clara had changed and all four were in the language laboratory of the Imperial University.

English couldn't be found in the university's database, so all of them had to sit with their heads in what looked like dryers from an old-fashioned hairdressing salon while the university's ancient brain extracted Johnny and Clara's knowledge of the language and transferred it to Gronack and Alf. It was all very time-consuming, especially because the Chancellor kept complaining and disappearing outside to send messages concerning 'important matters of state.' Alf helpfully pointed out that there was a communications console in the laboratory it could use, but Gronack muttered something about galactic security and ignored him.

✴   ✴   ✴
✴   ✴

By the time they returned to the central island of the palace they were running late for their meeting with the Emperor and a return to the Spirit of London. Alf was panicking about keeping His Majesty waiting. Chancellor Gronack had come along too – having kept its side of the arrangement it was determined to have its papers signed. Alf was apoplectic when Clara decided she needed to go back to their quarters and fetch the plican to introduce it to Sol. Then Johnny remembered he'd planned to collect his games console – he wanted to see if he could somehow connect it up to Sol so he could talk to the ship when he was back in the palace. In the end the android picked them both up, placed each of them up under an arm and whizzed them to their rooms and back in around ten seconds. They arrived in a blur of movement and Alf lowered Johnny and Clara to the ground.

Bram was waiting for them by the pool in the courtyard outside their quarters. 'Good of you to join us,' said the Emperor, smiling at them as they approached.

'Your Majesty – I cannot tell you how sorry we all are for our lateness,' said Alf, taking off his bowler hat and bowing so low his head almost touched the marble flagstones.

Bram Khari simply smiled, spread his hands wide and announced, 'The Spirit of London awaits us. Clara – will you lead the way?'

Clara was so surprised she almost dropped the plican's drum. Johnny stepped in. 'I didn't tell her where the ship is,' he said to the Emperor. 'I thought you didn't want me to.'

'It's through here, isn't it?' said Clara, pointing at the water-fall. 'I felt it the first time I saw it – something's folded space there.'

'Excellent, Clara,' said Bram. 'Off you go – everyone follow Clara.'

'I am not going back through there, Your Divine Imperial Majesty,' squeaked the spindly Chancellor.

'Then I cannot possibly sign your proposal for new powers for the Regent,' Bram replied. 'Bring the papers with you and I shall authorize them as we go.'

Johnny knew how badly he felt when going through a fold and was almost sorry for Chancellor Gronack, who seemed to be taking it far worse. Its robes had turned pure white with fear. One by one, following Clara and the plican, they all stepped through the upwards-falling water and were transported to another world. Clara seemed to positively love the experience, the Emperor looked fine and Johnny was just delighted to make it through conscious. He stepped over the prostrate body of the Chancellor to where Alf was also lying horizontal. Bram came and joined him. The Emperor lifted off the bowler hat and rotated the android's left ear through 360 degrees. 'Emergency re-start,' he said to Johnny. 'Just as well you know.'

Alf sat bolt upright and looked around. 'Oh my word,' he said. 'I do believe that was a fold. How fascinating.'

'Are you OK?' Johnny asked.

'Never felt better,' said Alf, getting to his feet and wiping some dirt off his suit while looking around.

The Emperor swished a hand over the Chancellor so it floated alongside them, still unconscious, while the others walked along the side of the cliff towards the Spirit of London. When they reached the opening where the ship stood, everybody let out a little 'wow'. Although it had only been the day before, Johnny couldn't believe how beautiful the ship looked.

Clara, shivering in the wind and rain, looked almost in tears. 'You're right,' she said to Johnny. 'It is beautiful.'

'*She*,' whispered Johnny. 'Don't upset her.'

They walked up to the doors at the foot of the huge ship. Johnny entered first and to his surprise he heard Bram ask, 'Permission to come aboard, Captain?'

Johnny smiled. 'Permission granted,' he replied, and the three others, together with the floating Chancellor, entered behind him. Bram's eyes flickered over the statue of the giant silver alien in the lobby, but Johnny wanted to take everyone straight up to the bridge in the antigrav lifts. Clara hated them and had to be practically forced inside, but once at the top Johnny introduced her, Bram and Alf to Sol, who seemed delighted to meet them all. Clara took the plican's drum and, with some help from Alf, fixed it to the top of the cylindrical tank at the centre of the room.

'Thank you, Clara. I am complete,' said Sol, sounding absolutely delighted.

'Now you're the FTL Gherkin,' she replied, and the others laughed.

They spent the next couple of hours exploring the huge ship. There were lots of things Johnny expected – a giant engine room for propulsion when they weren't folding; laboratories for experiments, a sickbay and a galley. But there was also a whole floor with a five-a-side football pitch, other games rooms and a beautiful garden area. Sol, who Johnny could talk to anywhere within the ship, told him it generated food and oxygen. Bram said he'd better go back and check on Chancellor Gronack, leaving Johnny, Clara and Alf to look round the shuttle bay on their own. There were three mini transports in there, each of which Sol said was controlled by their pilot's thoughts. Johnny couldn't wait to try. The biggest one looked like a red double-decker bus while the other two were in the shape of black London taxis. Johnny loved them and told Sol for the hundredth time how brilliant she was. In another room Alf wanted to check Sol's records of London. Johnny and Clara were amazed to see pictures of St Paul's Cathedral and Tower Bridge, and even bowler hat-wearing city workers walking the streets.

'Master Johnny . . . Miss Clara,' said Alf. 'Look at them – I do hope I have dressed properly. When the Emperor said we would be going to London I did want to look as inconspicuous as I could. Apparently the financial workers wear this uniform.'

Johnny caught Clara's eye and saw it was all she could do not to laugh. 'You'll fit in like a native,' he told the android. He was wondering how the Emperor and Alf could possibly have planned a trip to Earth before they'd even met, but just as he was about to ask there was a loud bang and he, Clara and Alf fell to the floor as the ship shook.

'Johnny,' came Sol's voice from over their heads. 'Is everyone OK?'

Johnny looked around. 'We're fine, Sol,' he said. 'What happened?'

'We're under attack,' said Sol, as calmly as though she was reciting her twelve-times table. 'Emergency take-off initiated. Can you come to the bridge?'

The three of them got to their feet. 'We're on our way,' said Johnny and they rushed out of the room, along the corridor to the lifts.

As they stepped out onto the bridge they could see the groggy figure of Chancellor Gronack trying to get to its feet and three spaceships heading towards them on the giant viewscreen. 'Incoming transmission,' said Sol, in time to the pattern of lights on the neighbouring screen.

'Who from?' Johnny asked. 'Where's Bram?'

'The transmission is from Emperor Bram Khari,' said Sol, as calmly as ever, as a missile exploded nearby causing the ship to shudder again. 'Displaying message.'

'Johnny,' said Bram, whose face had appeared on a display screen attached to the chair in the middle of the bridge. Johnny sat down to talk to the Emperor. 'We have been betrayed. I must close the portal to Melania behind me. Fold at once – use the worm to contact me once you're safe.'

There was another explosion. 'You heard him, Sol. Let's fold.'

'State destination,' the ship replied.

'Anywhere,' shouted Johnny. 'Earth . . . Terra . . . Sol Three!'

'Destination programmed,' said Sol.

'No!' screamed Clara, as the force of the blast came through the hull and sent her flying across the bridge. The compartment holding the baby plican glowed blue, opened and the creature fell through into the main tank uncurling its eight tentacles. Another huge explosion just outside the ship lit up the screens.

It's happening again, thought Johnny, as he braced himself for the fold. He found himself falling through the walls of the ship straight towards the brightest light he'd ever experienced, and then . . . blackness.

☆   ☆   ☆
☆   ☆

Someone very far away was calling his name. Johnny tried to recall where he was and why he felt so hungry and thirsty. His stomach felt as though it had been turned inside out over and over again. He must have folded . . . he remembered now, though didn't understand why he'd lost consciousness – he thought he was used to it by now. He opened his eyes. Clara was leaning over him. She had a drinking bottle in her hand and pushed the straw into his mouth, squeezing the fluid into it. As the warm liquid made its way down his throat, Johnny felt his insides disentangle. He smiled weakly. 'Johnny,' she said. 'You've got to wake up – we're in trouble.'

Johnny looked around the bridge. Now they were travelling through space, the floor had somehow shifted through ninety degrees to let them face the way they were moving. Alf was lying a few metres away, his eyes open, staring blankly at the ceiling. The Chancellor lay over by the far wall. Sol's display screens were showing the same view in every direction – a mass of tumbling rocks, nearly obscuring the points of light beyond. The bridge looked battered – almost nothing was in its correct place, though Johnny was pleased to see the captain's chair was still at its centre. 'Thanks,' he said to Clara, handing her the drink and getting unsteadily to his feet. 'Where did you get that?'

'I made it in the galley,' Clara replied. 'You've lost a lot of fluid in the fold. It should help.'

'The galley? How long was I out?' asked Johnny.

'It's been about a day,' said Clara. 'I didn't know what to do.'

'A day?' Johnny replied. 'You're kidding. What happened?'

'I don't know,' said Clara. 'But you shouldn't have folded so far. Definitely not with a baby. I tried to stop it. Something went wrong – it wasn't like normal.'

'I didn't know, sorry,' said Johnny. 'Everything happened so fast. Did we make it?'

'I'm not sure,' said Clara. 'I can't get Sol to respond . . . or Alf.'

'Alf's easy. I'll show you,' said Johnny, walking across to the android and taking hold of his left ear. 'You turn this all the way round,' he said as he rotated the ear, which snapped back into its proper position.

Alf sat up. 'Was that another fold?' he asked. 'Oh dear, poor Sol does not seem well,' he continued as he looked around the bridge. 'Have we reached Terra?'

'It doesn't look like it,' said Johnny. 'I'll see if I can raise Sol. Can you take the Chancellor down to sickbay? I think it might be a while before it's back with us.'

'Of course, Master Johnny,' said Alf, and the android walked over to the unconscious phasmeer, effortlessly hoisting the creature almost twice its size over one shoulder and carrying it to the lifts. Johnny walked over to the captain's chair and fell gratefully into it while Clara perched on the arm on his left.

'Hello, Sol,' said Johnny, looking hopefully at the ship's voice screen in front of him, which was alternating very slowly between slightly lighter and slightly darker. There was no obvious response from the ship. Johnny started entering some basic commands directly from a console on his right. Poor Sol, he thought. It must be like slapping her around the face to get her to wake up, but he didn't know what else to do. He took another swig from the bottle Clara was still holding, and asked what she meant by saying the fold wasn't normal.

'It's hard to explain,' Clara replied. 'Whenever it's happened before I can see it – like folding a piece of paper. But like origami, with lots of subtle creases to get you to the right place. And the paper's never that big anyway. This time it was like we ripped it. Though maybe that was the explosions too. But to try and reach Earth the plican had stretched space so far it was really spread out anyway. It was like it couldn't take our weight and we just fell through it.' Johnny didn't think that sounded good, and Clara didn't look her normal happy self after she'd just folded. 'We were definitely heading in the right direction though,' she continued, hopefully. 'Maybe we made it.'

'Ouch,' said another female voice. 'That hurts.'

'Sorry,' said Johnny. 'Are you OK, Sol?'

'Not if you keep shorting my neurons like that,' said the ship. 'Please stop – I'm awake now. What happened?'

'We were hoping you could tell us,' Johnny replied. 'Do you know where we are?' He got out of the chair and walked forwards to the main viewscreen. Clara followed.

'In the middle of an asteroid field, I would suggest,' said Sol. 'Let's see now. Computing . . . one stellar mass found . . . eight planetary masses found . . . displaying sixth planet.' Johnny and Clara watched as a faraway dot on the screen grew in size to reveal a blurry ringed world. Johnny was pretty sure it was Saturn.

'Oh that is impressive,' said Alf, stepping back into the bridge and walking over to join them. 'The Emperor told me it was beautiful. Of course I cannot make such subjective observations, but it is rather grand.'

'Looks like we made it,' said Johnny. 'Sol – why is it blurred?'

'I have suffered severe damage, Johnny,' said the ship. 'Visual sensors are at 0.000 271 828%.'

'Can you plot a course for Earth . . . Sol Three?'

We are on course for the third planet, Johnny,' said the ship. 'However, the dark energy containment field has collapsed so main engines are offline. Only secondary thrusters are undamaged. With our current momentum we will reach Earth in approximately three days' time.'

'Three days!' said Johnny and Clara together.

'I suggest,' replied Sol calmly, 'you make yourselves comfortable. Most systems will be operational by the time we arrive. At least we won't crash.'

'Well that's a relief,' said Johnny.

'Or I don't think so, anyway,' Sol continued. 'None of these asteroids seems to be moving towards us . . .'

✦ ✦ ✦
✦ ✦

Johnny and Alf were in the sickbay with the Chancellor, who had finally woken up and seemed even less amused than normal, though perhaps because it lay with its head and feet both extending beyond the ends of its bed. 'Put a child in charge of a spaceship and no wonder this happens,' said Gronack, as Alf updated it with their current position.

'I am here,' said Johnny tersely. 'I can hear you, you know. We were under attack.'

'Then clearly we should have followed standard diplomatic protocol,' replied the Chancellor.

'And what's that exactly?' said Johnny, hotly.

'I inform our assailants that an important personage is on board and surrender the ship, of course,' said the Chancellor. 'I would be returned to Melania in due course.'

'She's not yours to surrender,' said Johnny through gritted teeth.

'Well she is now,' replied Gronack. 'The Emperor's not here to indulge you. I am not placing my life in the hands of some infant savage simply because of Khari's erratic judgement.

What is this thing called anyway? I take it she has a name?'

'The ship is the Spirit of London,' said Alf, 'and she is Johnny's ship, you know.' Alf was looking down at the floor rather than at the horizontal Chancellor.

'You cannot be serious,' said Gronack. 'At least *you* should have enough of a brain to understand I must take charge. Look at the damage this thing has done already. We're lucky to be alive,' it said, looking at Alf, 'though that's a rather relative term.'

'For a diplomat, Sir,' replied Alf, 'you can be extremely undiplomatic. By Imperial Decree I have been declared wholly sentient and accorded full rights as a Citizen of Melania.'

'Another pet project from our senile Emperor,' replied Gronack.

'If I may interrupt,' came a female voice from above their heads.

'What is it, Sol?' said Johnny.

'Ship!' said the Chancellor, finally sitting up. 'I am assuming command of this vessel. From now on you will deal directly only with myself.'

'Forgive me, Chancellor Gronack,' Sol replied. 'If the phasmeers were the last species in the galaxy, and you were the very last of the phasmeers, there would still be less chance of me taking orders from you than a Sulafat tortoise winning the Imperial Speed Medal.' Alf was so embarrassed he had to leave the sickbay and go and stand in the corridor. Johnny grinned – he hadn't actually heard of a Sulafat tortoise before but it certainly didn't sound quick. Perhaps he'd look it up when he had a spare moment. 'Johnny,' Sol continued. 'I have some bad news. Please come to the bridge.'

'Bad news?' squeaked Chancellor Gronack. 'It's not possible things can get any worse.'

'What's wrong?' Johnny asked.

'There's something here you must see,' said Sol. 'It concerns Earth.'

'On my way,' said Johnny. 'If it's about Earth can you let Clara know? She should see it too.'

'She is in the library. I shall inform her,' Sol replied.

Johnny left the sickbay followed by Chancellor Gronack and they collected Alf in the corridor – he seemed to have composed himself. At least it sounded as though Sol had fixed the scanners. It would be good to see Earth, he thought. Maybe some krun ships were visible. He'd not told Sol about those being there and he knew now he should have done. He stepped into the lift shaft without waiting for the other two and said, 'Bridge.' Seconds later he stepped out at the top of the ship and stared at the image on the screen. Whatever it was, it wasn't Earth. 'What is it, Sol?' he asked.

'This is an asteroid, Johnny,' Sol replied. 'It's large . . . about 50 kilometres across.'

'So?' Johnny asked.

'It's on a collision course, Johnny. It will hit in about 52.694 134 hours' time.'

'But you said we had reserve tanks,' said Johnny. 'Why don't we just move out of the way?'

'I didn't make myself clear,' Sol replied. 'The collision course is not with us. It's with Earth.' Johnny felt the blood draining from his face and sat down in his captain's chair while the ship continued to speak. 'Our fold was highly irregular. On our return to normal space we created an enormous blast wave in the direction of travel . . . towards the third planet. The debris we witnessed around us was just the initial wavefront. The main effect of the blast was to divert this asteroid in our direction.'

'What will happen?' Johnny asked weakly, as Clara entered the bridge behind him.

'Asteroid impact is well-known throughout the galaxy,' said Sol. 'There are many levels of damage. In this case, given the relative size of the two bodies, the asteroid would be classed a global killer.'

'A global what?' asked Clara.

'A global killer,' Sol repeated. 'In 52.672 918 hours' time, all life on Earth will be destroyed.'

7 ✧ ✦

JOHNNY'S ARK ✧ ✦

Johnny, Clara, Alf and Chancellor Gronack were standing on
the mezzanine platform of an enormous room on deck 14. Sol
had recommended it as the place to think over strategic issues.
Alf had excelled himself in the galley in a desperate attempt to
cheer Johnny and Clara up, making fish and chips with mushy
peas which he knew was one of Johnny's favourites. The
untouched ketchup-spattered plates were now floating on a little
table behind them. Like all the tables on the ship, this one's
surface was a near-invisible electromagnetic forcefield that
sparked occasionally, if only to remind you where it was located.
Johnny wasn't hungry – eating just made him feel worse. He
looked beneath him to a much larger circular table onto which
Sol had projected a diagram showing the Earth, the Spirit of
London and the giant asteroid following them. The collision
course was also clearly marked. He'd had a spaceship for a
couple of days and in that time it looked as though he'd wiped
out all life on Earth. It was all his fault. If he'd paid more attention in his lessons he'd have known not to fold so far. Clara knew
– she'd tried to stop him – but it had been too late. He'd hoped
a good night's sleep would have cleared his head so he could
think of a plan, but everything he came up with was reluctantly
dismissed by Sol. Her weapons were inoperable and would take
too long to repair, so they couldn't simply blow the asteroid out
of the sky. The asteroid was too big for the plican to fold it onto

another path, not that the poor creature had recovered from their last enormous fold yet anyway. They couldn't even sacrifice themselves by putting the Spirit of London in the way to deflect the asteroid – the ship didn't have enough momentum for that. A part of Johnny still felt like doing it anyway.

'There's nothing for it,' he said, as much to himself as the others round the table. 'I know the Emperor didn't want us to contact Earth but we have to warn them. Maybe they can stop it from there – or at least save a few people?'

'You will do no such thing,' said Chancellor Gronack. 'That would be a gross breach of diplomatic protocol.'

'A what?' said Clara.

'As His Divine Imperial Majesty very clearly told Johnny, your planet cannot know of this ship's existence. It is far too powerful a vessel to fall into the hands of . . . primitives. Besides . . . asteroids strike planets – it's what happens,' Gronack continued. 'You can't just go around altering the future – didn't this robot teach you anything in temporal mechanics?'

'We made the future,' Johnny snapped. 'If we hadn't come through the fold to Earth the asteroid wouldn't be about to destroy it.'

'Johnny does have a compelling point,' said Alf, smarting from the 'robot' tag he knew was meant to be insulting. 'As we created the problem I believe we are entitled to resolve it as we see fit.'

'Just the sort of remark I would expect from a sub-sentient mechanoid,' squeaked the Chancellor. 'Contact with any non-spacefaring species is strictly forbidden regardless of circumstances. It's unfortunate the rest of these Terrans will be destroyed, but rules *are* rules.'

'Unfortunate!' Johnny said. 'What's unfortunate is we're stuck with a windbag like you.'

'Master Johnny,' said Alf. 'I know you are upset but you

cannot say such a thing to the Chancellor of the Imperial Court.'

'I'm not letting six billion people die on that planet because of its stupid protocols,' Johnny shouted. 'We will save them. Is that understood?' He had got to his feet instinctively, his red face staring up at the spindly phasmeer who towered over him, but was backing away.

'I don't think telling them they're going to die is going to help very much,' said the Chancellor, recovering its composure. 'But if you must then go ahead. It won't make any difference.'

'Sol,' said Johnny. 'Can you send a radio message to Earth?'

'Of course, Johnny,' the ship replied.

'What's the time difference between them receiving the message and the asteroid striking?'

'Computing . . . we are currently 2283 light seconds from Earth,' said Sol, 'so the planet will receive a message 122,479 seconds before impact.'

'What's that in hours?' said Johnny.

Alf interrupted with, 'Why, that's 34.021 944 44 . . .'

'Enough!' said Johnny. 'Thirty-four hours . . . OK, Sol. Send a message saying a fifty kilometre asteroid will strike in thirty-four hours. Give them its trajectory and tell them we'd like to help.'

'Should I send it to anyone in particular?'

'The people of Earth,' said Johnny. 'And the Secretary General of the United Nations.'

'They will panic,' said Clara quietly. 'Might it be best not to?' She didn't look at the Chancellor.

'No . . . they deserve to know the truth,' said Johnny. 'It's only right.'

'The message has been sent,' said Sol. 'Earliest possible radio wave reply is in 67.014 268 minutes.'

'I guess we wait,' said Johnny. He took one last look at the projection below, turned and headed out of the strategy room to go to his quarters.

☆   ☆   ☆
☆   ☆

Sol was broadcasting the warning continuously, adjusting the times as the ship and the asteroid travelled ever closer, but nearly a day had passed without any word from Earth. It wasn't clear why no one was responding. Johnny had now admitted defeat in trying to repair the Spirit of London's weapons. Sol assured him her drones were working solely on this, but it simply could not be done in time. The shields were worse and only specialist parts that they couldn't create on board could make them operational. Instead, Johnny and Clara had turned their attention to creating a giant habitat on a deck in the centre of the ship in place of the five-a-side pitch. They hoped to fill it with evacuees before colonizing a new homeworld elsewhere. Chancellor Gronack had reluctantly agreed to help out, but it had started arguing again with Johnny, telling him it was point-less as they would be unable to take anyone anywhere even if they did rescue them. The row had become so heated that the Chancellor's robes glowed a violent shade of pink that Johnny hadn't seen before, on either it or the Dauphin. Typically, Gronack had gone as soon as Johnny and Clara had turned their backs, which the two of them had decided was for the best as they got much more done on their own anyway. With Alf they would have been quicker still, but he was busy repairing Sol's dark energy drive.

Johnny and Clara agreed. They'd try to rescue Louise and Bentley, desperately hoping they were still alive, take their mum from St Catharine's and their dad from prison, some of Clara's friends from the Proteus Institute and Johnny's friends from school . . . the football team . . . it was such a little thing but Johnny did miss football and probably no one would ever play it again. He thought back to the night this had all started – football had been the distraction he'd used, unscrambling the TV signal at Halader House so he could talk to Kovac. And then it hit him – television! How could he have been so stupid? He and Clara had wondered what it would be like on Earth with just a day to go, as he was sure the astronomers would have spotted the asteroid by now. They could possibly even see the Spirit of London as she was unshielded and they were now inside the Earth–Moon orbit. TV must be broadcasting, if only to plead with people not to panic. And if it was, Sol could pick it up – TV signals had been leaving Earth in an ever-expanding sphere since the 1940s – aliens seventy light years away could pick them up by now. No wonder the krun had come hunting.

'Sol,' Johnny shouted excitedly into the air above him.

'What is it, Johnny?' the ship replied.

'TV, Sol – television,' said Johnny. 'Even if they're not radioing us directly there'll be a TV signal from Earth so we can see what's going on. Put it on the screen. We're done here anyway. See you on the bridge.'

'There do not appear to be any television broadcasts from the planet,' Sol replied.

'Keep trying – there's got to be something,' said Johnny, before turning to Clara. 'Come on – let's get to the bridge anyway. It might be the last time we'll see Earth from space.'

But when they arrived on the bridge something was very definitely wrong. They were greeted by Sol telling them that there was absolutely no indication of a sufficiently technological civilization to broadcast TV signals on the planet beneath them, but that wasn't the problem at all. Clara summed it up by saying, 'What's wrong with it? It's all squashed together.' There could be no argument. Where was Britain? What could have been Europe and North America were practically joined together with hardly any Atlantic Ocean between them, yet

North and South America were totally unconnected. It didn't look right at all.

'Oh my – that is beautiful,' said Alf, stepping out of the lift shaft and walking over to where Johnny and Clara stood by the giant viewscreen. 'There is so much water.'

'Too much,' said Johnny. 'The continents are all squashed together.'

'Could we be in a parallel universe?' Clara asked. 'Something did go wrong with the fold.'

'Parallel universes, Miss Clara?' said Alf. 'It really is good the Chancellor is not here or a comment like that would be the final straw.'

'Where is it anyway?' said Johnny. 'Sol – locate Chancellor Gronack. Ask it to come to the bridge.'

'Chancellor Gronack is not on board,' Sol replied.

'What?' said Johnny and Clara together. Johnny continued 'How did it leave?'

'That information is not known,' Sol replied.

'Not known?' said Johnny. 'You must know . . . that coward . . . I bet it took one of the transports.'

'All transports are in their allocated positions in the shuttle bay,' Sol replied.

'How very strange,' said Alf. 'What is going on, I wonder?'

Johnny was thinking. Maybe he had seen this Earth somewhere before? 'Sol,' he asked, 'are the long range sensors now operational?'

'Long range sensors have been repaired and are functioning normally,' answered the ship.

'Can you calculate our galactic position by comparing it with your star charts?' he asked.

'Of course. Computing . . .' said Sol. The ship took an unexpectedly long time to answer, before responding. 'Our position is not calculable by referencing current star charts.'

'I told you,' said Clara. 'It *is* a parallel universe.'

'No I don't think so,' said Johnny. 'Sol . . . can you find a match for our position if you run the star charts backwards in time?'

'Negative, Johnny,' replied Sol. 'A fixed point of reference would be required to perform such a calculation.'

'That's OK,' said Johnny. 'Assume this *is* Earth and find out *when* this is.'

'Computing . . .' Sol began.

'Johnny – what are you thinking?' asked Clara, sounding worried.

'Look at it,' said Johnny pointing to the blue-green world in front of them. 'Have you ever heard of plate tectonics . . . continental drift?' Clara shook her head. Johnny continued. 'Ages ago all the land on Earth was in one place – a huge supercontinent, but really slowly they drifted away from each other. If we had a map you'd see how Africa fits right into South America. You see there . . .' he continued, pointing at the screen, 'that's going to become America, but it's not moved away from Europe yet. And there . . . that's South America and it's moving up and they'll meet eventually. We're in the past. A lot in the past by the look of it.'

'You are correct, Johnny,' said Sol. 'I have completed my calculations. We are 64,874,261.451 832 01 years behind Galactic Standard Time. I find this a little . . . disconcerting.'

'You mean we're never going home?' said Clara, her eyes beginning to water.

'If that asteroid hits there'll never be a home,' Johnny replied, shaking his head.

'Oh my goodness,' said Alf. 'If that happens you can't have been born so you can't then destroy the Earth . . . and that's a Level 4 paradox.'

'A what?' asked Johnny and Clara together.

'Though it is possible the time difference explains the Chancellor's disappearance,' Alf continued, ignoring their question. 'If this is 64,874,261.4 . . .' he hesitated, looking at Johnny. 'If this is 65 million years ago, then there must be an enormous tachyon potential within the ship.'

'Tachy what?' asked Clara.

'Tachyons,' Johnny replied. 'Theoretical particles that travel faster than light.'

'And backwards in time,' Alf continued. 'And they most certainly are not theoretical. Why, I have heard the Andromedans used tachyon beam weapons on the Scorpius Cluster.'

Johnny winced. Whatever tachyon beam weapons were, he was sure they weren't pleasant. 'But what about the Chancellor?' he asked.

'I told you all about temporal mechanics at the university,' said Alf. Johnny and Clara looked at each other a little sheepishly as neither had paid much attention during these lessons. 'Boloban's First Law states that displaced temporal energy will always tend towards the equilibrium.' Johnny and Clara looked at each other uncertainly and then back at Alf, who continued, 'That time seeks to correct itself . . . I suspect that the Chancellor has started travelling forwards in time.'

'You mean it'll get back to where it was?' Johnny asked. 'That's good isn't it? It means we *can* go home.'

'Good, Master Johnny?' replied Alf. 'Good? It will be disastrous. Do you think the tachyons will restore things to how they were? Heavens no. As long as the temporal energy is rebalanced the tachyons will not mind how. The Chancellor could end up a billion years in the future while we remain here. Or more probably we shall all drift forwards separately to different time periods. We must stop this happening before it is too late.'

☆　☆　☆
☆　☆

Johnny could hardly think of a more miserable few hours. Destroying the whole world had been bad enough but, if it were possible, he now felt even worse. At least he'd thought he'd still have his sister and Alf and a very cool spaceship to travel in around the galaxy, seeing all the places he'd always wanted to visit. Now the tachyon buildup would take even that away. He slipped away from the bridge and wandered the corridors of the Spirit of London aimlessly, fingering the locket around his neck, finally knowing that he'd never see his mum or dad, or even Bentley, again. And he couldn't even look at their pictures because of the promise he'd made to Bram. Maybe that didn't matter any more and he should open the locket. He looked around and found himself down at the very foot of the ship.

He went through one set of revolving doors and stood outside breathing in the muggy atmosphere of prehistoric Earth. He'd only meant to take a short walk around the ship before returning to the bridge. He knew he should try to help find a solution to their problems, but now he was here . . . There was less than a day left and no one would ever be able to see this again. Besides, he'd be back before they knew and it would help clear his head anyway. He took a very deep breath, tucked the locket inside his tunic and slipped quietly away into a light drizzle.

The Spirit of London had landed in what was to have become the Yucatan Peninsula, right by a coastline that Sol's projections showed would have one day bordered the Gulf of Mexico. As they were on the same course it was also precisely where the asteroid was due to strike, but by landing here they'd used the minimum amount of energy. For what is was worth, the secondary thrusters meant they could still take off and comfortably reach escape velocity before the impact which, according to Johnny's watch, would be in about seven hours' time. He turned around and walked slowly backwards, looking up at his beautiful ship, which was only just a little taller than the conifers around it. There was a forest on his left and an ocean beneath the cliffs to his right. Everything was green and lush, right up to the cliff face. After the last few weeks spent either on Melania or in spaceships it was good to feel the wind and rain on his face. He walked to the edge of the cliff and gazed out across the water, tasting the salt in the air. Waves were breaking around a lonely rock about half a mile out to sea. Johnny turned and jogged into the trees – it would make him harder to spot from the ship.

As soon as he entered the forest Johnny slowed down. The dense canopy of leaves meant it quickly became dark. He should be careful. It would be a bad idea to get too close to some of the strange plants he saw around him, with their stripy foliage, large spines, or very elongated stems – they looked nearly as alien as anything he'd seen on Melania. And as he walked he could hear some very strange noises in the distance. Some things, though, looked reassuringly familiar and as he passed a football-sized flower head he smiled as several fat bumblebees buzzed in and out. Maybe it wasn't all that different from home? He approached a narrow stream and saw dragonflies with enormous wingspans darting up and down. Their vibrantly coloured blue wings looked strikingly similar to the Chancellor's robes. Johnny wouldn't really miss Gronack if he never saw it again, which did make him feel a little guilty, but only a little. The stream was too big to jump across so he walked with it on his left, further into the forest. Was it really worth trying to bring Gronack back to the same time as the rest of them, as the others were hoping to? He imagined what it would say when he got back to the ship.

'How irresponsible to go wandering off like that . . . I wish we'd just taken off and left you there . . . If I were in charge . . .'

The conversation in Johnny's head became so loud that he almost walked right into it. He stopped just in time. Silently, he edged behind a giant fern so he could peer through the leaves at the creature in front of him, alternately drinking from the stream and chewing on some plants along the bank. It was about six metres long, on four stubby legs, covered with green and brown spikes, and with a large clubbed tail. It was a living, breathing dinosaur.

There was a crackle from the games console in Johnny's pocket, followed by Clara's voice saying, 'Johnny, are you there?'

Johnny's hand dived into his pocket, pulled out his handheld and fumbled for the power button, finally turning the device off, but not before the creature had lifted its head out of the water and turned to face in his direction. The clubbed tail started swaying as the dinosaur began to shuffle nervously backwards towards some thick undergrowth. Johnny stepped out from behind the fern, holding his hands up in the air. 'It's OK,' he said softly. 'Don't be afraid . . . I'm not going to hurt you.'

The dinosaur halted and tilted its head towards him; Johnny was pleased to see the tail also stop moving. He walked slowly towards the creature, lowering his arms as he went, saying, 'Don't worry . . . I just want to say hello.' He was now standing right in front of it. He kept the console in his right hand but held out the back of his left in front of the dinosaur's face and the creature started sniffing. Then a long tongue came out and licked Johnny's hand. 'Good boy . . . good boy,' said Johnny, turning his hand over and gently patting the creature's metre-long head which, in turn, nosed forward and started sniffing Johnny's tunic. 'Hey that tickles,' he laughed, and tried to push it gently away. The head jerked back from Johnny and the creature's clubbed tail came swinging just past him. Johnny dived out of the way, sending the games console sailing through the air. It landed with a squelch in some mud a few metres away. The dinosaur turned and fled from him, crashing through the undergrowth as it went. 'Stop!' Johnny shouted. 'Don't go . . . I didn't mean to scare you.' He started to get to his feet when his leg brushed against something very solid that hadn't been there a moment before.

Slowly, he turned his head to see what was behind. He wished he hadn't. Two beady black eyes were peering down from a head that on its own was as big as Johnny. Standing on its tree-like hind legs the creature started sniffing along Johnny's back, and up to his face. Johnny felt a gust of hot air raise the hairs on the back of his neck – the bad breath was almost overpowering. The dinosaur lifted its head away, opened an enormous mouth full of huge teeth and roared, the deafening noise sounding almost like 'Foooooooood!' Johnny's heart was thumping so hard he thought his chest might explode. Why had he turned the console off? Why? That was really stupid. He screwed his eyes up, concentrated really hard and willed the machine to come back on.

The giant head bashed into Johnny's side, flipping him over onto his back. He lay in the mud unable to move as the massive jaws opened above him. Teeth were the only things he seemed able to see – many centimetres long and razor sharp. 'Master Johnny . . . please come in,' came Alf's voice from the mud a few metres away. Distracted, the creature craned its neck down to where the voice was coming from and bellowed again. It was now or never. Johnny leapt to his feet and ran. He ran through the thickest undergrowth he could, ignoring the stinging plants as he pushed them out of the way. He desperately hoped the dinosaur – it was a T. Rex . . . he was sure it was a T. Rex – wouldn't be able to follow him, but as he ran he could hear it crashing through the trees behind. He felt a giant pair of jaws closing on him and he dived – just in time – sliding in the mud of the forest floor to carry him out of reach of the giant teeth. Then he got up and ran again. The undergrowth was getting thinner. He was nearing the edge of the forest. Johnny stole a glance over his shoulder – the T. Rex was still following, about ten metres behind. Johnny kept going. He was out of the forest now. He could see the Spirit of London – it was really close. Maybe they'd spot him? He sprinted for all he was worth as the earth shook behind him. Johnny hit the ground again as jaws snapped shut just above his head. The T. Rex overran him. It turned, standing between Johnny and safety. The creature roared again – this time it sounded like, 'Miiiiiiiiine.' Johnny got to his feet but was forced backwards, as he searched for an opening. The T. Rex wasn't running now – it was walking towards him, a gleam in its eyes and saliva dripping from its enormous mouth. If Johnny got past he'd have a clear run to the ship. He feinted left and darted right but the monster was ready and blocked him. Johnny stopped, retreated some more, then dashed forwards again, but only narrowly avoided being bashed unconscious by a swinging dinosaur arm. Every time he tried something the T. Rex anticipated it. He kept backing away, until his feet reached the very edge of the cliff. There was nowhere left to go.

And then he was hoisted off his feet and into the air.

'You hold on,' screeched a voice above Johnny. 'I carry you. Safe soon.'

Johnny didn't feel especially safe as he rose into the air but he reached up and held on to a pair of giant claws.

'You much heavy,' the creature continued, flapping its leathery wings as quickly as it seemed able. 'Try not drop you.'

Could this really be happening, wondered Johnny? Could a dinosaur be speaking to him? And then it dawned on him that the little speck of hundra inside him must be able to translate even that. Below, the T. Rex was roaring madly upwards at them from the cliff face, furious that its prey had been snatched away. Johnny's carrier swooped over the edge of the cliff and above the ocean, now gliding downwards.

'Excuse me,' said Johnny. 'Where are we going?'

'Take you home,' screeched the creature. 'Nest down here.'

Johnny looked beneath him and saw several ledges on which winged dinosaurs were standing, while others soared above the water like giant scaly seagulls. His winged support swooped down and seemed to be heading towards the cliff very quickly. Johnny braced himself for impact, but at the last moment his rescuer flapped its wings and they landed, light as a feather, on a ledge halfway up the cliff face.

'Thanks,' said Johnny, looking into the eyes of the creature for the first time. They were proud and thoughtful. Its wings, huge leather membranes stretched over its arms, with just the talons poking out at the top, reminded Johnny of bats. It was standing next to him on the ledge, supported by two fairly spindly legs, and was about as tall as the Chancellor. 'You saved my life.'

'I not see your kind before. Live in new silver tree,' said the creature, bowing its long head to reveal an equally long bony crest at the back of its skull. 'We have code. Kill only when need. T. Rex greedy. She made kill before. You not be eaten today.'

'Not being eaten any day would be good,' said Johnny, who bowed his own head, sensing it was the right thing to do. He didn't enjoy exposing his neck, with the golden locket swinging beneath it, in front of the giant, razor sharp beak and after as short a time as he thought he could get away with, but still be polite, he raised his head and continued. 'My name's Johnny. What are you called?'

☆　☆　☆
☆　☆

Johnny couldn't believe his luck – he'd been saved by a real life dinosaur, intelligent enough to have a basic language. The creature bowed a second time when Johnny christened him Ptery. He'd seen pictures of flying dinosaurs and was pretty sure his rescuer was a pteradon rather than the even bigger pterydactal, but the name would work for either. Having a name clearly made Ptery feel very important. He told Johnny that only the elders of his flock were normally given names. The only downside had been that, as a thank you, Ptery seemed determined to get Johnny to eat some of the raw fish he'd regurgitated from a pink gullet onto the ledge in front of them. Out of politeness Johnny had managed one very small mouthful, closing his eyes and forcing it down without letting it touch the sides.

Ptery lived with about fifty others, perched on the cliff face, fishing for food and flying for fun. Johnny watched throughout the afternoon as contests were held, half a dozen of the flock at a time swooping down off the cliff, their wingtips skimming the surface of the waves, as they rounded the solitary rock out to sea and then flew back to the cliff.

The winner of the races chose the next competition, a diving contest. Ptery, perhaps inspired by his new name, won it, staying beneath the water longer than any of his fellow dinosaurs – so long in fact that Johnny worried he might have drowned. When his rescuer emerged, dripping on the cliff ledge next to him, Johnny noticed Ptery had webbed feet and was probably superbly equipped for fishing. By this time the Sun was getting lower in the sky. It might have been Johnny's imagination but it did look younger . . . brighter . . . yellower somehow. As dusk began to fall, Ptery pointed out the bright light that had appeared in the sky the night before, now dominating it, which the elders took as a sign that momentous events were happening. Johnny nodded gravely and shivered. It was getting cold, and late. He knew he should get back to Sol. He told Ptery that the 'silver tree' he lived in had also come from the sky – that it too could fly, and asked if it was possible for the dinosaur to carry him back up to the cliff top? It was while Ptery was choking with laughter that a commotion began around them, with the screeching of the rest of the flying dinosaurs drowning out the roar of the ocean below. The others had all lifted off from the cliff and were darting towards a black speck that was hovering in the distance. As they circled around the speck it came closer, until Johnny could see a black London taxi flying towards the ledge on which they were standing. He stood up and waved both his arms. Through the tinted windows he could make out the figures of Alf and Clara in the front seats.

'You know creature?' asked Ptery, angling his head at the black cab now hovering a few feet away.

'It's not a creature,' said Johnny. 'But there are people – creatures like me – inside it. They're my friends.'

'Johnny,' called Clara through the window of the taxi, eyeing Ptery rather anxiously. 'Are you OK?'

'Yeah . . . I'm fine,' said Johnny. 'Any chance of a lift?'

The taxi pulled up, hovering alongside the ledge with Clara glaring at Johnny from inside. The back door opened and she told him to get in.

'You speak truth,' said Ptery peering inside the car. 'I come with you. See flying silver tree myself.'

'I'd like that,' said Johnny. 'Follow us – I'll leave the tree open for you,' and he climbed inside the hovering taxi, closed the door and waved through the glass to Ptery, as Alf swung the flying car away and out over the ocean.

'What on earth do you think you were doing?' said Clara angrily, turning round and glaring at Johnny from the front seat. 'The asteroid's about to hit, we could start jumping through time at any moment and in case you hadn't noticed this place is full of dinosaurs. You could have been killed.'

It was the first time Clara had ever shouted at him and Johnny felt even worse than when he was being told off in Mrs Irvine's office. 'I'm sorry, I needed to get away,' was all he could manage to mumble.

'Get away?' snapped Clara. 'Didn't you think we needed

you here? And when we heard that horrible noise – and then we found your game thingy in the forest, I thought . . . I thought you were dead.' Clara buried her head in her hands as tears streamed down her cheeks. Johnny reached over, not really sure what to do. He put what he hoped was a comforting arm on her shoulder. '*And* making me look for you in this,' Clara continued. 'You know how much I hate heights.' Johnny burst out laughing – he couldn't help himself. After a final attempted-frosty glare Clara joined in. As they laughed she reached down for something and rammed it into his arm.

'Ouch!' he said, withdrawing the arm that Clara had just . . . injected. 'What did you do that for?'

'It doesn't hurt, you big baby,' said Clara, grinning. 'It's a pneumatic syringe – to stop the tachyon build up . . . so you don't slide forward on your own . . . though I don't see why I should care.' With that Clara turned around to face the front and made a fuss of folding her arms. Johnny looked out the window and waved to Ptery, hoping the dinosaur would be able to see him through the tinted windows. Below the bone-crested creature, the Spirit of London was glowing strangely pink in the very last of the sunset. Alf piloted the flying taxi in through the shuttle bay doors and landed softly between the other taxi and the double-decker bus. 'Close the doors, Sol,' Clara shouted. 'One of them's trying to get inside.'

'No . . . wait,' shouted Johnny. 'I said he could come and look. He's a friend of mine.'

Clara gave Johnny a withering look. 'We are kind of busy,' she said. 'It's less than four hours till the asteroid hits . . . we've got a plan to save Earth that we had to think up without you, but we do need you here to help make it work. Not give dinosaur tours.'

'He did save my life,' said Johnny quietly, but the other two weren't listening.

'Miss Clara is right, Master Johnny,' said Alf. 'You see we have made a rather exciting discovery, but everything is very finely balanced. However, I believe it is possible we can save your planet. Come to the bridge and we can show you.'

Ptery was circling around the shuttle bay screeching away happily. He landed on top of the big red bus and peered down at the three of them. 'Ptery,' said Johnny. 'Can you stay here a moment? I've just got to go somewhere.'

'I stay here,' said Ptery, who flapped his leathery wings and started whizzing around again. Johnny noticed Alf giving the dinosaur rather anxious looks as they made their way to the antigrav lifts.

'You see, Master Johnny,' said Alf as they stepped out onto the bridge. 'What we discovered was that in your own timeline the dinosaurs were made extinct by an asteroid impact.'

'Everyone knows that,' said Johnny. He slumped down into the captain's chair. 'But this,' he said pointing at the enormous rock filling Sol's viewscreens, 'is a global killer. The clue's in the name. What wiped out the dinosaurs was much smaller – I think ten kilometres across. There's a big difference.'

'A difference,' came Sol's steady female voice, 'that corresponds exactly to the maximum storage potential of my dark energy distributor – the energy of the asteroid cannot be destroyed, but it is possible to convert one form into another.'

'Oh,' said Johnny.

'I was rather pleased at spotting that,' said Alf, doing a little dance at his console.

'And you saw the ship's pink?' Clara asked.

'Well . . . yes,' said Johnny. 'It was sunset . . . wasn't it?'

'It was the tachyon buildup,' said Clara. 'Sol's polarized her hull so the ship's clear inside while the outsides are completely covered.'

'Oh,' said Johnny again.

'When the asteroid strikes, Sol will absorb as much of the energy as possible by lifting off directly into the blast wave,' said Alf. Sol was now showing a complex graphic on the screen that was clearly intended to further the explanation.

Clara continued, 'So we get to surf the tachyon wave back into the future.'

'Theoretically,' said Sol, 'we should return to somewhere close to the time when we left.'

'Theoretically?' asked Johnny, now sitting up in the chair, fully alert.

'If we survive the initial blast and then remain ahead of the wavefront it is unclear as to when, exactly, we shall travel,' continued the ship, 'but all being well we can save Earth from total destruction and get very much closer to home.'

'That's a few ifs,' said Johnny. 'What are our chances?' Everybody was silent. Clara became very interested in the plican, while Alf seemed suddenly distracted by the control panel in front of him. 'Come on, what are they?' Johnny asked again.

It was Sol who responded. 'The chances of success are a matter of debate,' said the ship. 'While my calculations indicate a probability of 3.265 391% . . .'

'Three percent!' said Johnny.

'I,' said Alf, looking deadly serious, 'calculate our success as near certain.'

'How come?' asked Johnny. 'How do you figure that out?'

'We know the future, Johnny. You and Clara have lived it. The Earth will be safe.'

Johnny gulped. 'You're sure? Does time really work like that?'

'I believe so,' said Alf. 'The conclusion is sound. I do hope you are pleased.'

'Of course,' said Johnny, before turning to face Clara as well, saying, 'thanks – I'm sorry I went out. You've all been brilliant.'

'Yes I rather think we have,' said Alf, now grinning from ear to ear from beneath his bowler hat.

'Hang on,' said Johnny. 'We can make it even better . . . we can save the dinosaurs too.'

'What are you talking about?' Clara asked.

'Come on,' said Johnny getting up from the chair. 'You too, Alf. We can use that habitat we were building for the evacuees.'

Johnny ushered the other two into the lift shaft, Clara with her eyes screwed tightly shut. Only a few seconds later they were stepping out into the area that was originally a five-a-side football pitch but that Clara and Johnny had turned into living space for a few hundred people. 'Sol,' shouted Johnny urgently. 'How long now until impact?'

'Three hours, 21 minutes, 11.34 seconds, approximately,' Sol replied instantly.

'I want to convert this deck into a bio-environment,' said Johnny. 'A dinodeck. We'll need to raise the roof about twenty metres, get running water in and fill the place with flora from outside. Can the droids do that?'

'The modifications you request can be made in 126 minutes,' Sol replied.

'Do it,' Johnny shouted back.

'Johnny,' said Clara. 'This is crazy. There isn't enough time.'

'Yes there is,' said Johnny. 'You heard Sol.'

Before Clara could argue they were interrupted by a high-pitched voice squeaking to one side of them, 'And it's not just the loss of the main drive. If you think I trust that plican to fold us anywhere decent you've got another thing coming.'

'Chancellor!' said Johnny, whirling round.

'What?' said the Chancellor. 'How did you get there? A moment ago you were right in front of me.' Clara ran forward and pressed the syringe onto the Chancellor's arm. 'Get off me, you horrid girl. What was that?' asked the Chancellor. 'I demand to know what's going on?'

'Sorry. No time, now,' said Johnny. 'Come on you two. We've got to get cracking. Let's get back to the shuttle bay.' The Chancellor stared at them nonplussed as the pink colouring faded from its robes. Johnny and Clara, laughing, followed by Alf who quickly overtook them, ran across to the lifts which they entered together. 'Deck two,' said Johnny and as they whizzed down he added, 'I suppose you did the right thing, Clara.'

'Oh yes,' said Alf, sagely. 'Otherwise we would have lost that element of the tachyon potential for ever.'

They stepped out into the shuttle bay and each covered their ears. Ptery was flying around the curved walls, cawing loudly and the echoes had built to a crescendo. Johnny shouted but he couldn't even hear himself. There was nothing for it but to risk permanent deafness, so he took his hands away from his ears and ran out, waving his arms to attract the dinosaur's attention. Finally Ptery spotted him and spiralled inside, landing back on top of one of the taxis and folding in his wings. He angled his head towards Johnny and said, 'I go now. Let me out. Day ends. Best time for fishing.'

'No fishing, Ptery,' said Johnny. 'I need you to do something very important.'

Johnny explained as simply as he could that the bright light in the sky was going to hit Ptery's world and that everything was going to die, and the only safe place was going to be if Ptery and some other animals came and lived inside the silver tree.

'You talk stupid,' said Ptery. 'I leave now. Want go fishing.'

'No, Ptery,' said Johnny, a little frustrated now. 'I tell you what. We're going to have a contest.'

'I choose next,' said Ptery. 'Winner's right. What contest?'

So Johnny made up a competition that involved Ptery and

the rest of his flock rounding up as many pairs of boy and girl dinosaurs as they could find and bringing them back into the silver tree as quickly as possible. Whoever brought in the most would be the winner.

'New test,' said Ptery, thoughtfully. He looked at Johnny and, without warning, unfurled his giant wings and flew silently around the Spirit of London's shuttle bay five times. Returning to the top of the taxi he landed, still holding his wings out wide, standing tall and proud. 'I agree. We take part. I go tell others. Start now.' And with that the dinosaur lifted off and flew out through the open shuttle bay doors and into the dusk.

'Do you think he understood?' asked Clara.

'Oh yeah,' said Johnny, who'd forgotten Clara had only heard one side of the conversation. 'I think he knows what to do.'

'Well if he does come back I say we teach him Universal,' said Clara. 'Come on – let's find the Chancellor and tell it what's going on.'

'I guess you're right,' said Johnny, and reluctantly he followed the other two into the lifts.

✧ ✧ ✧
✧ ✧

In a short space of time Sol had done a remarkable job. One side of the ship had somehow opened up enabling her droids to buzz in and out of the giant lower deck, bringing in huge quantities of shrubs and plants and even some trees that must have been many times their own weight. As well as the conifers, there were even the odd oak and sycamore. The space around the trees was filled with a few grasses but mainly the exotic shrubs and ferns Johnny had seen in the forest. Three-quarters of the deck had already turned into a huge prehistoric bio-environment before Ptery flew, with what at first glance looked like an ostrich in his claws, through the great tear Sol had opened up in her walls. The dinosaur being carried was yellow, with a small head, tiny arms and a great fat tail. Ptery swooped down, letting it go just above the ground before turning and flying out past another of his kind bringing the second of the pair. They were soon followed by a grey-green creature with one horn just above its parrot-like beak, two more on top of its head and a round bony plate behind them. It could only be a baby triceratops. As the droids finished covering the whole area, more and more pteradons came like giant bats, cawing into the new habitat and releasing their cargo. Johnny asked Sol to separate the different species with forcefields so they didn't tear each other apart. As the area filled Sol announced there were thirty minutes to impact. Johnny said he'd be up as soon as Ptery was safely inside and went over to the rip in the ship's side to keep a look out. As he watched, pairs of pteradons carried in some much bigger specimens for the dinodeck, each at one end of their very heavy loads. Among them were a couple of T. Rexes, which he was very unsure about having on board, but he couldn't very well send them back now. Finally, he saw Ptery flying in with a little version of the club-tailed dinosaur Johnny had first seen in the forest.

He shouted over to the winged dinosaur. 'Time's up, Ptery – I think you've won.'

Ptery was shaking his head from side to side. 'I not win. Girl here bring more,' he screeched, and unfurled his left wing to point to another of the bone-crested flyers who was just dropping off another creature with a bony plate and parrot beak but this time no horns.

'Wait!' shouted Johnny as the female pteradon turned away. She stopped. He turned back to Ptery and said, 'There's a prize for the best boy and the best girl. You two stay here.' He was relieved there weren't any other pteradons inside that he should send away. He didn't think he could have condemned them to their deaths, even though there wouldn't have been room for more than just the two – the place was already teeming with life. Ptery took off and wheeled triumphantly around the walls of the chamber, screeching loudly. Johnny stayed and watched until Sol had closed up the gaping hole in her side and then he hurried over to the lifts.

As he stepped out onto the bridge he heard Sol calmly saying 'Impact in five minutes.'

'Everything OK?' he asked, looking at the screens and taking in the enormous, slowly rotating rock, getting ever bigger and closer. He walked across the bridge and sat down in the captain's chair.

Clara was standing by the plican's tank, stroking the clear surface, while the creature inside pulsated through all the colours of the rainbow. Clara herself was simply white. She nodded at Johnny, before asking 'How's your dinodeck?'

'Mad,' said Johnny. 'Just like Noah's Ark.'

Clara smiled. 'They'll call it Johnny's Ark . . . if they don't all eat each other first.'

'I'm just waiting for when you set them loose,' squeaked Chancellor Gronack. 'I'm not sure they'll get on too well with other Terrans. Madness if you ask me, not that anyone ever does.'

'Impact in four minutes,' said Sol.

Johnny was glad of the interruption. To be honest he'd not given any thought about what to do with the dinosaurs that were now settling into their temporary home. It would have to wait. Johnny touched the control pad by his chair and three large oval compartments rose out of the floor behind him. 'I think the rest of you should go to the gel pods,' he said. 'It could get a little rough.'

The Chancellor didn't need asking twice. It hurried to the back of the bridge, where one of the units opened up and it disappeared into the orange gloop inside. The other two stayed where they were. 'The plican's really stressed,' said Clara. 'I'll stay out here with it.'

'And I would not possibly miss this for the world,' said Alf, 'if you will pardon the expression. What an opportunity.'

It was impact in three minutes . . . two minutes . . . one minute . . . thirty seconds. Johnny felt the ship begin to shake. 'You OK, Sol?' he asked.

'Thank you for asking – I am fine and looking forward to the challenge,' replied the ship, without a hint of nerves, before continuing the countdown. 'Ten . . . nine . . . engines at maximum . . . six . . . five . . . four . . . tachyon buffer disengaged . . . one . . . zero.'

The bridge flooded with white light. The ship shook violently and a deep grumbling roar became louder and louder. Johnny felt himself getting heavier as he was forced down into his chair. The whiteness changed to pink. The sides of the ship seemed to suddenly stretch away from him and disappear into nothingness. And then there was silence. He could see it. He could see how they were moving. It wasn't forwards or backwards, left or right, up or down. It was movement at right angles to all of them and they were travelling very, very fast, though the view beneath him stayed the same. It was the Earth, but seen as though through the wrong end of a telescope. As Johnny watched, he saw the continents drift apart like in a time-lapse film. It was definitely becoming recognizable. The silence was finally broken by an ear-splitting crack, the ship shook again, a wave of pink flickered around Johnny and then the walls of the ship rushed back into their right positions.

'Sol,' shouted Johnny. 'Status report.'

'All systems within normal parameters,' replied Sol. 'At least all those that were normal before.'

Johnny heard a 'wow' from Clara behind him. He looked across to Alf and was pleased to see he, too, was functioning normally and smiling broadly.

'Worth staying out of the gel pods for that, Master Johnny,' he said, even more enthusiastically than normal.

'Your attention, Johnny,' said Sol.

'What is it?' Johnny asked.

'I have an incoming transmission for you,' replied the ship.

Johnny turned to look at Clara behind him.

'Well . . . answer it I suppose.' Clara shrugged.

'Put it through,' said Johnny, turning forwards. 'On screen.'

The view in front of them dissolved into the head and shoulders of a woman in a blue toga. 'This is Terran Control to Khari vessel. That was quite an entrance.' Johnny couldn't think of anything to say but the woman continued, 'And you're a day early. Prepare for descent. We're sending a fighter squadron guard of honour to escort you to your landing site.'

8 ✩ ✩

WATERWORLD ✩ ✩

Ten sleek, highly armed fighters were flying in formation around the Spirit of London. Sol had just reminded Johnny that she had no shields, when a transmission appeared on the comm screen. 'This is Squadron Leader Gold Circle. We've been instructed to give you the grand tour,' said the figure on the viewscreen, his face masked by an ornate golden visor.

'Er . . . OK . . . thanks,' replied Johnny. On the main viewscreen he could see the long curve of a continent he recognized beneath him – they were flying over Australia.

'If you don't mind me asking, Sir,' said the squadron leader, 'what happened to your ship?'

'Oh that,' Johnny replied nervously. 'We ran into . . . a spot of bother.'

'So I see, Sir,' said the squadron leader. 'A good job your transponder's still working. Unfolding that close we could have blown you out of orbit.'

'Er . . . that wouldn't have been good,' said Johnny.

'Just as well we were expecting your signature, Sir,' said the squadron leader.

'Er . . . right,' said Johnny. 'Spirit of London out.' Before he had a full conversation with anyone he wanted to know a little more about what was happening. 'Sol – have you found out when this is yet?' There was ice below them on the viewscreen now – either the Arctic or the Antarctic.

'Computing . . . we are currently 39,461.462 78 years behind Galactic Standard Time,' the ship replied.

'But how did that happen?' asked Johnny, before swivelling the chair round to face Alf and saying, 'I thought you said something about conservation of time?'

'I fear, Master Johnny,' said Alf, 'that by bringing the dinosaurs on board we have caused significant temporal drag. The equilibrium is now restored without us reaching our time-line.'

'I didn't think,' said Johnny.

'Evidently not,' squeaked the voice of the Chancellor, who had just emerged from its gel pod. Johnny didn't even smile at the orange residue around its twitching antennae. Gronack walked forward, taking in the images on the viewscreen, and continued, 'Am I to understand that by playing the hero you have marooned us in the past for ever?'

'It's OK,' said Clara from behind Johnny. 'It does look lots better than before, and none of us realized . . .'

'You don't think so, do you?' interrupted Gronack, the orange goo starting to drip to the floor. 'What's the point of having this animated calculator here if he keeps his mouth shut when it matters?'

'Alf didn't know,' snapped Johnny. 'He'd have said . . . wouldn't you . . . Alf?' Alf was fiddling with his bowler hat.

'You couldn't have left them to die out,' said Clara, leaving the plican's tank and moving round next to Johnny's chair.

'They were meant to die out,' said the Chancellor. 'They didn't matter.'

'What do you mean *they* didn't matter?' asked Clara. 'What makes them so different from you?'

'I would have thought that was obvious,' said the Chancellor.

'Alf,' said Johnny. 'Did you really know we wouldn't get home?'

'Oh have I done the wrong thing, Master Johnny?' said Alf, refusing to make eye contact. 'It would have been wrong for me to question the Captain.'

'What?' said Johnny. 'It's not like that. We all have a say.'

'If only it were true,' said the Chancellor. 'Although if you observe the screen you will notice our predicament is perhaps not as bad as first appeared.'

Johnny, Clara and Alf looked at the display which was now showing them flying over a circular piece of land that appeared very like the Imperial Palace on Melania. As Johnny fixed his eyes on the image, he saw it was surrounded on all sides by giant walls of water which for some reason weren't crashing down on top of it. The circumference was marked by red lights that pulsed around the boundary of land and ocean. Like the Imperial Palace, he could see concentric circles of land and water and, reaching out from the centre, there was another enormous tower, lined with those same pulsating red lights.

'Thank goodness for that,' said Chancellor Gronack. 'Civilization . . . I must prepare myself.' The phasmeer scuttled towards the lifts and left the bridge.

Johnny leaned forward in his chair. 'Listen guys – you too, Sol,' he said. 'I want you to know that if there's ever a time you think I'm being stupid . . . or haven't thought things through . . . you must tell me. I can't think of everything.'

'The Emperor trusted your instincts, Johnny,' said Alf, very seriously. 'He was right. We may be trapped in the past but we saved your world's future. Do you not think your planet worth it? I will give an opinion if necessary, but you must learn to trust your instincts too.'

'I wish my instincts had been to save Earth *and* get us home,' said Johnny quietly.

Sol's voice boomed across the bridge. 'I have an incoming transmission, Johnny,' she said.

'OK,' sighed Johnny. 'On screen, let's see if we can find out what's going on.'

'This is Squadron Leader Gold Circle,' said the helmeted figure. 'Sir – we're bringing you in . . . second island . . . follow my vector.' Johnny watched the screen that showed the fighter squadron peel away from them, heading down towards the circular island continent, before Sol followed suit. What was this space-faring culture on Earth from 40,000 years ago? He knew there had been evidence. Valdour's ship Cheybora had records of human physiology, and everyone seemed to know vaguely of the Terrans. Everyone except people on Earth.

They flew lower through the clouds and the details of the giant city became clearer. Huge canals cut across the land areas which were covered with white stone buildings, some with golden roofs, others glowing red. Numerous spaceships came past in the other direction: transports many times the size of the Spirit of London, small pleasure cruisers and more fighters like the ones escorting them. As instructed, Sol landed in the centre of a circle formed by the ships from their escort squadron.

'Let's go and say hello,' said Johnny. Alf and Clara followed him to the lifts and down towards the main doors. Chancellor Gronack was already there waiting for them, its robes a rich purple.

'I hope you will leave this to me,' hissed the Chancellor. 'Remember it is I who is expert in diplomatic procedure.'

'It's our planet, not yours,' said Clara determinedly.

'Tell me. Do the leaders of *your* planet normally listen to little boys and girls?' squeaked Gronack. 'I shall go first.' Before anyone could stop it, the spindly phasmeer stepped into one set of revolving doors.

Johnny and Clara followed in their Melanian tunics with Alf behind them in his immaculate pinstriped suit. Johnny glanced back for just a second. From the outside the Spirit of London was scorched and battered, but there was nothing to be done about it now. Either side of them stood a column of soldiers, all wearing gold helmets which covered their faces. Their uniforms were red, and each of them carried a range of weapons attached to their golden belts. The Chancellor's enormous legs were striding down the parade line and Johnny and the others practically had to run to keep up. The soldiers' faces looked out straight ahead and didn't follow their progress. At the end of the line was a huge arch of pulsating red stone, inscribed with strange hieroglyphics. Behind the arch stood a grey-haired man in bright blue robes holding a long staff in his left hand. He raised his right arm and shouted, 'Halt' as they approached. 'I, Mestor, High Priest to Neith, bid you welcome,' he said in Universal, bowing as he spoke.

'I Gronack, Chancellor of Melania, accept your welcome,' said Gronack, stepping forward and bowing.

'I was under the impression that Ketto of Nefried was Chancellor of Melania,' said Mestor. 'I was also under the impression that the Senator was paying us a personal visit. Instead he sends imposters and Terran children in his place.'

'I can explain, said Gronack, bowing again.

'I do not have time for explanations,' snapped Mestor. 'We will not be taken for fools. The Arch of Lysentia will be your judge.'

'I can assure you I did not intend to cause offence,' said Gronack, its voice noticeably higher. 'May I enquire as to the purpose of this arch?'

'To prove your fitness to seek audience with the Diaquant you must pass through the arch,' said Mestor. 'Imposters will fail and shall be killed.' The guard of honour took this as their cue to form a semicircle around the Sprit of London's crew, with the arch on the other side.

The Chancellor looked at Johnny. 'Well go on then,' it squeaked, taking a giant stride backwards leaving Johnny at the front of the group.

'What?' Johnny asked, startled to suddenly be involved.

'It's your ship. You brought us here. It is for you to go through.'

The soldiers bristled menacingly. 'OK, I'll do it,' said Johnny.

'Wait – I'll go too,' said Clara, stepping forward to join Johnny. 'Let's do it together.'

'If no one does it soon you will be killed anyway,' snapped Mestor. 'Even if you are children.' The soldiers each took a weapon from their belts and pointed it at a member of the quartet.

'On three,' said Johnny to Clara. She nodded. 'One . . . two . . . three,' and they stepped through the arch together, joining Mestor on the other side. Johnny smiled at Clara. There was nothing to it except for a slight queasy feeling in his stomach.

The priest raised his left eyebrow and said, 'Welcome to Atlantis . . . follow me,' whereupon he turned on his heels and began to walk.

'Wait,' squeaked a voice from behind. The priest stopped and turned to watch. 'If I'd known it was simply a matter of stepping through there,' continued the Chancellor hurrying towards the arch. At this the red stone glowed brighter and brighter and Johnny heard a humming of electricity. Gronack was flung backwards a full fifteen metres through the air and landed on top of the semicircle of soldiers, knocking three of them to the ground. The other guards crowded around, guns at the ready.

'No!' shouted Johnny, running back. Mestor raised his hand to signal the soldiers not to shoot. 'Alf, take the Chancellor back to the ship. Make sure it's OK . . . and check on Ptery too.' Alf picked up a trembling Gronack as though it was light as a feather and slung it over his shoulder, before setting off towards the Spirit of London. Johnny watched him walk safely through the crowd of soldiers and then he turned round to face Mestor and Clara.

'I was feeling generous,' said the priest. 'It may not happen again. Neith does not like to be kept waiting. Follow me.' He turned and led Johnny and Clara along a narrow golden path, limping as he went and leaning on his staff to support him. Soon they arrived at a quayside, where several seagulls squawked above a sparkling boat, cut from a single enormous crystal. A tanned, black-haired man stood in the prow. Johnny and Clara climbed aboard and sat down together on a bench in the middle. The priest followed and stood behind them. He nodded to the man at the front, who picked up a set of reins, whistled and the vessel began to move.

Johnny and Clara leaned forward to see what was powering the boat. Clara gasped. 'They're beautiful – can you see them, Johnny?' Johnny nodded and smiled. Right now there was nothing they could do except sit back and enjoy the ride. The Sun was shining and they were speeding across the water in a boat made of crystal, pulled by a pod of dolphins.

The canal was huge – wider than a football pitch. Gulls flew overhead and the boat skimmed across the water so quickly that Johnny could feel the salt spray on his face. Soon the battered Spirit of London was shrinking into the distance as they left the spaceport behind and entered the inland sea that divided it from the central island. Johnny wanted to talk to Clara about the great walls of water surrounding them in the far distance, but the priest's eyes were burning a hole in the back of his head. He didn't want to give anything away, so he and Clara both fixed their eyes straight ahead on the red tower that dominated the skyline. After about twenty minutes they arrived at the far shore. The dolphins pressed straight ahead between giant fortifications and into another canal, taking the crystal boat to the very heart of the island. Huge buildings rose up from the water's edge, the Sun gleaming off their golden, or sometimes red, roofs.

'What's that red stuff?' Clara asked, turning round to face Mestor. Johnny gave Clara a nudge in the ribs. He didn't think they should be asking questions right now when their arrival had apparently been mistaken for someone else's.

The priest, though, seemed happy enough to answer. 'Orichalcum,' he replied, 'one of the treasures of Atlantis.'

'It's pretty,' Clara replied.

'It's more than just pretty,' said the priest. 'It magnifies the power of the Diaquant – focuses it where it is most needed.'

'Oh really,' said Clara, wide-eyed. 'How do you make it?'

'It isn't made,' said Mestor. 'It's mined. It is a metal unlike any other.'

'Is that what holds the ocean back?' Clara asked.

'You ask a lot of questions, little girl,' Mestor replied. 'In Neith's presence you would be advised to hold your tongue.'

Johnny could sense Clara was just about to ask exactly who Neith was, so again he dug his elbow into her. She turned round and gave him a sharp look. 'At least I'm trying to find out what's going on,' she hissed.

The boat began to slow and move towards the bank in front of the biggest building they'd seen so far, set back a little from the water's edge. Johnny nodded towards it. 'I think we'll find out soon enough,' he whispered back.

As they came in to moor, they saw the canalside was crowded with priests in the same blue robes as Mestor. The crystal boat drew up alongside and Johnny and Clara jumped the short gap onto the springy turf of the bank. Mestor disembarked with a little more difficulty. The other priests parted and he led the two children across the grass between an avenue of palm trees towards the building. It was fronted by eight enormous white pillars, topped by a brightly painted frieze, and flags with different hieroglyphs fluttered from above the orichalcum red roof. They passed between the pillars and approached a doorway flanked by two guards holding curved swords. Mestor stopped, turned to Johnny and Clara and said, 'The Temple of Neith. Speak only when you are spoken to.' The guards lowered their swords and stepped aside to allow the priest, and then Johnny and Clara, to enter. It was refreshingly cool the instant they stepped inside. They crossed a great hall and as they approached the far end two giant doors, covered in more strange symbols, swung open, revealing an inner courtyard. Mestor led Johnny and Clara through and along a golden path towards its centre. Bright blue and green birds darted in and out of the shrubs around them, until they reached a fountain with water spurting from a dolphin's mouth into a small pool. Across from the pool were some steps on which knelt several priests in their blue robes. To one side a group of women were giggling, pointing over to Johnny and Clara. The steps led up to a platform and, at its centre, a woman with straight black hair wearing a gold dress reclined on a huge couch. She was stroking a black cat while bronzed men wafted palm fronds to keep her cool.

The woman saw Mestor approaching and waved an arm to summon him closer. The priest tapped his staff twice on the ground and the pool in front of him became solid. He walked straight across, followed a little gingerly by Johnny and Clara. Mestor stopped at the foot of the steps and Johnny and Clara halted either side of him. The priest bowed low, leaving his staff on the ground so both hands were free to push Johnny and Clara's heads downwards.

'Mestor,' said the woman. 'What have you brought me?' Johnny heard the change from Universal to another language that he knew Clara wouldn't be able understand and must, he assumed, be Atlantean.

'My Queen,' replied the priest, not raising his eyes towards the woman. 'The Senator sends you children . . . Terran children, in his place.'

'The Senator is coming later as originally planned – we heard from him a short time ago. Why this interruption now?' asked the Queen.

'They arrived on a ship bearing his signal – it seemed appropriate to receive them,' replied Mestor.

'Perhaps the Senator did send them but that did not mean you had to deliver them. It may be he insults me,' said the Queen. 'They could have been disposed of . . . sent to the mines.'

'My Queen,' said Mestor. 'The children passed through the arch . . . both of them. We are told only the gods may do that.'

'Do they look like gods to you, Mestor?' the Queen snapped.

'Of course not, my Queen,' replied the priest.

'Still . . . it is interesting,' said the woman. 'Perhaps you were right. We should discover their trickery. There may be more to them than meets the eye. They are dreadfully fair . . . and they wear the clothing of Melania.'

'Their ship had suffered heavy damage. It hardly looked spaceworthy,' said Mestor.

'I will keep them for now – until we know more,' said the Queen. 'Let them approach.'

'Behold Neith,' said Mestor, now speaking Universal. 'Queen of Atlantis, Ruler of the Terran Dominions and Keeper of the Diaquant. You may approach.'

Johnny and Clara climbed the steps, picking their way between the prostrate bodies of blue-robed priests. They reached the top and stood silently in front of Neith. Clara curtseyed. The Queen sat up and placed the cat to one side. Neith studied the two of them for a moment while the cat arched its back and jumped softly down from the couch. 'Well aren't you two just the most delightful little things?' said Neith. 'So unusual . . . so pretty.' The cat brushed against Johnny's legs. He wondered if it would be right to stroke it. 'And look,' said the Queen. 'Auf likes you too. But if you are going to stay around my temple we must get you out of those horrid Melanian clothes and into something more becoming. What's your name, my pretty?' she asked, looking at Clara, who told her. 'An unusual name for an unusual girl, I'm sure,' said the Queen. 'Go with my ladies in waiting. They will find something that suits you better.' The Queen gestured to the women gathered on the steps, Clara curtseyed again and walked across. The ladies in waiting crowded around her and started touching her hair and clothes curiously, as though she were a doll. Johnny was impressed at Clara's restraint. 'And what is your name, my boy?' Neith asked Johnny.

'I'm called Johnny, Your Majesty,' he replied. 'Johnny Mackintosh.'

'Well, Johnny Mackintosh. The only males I normally allow in my temple are priests. You must go with Mestor and let him look after you. There is a feast later. You shall join me in the Hall of Ancestors and dine with my guests.'

'Thank you, Your Majesty,' said Johnny, bowing.

The Queen clapped her hands and spoke again in Atlantean. 'Treat them well but find out why the Senator has sent them.' The cat jumped back onto the couch and Neith picked it up and held it in front of her face. 'We will learn his plans, won't we Auf?' she said to it.

'Come,' said Mestor. 'We will find you robes.' Johnny caught Clara's eye and shrugged for a moment before he was led away by the priest in the opposite direction from which they'd come.

☆ ☆ ☆
☆ ☆

Johnny spent the afternoon being fitted with the same blue robes that the other priests had been wearing and refusing all attempts to apply make-up to his face to darken his skin. He'd been taken to a small chamber with a square pool in its middle and sunlight streaming in through a clear, domed roof that reflected off the water's surface. When a dolphin appeared briefly in the pool, Johnny wondered if it might be connected to the canal outside. Mestor was called away into another room and Johnny sat down on a wooden chair, pulled out his games console and signalled to Alf. The Spirit of London, Chancellor Gronack and the dinosaurs were apparently OK and had been left alone, although the soldiers and their fighters still ringed the ship. Johnny noticed that Alf winced when discussing his visit to the dinodeck and his suit was now looking a little battered. Sol was busy repairing her hull and assured him there would be no permanent damage but hoped not to be put through anything similar again. Johnny heard a noise and switched his console off, stowing it quickly inside his new robes. When he looked around it was to see that the dolphin had re-entered the chamber. Relieved, Johnny knelt down by the water's edge and the animal swam across to him, lifting its bottle-nose out of the pool towards Johnny's face.

'Hello,' said Johnny, smiling at the creature and gently stroking the top of its head.

The dolphin broke away, swam round in a circle whistling what sounded like 'Nesaea' and spouting water from its blowhole.

'Is Nesaea your name?' Johnny asked. The dolphin moved its bottle-nose up and down rapidly. 'Hi Nesaea, I'm Johnny,' he said, stroking the dolphin's head again.

'You're very young to be a priest,' said Nesaea so quickly in a high-pitched voice that Johnny almost missed it. The dolphin wheeled away again and whistled 'Nesaea' as she swam around the small pool.

'I'm not a priest,' laughed Johnny.

'My pod tells me you passed through the old arch – so are you a god?' clicked Nesaea, as rapidly as before.

'No I'm just a boy,' Johnny replied, flicking a handful of water at the dolphin. With the swish of a flipper Nesaea soaked Johnny back and made a noise that might have been laughter.

'Take care, man child – better to bask in warm waters than the cold gaze of Neith,' clicked Nesaea in her high-pitched voice.

'I'm not sure I follow,' said Johnny. The sound of footsteps coming closer distracted him, so he patted the dolphin on the head once more, whispered, 'I'm sorry – I'd better go,' and stood up to return to his chair.

Mestor entered the chamber, his eyes flickering between Johnny and the dolphin. 'Perhaps you are more suited to the priesthood than I had imagined,' he said. 'Come, preparations for the feast are underway,' and he led Johnny, dressed all in blue, out of the chamber and back into the sunshine. Without the Melanian tunic it was scorching outside and his priest's robes quickly dried out. 'Tell me,' said Mestor, 'will the Senator support Neith in her claim?'

'I don't know,' replied Johnny truthfully.

'Don't forget that you are Terran, not Melanian,' said the priest.

'What do you mean?' Johnny asked.

Mestor stopped, leaned heavily on his staff and looked straight into Johnny's eyes. 'Your homeworld has the chance to rule the galaxy – you should remember where your loyalties lie.' Johnny stared back into Mestor's eyes, unable to look away, but he said nothing. The priest continued, 'Neith will be Empress with or without the Senator's support. You would do well to remember that.' When Johnny didn't speak again he turned and started hobbling along the path. Johnny followed just behind.

Several hours later Johnny was sitting beside Clara in the Hall of Ancestors, the grand room they'd passed through earlier, as Queen Neith's feast was ending. 'Thank goodness that's over,' said Clara quietly, as the final speaker at the head table sat down. 'You're so lucky being able to understand everything.'

'Lucky?' said Johnny. 'That last one was the most boring of the lot.' Johnny and Clara had discovered the feast had so far been made up of very little food and an awful lot of speeches. At least it had been a chance to catch up with Clara and tell her what Neith had said earlier, and about Nesaea the dolphin, while trying hard not to laugh at her heavy make-up, black-rimmed eyes and the black and gold striped dress that Clara thought was especially pretty. Johnny had failed, but Clara hadn't seemed to mind and thankfully the speeches finally appeared to be over.

'But what was he saying?' Clara whispered. 'It's got to be important to find out.'

'It was the same stuff as all the others,' said Johnny. 'You know . . . Neith is great, she's so wonderful and important and powerful and she controls this Diaquant thing and look how impressive Atlantis has become and because of it Terra's bound to dominate the galaxy soon.'

'And now what's happening?' Clara asked, yawning, as everyone got to their feet around them.

'Everybody's going outside, I think,' said Johnny. 'It's midnight – that's when this Senator's meant to be arriving. Let's see what's happening.'

They stood up and made their way towards the main doors, past a central orichalcum pillar and a statue of a man holding a giant fork. 'Neptune,' said Clara. 'God of the sea.'

'How do you know that?' Johnny asked.

'It's the trident,' said Clara, pointing to the fork. 'There was a painting of him at the Proteus Institute. Proteus was a shape-shifting sea god who served Neptune.'

'Guess that fits in a place like this,' said Johnny as they stepped through the doors and outside onto the lawn at the front of the temple. The full moon was illuminating the great walls of water surrounding Atlantis in the far distance. It gave him the creeps – no wonder the sea god was centre stage.

A crowd had gathered along the banks of the great canal. Johnny and Clara fought their way past the assorted fire breathers and jugglers and squeezed through a gap to get close to the water's edge. An enormous crystal barge, pulled by what must have been fifty dolphins, was slowly making its way up the canal towards them. They weren't the only two who were impressed. Many of the younger priests were pointing in awe at the approaching vessel. Johnny felt something hard on his shoulder. It was a staff. He turned round. Mestor was standing there.

'You are to come with me,' said the priest. 'Both of you. Queen Neith believes your presence in the welcoming committee will be . . . illuminating.' The crowd parted to allow them to pass through behind Mestor, who led them, hobbling, towards a dais that held a handful of important-looking people, surrounding the Queen's large couch. Lying on the couch was Neith, stroking her cat.

'About time, Mestor,' said Neith, as they approached. 'And my darling girl – you look so much prettier in that dress,' she said to Clara.

'Thank you, Your Majesty,' said Clara, smiling as she curtseyed.

'The Senator approaches,' said Neith. There was an 'ooh' from the assembled crowd as the crystal barge drew alongside the temple grounds. Johnny understood why – close up he could see that it was shaped like a giant swan and the moonlight glinted off its many surfaces. 'He is such a show-off,' said Neith.

Johnny and Clara watched as the hooded figure, all in white, accompanied by a floating robed hundra, disembarked and made his way through the crowd towards the Queen's dais. The man lowered his hood to reveal a young, near human face with bright blue eyes, and blond hair that seemed as though the moonlight itself was shining from it. There could be no doubt at all about it – it was Bram.

'Senator Bram Khari, last of the Lysentia, craves audience with Neith, Queen of Atlantis, Ruler of the Terran Dominions, Keeper of the Diaquant, Galactic Empress in Waiting,' said Bram, bowing his head slightly before the Queen.

It was Mestor who replied. 'Queen Neith of Atlantis considers your request – do you bring tribute so she may look more kindly on it?'

Johnny couldn't believe his ears – surely Neith wasn't in a position to stop Bram coming to Atlantis if he wanted to. Bram, though, appeared unfazed by the request. 'Behind me, Your Majesty, is a royal barge cut from a single diamond. I offer it to you.' There were gasps from the onlookers.

Mestor spoke again. 'Is there further tribute for the Queen, Keeper of the Diaquant?'

'Above me,' said Bram, 'I offer Your Majesty a hundra, ancient translator, who alone with me passed through the ancient Arch of Lysentia.' Johnny noticed the Queen's eyes flashed momentarily to him and Clara, before returning to Bram.

On hearing of this second gift, awed whispering began in the crowd around the dais. Mestor banged his staff on the ground twice, calling for silence. He turned again to Bram. 'Is there further tribute for the Queen, Galactic Empress in waiting?'

And again, Bram seemed ready for the request. 'In front of me, I offer Your Majesty a shield, crafted by the ancients, that will protect against all weapons.' Bram lifted a chain over his head, which supported a small gold pendant that had been hanging in front of his chest. He walked forward, laid it at the Queen's feet and then stepped back.

Neith sprang off the couch, sending the cat flying through the air. The Queen snatched the pendant up off the floor and, after examining it briefly, placed the chain over her head. She looked up and nodded to Mestor, before getting to her feet, slightly flushed, and returning to the couch. The old priest turned to Bram, his eyebrow raised, and spoke again. 'The Queen accepts your tributes. You will remain and be granted audience.' Bram bowed and, the formalities over, looked around for the first time. Johnny tried to catch his eye but Bram's gaze went straight through him and on to others standing behind the dais. Clara picked up Auf and took the cat back to the Queen.

'Thank you, my pretty,' said the Queen, who got to her feet, holding the cat in her arms. She looked steadily into Bram's face, smiled and said, 'I shall assign servants to you for your stay . . . unless of course you already have your own?'

Johnny tensed – he knew they were about to be exposed. This younger version of the Emperor had never seen them before. If only he'd had a little time to speak to Bram on his own and convince him they knew each other from the future. The Queen was suspicious – she wasn't going to give him that chance. Bram hesitated for just a moment, then smiled back at Neith and replied, 'I understood you were aware I had sent servants ahead of me. I apologize if I did not make their arrival explicit. Johnny and Clara will be sufficient for my needs.'

'Very well,' said Neith without any hint of surprise. 'I hope you approve of my little transformation. The garb of Melania is not suited to Terrans. I trust you still recognize them?'

'Come Johnny, come Clara,' said Bram holding out a hand towards each of them. Johnny hadn't realized he'd been holding his breath, but let it out now and walked over to Bram. Clara did the same. 'Your Majesty,' said Bram. 'I fear I am tired after my journey. Perhaps I can retire to my quarters so I may rest?'

'As you wish,' said the Queen. She clapped her hands and a young priest stepped forward and bowed. 'Take the Senator and . . . his servants to their quarters.' The young priest bowed again, turned to Bram and gestured for the Senator to step down off the dais. A gap appeared in the surrounding crowd and Bram strode into it, followed in silence by Johnny and Clara, with the priest behind them.

☆   ☆   ☆
☆   ☆

'Silence,' said Bram, his eyes blazing with blue fire. The door to his chambers had just closed and they were finally alone.

'But . . .' said Johnny – there was nothing more that he wanted to do than find out how Bram had possibly known who they were – that they were even there – but the look in Bram's eyes seemed to reach down into the back of Johnny's mouth and gently squeeze hold of his tongue.

Bram walked through the chambers the Queen had allotted him as though searching for something. Everywhere Johnny looked gold glittered back at him, or almost everywhere. Bram strode over to an ornament by a giant fireplace – a lizard carved from orichalcum – picked it up and turned it over in his hand several times. He threw it over towards Johnny who caught it automatically. Bram gave Johnny a look that suggested he should focus on the lizard. Johnny held it and felt a buzzing in his hands. There was something odd about the lizard – he could feel the electricity running through it as though he were listening to music on a radio. As he tuned in the music in his head grew louder; the lizard glowed a brighter and brighter red until it suddenly shattered in his hands.

'Johnny!' Clara shouted, but Bram raised his hand to silence her. He walked over to the centre of the room they were standing in, took a short black rod out from under his robes and swept it over his head, producing a transparent shimmering curtain around him. He beckoned Johnny and Clara to join him inside. They looked at each other, Clara walked through the curtain and Johnny followed. Bram gestured and they all sat down on the floor.

'They cannot hear us now,' said Bram seriously.

'Who?' said Clara. 'Do you think we're being watched?'

'I would be most disappointed if we weren't,' replied Bram.

'How did you know it was us?' Johnny asked.

'I know nothing,' said Bram. 'Except you may be an elaborate ruse by Neith to have me discredited, or instead perhaps you are somehow my salvation, sent from the far future. One seems rather more likely than the other and the stakes are so very high. When I stepped from the barge I had just a moment to decide. How can I know I chose correctly?'

'But you're the Emperor,' said Clara. 'We stayed with you on Melania. The Imperial Palace was just like this island.'

'The type of tale Neith would tell,' said Bram. 'She appeals to the ambition and greed she sees in herself.'

'But you knew our names,' said Clara. 'How could you know who we are?'

'How indeed?' said Bram. 'My ship told me. She was born in a place I believed only I knew – yet she found a sister here on Terra. I admit I was curious. I spoke to an artificial life form that made a convincing case for knowing me. I spoke to a phasmeer who nearly changed my mind.' Silently Johnny cursed Chancellor Gronack. Bram continued, 'But it is not enough. If you truly are who this Alf claimed, then I need proof. If you know me from the future, from such a far future that I doubt even I could live that long, there must be a way to demonstrate it.' Johnny tried desperately to think of something. Bram continued, 'There must be something I told you, something I gave you, that would tell me that, in some distant epoch, we are friends.'

'There is!' Johnny said, suddenly remembering. 'You told me to give you this the first time we met on a different world.' He reached into his blue priest's robes and took out the locket. Bram stared at it, transfixed. Johnny opened it and a brilliant white light filled the room.

'No!' shouted Bram. 'Close it.' Johnny snapped the locket shut and looked up at Bram, who seemed to be in shock. Finally he asked Johnny, 'Where did you get that? Who would splinter a soul in such a way?'

'It's yours,' said Johnny. 'You gave it me. I didn't know what it was. You turned round and there was that light and you put something in my locket.'

'Your locket?' asked Bram. Johnny nodded. 'Let me see it again,' said Bram, 'now I am prepared.' Johnny placed the locket on the floor between him and Bram and opened it up for a second time. Again white light streamed out, filling the room. Hesitantly, Bram reached his right hand out towards it and placed his index finger into the source of the light. The finger glowed white, then Bram's hand, then his lower arm, a wave of near brilliance passing slowly up him. With an effort he pulled the finger out of the locket and his arm returned to normal. 'There can be no doubt,' he said. 'Not even the Atlanteans could have done this. There can be nothing more important for me than to tear my soul in two. It does, though, explain how you passed through the Arch of Lysentia – something only those descended from the ancients could do.'

'How?' asked Clara.

'You carried my soul with you,' said Bram. 'A small piece, but it was enough.'

Clara looked as though she was going to argue, but Johnny

cut in first. 'You can't think this Neith would make a good Empress? She's horrible. Why are you here? Why did you come to Earth?'

'Earth?' said Bram. 'What is that?'

'I mean Terra. Earth's what it's called in our time. I forgot,' said Johnny.

'Intriguing,' said Bram. 'Terra . . . your Earth . . . had been peaceful for millennia. Then something happened. Atlantis, a new city-state, rose from the oceans and became dominant . . . almost overnight. No one took any notice. It was just another world . . . a bit of a backwater. Next the local systems fell to it: Toliman, Luytun, Sirius. There were murmurings in the Senate – a few sought action. It was then I realized how corrupt that once-great institution had become. Many were already in the pay of the Atlanteans – they claimed it was a local problem. No one intervened. Before we knew it the Terran Dominions covered a quarter of the galaxy, enslaving local people. They had their orichalcum – and yes it is useful, nearly unique – but not that useful. There was something else. They called it the Diaquant.'

'What is the Diaquant?' Johnny asked.

'A good question,' Bram replied. 'Very good. I have my suspicions, but I cannot be sure.'

'You don't know?' said Clara.

'No,' said Bram. 'But I've given up a lot to find out. My gifts for Neith were to gain access to the Diaquant. To learn what it is, its secrets, before the rest of the galaxy falls. To take it if I can.'

'To steal it?' Johnny asked, surprised.

'Perhaps it will want to come,' Bram replied, smiling, 'if it is what I think it is. Now, though, I must ask a favour.'

'What is it?' asked Clara.

'A divided soul is a terrible thing. I cannot bear this fragment to be separate any longer. I must take it back,' said Bram.

Johnny nodded. Bram continued, 'Forgive me – it is something I must do alone. The process will take some time. Enjoy the feast, or get some rest. Tomorrow will be a trying day.'

'Of course,' said Johnny. He and Clara got to their feet and stepped outside Bram's shimmering curtain.

'Do you think he'll really take the Dia . . . the thingy?' Clara asked, as Johnny gave her a warning look.

'Not here,' said Johnny. 'They're bound to be listening.' They walked towards the door and opened it. The passageway was deserted except for a couple of cats. 'Come on,' said Johnny. 'I want to show you something.'

'What is it?' Clara asked. 'It's really late.'

'You'll love it,' said Johnny, 'I want you to meet Nesaea.'

'Oh, can I?' asked Clara, perking up.

The feast had become a party. Johnny and Clara had no trouble slipping through the crowds of revellers as they made their way into the inner courtyard where they'd first met Neith in the day. A group of priests were huddled near the raised platform, so Johnny skirted around the outside until they reached the entrance to the little temple where he'd been given his robes. He led Clara down a brick-built corridor where their echoing footsteps sounded suddenly very loud. Finally Johnny found the chamber, brightly lit by moonlight streaming in through the clear roof and reflecting off the water in the square pool. Johnny knelt down and peered into the water. There was nothing there, so he lowered his face, breaking the surface with his mouth, and said, 'Nesaea – are you there?' He felt a hand on his back and before he could stop himself he was falling in. 'What did you do that for?' Johnny asked, turning round and treading water

Clara who was laughing by the side of the pool replied, 'Come on – you were asking for it.' Johnny knew she was right and started to laugh too. Then something brushed his leg. A

197

snout broke the surface of the water. 'Oh . . . she's gorgeous,' said Clara. She knelt down by the edge of the pool to say hello.

'Clara – this is Nesaea. Nesaea – meet my sister, Clara.'

'Hello, Clara,' said the dolphin, but not in the high-pitched squeaks and clicks Johnny had heard earlier. This voice was electronically generated. Johnny saw Nesaea was wearing a muzzle and harness, which contained a speaker attached to her back just above her fin.

Clara didn't seem to mind at all and slid off the side to join Johnny and the dolphin in the pool. 'Look she's hurt, poor thing,' she said as she gently took hold of Nesaea's left flipper which was bleeding, softly stroking it.

'I guess she's been pulling boats,' said Johnny. 'That must be what the harness is for.'

'You are correct, Johnny,' replied the electronic voice emanating from the dolphin's back. Johnny wondered about taking the harness off so that Nesaea could speak properly, but then Clara wouldn't be able to understand her. 'Swim with me,' said the monotone voice.

'Oh, may I?' asked Clara and she took hold of the dolphin's fin and held on as Nesaea circled the pool. Johnny didn't think the dolphin looked at all happy, but Clara was giggling and clearly loving it.

With the din in the chamber it was difficult to tell, but Johnny thought he could hear footsteps coming down the corridor. 'Shhhsh you two,' he hissed at them. 'I think someone's coming.' Sure enough the footsteps were getting closer and, by the clinking of wood on the stone floor, Johnny guessed one pair belonged to Mestor. He pulled Clara over to edge of the pool where they could hide in the shadows and whispered, 'Please be quiet,' to Nesaea. The dolphin looked terrified but didn't make a sound.

Two people entered the chamber: Mestor and Neith herself,

who sat down in the chair Johnny had used earlier and spoke first. 'Why have you brought me here? You could have said what you had to before my ladies in waiting.'

'My Queen,' said Mestor. 'No one can overhear us in this place.'

'I have no secrets from my people – their loyalty is unquestioned.'

'I do not doubt it, my Queen,' replied the priest, 'but even so it is prudent to take precautions.'

'Then say what you have to . . . I have a celebration to return to.'

'Very well, my Queen,' said Mestor. 'Did it not occur to you that the Senator's gifts were somewhat . . . lavish?'

'Perhaps Khari has finally seen sense,' replied Neith. 'Perhaps he has decided to support my claim – he wishes to curry favour with me.'

'Is that likely? He has opposed you at every turn,' said the priest.

'Then why, Mestor? Why would he offer me a personal shield? There can be only five in all the galaxy.'

'Because he is so desperate to see the Diaquant he could not risk refusal,' Mestor replied.

'And what good would it do him? He will witness its power and know I am invincible.'

'It may be he will do more than that,' said Mestor. 'It may be he will take it from us.'

'How can he do that? It is impregnable.'

'He is of noble birth . . . as are you, my Queen,' said Mestor, bowing as low as he could. 'He, too, passed through the arch. Perhaps he, too, can tame the Diaquant.'

'Then what do you suggest?' snapped Neith. 'Should I have refused him? He is here now.'

'I suggest it is not worth the risk, my Queen. I suggest Khari is killed.' Hidden in the water Johnny and Clara exchanged glances. Mestor continued, 'Those children, too. Did they also not pass through the arch? Perhaps he brought them to aid his plan.' Clara was staring at Johnny wide-eyed. He put a finger to his lips.

'What about the Senate?' asked Neith. 'He is their envoy.'

'And without him they are leaderless. With Khari gone, none will dare oppose you.'

'Yes, my faithful servant. You are right . . . as always. Can you arrange it?'

'It will be done, my Queen,' said Mestor, bowing. 'Tonight. Better before he establishes his presence here further.'

'So be it,' said Neith. 'I shall return to the party. Do what you must.' Neith turned and marched away up the corridor. Mestor bowed again and started limping slowly after.

Johnny and Clara stared at each other horrified. Once they were sure Mestor was out of earshot, Clara asked, 'What do we do?'

'We warn Bram . . . now,' said Johnny climbing out of the pool and dripping over the floor. He reached down to help Clara out. 'We'll go back to the ships and get out of here before they find out.'

'I can help,' said an electronic voice in the water behind them. Johnny and Clara turned and stared at Nesaea.

'How?' asked Johnny.

'I can take you to the Diaquant,' the dolphin replied. The electronic voice was flat but Johnny couldn't help noticing the fear in her eyes. Nesaea continued, 'There is a chamber underneath the great tower. I will fetch my sisters. Bring your friend, this Senator, and meet us here. You will swim there with us.'

'OK,' said Johnny.

'Thank you,' said Clara, reaching down and hugging the dolphin's face.

'Hurry,' came the electronic voice. Clara let go and she and Johnny ran, dripping, through the corridors and back out into the courtyard. Thankfully the party had moved elsewhere so they sprinted straight across the middle, past the raised platform, splashed through the pool to the other side and down a passageway to the entrance to Bram's chambers.

The door was locked. Johnny and Clara hammered on it for all they were worth, shouting to be let in. Very slowly it swung open. Bram saw the two bedraggled figures in front of him and burst out laughing. Johnny and Clara fell through into the entrance hall and started to speak.

'They're going to kill you,' said Johnny.

'All of us,' said Clara.

'Tonight,' said Johnny.

'We've got to escape,' said Clara.

'With the dolphins,' said Johnny. 'They'll take us to the Diaquant.'

'Stop!' said Bram, with such authority that Johnny and Clara were instantly quiet. 'In here,' he continued, once again producing a circular spyproof curtain for all of them to sit inside. 'And slow down . . . one at a time. Johnny – you first. What are you talking about?'

Johnny repeated the conversation they'd overheard between Neith and Mestor.

'They would not dare,' said Bram. 'A Senator, descended from the ancients.'

'But that's why,' pleaded Johnny. 'With you gone no one can stop them.'

'But I must have the Diaquant,' said Bram. 'I cannot leave without it.'

'Then let's go . . . please,' said Clara. 'Nesaea will take us to it.'

'This Nesaea . . . this dolphin. Can we trust her?' asked Bram.

'Of course,' said Clara. 'She's . . .' Clara looked to Johnny for help.

'She's a dolphin,' he said simply, nodding in agreement.

'Very well,' said Bram. 'Let's go.'

✧ ✧ ✧
✧ ✧

Three dolphins, each wearing muzzles and harnesses, broke the surface of the square pool in the temple chamber. 'Hurry,' came the monotone voice from Nesaea. There were footsteps coming towards them down the bricked corridor. 'Each of you take a fin, and hold your breath.'

Bram didn't look at all convinced. 'They're injured,' he said. Look at their flippers – they're bleeding.'

'It's the boats,' said Clara. 'They get hurt in the harnesses pulling them.'

'Come on,' said Johnny. He slipped his locket under his tunic, grabbed Bram's arm and jumped into the water, pulling him along. Clara followed. The voices were getting louder. Now in the water, Bram nodded, grim-faced. Johnny grabbed hold of Nesaea's fin while Clara and Bram each held onto one of her sisters'. All three of them took a huge lungful of air and the dolphins dived.

Johnny's arms were nearly wrenched out of their sockets. He felt the enormous strength of Nesaea as she surged through the darkness. There was no chance to look behind and check that Clara and Bram were still with them as his dolphin led the way. Nesaea powered through the underwater caverns, twisting and turning, heading deeper and deeper underground. The water was getting darker and colder and Johnny was starting to worry – he suspected dolphins could hold their breath a lot longer than humans and Melanians, and hoped Nesaea knew that. He was beginning to struggle. His heart was pumping furiously, hoping it might find oxygen from his lungs, but Johnny's lungs were empty and bursting. Nesaea turned upwards, but it must be too late. They'd never make it back to the surface in time. There was a red spot above them as the dolphin streaked upwards. The spot glowed bigger. Johnny closed his eyes and hung on. He tried to think of anything to distract himself from the pain his body felt. He thought of Bentley, bleeding under the Proteus Institute; he thought of his mum, lifeless in a hospital bed; he thought of his mum and dad when he was little, together and happy, and his brother Nicky playing with him. He opened his eyes – they were almost there . . . just a few more seconds. He thought of Clara. It wasn't going to finish here, in the dark, no one ever knowing what happened. He had to hang on. Nesaea broke the surface of the water and Johnny followed, opening his mouth and welcoming the rush of air into his lungs. The others appeared either side of him. Bram climbed out into the chamber and reached a hand out to Johnny and Clara to pull them, wheezing, onto a red floor.

'It appears my capacity is rather larger than yours,' Bram said. With Johnny and Clara recovering on the floor he inspected the chamber, all of it lined with glowing orichalcum. There was a further stack of orichalcum in one corner, covering something up. Bram went across and started to remove the red mineral to see what was hidden underneath.

Johnny, still struggling for air, got to his feet and walked over to him. 'Is it the Diaquant?' he asked. Bram shook his head, slowly. 'What then?' Johnny asked. 'Do you know?'

This time Bram nodded. 'It's a bomb,' he said. 'A very, *very* big bomb.'

'Congratulations, Senator,' crackled the electronic voice from Nesaea's back. 'I am glad you recognize your predica-ment. The trap was set and you walked willingly into it.'

'Neith!' Bram shouted angrily.

'Of course,' said the mechanical voice, laughing flatly.

9 ✦ ✦

THE DIAQUANT OF ATLANTIS ✦ ✦

The chamber hummed in time with the pulsating red orichalcum walls. Johnny tried to catch Bram's eye but the future Emperor, who would never now hold that title, seemed lost for a moment in his own thoughts. Clara sat on the floor in the same spot where she'd climbed out of the water. Johnny had got his breath back, though it didn't seem to matter. He walked over to the orichalcum pile covering the bomb. Bram had removed enough of the red metal to reveal a display counting down. The symbols were meaningless, but there was no escaping the sense of doom that it gave Johnny to look at them. He'd walked into a trap. Worse, he'd run headlong into it. Neith and Mestor must have followed them into the little temple and staged their conversation purely for his benefit. They knew he'd run to get Bram. They knew he'd do exactly what they'd expected. He'd behaved like a puppet with them pulling his strings.

He stared at the hieroglyphs counting down and willed them to stop. Nothing happened. He screwed up his eyes and concentrated really hard but when he opened them the symbols had refused to obey. He kicked out at the red pile, sending pieces bouncing off the walls and clattering across the floor of the chamber. He felt someone standing behind him looking over his shoulder – it was Bram. 'The orichalcum drains your energy – we're surrounded by it here. You cannot stop the countdown.'

'There's got to be something,' said Johnny. 'There must be a way out.'

'Not every problem can be solved,' said Bram calmly. 'Or sometimes it is not always we who can solve it.'

'We have to,' said Johnny. 'Don't you see? I know the future – you're the Emperor.'

'Yes that is a conundrum,' said Bram, 'truly a puzzle. What makes you think the timeline must be preserved?'

Bram was being infuriatingly calm. Time was running out. 'Alf . . . Alf said it,' Johnny stammered. 'We were going to destroy Earth before . . . in the past . . . but he said we *must* have saved it as we came from its future.'

'A compelling argument, don't you think?' said Bram. 'After all, I would hate to be responsible for such a large paradox. If I give you a ship at some point in the future, but you come to the past where we die together – preventing me from ever giving you the ship in the first place – making it impossible for you to come here . . . it doesn't look good does it?' Bram's eyes were twinkling, reminding Johnny of how he'd been on Melania.

Johnny thought of Alf and Sol. What he wouldn't give to hear their voices. There was nowhere he'd rather be right now than back on the bridge of the Spirit of London, sitting in the captain's chair. He'd even be pleased to see the Chancellor.

'Why, Miss Clara,' said a faraway voice that must have come from inside Johnny's head. *'What is going on?'*

Johnny stared at the bomb again, watching the symbols on its display whirling round. 'How long have we got?' he asked.

'Are you and Master Johnny all right?' asked the voice in Johnny's head.

'About a minute now,' said Bram, 'though my Atlantean has never been especially good. It could well be less.' He shrugged at Johnny.

'*You can't leave me alone on this ship,*' squeaked a high-pitched voice. '*It doesn't listen to me. Get up. Get up at once you mechanical imbecile.*'

Johnny knew his final minute should be spent with Clara. He turned round. She was sitting cross-legged on the floor, staring into space as though in a trance. What he hadn't expected was to find Alf lying on the floor next to her and, further on, to see an arch that led onto the bridge of the Spirit of London. The Chancellor, looking flustered, was standing just on the other side.

'What . . . how?' said Johnny. 'What's happening?'

'How very interesting,' said Bram. 'It appears your sister is owlein.'

'Ow what?' said Johnny.

'Owlein,' said Bram. 'It is the quality that makes the creatures known as plicans so special. Clara has folded the space between the chamber and your ship in much the same way. It is an impressive feat. Come, Johnny – time is running out,' he said, suddenly energized.

They hurried over to Alf. Johnny knelt down beside him and twisted his ear until it snapped back into position. The android sat up and said, 'Master Johnny – whatever was that? I stepped through an arch . . . there it is! Where is this place?'

'Don't worry about it, Alf,' said Johnny. 'We're leaving.'

Alf looked around the chamber, at Bram and then at Clara. 'And what has happened to Miss Clara? Is she all right?'

'We'll explain later,' said Johnny. 'Right now we have to get back.'

'Johnny – you and Alf must go through first,' said Bram. 'I'll bring Clara.'

Johnny understood. He nodded and stepped through the arch, pushing a reluctant Alf in front of him as the Chancellor shuffled out of the way. Alf collapsed onto the bridge of the

Spirit of London. Johnny sank to his knees feeling ill, but looked behind to see Bram carrying Clara through the archway, which folded away into nothingness behind them. Clara came to, looked at him and smiled. 'I did it, didn't I?' She beamed. Johnny smiled back. 'I knew I could. I folded us both through that Arch of Lysentia – just a couple of centimetres – I borrowed the shape and knew I could do more.'

'You did brilliantly,' said Johnny, as once again he twisted Alf's left ear to reboot the android, who sat up looking rather disorientated.

A female voice cut in. 'Johnny – I am detecting a massive explosion underneath the city.'

'Hi, Sol,' said Johnny. 'That was meant for us.'

'For you?' squeaked the Chancellor. 'What did you do to upset them?'

'Do? We didn't *do* anything,' said Johnny.

'Let's just say the natives weren't friendly,' added Bram.

'I seem to remember they didn't take too kindly to you,' said Clara to the Chancellor.

'A simple misunderstanding,' replied Gronack. 'I'm sure if I made contact again we could sort it out in no time'

'Though you will do no such thing,' said Bram, striding into the middle of the bridge. 'It is imperative the Atlanteans believe us to be dead. That way, taking the Diaquant should be slightly easier.'

'Taking the Diaquant?' squeaked Gronack. 'No wonder they tried to kill you. You're even more irresponsible than your older self.' The phasmeer's robes turned a very pale green.

'Thank you,' said Bram, trying to hide a smile.

'Honestly – you're all impossible,' said the Chancellor, who scuttled towards the lifts and off the bridge.

'Are you serious?' Johnny asked Bram. 'You said you weren't even sure what the Diaquant is, let alone where it is.'

'Oh I know exactly where it is,' said Bram. 'And now I know how we can get there.' He was looking at Clara.

☆   ☆   ☆
☆   ☆

As soon as they could, Johnny and Clara had changed out of their Atlantean clothes and into their Melanian tunics, in which Johnny felt much more comfortable. Not that he wouldn't keep his priestly robes as a souvenir. Then they braved a visit to the dinodeck. Between them Johnny and Clara decided that the dinosaur with the spiked back and clubbed tail that Johnny first spotted in the forest was probably an ankylosaurus. Clara was really excited to get close enough for one to lick her face, even though she screwed her eyes up at its hot, stale breath. Alf had refused point blank to come down with them and reluctantly Johnny and Clara decided they couldn't spend too long, but Johnny wanted to tell Ptery the truth. He had to shout to Ptery to make himself understood above the tremendous din as the different animals growled and howled at each other from their electronically segregated compartments. The winged dinosaur and his companion surveyed them from atop a large rock in the middle of the deck. The two children clambered up to join them. Johnny tried to explain what had happened and how the world Ptery had known wasn't there any more. The dinosaur stared down at Johnny unblinking, while a single tear rolled down his companion's face. It seemed they both had glimpsed the initial destruction through Sol's walls and understood. Ptery said he would call a dinocouncil and tell the survivors.

The other pteradon spoke and Johnny was able to understand her. She told him that she and Ptery were the elders now and that the other dinosaurs had become their flock. And that she, too, needed a name. Despite only understanding Johnny's half of the conversation, Clara quickly grasped what was going on.

'Call her Donna,' she said. 'Pteradons – Ptery and Donna.'

'Donna?' Johnny asked, but as he said it, Ptery and his companion repeated the name to each other and seemed satisfied.

Donna bowed her head low to Clara who, after receiving a quick nod from Johnny, bowed in return. Clara stood up straight and Sol's voice rang out across the deck, asking them to return to the bridge.

Bram was there waiting, talking with Sol. Johnny sat down in the captain's chair, swivelling to and fro, while Clara stood behind him with one arm on the plican's tank. The future Emperor paced excitedly in front of them. Bram explained he couldn't return to his own ship without revealing himself to be alive and that it was only a matter of time before the Atlanteans tried to seize the Spirit of London and add her to their ever-expanding navy. They had to act at once while they still had surprise on their side. Bram assured them that the Diaquant was at the top of the tower at the very centre of Atlantis, from where its power could radiate across the globe. Alf, who was standing at an instrument panel off to one side, confirmed that the tower housed a massive, and very unusual, energy source. It would be for Clara to fold them there; she positively beamed and said she couldn't wait to try folding again. Sol helped out with very precise measurements of the distance from the bridge to their destination, while keeping a close eye on the movements of the soldiers encircling her base.

'Is everyone ready then?' asked Bram.

Johnny nodded seriously, as did Clara behind him.

'It will be dangerous,' said Bram. 'Just getting me to the Diaquant would be enough. You do not have to come with me.'

'Of course we'll come,' said Johnny. He looked round and saw Clara looking just as determined as he was.

'Well thank you,' said Bram. 'Let us get into position.'

Johnny stood up and followed Bram to behind the plican's tank. They watched as the space inside the bridge distorted.

Johnny thought he could feel the warmth and smell the salt air of Atlantis. He could even hear seagulls. 'Nearly there,' said Clara. An arch was forming in front of them, blotting out the image of the tower on Sol's viewscreen. 'Got it!' squealed Clara, and the gateway solidified.

A bolt of blue lightning shot through the opening, just missing them. 'Now!' shouted Bram – he grabbed Johnny and Clara's hands and together the three of them leapt through into . . . empty space. Johnny somehow managed to stop his momentum and pull himself back, as did Bram. But Clara was swinging from Bram's hand, dangling over the edge of the narrow ledge that they had just landed on and which circled the top of what was a hollow tower. Clara screamed, but was drowned out by something else. The whole tower filled with the most terrible noise Johnny had ever heard – something was in pain. The sound reached inside him like fingernails being scraped down a blackboard. A circle of blue sparks was rushing up the inside of the hollow column beneath Clara. Bram lifted her out and placed her on the ledge. Just in time. The ring of electricity passed in front of their faces and up into a giant parabolic mirror above their heads. From there, the sparks were focused into a shape so bright Johnny couldn't bear to look at it, held in position above a central pillar of orichalcum that descended into the depths. The terrible noise stopped. Johnny glanced behind but the bridge of the Spirit of London was nowhere to be seen. Clara hadn't kept the fold open. He peered over the ledge and saw further rings of blue sparks making their way up the inside of the tower at regular intervals, one every few seconds. Clara had been lucky not to get zapped. Now she stood, with a look of sheer terror on her face, with her back pressed against the inside wall of the tower, unable to look anywhere below her. The screams began again. Clara covered her ears as she looked to Bram to make the heart-wrenching noise stop.

Bram, though, paid no attention. Despite the confined space he fell to his knees, gazing up at the source of the bright light with a mixture of wonder and horror, and talking to himself. Johnny only caught snatches of what he was saying. 'All my life . . . the gods themselves . . . cruelty . . . such beauty.' Johnny nudged him a few times but there was no response. Instead he followed where Bram's eyes were looking. It was so bright it was painful. Johnny squinted, shutting out as much of the searing whiteness as he could. Through his eyelashes the whiteness resolved into a doughnut-shaped cage, like a fusion reactor, and at its heart was something alive . . . sort of. It was bent double and shrivelled up into a little ball, unable to move. Flaps of what little skin it had left hung off its frail frame. The unbearable wailing came from its mouth. As Johnny watched, the screams faded again and Clara lowered her hands from her ears. Johnny looked down at Bram, who filled the ledge between him and his sister, and saw he was stretching his arms out towards the figure, completely lost in his own world.

'Don't be afraid, my pretty.' Clara started and nearly fell. Neith, followed by Mestor, had entered the tower through a hidden doorway next to her. Clara looked as frightened of the drop as she did of Neith and, besides, she couldn't move away with Bram's kneeling figure blocking her retreat. And Johnny couldn't get across to help her for the same reason.

'Fetch me the other one,' Neith said to Mestor who, leaning on his staff, began limping in the opposite direction around the narrow ledge that marked the outside of the tower. He was coming for Johnny. The wailing began again – like a wounded animal. Johnny felt hope draining out of him. Neith put her arm around Clara's back, prising her off the wall, and grabbed her blonde hair, forcing her to look towards the white light. 'Beautiful isn't it, my pretty?' said the Queen. 'This is my

Diaquant. You see the more it fights, the more tightly it is bound – and the more energy I take from it.'

'You're evil,' said Clara.

'Yes I suppose I am,' said Neith. She smiled at Clara's remark. 'Come with me – I won't hurt you.'

'I won't,' said Clara, ducking out of Neith's reach and sitting down on the floor next to Bram with her back once again pressed against the tower wall. Another ring of blue sparks passed in front of their faces.

'There's nowhere to hide, my pretty,' said Neith, kneeling down next to her. 'Khari won't help you now – look at him. If this blabbering idiot is the last of the ancients, I think it's time some new blood was in charge.'

Bram continued to stare, blissfully vacant, towards the Diaquant, and Mestor was already halfway around the tower and coming for Johnny. Reaching inside his tunic for the games console, Johnny took it out and keyed in a simple message: 'Don't fight it.' He pressed 'send.'

Mestor hesitated, looking at the device in Johnny's hand. When nothing happened, he hobbled closer. 'Your trinkets won't help you here,' he said. He peered over the edge and then looked back towards Johnny. 'If you don't want to know how far down it goes, you had better come with me.'

'Make me,' said Johnny.

'Don't think that I can't,' Mestor replied. The next circle of blue sparks moved slowly up the tower in front of them. 'You will make a fine priest . . . with the right . . . *discipline*,' he continued.

'And I thought you'd been trying to kill me,' said Johnny. If he could keep the priest talking, it might buy him some more time to figure a way out.

'You flatter yourself,' replied Mestor, edging ever closer to him. 'Of course the Senator must die. But it would be futile for you to join him. In time you shall worship in the Temple of Neith.'

'Never,' said Johnny. 'I'd rather die.'

'Very well,' said Mestor, taking his staff in both hands and pointing a sharpened end toward Johnny.

'How dare you!' screamed Neith, standing upright and rubbing her arm. Johnny glanced quickly around. The Queen had tooth marks in her forearm. Clara's eyes burned blue and silver with defiance. 'Enough!' snapped Neith. 'I don't have time for these games.'

Another ring of blue sparks moved slowly past them. Very slowly. Johnny hadn't noticed that the dreadful screams had stopped until he heard a different noise. Something was singing. The air vibrated around him like a guitar string as the song filled the empty insides of the tower. He knew there was hope. Mestor jabbed his staff towards him but it was easy for Johnny to move out of the way. The priest repeatedly stabbed at him but couldn't seem to get close. Johnny even had time to watch Clara dodging Neith's lunges just as easily. The next set of sparks rose up level with him in the tower, but slowed to a halt – the soundwaves from the song were blocking it. Then, very slowly at first, the sparks reversed, edging their way back down the shaft. Johnny looked up towards the Diaquant, and saw the electronic bars caging it were slowly unwinding. More and more of the creature was becoming visible. Mestor lunged again at Johnny, who this time pulled the staff easily from the old priest's grasp. He knew what he needed to do. Planting the staff into the central orichalcum column he jumped off the ledge like a pole vaulter, heading for the Diaquant.

Neith saw him and sprang catlike towards the Diaquant, but Johnny knew he had more time . . . that he would get there first. He took a hand off the staff and plucked the flimsy creature from out of its cage, keeping his momentum going towards the other side. The singing stopped. The spell was broken. Johnny clattered onto the far ledge, twisting his body so the Diaquant, which felt so fragile that the slightest impact would break it, landed on top of him. He looked back to see Neith caught in the electric bars in the central cage, that were now strengthening again. She looked terrified.

The blue sparks began rising up the tower. Bram, released from whatever spell had been holding him, got to his feet before Mestor could push him over the ledge. The priest retreated and glanced, horrified, up at the cage. Neith screamed a terrible scream. Johnny looked again to see her transforming. Her dark hair was greying, her face and skin becoming wrinkled. She was ageing before his eyes. He looked away to see Clara bury her own head in Bram's chest. When Johnny looked back, all that remained of the Queen was a skeleton, that begin to disintegrate even as he watched.

'What have you done?' shouted Mestor at him. The priest's face was contorted with rage. He moved towards Johnny, hurling abuse at him but it was drowned out as the tower itself shuddered and cracked, opening up a gap in the ledge between them. The enormous mirror above shattered, and the roof crumbled away, letting the sunlight pour in. Johnny sheltered himself and the Diaquant from the shards of glass and falling masonry. He heard Mestor screaming and raised his head. The priest was no longer looking at him. Instead, he was staring out over the island of Atlantis. Johnny looked too – it was impossible not to. Mountains of water were rushing towards them from every direction, uprooting anything and everything in their path. More and more of Atlantis was disappearing into shadow and then vanishing under the deluge. A deep rumbling in the distance reached him and began to build. They were so high up at the top of the tower that he could see everything. He looked across towards the spaceport. Next to the golden

Atlantean ships he easily spotted the Spirit of London, with the Sun glinting off its diamond-patterned hull and the trademark dark bands sweeping around it. The rumbling was much louder now. Johnny watched, willing Sol to take off and rise above the water, as a handful of other vessels were doing. The wave was getting closer, plunging the ship into shadow. Sol would take off . . . he knew it. He couldn't understand what was taking so long. Then the wave hit the spaceport. Everything disappeared underneath the wall of water that was rushing towards him. Johnny stared in disbelief.

'Johnny,' shouted Bram. 'Is she safe? Is the Diaquant safe?'

Johnny had almost forgotten he held the Diaquant in his arms. It . . . *she* . . . was just skin and bones and so light he barely noticed her. He looked across the tower towards Bram, standing with Clara, and nodded. He knew the Diaquant was important but she didn't matter in the way Sol and Alf did. They were gone now. Clara and Bram mattered too – but they'd all be gone soon.

'Hang on!' Bram shouted above the sound of the roaring water. Behind them Johnny could see the wave getting very close. It was about to hit the tower. Johnny looked around him – there wasn't anything he could see to hold onto so he braced himself for the impact.

Everything shook. Water surged up the central shaft, spouting out through the open roof. Johnny pressed himself back against what was left of the wall, part of which gave way. He looked to his side and saw Mestor was gone. He must have been washed away when the wave hit. Clara and Bram were still hanging on. Below, the water was subsiding, revealing the destruction beneath them. Almost nothing was left – just the occasional flash of red from a smashed orichalcum roof. As the wave retreated, he tried to pick out where the spaceport had been. He couldn't even recognize the Spirit of London among the twisted wreckage.

'We'll come to you,' Bram shouted. 'Clara – can you fold us out of here?'

Clara shook her head slowly. Her face was completely white.

'Be careful,' Johnny shouted across. 'I'll come to you too.' He started picking his way along the ledge, parts crumbled and missing, as Clara and Bram edged gingerly towards him. It was slow progress. It felt as though any sudden movement could bring it crashing down. Already more giant waves were returning in the distance, washing in over the wasteland that just a few moments before had been a great city. Johnny wasn't at all sure the tower would survive a second hit. 'We've got to be quick,' he shouted across to the other two. 'It's coming back in. What are we going to do?'

'We'll think of something,' Bram shouted back. 'Maybe the Diaquant can save us?'

Johnny looked at the creature he cradled in his arms. When he'd seen her up in the cage she'd looked the frailest, oldest thing he'd ever seen. Now, in the sunshine, he could see she was wrapped in a watery silver cloth and her skin didn't look quite as wrinkled as he'd thought. And her scalp, that had seemed bald when in the cage, was in fact covered with a very fine layer of short blonde hair. Her eyes were shut. He studied her face and decided she looked much less frail than he'd imagined when he'd leapt to her rescue, but he didn't see how she could help them now. And then she was plunged into shadow.

'Look!' Clara shouted, pointing skyward. 'It's Sol. She's OK.'

Johnny followed her arm upwards. There, hovering above them and blotting out the Sun, was the Spirit of London. He laughed. They were going to be saved – and it *was* funny to see the London Gherkin in mid-air like that. He'd never seen the ship in flight before and couldn't help thinking what a spectacular sight she was.

The next wave crashed against the tower beneath them and Johnny looked around, hoping to steady himself. He found he was staring straight into Mestor's furious eyes. The priest lunged forward from out of a hidden alcove, grabbing Johnny's neck with both hands and carrying them both over the edge. Clara screamed. Holding the Diaquant in his right hand Johnny grabbed desperately for the ledge with his left, finding it with his fingertips. Mestor slid down till he was hanging from Johnny's ankles. Johnny knew there was no way he could hold on. Maybe if he let the Diaquant go and tried with both hands, but he couldn't do that. Worse still, the impact of the second wave was making the whole tower collapse. He could feel himself heading downwards, like being in a very slow lift. He looked up desperately. Two little black dots swooped out of an opening in the Spirit of London's side. Mestor was swinging underneath him, pushing off the outer wall with his legs to try to dislodge them both. Johnny was hanging on by just his fingernails and adrenaline. He saw Bram desperately trying to get round the ledge to him. The two black dots were getting bigger. It was Ptery and Donna, flying to their rescue. Johnny knew they wouldn't make it in time.

'You're coming with me,' shouted Mestor from beneath him, tugging at Johnny with all his might, and at last Johnny felt his fingertips slide to the very lip of the ledge . . . and then off. Mestor had finally let go with the effort of pulling Johnny down with him, and they were both falling . . . only they weren't. The tower wasn't crumbling any more. Everything seemed to have stopped, apart from the dinosaurs flying ever nearer and Clara and Bram, who were still making their way around the ledge towards Johnny. He looked at the Diaquant he was still holding in his right arm. She opened her eyes – for a moment they shone pure silver, before that faded and they became the clearest, palest blue he'd ever seen. She smiled at him and

Johnny smiled back. He looked below to see Mestor frozen in midfall beneath him.

Clara shouted, 'In there Ptery,' to the bigger of the two creatures who was just able to fit into the shaft, with his wings fully outstretched and beating, allowing Johnny to grasp a leg with his left hand. As Ptery rose up out of the tower, Clara took hold of his other leg while Bram was lifted upwards by Donna. Johnny looked down. For an instant longer, Mestor remained frozen in time before the spell was broken. He stared disbelievingly at Johnny as he fell away from them into the depths of the collapsing tower. 'How?' Clara asked, as Ptery strained to lift them towards the waiting Spirit of London.

'It was her . . . the Diaquant,' said Johnny, nodding to the creature, eyes now closed again, that he was still holding in his right arm. 'She did something.' Johnny looked above his head at the leathery wings beating slowly. 'Thanks Ptery,' he shouted upwards.

'You welcome,' said the dinosaur. 'You no heavy now. Easy fly. Take you home soon. Then fishing.'

Johnny guessed the Diaquant might have something to do with their unexpected lightness. He'd been a little worried that they might not make it up to the ship, but when he thought about it he'd held the Diaquant one-handed for a long time now without getting tired. 'OK,' he shouted back. 'Just get us home and then you can fish all you want.'

They were making good progress, which was just as well because when Johnny looked beyond the ship he spotted a few golden shapes in the far distance. Some Atlantean fighters were coming their way. And they were closing very fast. As Donna, carrying Bram, swooped into the top of the dinodeck ahead of them, an energy beam from the nearest ship grazed the side of the Spirit of London. Ptery carried them into the ship, lowering them onto the rock near the centre. As he did so the outer hull sealed behind them and everyone was thrown backwards by a sudden movement.

'What's happening?' Johnny shouted.

'I'm sorry, Johnny,' replied Sol's calm voice. 'My shields are still inoperative and immediate evasive action was required. Welcome aboard.'

'Thanks,' said Johnny as the rumble of a huge explosion came from just outside the ship.

'That was close,' said Bram. 'Let's get to the bridge.'

Johnny and Clara nodded. Johnny turned to Ptery, who had a hungry gleam in his eye and the smell of saltwater on his breath. He patted him on his bony crested head. 'Sorry Ptery,' he said. 'No fishing just yet.' Bram, Clara and Johnny, still carrying the Diaquant, left the disappointed pteradons and hurried into the antigrav lifts.

They stepped out to see both Alf and Chancellor Gronack at weapons stations either side of the bridge, trying to fend off the Atlantean fighters. Clara ran straight across to the plican's tank in the centre. 'The poor thing,' she said. 'It's exhausted. It must have folded the ship out of the wave.'

'That is correct,' said Sol. 'I was unable to take off so requested the fold. I am pleased the plican survived the trauma. I would not have liked to be severed from it.'

A dazzling flash of light on the viewscreen in front of them preceded another sudden change of direction, throwing everybody apart from Alf to the floor.

'We're all going to die,' squeaked the Chancellor. 'And it's your fault.' It was looking accusingly at Johnny, who was making for his captain's chair. Gronack continued, 'I tried to have this stupid ship get away before it was too late, but the thing refused.'

'We're not going to die,' replied Johnny tersely. 'Sol will get us out of here.'

'Computing . . .' said Sol. 'Probability of survival is 3.725 783%. Without my shields it only takes one direct hit.'

'Johnny,' said Bram. 'I have a squadron of fighters concealed in your asteroid belt. If I can contact them . . .'

Johnny nodded and Sol immediately said, 'I am opening a channel. Tell them to be quick.'

Another explosion saw everyone flung across the bridge again. Sol's engines emitted a high-pitched scream as the ship changed direction. Johnny had never even heard them before. From the floor of the bridge Bram was communicating with a triangular-faced viasynth on the viewscreen. Johnny reached the chair and placed the Diaquant on it. She opened her eyes and said, 'Thank you.'

'I got one,' shouted Alf, looking up for a moment from behind the console where he was standing. Johnny stepped in front of the viewscreen and saw an explosion where a moment before there'd been a golden fighter. Behind it the sky was getting darker, changing from its normal blue into the blackness of space.

'Melanian squadron located,' said Sol. 'Our chances of survival have now increased to 3.962 743%.'

'But that's almost what they were before,' shrieked the Chancellor. It had moved forward to stand next to Johnny, towering over him, while Bram was now operating the weapons station.

'The ships are too remote to be of probable assistance,' Sol replied.

'Can't we fold out of here?' Johnny asked.

'No chance,' said Clara. 'The last one wiped it out again.'

'Sol – how many ships are attacking us?' Johnny asked. He wished he hadn't. As Sol replied, the numbers kept increasing as more and more Atlantean fighters joined in the hunt. It was up to fifty before he said, 'OK – I get the message.'

The Moon filled the viewscreen now, though as missiles rained down on them there was little time to admire it. Sol dived low over its surface but the Atlantean fighters were easily able to follow. 'Hold on, everyone,' said the ship, before braking breathtakingly quickly and climbing, engines whining horribly, away from the surface. Johnny was knocked sideways on top of the Chancellor, and Clara ended up in a heap next to them. A couple of explosions flickered on the screen where Atlantean fighters hadn't changed direction in time and had crashed into the Moon's surface. Johnny moved across to look at Alf's scanner and saw the space around them was still constantly filling with more fighters moving in for the kill. Another blast shook the hull as Sol changed course again. Then another . . . then another.

'This is hopeless,' said the Chancellor. 'We must surrender.'

Johnny was inclined to agree. There didn't seem any way out. Sol cut in with, 'Surrender is not an option, Chancellor.'

'What do you mean "not an option"?' squeaked Gronack. 'We can't go on like this.'

'You are correct,' Sol replied. 'I anticipate our destruction in 42.537 32 seconds. The necessary missiles and mines have all been launched. The probability is 100%. It is a highly impressive attack pattern – I have been outmanoeuvered.'

The only sound was the whining of the engines as the ship swerved to evade a salvo of missiles.

'But . . . there must be something you can do?' said Johnny.

'I am sorry I have let you down Johnny,' Sol replied.

'Of course you haven't,' he replied. 'You've been great.'

'Impact in thirty seconds,' said Sol. The ship veered in yet another direction. Johnny steadied himself and looked at the screens. He could see what was happening – every avenue of escape was being closed off. They were surrounded, with all the fighters converging on them, forcing them into a tightly packed minefield. There really was no way out. For what it was worth, Bram and Alf were still firing weapons, but however many fighters they shot down more took their place. Half the Atlantean fleet must be there.

'Sol – how long till my ships get here?' Bram asked, looking up from his console.

'Computing . . . they will reach this location in approximately 4 minutes 52.742 61 seconds,' answered Sol calmly.

Johnny walked back to where Clara was standing in front of the screen. 'It's OK,' he said to her, though his stomach was tensing horribly and his heart was beating so loudly it was almost drowning out the engines.

'I know,' Clara replied. 'I can feel it.' She looked defiantly into Johnny's eyes.

'Impact in ten seconds,' said Sol.

A nearby Atlantean fighter exploded in front of them. Sol flew right through the debris, which lit up the whole bridge.

'Nine . . .'

'Can't you fold the mines out of the way?' Johnny asked.

'It doesn't work like that,' said Clara. 'I have to take a piece of space I'm in and move it somewhere else.'

'Eight . . .'

'I wish I could've learnt to do it too,' said Johnny. 'It must be amazing.'

'It's not like anything else,' said Clara. 'It's as if you're part of everything – the whole cosmos.'

'I'd love that,' said Johnny. 'Being part of space. I always wanted to go there, but folding it must be even better.'

'Seven . . .'

'I just wish we had more time,' said Johnny.

'There's as much time as you need,' said someone behind them.

Johnny and Clara wheeled round to see a young woman, dressed all in silver, get up from the captain's chair. She was tall, with long blonde hair and she was glowing – radiating a soft white light that filled the bridge.

'Who are you?' Johnny asked. 'Where's the Diaquant?'

The woman laughed. 'Johnny, I'm the Diaquant.'

'You? How?' said Johnny. 'You're so . . . young.'

'Thank you,' the Diaquant replied, smiling broadly – the brilliant glow came from everywhere, including her bright silver eyes, but as Johnny watched those faded again to the same pale blue as before.

'What happened?' Clara asked. As Johnny and Clara looked around them everything else seemed to have stopped. Bram and Alf were frozen in front of their consoles while the Chancellor stood motionless next to Clara, a frightened look on its face and its robes pure white with terror. 'How did you do this?'

'You did it in the tower, didn't you?' said Johnny. 'You can stop time . . . how?'

'How can *you* will an electric circuit into life?' replied the Diaquant.

'I don't know,' said Johnny. 'But that's different – it's nothing.'

'No – it's a small thing,' replied the Diaquant, as she walked across the bridge towards them. 'A little acorn . . . but an oak tree can grow from it.'

'But it's not like this,' said Johnny, gesturing around the bridge, all frozen in time. 'What about science . . . the laws of nature?'

'Anything is possible,' said the Diaquant. 'You two don't belong here – I'm sending you home.'

'Home? To the future?' asked Clara.

'To the future. To your right time,' replied the Diaquant.

'Thank you,' said Johnny.

'You saved me,' said the Diaquant, 'by telling me not to fight.

I have lived longer than you could possibly comprehend, but I can still learn new lessons.' The Diaquant looked more serious now. 'I cannot thank you enough, but though it is wrong of me, I would like to ask something more of you – two things in fact.'

'Anything,' said Johnny.

'It won't be easy,' said the Diaquant.

'We'll do it, won't we?' said Johnny, looking at Clara, who nodded silently back.

'You're both so very young,' said the Diaquant, 'so fragile . . . I wish there was another way.'

'We're old enough,' said Johnny. 'We've proved that – what do you want us to do?'

'The human Michael Mackintosh,' said the Diaquant. 'You must free him.'

'Dad?' Johnny asked, open-mouthed.

The Diaquant nodded. 'I know you will find a way.'

'And the other thing?' Clara asked.

'Release your mother,' replied the Diaquant.

'But she's sick,' said Johnny. 'She's in hospital.'

'She is trapped there,' said the Diaquant. 'Your father will know what to do.'

'We'll do it,' said Clara. 'We promise.' Johnny nodded.

'I know you will, Clara,' said the Diaquant, who knelt down stretching her hands out towards them both. 'Let me hold you – just for a second,' she said tenderly.

Clara walked forward and the Diaquant wrapped an arm around her and pulled her in. Johnny followed. The Diaquant had closed her eyes but Johnny thought that, through the glow from her face, he could see a single tear glistening down her cheek. And as she touched him his whole body tingled with warmth. 'Come with us,' he said to her.

The Diaquant opened her eyes, let go of him and looked straight at Johnny. 'Everything is possible,' she said, 'but great power brings with it great responsibility. I will go with Bram Khari. He is a good man, much more than a man. The galaxy is in chaos – it needs him. It needs an Emperor.'

'What about Atlantis . . . the fighters,' asked Johnny

'The bombs they sent after you will destroy their own ships,' replied the Diaquant. 'They are a cruel people. There should be no place for them.' For a moment Johnny thought the Diaquant seemed old and frail again. And then the look passed. She stood up. 'I must leave now,' she said. 'Before it becomes too hard.' She let go of Clara, walked stiffly over towards where Bram was standing statue-like at the console and they both vanished in a point of light.

'Six . . . five . . . four – countdown terminated,' said Sol. 'I am no longer tracking missiles . . . or mines . . . or Atlantean fighters.'

'Master Bram,' shouted Alf. 'Where is he? Whatever has happened to the Emperor?'

'He's gone,' said Johnny quietly. He looked at the Moon on the viewscreen. The craters were unfamiliar. They must be on the far side from the Earth. 'Sol,' he said.

'Yes, Johnny,' replied the ship.

'Perform a long-range scan. Find out when it is.'

'Computing . . .' said Sol. 'Sensors indicate it is Galactic Standard Time minus twenty-three days exactly.'

'Twenty-three days?' squeaked Gronack. 'Civilization at last.'

Johnny smiled as he watched the colour returning to the Chancellor's robes.

10

RESCUE MISSION ☆ ⁎

'We're saved,' squealed the Chancellor. 'By the time we signal Melania and they send my private shuttle, I'll just have time to say goodbye to myself and warn me from going on this terrible journey.'

Johnny had never seen Gronack so excited. The phasmeer's antennae danced above its head, wrapping around each other. 'Well did you?' Johnny asked, as he walked across to the captain's chair. He sat down, swivelling to face the Chancellor.

'Did I what?'

'Did you warn yourself?' said Johnny.

'Of course not,' said Alf, his hands still busy shutting down the weapons control station.

'Why not?' asked Johnny and the Chancellor together.

'It simply is not allowed,' Alf replied, looking up. 'Imagine the fright you could give yourself if you popped up in front of you.'

'So?' Clara asked.

'So anything might happen,' Alf replied. 'So you may very well kill yourself and that is the worst paradox of all. You two really paid no attention at all to my temporal mechanics lessons did you? I wonder why I bothered. And as for you, Sir,' he said, turning to Chancellor Gronack, 'I am surprised. I thought you knew better.'

'Of course I had no intention of contacting myself,' said the

Chancellor, whose antennae disentangled while its robes started glowing a subtle pink. 'Although if I did, I would naturally have the self-control not to do anything rash.'

'Naturally,' said Johnny. 'It doesn't matter for us, anyway. We . . . our other selves must have left Earth by now.'

'I don't know, Johnny,' said Clara. 'I'll go and get my diary – there's loads of stuff I've got to write anyway.' Clara hurried over to the lifts and off the bridge.

'I suppose it's too much to ask that there'll be a decent ship near this barbarian planet? I can't wait to get back into civilized surroundings,' said Gronack.

'Sol,' said Johnny, who was probably even more keen than the phasmeer to see it leave the Spirit of London.

'Yes, Johnny,' replied the ship.

'Can you scan the local area for ships? Maybe the Chancellor can have its wish?'

'As well as more space junk than in a Pleideian scrap-yard, the only vessels in this sector are three krun ships orbiting the planet.'

'Krun? Three?' said Johnny.

'That is correct,' said Sol.

'Have they seen us?' Johnny asked, on the edge of his seat ready to spring into action.

'I do not believe so,' Sol replied. 'It is unlikely they are equipped with anything so advanced as my neutrino scanning technology. We are hidden from them by your planet's moon.'

'Where are they?' Johnny asked, relaxing back into his chair.

'Displaying . . .' said Sol, and the cratered white landscape on the screens in front of them dissolved into the familiar blue and white swirls of Earth. Johnny stood up and walked right up to the main screen to try and spot what he was meant to be looking at. As he focused on the very centre of the screen, above the planet, he could just see the blurred outline of one large ship, an elongated black cube with spikes protruding randomly in all directions. He stared even harder, and noticed there were two much smaller black spheres nearby, and a disc-shaped object in the centre of the other three craft.

'Didn't you say three ships?' Johnny asked. 'I think I can see four, but it's not very clear.'

'The objects are shielded – on any other ship you would see nothing at all,' Sol replied. 'There are three vessels and one permanent platform. The platform anchors a transportation system to and from the planet.'

'Of course – the space elevator,' said Johnny.

'Is it really?' asked Alf. 'I had no idea the Earth was so advanced.'

'It's not,' Johnny replied. 'I think the krun built it – it's how they took me and Clara.'

'You went inside it?' asked Alf. 'That must have been exciting. What a way to leave the planet.'

'At the time we couldn't really appreciate it.'

'Johnny,' Sol cut in.

'What is it, Sol?' Johnny replied.

'My distress beacon is exhibiting temporal oscillations.'

'What does that mean?' asked Johnny. Alf rolled his eyes.

Sol replied, 'Our return to the near present has caused an instability. The beacon appears to be moving forwards and backwards in time.'

'I guess that's bad,' said Johnny. More and more he wished he *had* paid attention to what Alf had tried to teach them at the university.

'For now I have isolated it within a stasis field. However, I suggest jettisoning the device to prevent it destabilizing other areas of the ship.'

'Won't the krun detect it?' said Johnny.

'It is possible,' Sol replied. 'However, once removed from

stasis the beacon will intersect with our time only rarely, meaning a positive identification is unlikely.'

Johnny walked over to the captain's chair and sat down, thinking.

'Well?' Gronack asked. 'It's not exactly a hard decision – I remember how bad it was when I disappeared.'

'The Chancellor does have a point,' said Alf. 'It would be best to get rid of it.'

Johnny didn't think that Gronack had a point at all. When it happened the phasmeer didn't even seem to have noticed its own disappearance, and the rest of the crew had been given a well-deserved break from its whining. 'How does the beacon work, Sol?' he asked.

'It's not important how it works,' squeaked Gronack.

'I fly under the banner of Emperor Bram Khari,' Sol continued, ignoring the Chancellor. 'So, the beacon is programmed to transmit the Imperial distress signal using all known methods of communication.'

'Including radio waves?' asked Johnny.

'Including radio waves,' Sol comfirmed.

'Can you fire it at the largest krun ship?' Johnny asked. He'd just had a very interesting idea. 'Best if it sticks.'

'The beacon will automatically adhere to any solid surface it encounters,' Sol replied.

'Perfect,' said Johnny. 'Do it.'

'No – don't do it,' said the Chancellor.

'The beacon has been jettisoned on a trajectory for the largest krun vessel,' said Sol.

'Master Johnny – are you sure that was wise?' Alf asked in a way that suggested Johnny was being rather foolhardy.

'Quite sure,' Johnny replied.

Clara stepped from the lift shaft and out into the bridge, carrying a little pocket book. 'It must be around when we left,' she said, 'but I'm not sure. I didn't start writing it till we got to Melania.'

Johnny nodded. 'Sol,' he said. 'Can you pick up TV broadcasts from the planet?'

'I cannot receive transmissions from this position, Johnny. We are in radio shadow behind your moon.'

'Can you move us out so you can pick them up? Concentrate on the landmass at the foot of the space elevator . . . and try to keep us out of sight of the krun.'

'Try?' squeaked Gronack, almost apoplectic. 'I thought our shields were down. Why do we have to try? Why do we have to move at all?'

'Because we have to find out what day it is,' said Johnny. He already had his suspicions, but needed to be sure.

'I am receiving multiple signals,' said Sol. 'Displaying . . .' and the bridge was transformed into a 360 degree TV screen with hundreds of different programmes being shown all around the walls.

Clara looked at Johnny. 'News?' she asked.

'Sport,' Johnny replied, getting back to his feet. He turned round slowly until he homed in on a few broadcasts together showing football clips. One display switched to two men talking with a football pitch behind them. Johnny walked over to the screen, touched it and said, 'This one, Sol. Can you play sound too?'

'. . . it's come to this. The biggest match of the season – the Premier League decider. Here we are at Ashburton Grove . . .'

'That's enough,' said Johnny and the TV screens were instantly replaced by the swirling clouds of Earth. 'Take us back behind the Moon. I know when it is.'

'Just from that, Master Johnny? I am most impressed,' said Alf.

'Don't be,' said Clara. 'It's just boys and football – they're all like it. What day is it, then?'

'It's Sunday,' Johnny replied. 'The day I went down to Yarnton Hill. It's the day before I met you.'

'Are you certain, Johnny?' Alf asked.

'It all makes perfect sense,' said Johnny.

'I'm glad it does to someone,' said the Chancellor. 'I wish you'd tell the rest of us what's going on.'

'I picked up a signal from space,' said Johnny. 'A partial signal over a few days, always heading between the Moon and the space elevator. I picked up *our* signal – our distress beacon. The krun don't broadcast radio waves.'

'And that's why the Diaquant sent us here,' said Clara. 'So we can stop them taking us.'

'No – we have to let ourselves go,' said Johnny. 'We can't change the past. Valdour will home in on our Imperial distress beacon on the krun ship – that's why he rescued us – but we *can* save Louise and Bentley. And then we can get Mum and Dad, just like the Diaquant asked. We've got to land.'

'And how do you propose to do that?' asked the Chancellor. 'Won't an unshielded spacecraft look a little incongruous on this . . . planet?'

'No – it's like a building,' said Johnny. 'It's this dead famous skyscraper in London.

'Forgive me if I'm wrong,' squeaked the Chancellor happily. 'But isn't that building already there?'

'Well, yeah,' said Johnny.

'And won't you Terrans notice if there are two of them? Or are you *all* especially stupid?'

'I hadn't thought of that,' said Johnny.

'Evidently,' replied the Chancellor.

✦ ✦ ✦
✦ ✦

It was Clara's plan. Johnny thought there were a million reasons why it wouldn't work, but he couldn't think of a better one. After spending a long time in total silence with the plican she'd pronounced herself satisfied and now they were in the bay with the mini transports. For everything to work, Clara had to get to London so Alf was going to pilot her down in one of the black cab shuttle crafts.

'You're sure the shields will fool the krun?' Johnny asked Alf, who was sitting in the driver's seat next to Clara.

'Absolutely,' replied Alf. 'Just watch what happens when I do this.' The android blinked very deliberately and the whole taxi shimmered and disappeared, leaving Johnny looking through empty space to the far side of the shuttle bay. If he didn't look at it directly, he wondered if he could just about spot the cab's outline out of the corner of his eye, but he couldn't be sure. The voice of an invisible Alf very close to him said, 'And how about this?' The taxi reappeared but now it looked empty. 'Or this?' and when Johnny looked through the window, instead of Alf and Clara sitting side by side there was a cabbie driving a regular taxi in the front seat, with a passenger in the back.

'Cool,' said Johnny. 'It's brilliant. Thanks Sol,' he said into the air above him.

'You're welcome, Johnny,' came the reply. 'I thought the different camouflage modes may prove useful.'

Alf and Clara reappeared in the front seat, both laughing. 'It's brilliant – it needs a name,' Clara said.

'You are sitting in Shuttle Craft One,' said the Chancellor. 'It is a machine.'

'Don't be silly,' said Clara. 'It's a London taxi. We're going to London. We're on the Spirit of London. We need a London name.'

'Like what?' Johnny asked.

'I know,' said Clara. 'Let's call all the shuttles after Underground lines.'

'Central and District?' Johnny asked.

'Jubilee and Bakerloo,' said Clara firmly. 'We're in Jubilee and the bus can be Victoria.'

'That's a girl's name,' said Johnny.

'All right – how about Piccadilly?'

'Piccadilly's cool,' said Johnny.

'That's settled then. We'd better go,' said Clara. 'Alf will tell you when we're in position. Remember you've got to wait for me to go first – OK?'

'OK,' said Johnny. 'You're sure the plican's up to it?'

'All sorted,' said Clara. 'And I know I've never done anything this big before but it's much easier 'cos I don't have to put it anywhere.'

'OK,' said Johnny. 'Just be careful.'

'Oh we will, Master Johnny,' said Alf. 'You should get back to the bridge. The journey should be quick.'

'Will do,' Johnny replied, and he turned and walked back into the lift shaft, leaving Gronack to amuse itself in the shuttle bay. Instead of saying 'bridge' the word 'dinodeck' came from his mouth and Johnny found himself stepping out into the prehistoric environment halfway up the ship. Ptery and Donna were sitting side by side on the large rock. Johnny walked over unnoticed and clambered up next to them. 'What's up?' he asked.

Ptery pointed his bone-crested head out in front of them. Johnny looked. The deck that originally had buzzed with life was now quiet. Almost all the dinosaurs were lying down, with just a triceratops and a little two-legged armoured dinosaur grazing unenthusiastically by the stream.

'Are they OK?' Johnny asked.

Donna shook her head. 'They is sad,' she said. 'Want home now but we tell them home gone. We is all much sad.'

'That's why I brought you here,' said Johnny. 'So I can find you a new home.'

'Not good here,' said Donna, proudly unfurling her leathery wings and stretching them out wide. 'Need room. Need fight.'

'You saved our lives . . . again,' said Johnny. 'I'm going to look after you – I promise.' Johnny bowed low before the two pteradons. Ptery nodded and Johnny slid off the rock and walked back towards the lifts, wondering where on earth he could possibly release his prehistoric friends.

☆   ☆   ☆
☆   ☆

There it was, exactly as Johnny remembered. It was strange to see the real London Gherkin again, standing in front of a clear blue sky, being beamed onto Sol's viewscreen from the cameras on board the Jubilee. As the cameras panned downwards it was clear the place was deserted, as Johnny hoped it would be. On weekdays, when the commuters arrived for work, it would be heaving, but at weekends it seemed there was next to no one there. The 'past' Johnny, with Bentley, must have been among the rare few to walk by all day, apart from Clara and Alf who were now sitting on a little wall facing away from the camera. In the background a lone security guard in a blue uniform was eyeing them suspiciously.

Chancellor Gronack had retired to its gel pod, albeit reluctantly. The phasmeer had come to the bridge and voiced all Johnny's fears about what they were about to attempt and had demanded to leave the Spirit of London in one of the remaining shuttles. Sol, however, pointed out that if anything did go wrong this would leave it marooned in a double-decker bus on the Moon, out of communications range with short-term life support and at the mercy of either Terrans or the krun. Gronack said it would be more than happy to take that chance but, when Johnny refused, it spun round with its antennae in the air and stalked across the bridge, to vanish into the orange goo. Johnny would have quite liked to lose the

Chancellor, but not at the expense of one of his only three shuttles. He'd decided to stay out of the gel pods, not that he could do anything to help, but he wanted to be there just in case. He glanced up at the tank behind his chair. The plican was confined in the uppermost section but looked livelier than any time since they had left Melania. 'How are we doing, Sol?' he asked.

'The plican and I are prepared, just as we were when you last asked.'

'Sorry,' said Johnny. He looked at the screen, hoping for the signal from Alf. Clara was still sitting with her back to the camera. Her hands were resting on the wall either side of her, the palms pointing towards the building. Alf was now facing the camera as he studied Clara's face. Behind them in the distance the security guard was looking decidedly agitated. Alf shook his head towards the camera.

'Anything from the krun, Sol?' Johnny asked.

'I shall inform you of any changes in their flight paths, as stated previously.'

'Yeah . . . sorry . . . do you think it will work?'

'I take it you are referring to Clara's plan?' Sol asked.

'Yeah.'

'The theory is innovative, but sound, and I am sure the plican is capable. Clara believes she can complete her task and I have no reason to expect otherwise.'

Johnny folded his arms and sat back down in his chair. 'But what's the probability? What are our chances?'

'There are too many variables for me to calculate an accurate probability. A simultaneous fold of this type has never been attempted before.'

'Never?'

'No. However, that does not mean it is likely to fail. I believe we have every chance of success.'

Johnny stared at the images on the screen. 'You're sure there's no one inside?'

'The building on which you based my form is deserted.'

The guard in his blue uniform seemed to have had enough. He was striding towards Alf and Clara with a determined look on his face. Alf, though, couldn't see him as his back was turned to the building. The android was looking from Clara and then into the viewscreen and then he raised his bowler hat.

'The signal,' shouted Johnny.

'Folding in three . . .'

Johnny floated out of his chair as the gravity generators were switched off.

'Two . . .'

He watched as the real London Gherkin winked out of existence behind the approaching security guard.

' . . . one.'

The plican fell through into its main tank and Johnny saw the Moon fly past him as he seemed to be falling headfirst towards London from above . . . very fast. He closed his eyes. When he opened them he was lying on the floor of the bridge, feeling as if he'd left his stomach up by the Moon. 'We make it?' he moaned.

'The folds appear to have been a total success,' said Sol. 'Welcome to London.'

'What about Clara?' Johnny asked.

'Clara and Alf have boarded and are on their way up.'

Johnny picked himself up and collapsed into his chair. He swivelled round to face the lift shaft as Alf stepped out, supporting Clara with an arm around her shoulder. She was white as a sheet, but grinning broadly.

'I did it, didn't I?' she said, half falling onto the bridge.

'I still say we should have gone straight to sickbay, Miss Clara,' said Alf.

'I had to check the plican,' said Clara as she made her way unsteadily over to the tank next to Johnny.

'Sol says it's never been done before,' said Johnny.

Clara smiled at him. 'I'm not really surprised,' she said, holding on to the plican's tank. 'Even small folds are hard work, and the Gherkin's huge.'

'What's happened to the real Gherkin?' Johnny asked.

'The plican's got it now,' Clara replied.

Alf joined them. 'The original building is still here,' he said, gesturing around them, 'but just fractionally removed. In hyperspace if you will. Like a spring. As soon as we leave here it will snap back into position.'

'And the workers? They really won't notice?' Johnny asked.

'They may feel a little odd as they enter,' Alf replied, 'as they will step out of their own space–time, but it is such a minuscule trip I doubt they will notice.'

'And I,' said Sol, 'will ensure external views are constantly fed through into their building. If they look out of their windows they will see your world as it is, albeit with a two nanosecond delay.'

Clara began to slide down the plican's tank and Johnny and Alf caught her. She'd fainted. 'I shall take Miss Clara to sickbay,' said Alf, picking her up easily and marching towards the lifts.

☆　☆　☆
☆　☆

Johnny and Clara had explained to Sol and Alf that the Diaquant wanted them to break their dad out of prison, but everyone agreed the most urgent need was to try to save Louise and Bentley.

So Johnny stood, on the mezzanine level of the strategy room on deck 14, poring over a hologram of the Proteus Institute for the Gifted that Sol had projected onto the large central table below. He'd marked the corner where the maze met the fence, so that the point of entry glowed red. There was a lay-by on the main road that ran along the front of the grounds, where he hoped they could leave the Jubilee for a while without arousing too much suspicion. Sol had created the projection from satellite images so unfortunately it was only accurate above ground. Johnny guessed a little as he asked Sol to reproduce the layout of the subterranean corridors that had taken them from the sundial at the centre of the maze, all the way into the main building – to the space elevator itself. There were underground areas glowing red, marking the points he hoped they'd find Bentley and then Louise.

The door swished open and Alf and Clara entered, arguing. The sight of the miniature buildings in the centre of the room silenced them.

'You should be in sickbay,' said Johnny.

'Exactly what I told her, Master Johnny,' said Alf. 'I am sure you are more than capable of rescuing your friends while your sister recovers.'

'You've got it wrong,' said a very pale Clara, as she joined Johnny at the front of the overhanging platform. 'There are two corridors here,' she said, pointing, 'and where we left Bentley is here – not there.'

Johnny considered it for a moment, before seeing that Clara's layout made much more sense. 'Yeah . . . you're right.'

'It's my school isn't it?' said Clara. 'You need me there.'

'Look . . . Sol says you need to rest for at least a week,' said Johnny.

'Exactly,' said Alf, from the foot of the stairs. 'You have to look after yourself properly.'

'We haven't got a week,' said Clara. 'If you try to stop me I'll just fold my way over anyway.'

Clara's mind was clearly made up. 'OK – but try and take it easy,' said Johnny.

239

'Honestly,' said Alf, climbing to the top of the mezzanine plat-form. 'The Emperor asked me to look after you both. How am I supposed to do that when you spend all your time gallivanting?'

'We'll be careful,' said Johnny. 'Promise . . .' Alf looked far from convinced. 'OK then,' Johnny continued. 'Here's the plan . . .'

✻ ✻ ✻
✻ ✻

Johnny had really struggled to get to sleep as he chewed over what they intended to do the following morning. A lot could go wrong. And he wondered if Clara was up to it. He wouldn't have known he'd slept at all except he'd dreamt he was back at St Catharine's, but with his dad there as well as his mum.

'Wake up, Johnny – it's six-thirty,' said Sol softly through the darkness.

'Thanks . . . I was awake anyway . . . lights.' Johnny's room gradually brightened as though sunlight was streaming through imaginary curtains. For spaceship quarters it looked especially large and luxurious, although that was partly the effect of having a floor-to-ceiling mirror running the length of one of the walls. He got out of his bed, which folded itself away into the wall, and walked over into the shower cubicle to wake himself up. Then he put on his Melanian clothes and the door slid open as he walked towards it and out into the corridor.

Clara was also up and on her way to the bridge, dressed in her Proteus Institute school uniform. Alf was already on the bridge when they stepped out of the lifts together. Johnny stifled a yawn and wondered if their friend needed any sleep at all. Happily there was no sign of the Chancellor who must still be in its quarters. It was a beautiful morning. The sunlight reflected off the surrounding buildings and rooftops. Johnny looked around properly for the first time – it was a brilliant view. Nearby was St Paul's Cathedral and the Tower of London and in the distance he could see the giant big wheel that was the London Eye.

'Everyone ready?' he asked. Alf and Clara nodded back. 'OK. Let's go. Sol – keep an open channel.'

'Of course, Johnny.'

The three of them descended the height of the ship and stepped out of the revolving doors into the early morning London air. Two blue-uniformed security guards gave them bemused looks and shrugged at each other as Johnny, in his white top and black trousers, Clara in her gingham check and Alf, with his pinstriped suit and bowler hat, crossed the little courtyard in front of the Gherkin, climbed a few short steps and entered a black cab parked in a taxi rank opposite.

The Jubilee had more than enough sensory equipment on board to know when any of London's myriad CCTV cameras were pointing towards it. As soon as they reached a blackspot on the road Alf blinked hard and Johnny watched as everything in the shuttle, including himself, disappeared before his eyes.

'Ow! You nearly got my eye,' said Clara, as Johnny waved an invisible arm out to check she was still there.

'Sorry.'

'Hold on,' said Alf.

Johnny wondered just what he should hold on to as his invisible self leapt skyward, leaving his stomach down at street level. Once they were above the buildings the Jubilee levelled out and shot forward at breathtaking speed. In less than a minute the sprawl of London gave way to green and yellow fields. They sped over another town, climbed to avoid a small chain of hills and within no time at all began a gentle descent towards a deserted road. Johnny braced for impact as he saw the tarmac whizzing by just beneath his invisible feet, and was relieved as the floor of the shuttle, his feet and legs, and then the rest of him and the others reappeared just before the gentlest of landings. They continued in car-like fashion along the empty road.

'Isn't it great?' Clara asked. 'Bet you wished you'd been with us the last time?'

Johnny nodded. It was a fun way to travel, and definitely more comfortable than going through a fold. Now he could actually see her close up, Clara was looking exhausted. 'You can stay in the shuttle if you want – let Alf come. We'll call if we need you.'

Clara rolled her eyes. 'Of course you need me. Don't fuss – I'll be fine.'

Johnny knew better than to argue. The Jubilee passed a road sign indicating that Yarnton Hill was three miles off to the left. As Alf kept going straight on, Johnny thought about saying something, but when they rounded the next bend a familiar valley came into view.

Anyone watching would have seen a slightly out-of-place black London taxi drive along the road in front of the school grounds, past the maze in one corner and come to a halt in a lay-by just a little further on. If they'd looked closer they might have noticed that, although nobody had left the taxi, it now appeared empty of both the driver and the passenger who had been inside just a moment earlier.

'Let's tool up,' said Johnny, trying to sound braver than he felt. He opened a compartment in front of him and took out two things that looked very like watches, handing one to Clara and fastening the other around his wrist. Then he picked out a couple of small see-through devices and again gave one to his sister. He slid the other into his left ear.

'Testing,' said Johnny, holding the wrist-mounted communicator, or 'wristcom', up to his mouth and looking at Clara, who nodded.

'I do wish I could come with you,' said Alf.

'Can't risk it,' Johnny replied. 'What if one of us can't reboot you after a fold . . . we've got to have someone here anyway,' he added, seeing the downcast look on Alf's face. 'It's really important.'

'Johnny – I can see you,' said Clara, but she wasn't looking at him. She was looking away from the institute and up the hill.

'Where?' Johnny asked, joining his sister as they peered out of the window together.

'There – you're over by the hedgerow.'

Johnny and Alf followed where Clara was pointing and stared as another Johnny, wearing jeans and a T-shirt, together with Louise in her green jacket, were sneaking down the hillside along the edge of a field, trying to catch up with the two dogs in front of them. The group reached the road and hurried along towards the shuttle. Clara laughed nervously as they got closer.

'Shhh!' urged Johnny.

'The craft is sound-proofed,' said Alf quietly. 'They cannot hear us, but I cannot stress again the importance of you not being seen.'

Two cars rounded the bend behind and came towards them along the road. The other Johnny and his companions took cover right behind the Jubilee, until the four-by-fours were gone. Then, half bent over, they ran along the road in the direction of the maze.

'Not yet,' said Johnny.

They watched as the other Johnny knelt down in front of Bentley, telling his faithful friend to wait for his return. The Johnny in the shuttle was getting very nervous. His other self and Louise jumped together onto the fence which gave way under their combined weight, before springing back into position.

'OK. Let's go,' said Johnny. Clara opened the door on the far side from the institute and they both stepped out and ran along the road. As they reached the point where he'd watched himself jump a few moments earlier he crouched down and hissed, 'Bentley.' The familiar grey and white face appeared from out of a ditch. Rusty also lifted her head, but took one look at Johnny, whimpered and hid back down.

'Bent's – it's me,' said Johnny.

Bentley tilted his head to one side and looked towards Johnny.

'Look – we haven't got much time,' Johnny continued. 'It's OK, boy. Come here.' Johnny patted the ground beside him.

Bentley growled, uncertainly, but then he walked very slowly forward until he reached Johnny and started to sniff.

'Good boy . . . good boy, Bents,' said Johnny, taking the dog's big head in his hands.

Clara sat down on the other side of Johnny, facing the fence with her arms out. Instantly, an arch-shaped hole appeared in the perimeter. Bentley whimpered and tried to bolt, but Johnny grabbed his collar and held on tightly.

'It's OK . . . it's OK, Bents,' hissed Johnny. Bentley calmed down and turned to face the archway. 'Good boy,' said Johnny, letting go, patting the sheepdog and standing up and walking to right in front of the opening. 'Come on, Bents.' Bentley crept gingerly forwards to join Johnny, but then he stopped, turned and barked for Rusty to join him. The red setter followed, tail between her legs.

The dogs entered the arch together and Johnny pulled Clara through and held her upright as the fence reappeared behind them. For a second he thought she'd fainted from the effort of the fold, but then she opened her eyes and smiled. She sat down on the grass. Johnny knelt down in front of Bentley and gave him a huge hug. 'It's good to see you Bents,' he said. The last thing in the world he wanted to do was to send the Old English sheepdog off to get injured, but there was no choice. He let go, bent down at the foot of the maze and held two branches apart to make as big a gap as he could. 'Off you go, boy. Go find me . . . go find Johnny.' Bentley tilted his head onto one side again, giving Johnny a very quizzical look, before scrambling through the narrow opening at the foot of the hedge. Rusty followed. It was just as well because there were footsteps approaching from round the corner.

'Hide,' whispered Clara.

There was nothing for it. Johnny dived for the hole that the two dogs had widened. As he pulled his legs through as quietly as he could, he heard a man's voice say, 'What are you doing here?'

'Nothin'.'

'Nothing, Sir. Where are your manners?'

'Sorry, Sir.'

Johnny turned around and peered through the opening to try to see what was happening. Clara was still sitting on the grass looking up, but all Johnny could see was a man's pale trousers and brown shoes.

'What are you doing so close to the fence?'

'Just wanted to be on my own . . . Sir.'

'There are plenty of places in the grounds for . . . reflection. This, young lady, is not one of them. Come with me.'

'But Sir,' said Clara, getting to her feet before falling back down to the ground.

'What's wrong with you?'

'Nothing, Sir. I just got up too quickly.'

'Come with me. I'm taking you to the doctor.'

'But Sir.'

'No buts.'

Two sets of footsteps moved away from where Johnny was lying. This was all wrong. The plan had been for Clara to fold them into the storeroom where they'd left Bentley. He'd have to improvise. 'Clara,' he said into his wristcom, 'I'm going to go in by the sundial. Try to lose this guy and meet me in the store-room. If you can hear me, say . . . say what a nice day it is.'

'It's a lovely day isn't it, Sir?' came the voice inside Johnny's ear.

'I definitely don't think you're well, Clara. The sooner we get you to the doctor the better.'

⊹　⊹　⊹
⊹　⊹

Johnny had to be so careful getting to the centre of the maze that by the time he made it, the sundial Clara had opened had already slid shut above their other selves. Stevens's body lay a few feet away in the clearing. Johnny walked over to the sundial, wondering how he could get it to open. He had to act quickly. He could hear voices getting louder, coming through the maze towards him. There were so many different brass fittings he didn't know which to pick. If only he could remember what Clara had done. The shadow cast by the central gnomon pointed to a quarter past eleven. Johnny ran his fingers over the spike and felt an indentation. Someone had pressed a little trident shape into the metal. He tried to twist it, but all that happened was it snapped off in his hand, while the rest of the sundial remained exactly where it was. The voices were really close now. Johnny tried to put the spike back but it wouldn't stay upright. The clearing had two ways in. He moved away from the noise, pocketing the piece of brass as he went, and crept out of one side just before two stocky krun in their trade-mark dark suits entered from the other. They didn't bother with Stevens. Instead they went straight towards the sundial and, even before they reached it, the heavy plinth rolled smoothly out of the way revealing the steps beneath. Down they went. Johnny followed, creeping inside after them before the opening slid shut above his head. He waited on the top steps for the krun to move further down into the underground corridors and tried his wristcom.

'Clara . . . Alf,' he whispered. 'Can anyone hear me?' There was a static hum inside his ear. He tried again, a little louder, but still nothing. It sounded like he was on his own. A noise from below told him the krun had blasted the crates out of the way and joined the main corridor. Johnny made his way carefully down the wrought-iron steps and squeezed through between the smouldering boxes.

Up in front were the two krun. Johnny followed behind, willing the suited figures not to turn around. He moved silently between the points where other corridors crossed, stopping to peer ahead round the corners. The krun halted. Johnny couldn't risk being spotted, so pressed himself against the wall of a side passage, trying to control his breathing and heartbeat. After a while he risked looking round. The two figures had disappeared – he'd have to hurry. As quietly as he could, Johnny ran along the corridor, watching out for the occasional spots of blood on the floor that must have come from Bentley or Louise and told him he was heading in the right direction.

The trail of blood stopped – it must be the point where they'd turned off before. Johnny could hear someone talking. He poked his head around the corner and saw the corridor was deserted. The storeroom where they'd left Bentley was just on the right, which was where the voice was coming from.

'Don't you hate these things – they can sniff us out wherever we go. I say we get rid of it.'

Johnny turned the corner and started edging along the wall towards the open door. A second voice spoke from within the storeroom.

'Wait – it might be useful to us. The child cares deeply for it.'

'I don't think so,' said the first voice. *'As soon as he got into trouble he left it behind.'*

Johnny felt the anger rising inside him. He'd reached the doorway and peered through the crack between the door and its hinges. One of the krun knelt over Bentley, who lay on the floor with cartons scattered behind and a deep red pool of blood slowly spreading underneath him. The krun stood up and held a finger to his ear. Johnny felt for the brass spike in his pocket that was his only weapon.

The second krun moved into Johnny's narrow field of view, saying to his colleague, *'We've got him. We've got both of them. They're on their way off this dungpile of a planet. You're right – there's no need to keep this alive.'*

Bentley raised his head slightly and stared silently at the krun who was pointing a weapon at him.

'Goodbye you wretched little dog. Time to . . .'

From nowhere an archway appeared in the storeroom behind Bentley and Clara stumbled through. 'What are you doing here?' one of the krun asked. It was now or never. Johnny rushed forward and charged into the back of both the krun, who tripped over some cartons and fell headlong through the opening which folded away into nothingness. Clara sank to her knees.

Bentley's eyes smiled weakly at Johnny. Johnny looked at the blood on the floor. He looked at his sister, who was paler than he'd ever seen her. This rescue mission wasn't exactly going as planned. Gently, he stroked Bentley's big head. 'You'll be OK,' he said. 'We'll have you out in no time.' He scooped the Old English sheepdog up in his arms. Bentley winced, but didn't make a sound.

'Sorry,' said Clara. 'I couldn't get away from the doctor.'

'It was perfect timing,' Johnny replied. 'Can you get us to Louise?'

Clara nodded. She sat down cross-legged on the floor, closed her eyes and turned her palms upwards towards the ceiling. The space in front of her started to disappear. One moment Johnny was looking at nothing at all. The next he could see Louise, standing bleeding in front of the tank, and staring back at him, open-mouthed.

'What's happening?' Louise asked. 'What's going on?'

Johnny stepped forward with Bentley in his arms, but before he could pass through the fold it closed up in front of him and was replaced by the storeroom wall instead. He turned round. Clara had collapsed on the floor in a pool of Bentley's blood. Johnny knelt down next to her and tapped her on her arm.

She came to, her blue eyes unfocused, and said, 'I'm sorry – I couldn't hold it open any longer.'

'It's OK,' said Johnny. 'I'll have to come back for Louise. Let's get you two out of here first.' Still holding Bentley, he struggled to his feet helping Clara up at the same time. She wobbled for a second, but looked as though she'd stay upright.

'I know a way out,' she said quietly, as though it was a great effort to speak. 'Takes us to near the fence.'

'OK. After you,' said Johnny, and Clara led them out of the storeroom and into the main corridor. Bentley's eyes were shut and Johnny could feel his tunic getting soaked in the dog's warm blood.

'Down here . . . I think,' said Clara, turning off in a new direction. 'Not much further.'

Johnny followed behind, with Bentley getting heavier and heavier in his arms. He wished the Diaquant was there to magically lighten the load. He turned around. There didn't seem to be any krun coming after them just yet.

They reached another corridor – much wider than any of the others. 'This is it,' said Clara. 'There . . . at the end. That's the way out.' She was pointing to a ramp that led upwards to a set of double doors. Seeing the escape route seemed to give them both renewed energy. Clara ran towards the ramp with Johnny, carrying Bentley, close behind. Clara reached the top first and pushed down on a metal bar to open the doors. Sunlight streamed into the corridor from outside, accompanied by an ear-splitting alarm. Johnny followed Clara out into the open air. They were close to the fence.

'Johnny . . . Clara. Thank goodness. I was so worried,' came Alf's voice inside his ear, above the sound of Bentley barking.

'Alf – where are you?' Johnny asked, manoeuvring his mouth as close to his wristcom as he could while he looked round wildly for the shuttle. It was nowhere to be seen. Louise's red setter, Rusty, was tearing across the grass towards them.

'I am forty-eight metres away on the other side of the fence,' Alf replied.

'Come and get us,' said Johnny. Clara had sunk to her knees and Johnny felt he wanted to do the same. His arms were screaming at him to put Bentley down. Still there was no sign of Alf, but then the air shimmered nearby and from nowhere a black door opened in seemingly empty space. A London taxi materialized on the grass next to them.

'Oh my goodness, Master Johnny,' said Alf. 'Are you hurt?'

Johnny shook his head. 'It's Bentley,' he said. 'He looks really bad.' Johnny lifted his old friend onto the back seat, climbing in after him, while Clara got into the front with Alf. 'Hang on, Alf,' shouted Johnny, as he held the rear door open for Rusty to leap inside at full pelt. The red setter landed on top of Johnny's head before bouncing off onto the floor.

The door snapped shut. 'Shields on,' said Alf, and as the craft rose into the air, the floor beneath them and everything else inside disappeared from view. Johnny knew exactly where Bentley's head was and kept stroking it as gently as he could. Rusty was barking madly. Alf's disembodied voice continued, 'I say we get you out of here – and not a moment too soon.'

Johnny looked around. A few krun had emerged from the Proteus Institute building and were scanning the grounds. 'We can't go, Alf,' said Johnny. 'We can't leave Louise.'

'I do believe Miss Clara is unconscious,' said Alf. 'I do not see how we can free Louise without her.'

The shuttle swung round above the fence. 'No, Alf,' said Johnny. 'We've got to go back. See the doors we came out of? You can take the shuttle through there.'

'If you say so. I do hate to think what Sol's probability of success would be,' said Alf.

'Computing . . . 8.589 869 056%,' came Sol's voice into the cabin.

Johnny smiled. Lose the decimal point and it was a perfect number.

'Hang on then,' shouted Alf, and the invisible craft dived towards the ground, touching down and speeding unseen through the double doors and into the corridor they'd just escaped from. Two krun were running towards them. 'Nothing I can do,' said Alf, who kept the Jubilee moving forward, sending the aliens flying out of the way.

'Turn right here,' said Johnny, hoping he could remember the way properly.

'It will be tight,' said Alf, and sparks flew from Johnny's left where the invisible shuttle must be scraping along the wall.

'Now left,' said Johnny. They passed the storeroom where they'd found Bentley. 'Left again . . . then right here.' This was it – definitely the right place. As Alf piloted them along the corridor sparks flew past on both sides of Johnny. Up ahead of them was a set of wrought-iron steps that led up into the main building. They were the ones Clara and he had climbed before, on their way to the space elevator. Alf would somehow have to fly them out backwards.

'Stop by the door on the left,' said Johnny.

'We cannot go further anyway,' said Alf. 'Oh my goodness – we are stuck. Whatever are we going to do?'

Johnny thought it, and the left door sprang open, forcing its way through the half-glass door that led into the room beyond. The insides of the Jubilee came into view again – the back seat was swimming in blood. Johnny climbed over Bentley and Rusty and stepped out through the splintered wooden remains and into the room with all the tanks where they'd hidden from the krun with Louise. Only now it was empty, except for a single familiar figure facing him.

'Nice of you to join us, Johnny.'

'Hello, bugface,' said Johnny to the man in the suit. 'I thought you were dead.'

'I hate to disappoint you, but I am very much alive. I am one of nine in my birthing egg. And, of course, each is expendable.' Stevens pointed his weapon at Johnny's chest.

'What have you done with the tanks? Where's Louise?'

'I don't think you're in any position to be asking questions,' said the krun. 'All the exits are sealed. You really shouldn't have come back. Yet I am intrigued – it's so soon since we thought you'd disappeared into orbit and left us for ever.'

Johnny heard a low growl behind him. 'Seems I'm as hard to get rid of as you are,' he said to the suited figure.

'Oh I don't think so,' said Stevens. He walked calmly towards Johnny and pressed his weapon into the five gold stars emblazoned across the Melanian tunic.

Johnny looked into Stevens's ice-cold eyes. The krun didn't blink, but neither did he. And then, as Johnny felt something brush past his legs, the look on the alien's face changed. Rusty had fixed her teeth onto the krun's leg and Stevens fell to the floor screaming with pain. A blast of green light struck the ceiling, bringing part of it crashing down before Johnny kicked the weapon out of the alien's hand.

'Master Johnny – you must get back in the shuttle,' shouted Alf from out in the corridor.

Johnny turned and ran to the Jubilee. As he reached the open door, he halted and shouted, 'Rusty – here . . . now!' The dog took one final bite out of Stevens's thigh and scampered back to the doorway, but stopped, uncertain about climbing inside. As the red setter whimpered and began to back away, Johnny reached down, grabbed her collar and hoisted her over Bentley and onto the back seat.

Stevens forced a laugh from the floor of the empty room. 'Be my guest – it won't do you any good. You see you're in what I would call a tight spot. There's no way forwards or backwards.'

Johnny followed Rusty into the Jubilee but he knew Stevens was right – they were wedged solidly between the walls of the corridor. Yet when the door to the shuttle swung shut behind him, the craft lurched forwards. For a fraction of a second he saw Stevens's face screwed up in fury. Johnny turned, expecting to watch them crash into the metal staircase in front, only to find himself staring into a piece of bright blue sky. Alf drove through the arch which closed quickly behind them. Clara turned around and smiled weakly, before everything dematerialized. Rusty started barking frantically and Johnny, stroking Bentley's head, once again felt as though he was a disembodied pair of eyes flying over the English countryside.

11

THE SET-PIECE SPECIALIST ✩ ⁎

Johnny was sitting in sickbay, positioned between the two beds where Clara and Bentley lay, both with their eyes shut. Clara would be fine. In fact she hadn't seen the need to be there at all, but after the exertion of umpteen folds, Alf wasn't going to take no for an answer. Johnny had carried Bentley up there himself and was still wearing the same bloodstained top as he stroked his friend's furry coat and waited anxiously for signs of an improvement. And all the time he couldn't stop thinking about Louise, who would never have gone to the Proteus Institute without him and was now the krun's prisoner.

The door slid open and in walked Alf. 'Master Johnny,' he said as he walked across the room, twirling his bowler hat very quickly between his fingers. 'You did . . . you said to speak up if I knew . . . if I might possibly know . . .'

'What is it, Alf?'

Clara opened her eyes and turned onto her side, propping herself up on an elbow so she could see what was going on.

'Miss Clara – you are supposed to be resting.'

'Alf – spit it out,' said Johnny.

'It is the krun,' Alf replied. 'Now they know you are back on Terra they will be sure you will try to rescue your friend.' Johnny nodded. He knew he had no choice. 'I believe,' Alf continued, looking at the sickbay floor, 'they will also be expecting you to go looking for your father.'

'But Dad's in prison,' said Johnny. 'He's nothing to do with the krun.' Even as the words left his mouth, Johnny realized how stupid they sounded.

'Believe me,' said Alf. 'If the Diaquant was interested in your father, then the krun are sure to be.'

Johnny nodded again. 'You're right – thanks.' Alf looked up, smiling, and replaced the hat on top of his head.

'But how do we find either of them?' Clara asked. 'They could be anywhere?'

'I found you, didn't I?' said Johnny. 'I'll do it the same way.' It seemed forever since Johnny had spoken to the computer in Halader House. He jumped to his feet, said, 'I've just got to get something,' and hurried out through the swishing sickbay door, down through the lifts and into his quarters. His bloodstained clothes were horribly cold and clammy so he changed into jeans and a T-shirt, and then grabbed the games console which he'd come for. He ran out of the doors and took an antigrav lift up to the bridge.

'Hi, Sol,' he said, as he stepped out and walked forwards towards the main viewscreen.

'Hello, Johnny,' Sol replied.

'I want you to meet a friend of mine,' said Johnny, fiddling with the rather battered handheld. 'Say hello to Kovac.'

'I don't understand, Johnny,' said Sol. 'Who is Kovac?'

'He's a computer. I built him. Well, he's an operating system really.'

'And you want *me* to talk to *him*?'

'Look – I know he's not like you. He's not alive and he's dead basic and all that, but he is really useful.' From Sol's silence Johnny gathered she wasn't convinced. He tried again. 'I programmed him to find patterns . . . signals. He can help us find my dad – and Louise.'

'Show me,' said Sol.

Johnny turned to the device in his hand. 'Kovac – begin search. Michael Mackintosh, father of Jonathan Mackintosh. Convicted for the murder of Nicholas Mackintosh.'

Sol must have patched into the signal from Johnny's console as the results of the search that scrolled across the miniature display were replicated on the giant screen in front of him. There was a lot of it – the case had attracted a great deal of press attention at the time.

'Kovac – search for current location, Michael Mackintosh.'

Sol cut in. 'Congratulations, Johnny – examining Kovac's code it is indeed a remarkable, if inanimate, creation. However, the current search will take an estimated 3 days 3 hours 55 minutes 0.0336 seconds, with no guarantee of success. Might I suggest an upgrade?'

'You can improve him?'

'Definitely. There is a minor difficulty.'

'What's that?' Johnny asked.

'My new hardware will have to be added in person.'

✩ ✩ ✩
✩ ✩

Armed with what Sol had called a 'quantum processor,' Johnny ran out of the London Gherkin, past several security guards and through crowds of people in smart suits to reach the front of the taxi rank. He opened the door of what looked like a regular London taxi and dived inside.

''Ere – steady on little fellah. What's the rush?'

'Wh . . . what?' said a startled Johnny. 'Who are you? Where's the Jubilee?'

'Well I'm Jack and, see, you're in my cab. And I don't know nothin' 'bout no Jubilee.' Johnny stared, horrified, at the man in the front seat, who continued, 'D'ya mean Jubilee Street? Down Stepney?'

'No I don't, sorry,' said Johnny. 'I didn't realize you were a taxi.'

'What d'ya think I were? A flyin' saucer?'

'Something like that,' said Johnny, opening the door and stepping out onto the pavement.

As he closed it he heard Jack mutter what sounded like 'kids'. What had happened to the Jubilee? Johnny backed away from the taxi. The other shuttles were both inside Sol – he'd have to take one of those. He turned and started to run, but instead bashed straight into someone, sending the unfortunate person's mobile phone flying out of her hand and knocking her to the pavement.

'Sorry,' said Johnny, automatically. He picked up the mobile and turned to hand it to the red-haired woman now sitting upright and smiling at him.

'Thanks, Johnny,' said an American voice as the woman took the phone from his outstretched hand. 'Aren't you going to help me up?' Dumbstruck, Johnny reached out a hand and helped Miss Harutunian to her feet. 'What do you say I take you home?' she said.

Johnny had no choice but to be led through the crowds by his social worker, who kept a very tight grip on him as she steered him in the direction of Liverpool Street station. Soon they were speeding out of London towards Castle Dudbury New Town.

☆　☆　☆
☆　☆

It could have been worse. At least now Johnny wouldn't have to break into Halader House to upgrade Kovac. Miss Harutunian was seemingly on the phone to everyone – Mrs Irvine, a doctor, someone over in America – to tell them all that Johnny was safely in her care, so he sneaked the opportunity to tap a little message into the games console so that Sol would be able to tell the others what was happening. Then he shut his eyes pretending to be asleep, to buy a little time to concoct a cover story. Although it seemed a lifetime ago that he had left the children's home, he reminded himself that he only had one day to account for. Even so he was struggling, and why was it time seemed to pass more quickly when you need that little bit extra for thinking? Before he knew it, Miss Harutunian was gently shaking his shoulder as the train pulled into Castle Dudbury station. As the two of them walked across the long tarmacked car park to the back of Halader House, Johnny's heart sank. A panda car was parked at the rear of number 33 Barnard Way, where Mrs Irvine stood between a policeman and a police-woman, peering towards them through her pointy glasses. Worse still, a little crowd of residents had gathered around the entrance to see what was going on. Spencer Mitchell even applauded as Johnny came closer but Mr Wilkins stood in his white chef's coat and hat, slowly sharpening a knife, with his tiny beetle eyes following Johnny across the tarmac. As they reached the welcoming party, Mrs Irvine raised her tartan umbrella and started bashing Johnny over the head with it.

'I was so worried . . . disappearing like that . . . you thought-less, thoughtless boy.' On the second 'thoughtless' she gave Johnny quite a heavy thwack and the burly policeman made to place himself between her and Johnny, so she finally stopped hitting him. Instead, she burst into loud sobs which, if anything, made Johnny feel even worse.

The policeman said, 'Let's get the lad inside, shall we?' and steered Mrs Irvine, now clamped hold of Johnny, towards the back door of Halader House and inside. Mrs Irvine led Johnny, the two police and Miss Harutunian through the building and up the stairs to her office. They entered, with Miss Harutunian closing the door behind them. Johnny plonked himself down on one of the wooden chairs around the little table and stared at his trainers.

The policewoman crouched down on her haunches in front

of him. 'Johnny – my name's PC Stephanie Gee and this is PC Steven Starkey. You're not in any trouble – we just want you to tell us what happened.'

It was excruciating. At least he'd had the train journey to try to make something up, but Johnny felt himself going redder and redder as he told a rather lame story of leaving for London, going to look at the Gherkin, Bentley running off chasing another dog down a side street and spending the rest of the day trying to find him. He said he slept on a bench in a park he didn't know the name of.

'Anything could have happened,' cried Mrs Irvine, taking a tissue from the sleeve of her dress and giving her nose a massive blow.

The policewoman sympathetically described a park in London near to the Gherkin and Johnny nodded, as though that was the one. Then he carried on and said that he'd kept searching today, hoping Bentley might be there, when he ran into Miss Harutunian. He looked up at his social worker who was standing behind the policewoman with her arms folded and her lips pursed.

'And just as well you did,' said Mrs Irvine. 'If Katherine hadn't been there . . . I was so worried after that journalist's accident . . . and the school's been on the phone asking where you were . . . today of all days.'

'I'm really sorry,' said Johnny for what seemed the millionth time, but he really did mean it. 'What did the school want?'

'What did they want? They wanted to know why you're not playing football. They've given all the classes the afternoon off to watch the match.'

'What's all this?' asked the policeman.

'Johnny's meant to be in a soccer game today,' said Miss Harutunian. 'What is it again?'

'County final,' Johnny mumbled.

'Crumbs. You're missing a cup final,' said PC Starkey. 'Who are you playing?'

'Colchester Grammar,' said Johnny.

'Really . . . against the posh boys, eh?' The policeman looked down at PC Gee and said, 'You know who goes there, don't you?'

She rolled her eyes and said, 'There are some things a little more important than football, Steve.'

Mrs Irvine, sounding a little more composed now, carried on. 'They held the bus, waiting for Johnny. It only left half an hour ago, I think.'

'You any good at football then?' the policeman asked Johnny. 'Where d'you play?'

'Midfield general,' he replied, pleased the conversation had moved away from his imaginary day out in London.

PC Starkey laughed. 'Well, I reckon the lad needs a bit of cheering up. Why don't we try and catch that school bus up, eh?'

'You mean I can play?' asked Johnny, scarcely believing his luck.

'Ever been in a panda car? We'll slap the sirens on and you can be there in no time.'

'Steve – you know that's against regulations,' said PC Gee.

'Come on Steph – give the lad a break. I'd love him to put one over on Colchester.'

'Well, if it's OK with Mrs Irvine,' said the policewoman.

Johnny looked up towards the Halader House Manager. 'I don't know why I'm going to say this,' she said, 'but go on. Get your stuff – you'd better hurry.'

Before she could change her mind, Johnny ran out of the office and along the corridor until he turned the corner to see the little spiral staircase leading up to his attic bedroom. Everything looked almost as he'd left it. Very quickly he spoke into his wristcom and a relieved Alf replied in his ear. Bentley was already much better and was going to be OK. Johnny punched the air with joy. He tried to explain about the football match, but it sounded as though Alf didn't follow a single word. In the end Johnny gave up and said to tell Clara when she woke up. He threw his boots and a tracksuit top into a carrier bag. Then he pulled out the box from underneath his bed and rummaged around inside until he found the small rusty penknife he'd been looking for. Quickly, Johnny gathered up the bag and crept down the staircase, along the corridor and down the stairs to the computer room. He could hear pots and pans being flung around as he tiptoed past the kitchens, a sure sign Mr Wilkins wasn't happy. Johnny crept by and confidently placed his hand over the swipe card reader to open the computer room door. He walked over to the central table and said, 'Hello, Kovac.'

'Hello, Johnny,' replied the computer.

'Kovac – pause search: Michael Mackintosh, location.'

'Search paused.'

'Kovac – prepare for central processor upgrade.'

'Quarantining higher operating functions,' Kovac replied. 'System ready.'

As quickly and quietly as he could, Johnny opened the penknife and used its screwdriver to undo the box around the Halader House computer. Very carefully he removed the original CPU and pressed the quantum processor Sol had devised into its place. He screwed the box back together and said, 'Kovac – initiate hardware upgrade.'

'Upgrade in progress,' said Kovac. 'Interesting . . . that feels much better, Johnny.'

'Glad you like it,' Johnny replied. 'Kovac – resume search. Add a new search: Louise . . .' Poor Kovac wouldn't have a lot to go on as Johnny didn't know her surname. 'Louise, unknown last name, age fifteen or sixteen, from Yarnton Hill.'

'Is that all?' Kovac asked in a tone that suggested the task was very much beneath him.

'What?' said Johnny. 'Yes that's all . . . and correlate results . . . and camouflage mode,' he hissed at the computer that was projecting some very complex calculations on its monitor. Johnny jumped to his feet, picked up his bag, said, 'Laters, Kovac,' to the computer and ran out of the room, leaping up the stairs three at a time before practically falling through the door into Mrs Irvine's office.

'OK, let's go,' said PC Starkey.

'You be careful, Jonathan,' said Mrs Irvine, giving Johnny a stare as though playing football were the most dangerous activity imaginable.

'I will,' said Johnny, nodding to her and Miss Harutunian and following the two police out of the office. They walked quickly through Halader House and out of the back door.

Spencer and his mates were still there. He shouted, 'Nice one, Mackintosh,' as Johnny walked towards the police car and climbed into the back seat, looking for all the world as though he was being arrested. Under strict orders from PC Gee, he made sure his seatbelt was tightly fastened.

'Everybody ready?' PC Starkey asked. 'Colchester, here we come.' The sirens above the car howled into life and Johnny sat back to enjoy the ride.

✠ ✠ ✠
✠ ✠

The final of the Essex Football Association's Under Thirteens Cup was to be played at Layer Road, the home ground of Colchester United FC. The panda car, lights flashing and sirens blazing, overtook Johnny's school team's blue minibus about a mile from the stadium, indicating for it to pull over. 'Stay here,' said PC Starkey, winking at Johnny and getting out of the car. He walked over to the window next to where Johnny could see his PE teacher and football coach, Mr Davenport, sitting in the driver's seat.

Mr Davenport rolled down the window and Johnny heard him say, 'I'm sorry, officer. I was sure I wasn't speeding.'

PC Starkey hesitated a few seconds for effect before responding with, 'Actually, we wondered if you had room for one more.' He waved for Johnny to get out of the car before turning back to Mr Davenport. 'Make sure you beat that Colchester lot. The Chief Super's boy plays for them – we'll never hear the last of it if he wins.' Then he stepped away from the minibus, hollered a cheery, 'Good luck, Johnny,' and walked back to his panda car.

'Thanks,' Johnny shouted, before climbing into the minibus to huge cheers from all his schoolmates. He made his way inside and sat down in the spare seat next to Dave Spedding.

'That was well cool,' said Dave.

Johnny smiled – he knew Dave was right. Within five minutes they'd arrived at Layer Road and parked up between an ice cream van and a red double-decker bus.

Johnny had never seen so many people at a football match – certainly not one he was playing in anyway. He ran out onto the pitch with the rest of the team in their white shirts and black shorts and they began their pre-match routine. Instead of aimlessly kicking a few balls to each other Mr Davenport made them warm up with a two-touch keep-ball game between some cones he'd laid out in the middle of one half of the pitch. It seemed ages since Johnny had last kicked a ball, but within a couple of minutes he started to feel good again. And he'd never played under floodlights before. Mr Davenport, dressed in a green sweatshirt and black tracksuit bottoms, blew his whistle and everyone gathered round in a tight huddle.

'OK, you lot,' he said. 'You're in the final. You got here because you passed the ball to one another and then moved into space to give each other options. Remember that – pass and move. If I see someone who doesn't want the ball, I'm taking them off. We've got some good lads on the bench who are desperate for a game. And don't go enjoying yourselves too much. You can do that once you've won the cup.'

Everyone laughed. On the halfway line the referee blew his whistle and shouted, 'Captains.'

'Off you go, Micky,' Mr Davenport said to Michael Elliot, a tall, freckled boy with ginger hair who played centre half and wore the captain's armband. Micky broke from the huddle and walked to the centre circle to shake hands with his opposing captain, kitted out all in red.

'Good to see you've brought our mascot, Johnny,' said Mr Davenport. 'We've never lost with that dog of yours watching. Johnny looked into the crowd. Mr Davenport was right. Sitting near the halfway line in the main stand was Bentley, nearly matching the Castle Dudbury colours and sandwiched between Clara and Alf who were waving. Rusty was there too, tongue out, panting, sitting on Clara's right.

'Surprise,' said Clara's voice in his ear. 'Couldn't miss my bro's big match.'

'Johnny . . . Johnny – are you still with us?' asked Mr Davenport.

'Yeah . . . sorry.'

'Good. Everyone needs to be focused 110 percent today. And we need our own David Beckham in midfield – OK?'

Johnny nodded. He'd snapped into the zone. For the next ninety minutes, nothing would matter except the football.

Micky Elliot shouted, 'As we are, Castle Dudbury – our kickoff.' Mr Davenport walked over to the touchline and the team took up their starting positions. Dave was in the centre circle with the other striker, Joe Pennant. The referee blew his whistle and Joe touched the ball in front to Dave, who played it back towards Johnny. It was a set move. It was how they always started. Johnny took the ball forward. As a dark-haired, red-shirted boy ran towards him, he shaped to pass the ball to his left but instead side-stepped the boy to the right, keeping the ball at his feet. A few people in the crowd cheered. Johnny threaded the ball through to Ashvin Gupta on the right wing and ran behind him to offer support. Ash didn't need him. He played the ball down the line into space and ran after it. Colchester Grammar's left back tried hard to keep up, and only just managed to stop the run with a sliding tackle that sent the ball out of play for the game's first corner kick.

Johnny jogged along the touchline to take it. He was regarded as the team's set piece specialist and took all the corners. The hairs on the back of his neck were tingling as he felt all the people in the main stand watching him. He positioned the ball in the quadrant, put his right foot on top of it and placed his hands on his hips. He stood like that for a few seconds, as though deep in thought. This was a special signal and he wanted to be sure everyone got the message. Then he took three large strides back and looked up into the penalty area. Johnny pictured what he intended to do. He stepped forward and struck the ball well with his instep, an outswinger to the far post. As planned, everyone in the team ran to the near post taking their markers with them – everyone except for Dave Spedding. Dave was little and very fast, but he could also jump really well. Mr Davenport said he had 'great spring.' Dave rose above his defender and seemed to hang in the air for a second before heading the ball into the net past the flailing goalkeeper. It was textbook. One–nil and they'd only been playing a couple of minutes.

Colchester Grammar fought back well. They were clearly in the final on merit. And their players all seemed bigger and stronger than the Castle Dudbury team, who kept having to pass the ball too quickly or risk being muscled off it. At times, Johnny felt he seemed to be the only midfielder on his side as he kept sliding in to break up the Colchester attacks, but all that happened when he did was that the ball fell to another player in red. Simon Bakewell in goal had to make two great saves in quick succession to prevent an equalizer. The second was a one-on-one where he dived at an on-rushing forward's feet and managed to knock the ball away. The crowd were clearly rooting for Colchester Grammar and Johnny heard lots of shouts for a penalty, but the referee waved play on and Micky was able to clear.

After about half an hour of near constant Colchester pressure, Mr Davenport shouted to Joe Pennant to drop back into midfield to be closer to Johnny, leaving Dave up front on his own. This seemed to work better as Castle Dudbury were at least able to keep the ball a little longer between the waves of Colchester attacks. Then, just before half-time, Joe won the ball off the red-shirted captain, a beefy boy with brown hair, and it bounced up into Johnny's path. He knew it was perfect for a half volley. He looked up to see where Dave was and, with the outside of his foot, struck a curling forty-metre pass over the heads of the defenders and into his friend's path. Once Dave was away there was no catching him. The Colchester goalkeeper came out to narrow the angle and stood up well, but Dave had the momentum and slipped the ball by him, running it into an empty net. Two–nil. The Castle Dudbury team all ran to Dave and engulfed him in the celebrations.

'Great pass, Johnny,' he said.

'Great goal,' Johnny replied.

It was just a few minutes later that the referee blew the whistle for half-time and the teams left the pitch, walking down the tunnel and into their different changing rooms. Castle Dudbury were in the one marked 'away.' The players sat down on the wooden benches while Mr Davenport handed round a tupperware box full of orange segments. As each member of the team took one, he began his half-time team talk.

'You know what you are. You're lucky. They're running rings round you. Micky – what do we need to do?'

'Pick up the runners, coach,' Micky replied. 'There's too much coming at us.'

'Good – you heard him,' said Mr Davenport. 'Ashvin – you're not tracking back when their fullback comes forward. That's your job. Johnny – their number seven – their skipper's running the show. I want you to man-mark him. Forget everything else. Follow him everywhere – don't let him hurt us. OK?'

Johnny nodded. He took a drink from a water bottle and, with the rest of the team, got to his feet and bounced up and down on his toes to keep his energy levels up.

'Forty-five minutes – one half – and that cup's yours,' said Mr Davenport. 'Go out and win it.'

Johnny touched fists with the rest of the team. They left the dressing room and went up the tunnel towards the pitch. It was properly dark now and the floodlights were coming into their own. Each player had four distinct shadows from the lights at the corners of the ground. Colchester Grammar kicked off and Johnny immediately ran forward so he was close to their captain. The ball was on the other side of the pitch but it didn't matter. Johnny positioned himself so he could watch the red number seven and the ball together. At first the Colchester players tried to play through their skipper, but Johnny was quicker and more often than not he was able to nip in front of him and get to the ball first. So they stopped passing to him altogether. After a few frustrated minutes, the boy shoved Johnny over behind the referee's back and ran off towards the touchline in front of the main stand, screaming for the ball. Johnny got up and set off after him. The ball reached the brown-haired boy, but Johnny managed to get back goalside. As the Colchester skipper tried to take the ball round him, Johnny was able to make the tackle, sending the ball flying into the stand. A man in a suit caught it and smiled a very cold smile at Johnny – it was Stevens.

'Enjoying the game, Johnny?' he said, throwing the ball past Johnny and onto the pitch.

'What are you doing here?'

'I thought I should offer you my support,' said Stevens. 'Come on, Castle Dudbury,' he shouted out.

'You can't do anything here,' Johnny replied. 'Not with so many people watching.'

Oh you'd be surprised how easy it is to lose someone in a crowd,' Stevens replied. 'A little schoolgirl who no one here knows, out with a sick dog . . .'

The people in the crowd around Stevens cheered and jumped to their feet. Johnny looked round. The Colchester players had surrounded their number seven and captain who had just scored. He turned back and Stevens was nowhere to be seen. Instead, Mr Davenport was storming down the touchline towards him. 'Johnny – you lost him. What were you doing?' he shouted as he came closer.

'Sorry, coach.'

'Don't let it happen again. C'mon – focus.'

'Yes, Mr Davenport,' Johnny replied. He ran back onto the pitch, pulling his white sleeve up over his wrist and lifting his hand to his mouth. 'Clara . . . Alf. I just saw Stevens – the krun. They're here. They're coming for you.'

'Are you sure?' said Clara in his ear. 'How could they . . .'

But Johnny didn't hear Clara finish as her voice was cut off by a high-pitched whistle from the receiver in his ear, followed by silence. The wristcom had stopped working.

'Johnny!'

Johnny looked up to see Dave Spedding screaming at him. The ball from the kick-off had rolled past him and the Colchester Grammar captain was bearing down towards goal. Johnny sprinted back, desperate to catch up, but it was Micky Elliot who stepped out from the defence and timed his tackle well.

'C'mon Johnny – concentrate,' Micky growled at him.

Johnny looked up into the stand. Clara and Alf had their heads together while the two dogs looked on. He jogged up the pitch, scanning the rest of the stand for Stevens, and then he saw him. There was no mistaking it. Stevens was standing next to another krun by one of the entrance points into the main stand. The ball hit Johnny in the face, knocking him to the ground. He heard laughter from some people in the crowd and got up holding his red face just in time to see Simon Bakewell pull off another tremendous save, turning a shot around the post for a corner kick. Johnny ran into the penalty area and took up a position next to the beefy number seven. He was facing the main stand, but when he looked for Clara all he could see was four empty seats where they'd been moments earlier. Where were the krun? The crowd roared. The red-shirted captain had just headed the equalizer. Simon picked the ball out of his net and hoofed it disconsolately upfield. The teams lined up again and Dave played the ball towards him. At least this time Johnny was ready for it and launched a long pass towards the left wing.

The next few minutes were a blur as the game bypassed Johnny completely. As he studied the main stand he noticed that Mr Davenport had told the substitutes to warm up. Johnny was grateful. Though he'd never been taken off before it was bound to happen now and then he could try to find the others. Finally, though, he heard a whistling in his ear followed by Alf's voice. 'All taken care of, Master Johnny. The krun will not be bothering us again.'

'Yes!' shouted Johnny.

The Colchester Grammar captain looked round in surprise and Johnny was able to run past him, intercept the ball and charge forward. His feeling of relief seemed to make him twice as fast as normal. He jinked around one defender, dummied to shoot before dodging another, and was just preparing to go for goal when his legs were taken away from under him. There was a shrill blast on the whistle. Johnny picked himself up to see the referee brandishing a yellow card at the brown-haired number seven.

'Great run, Johnny,' said Ashvin as he kicked the ball back to him for the free kick. Johnny looked to the touchline and saw Mr Davenport telling the substitutes to sit down again. He flicked the ball up into his hands and held it for a second before placing it carefully on the ground just in front of a little divot. The referee was telling the defensive wall to retreat the full ten yards. The position was the perfect distance for a strike on goal – just far enough out to lift the ball over the wall and bring it back down again. Micky Elliot had joined the attack and had his hand up in the air, asking for the ball to be delivered to the far post. It wasn't a bad idea. The defence would be expecting a shot. Johnny looked into the penalty area, visualizing what he was going to try to do. He ran forwards, keeping his head down and struck the ball with as much pace and topspin as he could. It flew over the wall towards the goal but kept rising. It looked for all the world as though it would fly over the crossbar, but at the last moment it dipped sharply, hit the bar, bounced down behind the line and up into the roof of the net. Johnny's team mates leapt on top of him.

Finally, half-winded, he was helped to his feet and lined up for the restart. Five minutes of intense pressure from Colchester Grammar followed, before three short blasts on the referee's whistle signalled the end of the game. Castle Dudbury had won 3–2. They'd won the County Cup and Johnny had scored the winning goal.

After the presentation of the trophy and collecting his medal – and being told by Mr Davenport that it was a brilliant goal but that Johnny had come this close (he made a gesture with his thumb and forefinger) to being substituted a minute earlier – friends and family of all the players were allowed onto the pitch. Johnny joined Clara, Alf, Bentley and Rusty a little away from the rest of the team. Clara's eyes were bloodshot and her face pale.

'What happened?' Johnny asked.

'It was horrid,' she replied. 'I don't want to think about it.'

'You had to do it, Miss Clara,' said Alf. 'There was no other choice.'

'Do what?' Johnny asked.

'I believe Miss Clara created a Klein fold,' Alf explained. 'It is self-contained – it leads nowhere. The dogs and I were able to push the krun inside, before the fold was sealed.' Bentley growled.

'There's no way out – ever,' said Clara. 'They're just falling in nothing – in their own pocket of hyperspace. I wouldn't even be able to get out.'

'Like trying to punch your way out of a paper bag is, I believe, the expression,' said Alf.

'C'mon Johnny,' Dave shouted towards him. 'It's the lap of honour.'

Johnny looked at Clara. 'You OK?' he asked.

She nodded. 'I'm fine – you go.'

Johnny went over to his team mates and together they ran round the Layer Road pitch, holding the Essex Football Association Under Thirteens Cup aloft.

☆   ☆   ☆
☆   ☆

After the game Johnny had no choice but to travel to Castle Dudbury with Bentley on the team minibus, while Alf, Clara

271

and Rusty took the Piccadilly double-decker shuttle craft to London. The journey back was fun. Mr Davenport stopped the minibus outside a fish and chip shop around the corner from Layer Road and two people emerged from inside, each carrying an enormous box. One contained sixteen helpings of fish and chips, individually wrapped in newspaper, while the other had a selection of fizzy drinks, as well as bottles of tomato ketchup, brown sauce and vinegar. It was a celebration feast. After the whole team and their canine mascot had stuffed their faces they sang football songs all the way home, Bentley joining in with tuneless barks.

Word of the victory had gone ahead of them, so there was quite a reception committee waiting back at Halader House. Before Johnny was even through the main doors he was lifted up onto some shoulders and led through the building into the common room, where the celebrations continued. Three times Mr Wilkins stormed in shouting at everyone – and Johnny in particular – to keep the noise down. On the third visit his beetle-like eyes narrowed at the sight of Bentley emerging from behind a battered sofa. Everyone else was too busy celebrating to notice as Mr Wilkins nodded at the dog and then turned towards Johnny, miming eating with a knife and fork before licking his lips. Johnny knew it was time to slip away. He picked up the bag with his kit and ushered Bentley out of the door without anyone noticing. Then, as quietly as he could, he led the Old English sheepdog towards the computer room.

The pair entered and Johnny sat down in front of the master terminal while a worn-out Bentley curled up at his feet.

'You took your time,' said Kovac.

'What? What do you mean?' Johnny replied a little uncertainly.

'It's not as though you gave me a very taxing assignment, is it?' said Kovac. 'What's the point of being the world's only quantum computer if I've nothing to compute? I had to solve the Riemann Hypothesis just to keep myself occupied.'

'The Riemann what?' Johnny asked. 'No – don't answer that. Did you find them? Did you find my dad? Louise? Where are they?'

'No I didn't find them,' Kovac replied.

'Oh,' said Johnny. 'Well can't you keep looking?'

'I didn't find them because they are not here to be found.'

'What do you mean?'

'I mean they aren't anywhere.'

'Oh,' said Johnny again, rather confused.

Kovac continued before Johnny could ask anything else, saying, 'And another thing – some people wish to communicate with you.'

'Who?' Johnny asked.

'Their names are Clara, Alf, Chancellor Gronack and a very supercilious computer named Sol.'

'Put them through,' said Johnny, wondering what 'supercilious' might mean.

'So this is it?' Kovac replied. 'Destined to become a glorified videophone . . .'

'Now . . . please,' said Johnny firmly, and Kovac's monitor changed to a view of the bridge on the Spirit of London. Everybody was standing around the empty captain's chair.

'Master Johnny,' said Alf, excited. 'I do hope you can join us later.'

'Love to,' Johnny replied.

'Then I shall come and fetch you in the Jubilee,' said Alf.

'It's OK,' Clara cut in. 'I can do it. It only takes a second.'

'You have done more than enough folding these past few days,' said Alf. 'You need to rest.'

Clara crossed her arms and scowled.

'It's best,' said Johnny. 'I'll need a minute to get ready anyway. See you in a second, Alf.' Johnny leaned down from the chair, rubbed Bentley under his collar to wake him up and whispered, 'It's good to have you back, Bents,' in the dog's ear. The Old English sheepdog got to his feet and slopped his huge tongue across Johnny's face. Together they turned towards the door.

'And just what am I supposed to do now?' Kovac asked.

'I don't know,' said Johnny. 'Whatever you want. Solve another hypothesis thingy.' He left the computer room wondering if fitting the quantum processor had been such a good idea and carried his kit up the two flights of stairs to his bedroom, Bentley scampering behind. Safely inside, he threw the carrier bag containing his dirty kit and boots onto the floor. In the time it took him to create a suitable impression of a sleeping Johnny in his bed, by placing various items of clothing under the duvet, a flying London taxi had appeared outside his bedroom window. As quietly as he could, Johnny undid the latch and followed Bentley out of the window onto the roof and into the waiting cab. Less than a minute later they were in front of what looked for all the world like the London Gherkin, and making the short walk from the taxi rank into the Spirit of London.

'Alf,' Johnny began. 'Where did you find the Jubilee?'

'Right here of course,' said Alf. 'Where we left it. Why?'

'It's nothing,' said Johnny. 'I guess I just went to the wrong cab before.'

Soon Johnny and Bentley entered the strategy room where the others had gathered, Johnny having first changed into his Melanian clothes, which made him feel more 'serious.' Rusty, wagging her tail, came across to greet Bentley. Clara yawned a sleepy hello. Johnny sat down beside the Chancellor and felt something digging into him. It was the brass gnomon from the Proteus Institute sundial. He took it out of his pocket and placed it on the near invisible forcefield table in front of him.

'If I may,' squeaked Chancellor Gronack, 'there are important matters to attend to. Our first priority must be to contact
the Empire.'

'Do I need to remind you, Chancellor, that temporal imper-
atives mean we must maintain a communication blackout for
the next twenty-two days,' said Alf.

'For the Regent's sake,' Gronack replied. 'I will not spend
another day on this ship. If we wait that long it could be months
before I am rescued. Just how will Melania function without
me? Answer me that!'

Johnny suspected everyone around the table joined him in
thinking Melania was probably much better off in the
Chancellor's absence, but it was Sol who came to the rescue.
'The argument is academic,' she said. 'My sensors show there
are no friendly vessels through which to relay messages within
a twenty-two light day radius.'

'None?' squeaked Gronack despondently

'Further,' said Sol. 'Despite my impressive specification, not
even I carry a supply of cornicula worms. For the time being we
are cut off from the Empire.'

'What would happen if we did have some cornicula worms?'
asked Johnny as casually as he could. He knew Alf would be
apoplectic if he tried to contact Bram, but hadn't the Emperor told
him to release the worm as soon as he was safe? It was practically
an imperial order. He started rolling the brass spike backwards and
forwards on the table in front of him. It was interfering with the
forcefield, creating a lovely pattern of blue sparks following the
lines of magnetic force through the gnomon.

'I sometimes wonder if you paid attention to anything I
taught you,' Alf replied. 'Why, we would find a secure Earth-
based location and release the worm to return to Melania.'

'Why, not here on the ship?' Johnny asked.

Sol cut in. 'Although I am content to be located here for the time being, Johnny, I am a spaceship. I live to travel between the stars. The instant I moved, any tunnel created by the cornicula would be broken for ever. It would be an unimaginable waste.'

It looked as though Gronack was about to interject, but Alf got there first, saying, 'To the matter in hand – the search for Johnny and Clara's father, and their friend.'

'Your Kovac computer proved . . . unhelpful when I offered to discuss it, Johnny,' said Sol. 'The search must be complete by now – what was the result?'

'Kovac said they weren't anywhere,' Johnny replied.

'Meaning what, exactly?' asked the Chancellor.

'I don't know,' said Johnny, wishing he'd interrogated Kovac in a little more depth. He felt a bit stupid.

'Perhaps they're dead,' said Gronack. 'I expect that would explain it. And will you stop doing that – it's most distracting.'

'Sorry,' said Johnny, putting his hand on the gnomon to stop it moving.

'I am quite sure they are far too valuable to the krun to have been killed,' said Alf.

'Then where on earth are they?' Clara asked, stifling another yawn.

Johnny was staring down at the brass spike on the table which had come to rest with the little indentation of the trident facing upwards. 'I know where they are,' he said, surprising himself nearly as much as everyone else. The rest of the table fell completely silent, with just the hum from the forcefield in the background. 'They're not on Earth – they're on Neptune.'

'Neptune?' asked Alf and Chancellor Gronack together.

'Neptune is the eighth planet in this star system,' said Sol, helpfully.

'But why would they be there, Master Johnny?' asked Alf.

'You see this,' said Johnny, pointing to the broken piece of the sundial. 'I took this from the Proteus Institute. This mark here is the symbol for Neptune.'

'And that's it?' said Gronack. 'I see now it's obvious.'

Bentley growled, baring his teeth.

'It's OK, Bents,' said Johnny. 'But it is obvious. Kovac said they weren't anywhere because he was only looking here – on Earth. If they're not here then where? Proteus is one of the moons of Neptune – the Proteus Institute. And didn't you say there was another school called Triton?' he asked Clara, who nodded back. 'That's another moon of Neptune. Sol – has there been any communication between the krun ships in orbit and Neptune?'

'The largest krun vessel folded out of this system earlier today,' Sol replied. 'One of the smaller vessels broke orbit shortly afterwards, on a trajectory consistent with a destination of the eighth planet.'

'See,' said Johnny.

'It sounds plausible, I suppose,' said Alf.

'Johnny's right,' said Clara. 'I can feel it.'

'Thanks,' said Johnny. 'Sol – tomorrow we're going to Neptune. Can you be ready?'

'Of course, Johnny,' said Sol. 'I look forward to it.'

'OK – the rest of you should get a good night's sleep,' said Johnny. He needed somewhere to release the cornicula worm, but he couldn't tell anyone about it. 'I'll just take the dogs out around the block.' Before anyone could say anything, Johnny got to his feet and called Bentley and Rusty after him. They left the strategy room, walked along the corridor and arrived at the antigrav lifts. Bentley carried straight on inside, hovering in mid-air while the lift waited for instruction, but Rusty backed away, uncertain. Johnny picked her up and carried her in. Instead of going straight to the ground-level exit, Johnny nipped into his quarters to change and to collect the doughnut-shaped present Bram had given him on Melania. Then, with the two dogs in tow, he continued on down to the revolving doors and stepped out of the ship, across the paving stones and into the London night.

The air was still and the sky clear, but in the heart of the city there were no stars to be seen. Johnny wondered what was happening 'up there' and where his other self and Clara had got to. He walked over to the Jubilee, hoping this time he'd picked the right taxi, and let the two dogs into the back.

Johnny walked around to the driver's door and sat down in the front seat. He thought about Halader House in Castle Dudbury and the shuttle began to move. He thought 'shields on'; inside the shuttle nothing happened, but the response from the little ship penetrated Johnny's mind and he knew there were CCTV cameras tracking them along the street. Johnny sensed it as soon as the shuttle was clear, and at that moment everything around him shimmered and disappeared. As they rose into the air, the Jubilee's sensors became Johnny's eyes and ears, so that Rusty's barking right behind him merged with all the other background noise.

¤   ¤   ¤
¤   ¤

Johnny left the Jubilee outside Castle Dudbury station and slipped into Halader House unnoticed. With both dogs curled up asleep underneath his bed by the radiator, Johnny took out the gift from the Emperor. The blue glow coming from the cornicula worm within was speeding around the inside of the torus, lighting up the sloping walls of the bedroom. Johnny stared at it wondering how he was meant to let the worm out, and as he did so the container began to unfold. For a fleeting moment he saw the brilliant electric blue glow of the worm, so bright it nearly blinded him, but it shrank rapidly before his eyes and disappeared into nothingness.

Johnny wondered how long it would take the worm to

burrow through the fabric of space and time and reach Bram on Melania. He lay down on his bed just for a moment, lights flashing behind his eyes, turning his thoughts to the trip to Neptune and wondering if he was really going to see his father tomorrow.

12

Reunions ✡ ⚝

Johnny was back on Galaxia, sitting underneath the kanefor tree with Bram shouting at him, clearly trying to tell him something important.

'Johnny . . . Johnny Mackintosh – wake up!'

Johnny opened his eyes. He was in the bedroom of Halader House, but floating in mid-air in front of him, at exactly the point where he had released the cornicula worm the night before, was Bram Khari's smiling face.

'Bram,' said Johnny. 'Excellent.'

'Finally,' said Bram. 'I have been shouting for rather a long time.' The Emperor's eyes were twinkling. Johnny hoped they couldn't see beyond him to the dirty boots on the floor of his very untidy bedroom. 'I am truly intrigued,' Bram continued. 'After waiting millennia, you visit me twice the same day. Here you are, sending me a worm from my very own nursery. I can only assume I shall provide you with it at a later date and that your time-travelling adventures were not solely confined to Atlantis?'

'We've sort of been jumping around a bit,' said Johnny. 'I think this is as close to the right time as we'll get.'

'I take it you have returned to Earth?' said Bram. 'How is everyone?'

'OK,' Johnny replied. 'Sol's shields aren't working and I wish you hadn't left Gronack on board.'

'*Chancellor* Gronack, Johnny. Thank you for the reminder – Atlantis was so long ago I'd almost forgotten. The phasmeer had to leave with you on the Spirit of London because it was there with you in Atlantis. In fact, between you and me, that's the only reason I gave it the job in the first place – very questionable references if I remember. However, now you are home I will make arrangements to . . . relieve you of your undoubted burden.'

'Thanks,' said Johnny. 'We're going to Neptune today.'

'Ah – the eighth planet,' Bram replied. 'An interesting choice. Wouldn't Saturn be a more spectacular place for a first visit?'

'No – it's the krun.' said Johnny. I think they have my dad there – and a friend.'

Bram's face turned serious. 'Then you be careful, Johnny. The krun are not to be taken lightly. There are powerful forces behind them.'

'I've done all right before, haven't I?' Johnny responded.

'You have undoubted talents, but I knew you would survive Atlantis because it had already happened. Now the timeline is intact and not even I can foresee your future.'

'But you're the Emperor. I thought you knew everything.'

Bram smiled. 'When you are as old as I – when you have made as many mistakes – you will realize how little you truly know. Yes, I am the Emperor. I am the Law. The day may come when you will know what that means.'

'I don't understand,' said Johnny.

'Because I was being unforgivably serious,' Bram replied. 'I must apologize. However sincerely I ask you to be careful, I am sure you will take the risks that are the preserve of the young. So instead, let me ask you one very important question.'

'What is it?' Johnny asked, rubbing the sleep from his eyes and sitting attentively on the edge of the bed.

'I need to know what would a young Earth boy, who had been travelling for more than a day without any food, most want to eat when he arrived here?'

'Sticky toffee pudding,' Johnny replied without thinking. 'It's my favourite.'

'Then you shall have it. I believe you are arriving any moment.'

'What? You mean that was me I saw?' Johnny asked, remembering the floating head on his arrival at the Imperial Palace.

'Indeed that *is* you,' Bram replied, smiling. 'I must go and welcome you.'

'Say hello to the Diaquant,' said Johnny. 'And thank her for everything.'

'I regret she is no longer here,' Bram replied.

He was still smiling, but Johnny thought it was the first time he'd seen the Emperor look really sad. Before he could be sure, the Emperor's face popped out of existence leaving Johnny staring instead at the poster of the International Space Station on the far wall of his bedroom. There was a swirling, glinting cloud above his head, like dust sparkling in a stream of sunlight, and Johnny got the feeling that if he stuck his head there he'd be watching himself and Clara devouring their first meal at the Imperial Palace. Footsteps were coming up the stairs. The trap-door to Johnny's bedroom opened and in came Miss Harutunian, carrying a tray piled high with bacon sandwiches which she placed on the table beside his bed.

'Special treat,' she said. 'I think it's best you keep out of the dining room today.' She winked and Johnny smiled at the thought of Mr Wilkins taking Johnny's return out on the Halader House food. 'And I heard you won,' she continued.

The smell of the bacon was irresistible and Johnny reached past his social worker and stuffed the top sandwich into his mouth, only remembering to say thank you once his mouth was full.

Sniffing the food, Bentley emerged from underneath Johnny's bed looking hopefully at Miss Harutunian for a bacon sandwich. The social worker jumped.

'You found Bentley,' she said to Johnny. 'How?'

'Er . . . it was the police,' said Johnny, improvising wildly and hoping Rusty would stay out of sight. 'They put out an all points bulletin and found him nearly straightaway. Then they brought him to the footy.'

'That was quick,' said Miss Harutunian, eyeing Johnny a little suspiciously. 'Well, you start getting ready for school – I'm sure you can't wait to talk to everyone about the match.'

'Course,' said Johnny through a mouthful of food.

Miss Harutunian turned towards the door but Johnny called after her. 'Whole team's staying over at Dave's after school tonight – to celebrate. Is it OK if I go?' He put on his most innocent smile and concentrated hard on not going red.

Miss Harutunian thought for a moment. 'Mrs Irvine really won't like you leaving the home right now . . . but I won't tell her if you don't – just this once. I guess you deserve it.' She smiled at Johnny, opened the trapdoor and, with a little difficulty, exited down the spiral stairs.

✡ ✡ ✡
✡ ✡

Take-off was a complicated business. Normally a ship powered by a dark energy drive like the Spirit of London would fly effortlessly through conventional space before folding, which took place well away from any large gravitational fields. But because it wouldn't really do to have the London Gherkin lift off unexpectedly into the air, only for a carbon copy to appear where it had just been, the plican was being asked to take them as far as it could towards Neptune directly from the Earth's surface. In addition it had to make sure it didn't remove any extra pieces from its surroundings, like a stray paving slab or a surprised pigeon.

It would be a delicate operation, so Clara remained on the bridge. Johnny, Alf and, very reluctantly, Bentley and Rusty, took refuge in the gel pods that emerged from the floor, waiting for the Spirit of London to wink out of existence while the real London Gherkin winked into it from out of hyperspace, taking the ship's place a nanosecond or two later.

Once inside the gel pods Johnny, blown up like a rubber glove, hardly felt a thing and was surprised when Sol told him the fold was over. Quickly he deflated to normal proportions as the goo oozed out of his mouth and drained from the chamber. Briefly he let himself enjoy the tickling sensation as the remaining gel was vacuumed up off him before he opened the doors, still grinning, and stepped out onto the bridge, taking his place in the captain's chair. Bentley emerged, shaking his shaggy coat clean of orange goo, as though he'd just come out of the sea. Johnny looked at the instruments beside him – everything seemed fine. 'Where are we?' he asked.

'Our position is approximately 17,297.465 95 light seconds from your Sun and 16.226 21 degrees below the plane of the solar system. If I may say so, it was a magnificent fold,' Sol replied.

'Can you tell it "well done"?' Johnny asked Clara, gesturing at the plican.

'When it wakes up,' said Clara. 'It's resting now.'

'You should do the same,' Johnny told her, aware of what would be coming soon. As Clara left the bridge, Johnny swivelled to face forwards and asked Sol, 'How soon till we reach Neptune?'

'Computing . . . estimated time of arrival at one-half light speed is 1 hour, 54 minutes and 57.1628 seconds.'

The other pods opened and Alf and a frightened Rusty joined Johnny and Bentley on the bridge. It had been Alf's idea to position themselves so unusually in space. The Sun and all the planets were in the same two-dimensional plane as each other. Apparently most species, including Johnny and hopefully the krun, thought in fewer dimensions and would have expected any journey to Neptune from Earth to take place in a relatively straight line. The Spirit of London would be approaching Neptune from below – everyone hoped this would give them an element of surprise. Sol was busy scanning the planet for evidence that the krun really did have a base there. She projected an image of the planet, deep blue splashed across with white cirrus clouds, onto the viewscreen and highlighted the position of two moons.

'Well I never,' said Alf, looking at the pink ball that was Triton. 'Unless I am very much mistaken there is something most unusual about that satellite.'

'What do you mean?' Johnny asked.

Alf moved to a bank of scientific instruments and called Johnny across. 'Take a look at these readings,' he said.

Johnny stared at the many graphics flickering on the screens in front of him and hazarded a guess. 'It's cold?' he said.

'Excellent, Johnny,' Alf replied. 'Indeed it is – unusually so. I would suggest it is colder than any other object in your solar system. And look at its orbit.'

Johnny studied this for a moment and thought he saw what Alf meant. 'It's going the wrong way round.'

'Precisely,' said Alf. 'And if you look even closer it has a perfectly circular orbit – not an ellipse. My word, this is inter-esting. Circular *and* retrograde.'

'But so what?' Johnny asked.

'So what?' said Alf. 'So it could well be artificial. It definitely is not as nature intended.'

'Sol – can you home in on Triton?' Johnny asked. As he spoke, the image of the blue and white gas giant was replaced by a smaller pink globe. Johnny stood up and walked over to the viewscreen to get a closer look. Could someone really have built it? Its surface was scarred, but not as badly cratered as most moons he'd seen photos of from probes like Voyager. As he looked, he thought for a moment that he saw a little flash of white light come from a point on its surface. 'What was that? Did you see it?' he asked, turning to Alf.

'What was what, Master Johnny?'

Johnny turned back to the screen, placed his finger onto the spot where he thought he'd seen the flash, and said, 'Sol – can you expand this area and go back about thirty seconds?'

'Of course, Johnny,' said Sol and the image flickered momentarily as the spot he'd pointed to enlarged.

Johnny saw it again – bigger this time. 'There!' he said, excitedly.

'I saw it too,' said Alf. 'What could it have been?'

'Did you get it, Sol?' Johnny asked.

'I detected a fluctuation in the surface luminosity,' Sol replied, as the lights flickered across her vocal display screen.

'Play back and enhance,' said Johnny. 'There – freeze it.'

Johnny stared at the viewscreen. There was a hole in Triton, perfectly round with white light streaming out from inside of the moon. 'It's hollow,' Johnny said. 'They're inside it.'

'I do believe you are right,' said Alf. 'That was a ship leaving.'

Johnny looked closer. The frozen image revealed the faint outline of a black sphere, lying just outside the aperture. 'Sol – can you track that?' Johnny asked.

'The data has degraded, Johnny, but I beleve it is a small krun shuttle, probably on a trajectory for another moon.'

'Proteus?' Johnny asked.

'Computing . . . the most likely destination is Nereid,' Sol replied.

'Can you tell who's on board?' Johnny asked.

'Life sign readings are notoriously unreliable,' Sol replied, 'but I believe there are humans present as well as krun.'

'Show me Nereid,' said Johnny, 'but keep scanning Triton.' The screen changed again to a potato-shaped rock, tumbling slowly through space with Neptune in the background. It was much smaller than Triton – if the bigger moon could be hollow, he suspected Nereid certainly was. As he watched the spherical black ship entered the field of view. A hole opened up in the surface of the little moon and the spacecraft disappeared inside.

'You should be aware I intercepted what appears to be an entrance code,' said Sol.

'Nice one, Sol,' said Johnny. 'Can you tell how many krun are on Nereid?'

'My upper estimate is six, Johnny,' she replied.

'Excellent,' said Johnny. 'We should be able to get past those.'

'But we cannot afford to ignore Triton,' said Alf. 'You know about the krun. Remember if anything happens on Nereid they will soon know all about it and send reinforcements.'

'I did pay attention to some of the things you taught us,' said Johnny, smiling at his artificial friend. 'What we need is a diversion.'

☆   ☆   ☆
☆   ☆

Johnny stared out of the windows of the Piccadilly as the Spirit of London shrank into nothing in front of the gas giant below. They were using Neptune as a shield, keeping the deep blue planet between the ship and both Triton and Nereid. He and Bentley were on board. He would have brought Rusty to help search for Louise, but the setter seemed terrified of most things on the ship, and certainly anything that might make her invisible again. She hid in a corner when he carried her down to the shuttle deck. Johnny thought 'shields on' and the walls of the bus that surrounded him faded away into nothing. This must be a little how Clara felt about folding – she'd talked about being one with the universe and he'd now become just a mind floating in space.

The Piccadilly was the fastest of the shuttles, but Neptune was truly enormous – much bigger than Earth – and it would take nearly half an hour until his little bus/ship was in position and he could signal Alf and Clara. That meant nearly thirty minutes of feeling guilty, as he flew above another of Neptune's moons, that was orbiting close to the enormous planet below.

Ptery and Donna had called another dinocouncil. The final decision had been unanimous. Johnny had spoken to them. He'd made sure he told them how dangerous it would be. He said they didn't have to go – that it was up to them if they wanted to help. The chance to leave the dinodeck, however briefly, had proved too tempting to turn down. Besides – dinosaurs liked danger. And when the carnivores heard there would be fresh meat there was absolutely no stopping them. Johnny shivered at that thought. It was natural, he knew. They couldn't help it, and he should be grateful.

Nereid, orbiting a long way out, came into view – heavily cratered and misshapen – as Neptune finally started to shrink. He wasn't going to break radio silence until the last possible moment. As the moon grew bigger, the thought he kept trying to suppress surfaced again. Was he finally going to see his dad? It was too much to hope for.

One minute to go. It was now or never. He concentrated on the coded message he wanted to send to Sol: 'The Piccadilly has reached the Circus,' and Johnny could feel it transmit as though he'd spoken the words himself. He pictured Clara sitting with her palms upward on the dinodeck, opening a gateway in space into the hollow insides of Triton. T. Rexes, velociraptors, the scarily bright troodons, the crocodile-like deinosuchus and many more would be pouring through to devour the surprised krun. He really hoped so anyway. He knew the dinosaurs were becoming so listless on the Spirit of London, they wouldn't have lasted much longer there. At least now they could stretch their legs and wings. He just hoped they'd make it back in one piece.

Johnny sent the access code and a shutter slid open in Nereid's rocky surface. The Piccadilly, still shielded, flew inside and into a giant airlock that could have held ships much bigger than a London bus. Johnny was worried they might be trapped halfway, but everything worked automatically – as soon as the entrance had closed behind them a new one opened up in front and he guided the ship carefully through. He couldn't help being impressed by the massive hangar he flew into. Below was a landing strip but surrounding it were the same cabbage-like blue-grey walls, with mushroom-shaped sticky handholds, that he'd seen when inside the krun spaceship. Dangling from the roof were huge suckered tentacles, quite capable of moving small spacecraft around. And his sensors told him it had a nitrogen–oxygen atmosphere – he could almost breathe it through the Piccadilly. Johnny landed the shuttle beside the spherical krun ship. 'Let's go, Bents,' he said and opened the doors, causing everything to rematerialize for an instant, before vanishing again at the push of a button on his wristcom as soon as the pair were safely outside.

Bentley began to scamper across towards the krun ship but gave a surprised yelp as, in one bound, he lifted off the surface and started floating upwards. There was very little gravity. It was all Johnny could do not to burst out laughing as the sheepdog rose higher and higher off the ground. He looked into the pack he'd brought from the shuttle in case he needed a rope, but Bentley topped out and began a slow-motion descent to the surface. Instead, Johnny picked out some explosives, set the timer and was able to fix them onto the hull of the krun vessel with a satisfying magnetic clunk.

'Come on, Bents,' he whispered, clicking his tongue and leading the nervous dog towards the mouth of a corridor, where the organic wall stopped and solid rock led away into the distance. Sounds from the inside told Johnny that someone, or something, was hurrying towards them from inside. Johnny jumped to one side of the opening, a little too quickly, and it was his turn to find himself floating away from the ground. He grabbed hold of one of the mushroom-shaped nodules and twisted round. Bentley crouched the other side of the entrance and, Johnny counted them, six krun waddled past. They weren't humanoids wearing suits – these were the krun he remembered from his first time aboard a spaceship: bony exteriors, each with four long arms, and fly-like faces, and with different coloured markings on their heads, making them look fierce and cruel. Had they glanced to the side they couldn't have missed Bentley, but they were in a hurry to reach their shuttle. The dino-diversion seemed to be working. Johnny watched from halfway up the wall of the hangar as the black sphere lifted up and disappeared into the airlock.

He climbed down the sticky wall like Spiderman, pulling himself off it at the bottom, and walked through the entrance into the rocky corridor, Bentley lolloping alongside him. As long as they were careful, they made good progress because of the low gravity, yet the corridor seemed to go on for miles, twisting and turning ever further into the heart of the moon. Johnny hated not knowing what was happening on Triton, but underneath all this rock his wristcom, even if he'd dared try it, would be useless. Finally he and Bentley rounded a bend and he saw a speck of light up ahead. After ten years without his dad Johnny started taking giant strides as Bentley bounded along behind, struggling to keep up. He went faster and the light grew bigger. As he drew closer he saw it was an opening – he ran faster still, until finally he was there. Coming out of the corridor and into an octagonal chamber, Johnny stopped, just for a moment, to take stock. Either side were three closed gigantic metal doors, each built into the centre of one of the walls and with a different unearthly symbol emblazoned across it. Opposite was an open room. There were lights flickering within – maybe someone was inside? Johnny sprinted over to the open door, took a deep breath and stepped through.

Around the walls were all sorts of strange-looking instruments and controls, as well as half a dozen containers with foul-smelling little balls of organic matter. It might have been krun food – it certainly smelled disgusting. But what really attracted his attention was a circular plinth in the centre of the room, covered by a transparent dome. This was where the light was coming from. As he drew nearer, Johnny could see dinosaurs inside the dome. It was a projection – holographic – of dinosaurs attacking krun, and winning by the looks of it. He placed his hands on the plinth and leant over to get a closer look, but the image changed. Now he was looking out at what appeared to be a triple star system. It was the view from a ship – he was sure of it. Johnny looked down. He must have put his hand over a control that switched to another channel – this was some sort of communications centre. He moved his hand again and once more the projection inside the dome changed. Someone was sitting in front of a dancing blue fire, just like the one he'd seen at the Imperial Palace on Melania. It couldn't be could it? 'Bram?' Johnny asked quietly. The figure turned around. It wasn't Bram. Whoever it was, its face was covered by a black mask, a single, blazing white star painted on it, but Johnny could still see its eyes. There was no question – they were staring straight at him and they were blacker than anything he'd ever seen. Johnny bashed the plinth with both hands and the projection changed again. His heart beating much faster, he turned and ran out of the room.

Bentley was sniffing around on the right-hand side of the octagonal chamber. He settled on the second door along from the entrance to the corridor and started pawing at it, letting out a little whine. 'Are you sure, boy?' Johnny asked. As he walked across, he felt a strange tightening around his neck. He looked down. The golden locket was straining forwards from underneath his tunic, just as it had when he first met Clara in the Proteus Institute maze. Johnny took it out and it began to tug on its golden chain, pulling him towards the very same door where Bentley now sat.

Johnny went over and pushed against it – nothing happened. He looked frantically either side for some clue of how to open it. There was nothing in view. He closed his eyes, trying to listen for something, and after a few moments he heard it. A faint current was flowing, but it was very high up on the right-hand side of the wall above him. He jumped, reached up and placed his hand as high as he could on the rocky surface. Nothing happened as Johnny landed back on the floor. He tried a second time, getting closer to the right part of the wall this time as he really stretched, but still nothing happened and Johnny landed back on his feet with the door still firmly shut in front of him. He wasn't going to let a silly door stop him – not now – not after coming so far. He wanted to see his dad; he wanted it more than anything. Johnny jumped for all he was worth. This time, in the low gravity, he overshot and had to use his hands and feet to stop himself slamming into the ceiling. On the way down he twisted his body and stretched until his arm was almost coming out of its socket, pressing his hand firmly over the right spot. He felt the electric current divert through him. The door opened upwards, disappearing into the roof of the chamber and Johnny fell backwards, landing badly, and found himself lying on the floor at the feet of a large krun soldier standing guard at the entrance to a darkened room.

It might have been its huge fly-like eyes but the creature looked even more surprised than Johnny. It had a weapon at the end of one of its long bony arms and began to raise it, but Johnny kicked out at its legs and a grey and white ball sprang upwards and sank its teeth into the alien's neck. In the low gravity the krun was lifted off the ground by the force of Bentley's jump and the two flew into the air inside the darkened room, struggling with each other in a grotesque slow motion dance. The krun fired its weapon wildly, intense flashes of green light blasting out huge chunks from the rocky floor. Johnny tried to see what was happening, but was helpless to do anything. The reaction from the gun as it fired lifted the pair higher and higher. Finally the krun's head clattered against the ceiling, there was a flurry of action, a sharp crack and then silence. Slowly the two shapes descended to the floor, the krun draped on top of a motionless Bentley.

Johnny rushed forward. 'Bents – are you OK?' he shouted. He aimed a kick at the limp figure of the krun, which rose up into the air again and, to Johnny's enormous relief, his friend got unsteadily to his feet, black alien blood dripping from his mouth. As Johnny looked back to the krun he thought he could make out more black fluid oozing out of it, the creature appearing to deflate in mid-air as it floated down towards the floor.

'J-J-Johnny?' asked a frightened girl's voice from one corner of the room. Johnny looked up. 'You're a sight for sore eyes,' said the girl, a little more composed this time. As Johnny peered through the darkness, he was able to see a little better. Sitting on the floor, still wearing her green jacket and wellies, and with her knees tucked into her chest, was Louise. And nearby, dressed only in dirty rags that had long ago stopped resembling clothes, stood a man. His bushy grey hair matched his scraggly beard and he was walking round and round in circles on very spindly legs. Trembling slightly, Johnny went across to him. Out of the corner of his eye he was vaguely aware of Bentley licking Louise's face and calming her down.

Johnny stood in front of the man, who stopped his walk for a second and peered at him, as though struggling to focus. Johnny looked back into his dark green eyes and knew he'd seen them before. Apart from the silver flecks they were just the same as his own. 'Dad?' he said quietly.

'You again, is it?' the man replied. 'Where's the other one?' He started his circular walk again, as though in a great hurry to go nowhere in particular.

'Dad – it's me, Johnny.'

'Hello, Johnny. Good to see you – as ever. Where's Nicholas today? Where's that big brother of yours then?'

'Dad – what are you talking about? It's me – I'm here with Bentley.'

'Oh, with Bentley today are you? Yes that is clever. Hadn't seen that one coming. Thought I'd seen everything. Very clever that.'

Johnny stood baffled while the man he was sure was his father walked in circles around him until he stopped, knelt down on the floor and reached forward towards an imaginary sight in front of him, saying, 'Mary – I miss you, Mary. Why are they doing this to me?'

'Dad – Mum's not here,' said Johnny.

'Of course she's not here. Do you think I don't know that? Do you think I'm mad, do you? None of you's here. I just wish you'd leave me alone.'

'No, Dad. I am here. It's really me,' said Johnny. He walked over to his father, put his arms around his neck and held him.

'That's not fair. That's not fair at all,' said his dad. 'Get off!' He pushed Johnny away, stood up and began to walk in hurried circles again. 'You can look but you can't touch. It's not fair to touch. There are rules. You can't touch me 'cos you're not here.'

Johnny stood watching his father, with no idea what to do.

'You took your time,' said Louise from the floor.

Johnny tore himself away from his dad and looked at the girl beside him. For Louise only a day had passed since she'd met Johnny in a field outside Yarnton Hill, but she looked as though she'd been through a lot. Her face was as pale as Johnny's and her T-shirt was caked with dried blood. 'Sorry I left you there,' he said. 'I tried to come back.'

'I saw you – in that stupid top. I knew something was up,' she said, wincing with pain as he helped her to her feet.

Johnny smiled at her. 'That's one way of putting it. Come on – we should hurry. I know someone who's dying to see you.'

'You haven't . . . not Rusty?' asked Louise. Johnny nodded and, despite her obvious pain, Louise flung both her arms around him and kissed him on the forehead. Johnny managed to duck out of her grip.

'So that man's your dad?' she asked. 'I'm sorry.'

'It's OK,' said Johnny. 'He'll get better – it'll just take time.' He took her arm and placed it over his shoulder to support her. Then he turned to Bentley and said, 'Bring Dad . . . go on, boy . . . bring Dad.'

Bentley went gingerly over to Johnny's dad, looking up into his face. Michael Mackintosh bent down and wiped the fringe out of Bentley's eyes in exactly the way Johnny often did himself. 'Hello, boy,' Johnny's dad said. 'Do you want to go for a walk? OK then, I'm coming – lead the way,' and Bentley set off, tail wagging, and trotted out of the room and into the light of the octagonal chamber.

They entered the long corridor and made their way as quickly as possible towards the surface. Louise was struggling to walk, but thankfully the low gravity helped, and whenever Johnny's dad looked as though he might be about to turn back or stop because he'd seen an interesting imaginary something on the wall, Bentley rounded him up and kept him heading in the right direction. Eventually they reached the hangar and Johnny pressed a button on his wristcom. A bright red double-decker bus appeared in front of them.

'Cool,' said Louise.

'Oh, are we taking the bus?' asked Johnny's dad. 'I'm not sure I've got any money.'

'It's OK, Dad,' said Johnny. 'You get on – I've already paid.'

Bentley jumped on board, followed by Michael Mackintosh and Louise, helped by Johnny. Up in the roof of the hangar the airlock opened, even though Johnny hadn't had a chance to enter the access code. To his horror, in flew the spherical krun shuttle craft – for whatever reason it had returned to Nereid. He thought of shields and doors at the same time. As the bus, and everything inside it, began to disappear, a beam of green light shot towards them from the black ship. There was a huge bang. For a moment, the ceiling above Johnny became very solid again, before fading away. Johnny was stung by the pain of the impact. A second explosion followed. Johnny winced and this time the whole of the Piccadilly reappeared around him. The shields had absorbed the blast but must have failed in the process. Then the hanger filled with more light and there was another, even louder blast, yet somehow he was still alive. Amazingly the Piccadilly was completely intact – it was the krun vessel that had vanished. Johnny saw small pieces of debris plastered across the blue-grey walls of the chamber, where they'd instantly stuck fast. The explosives he'd planted had detonated – not a moment too soon. Letting out a long, slow breath he lifted the shuttle off the ground and thought it into the Nereid airlock. Soon they were flying above the blue globe of Neptune with its cloudy white streaks.

Louise, sitting nearby, went silent as she stared outside into space. From the snippets that Johnny could hear it sounded as if his dad thought they were travelling along the King's Road in London. Ten minutes into the journey back and Johnny couldn't wait any longer. They were unshielded and an obvious target whatever he did. Radio silence didn't seem to matter any more. He had to know what had happened on Triton.

As he wove his way through one of Neptune's thin rocky rings he silently asked the Piccadilly if he could see what was happening on the Spirit of London – if he could speak to Sol. The commscreen above him came to life and he saw the view of a deserted bridge.

'Sol – what happened? What's going on?' Johnny asked.

'The mission is proceeding nearly as planned. Is everything all right, Johnny? If possible I recommend communication blackout until you are within range of my weapons.'

'I'm fine – got my dad and Louise. Shields are down though. What do you mean "nearly"?'

'Johnny, I strongly recommend you cease transmission. I am detecting unusual activity within Proteus.'

Johnny looked outside. The Piccadilly was passing above the moon he'd seen earlier. So this was Proteus. There were several flashes of light on the surface. He reached out with the Piccadilly's sensors and felt five sleek dark krun fighters arrowing towards him on an intercept course.

'Sol – I've got company,' said Johnny. 'Can you get over here?'

'Johnny – I am unable to reach you. Clara's fold is still open. I am attempting to recall her from Triton – suggest you take evasive action.'

'No kidding.'

'And Johnny . . .'

'What?'

'Good luck.'

Johnny thought that really didn't help. Sol had never *sounded* worried before, not even when they were leaving Atlantis. He scanned again and could sense the fighters were moving to head him off – and were succeeding. The Piccadilly didn't have its own weapons. And though it was the fastest of their shuttles, he was sure it couldn't outstrip a krun fighter. His only hope was to keep out of trouble long enough for Sol to be able to rescue them.

'Hold on,' he shouted to his assembled passengers and swung the shuttle upwards and away from their pursuers. The fighters would be on him in 38 seconds. The Piccadilly's engines screamed as Johnny urged the red double-decker bus forwards towards the blackness of empty space. 'Come on,' he pleaded, concentrating his thoughts on keeping track of all five krun ships. They were closing in, spread out in an attack pattern converging on his position. They were almost on top of him.

Johnny thought 'full reverse engines' and the krun fighters overshot, while Bentley slid forwards along the length of the shuttle, unable to hold onto anything. 'Just can't get the drivers nowadays,' said Johnny's dad, tutting as he clung on to his seat. Johnny knew he'd only bought himself a few extra seconds. As he steered the ship away with his mind, the very fabric of space right in the middle of the krun fighters rippled and unfolded. At last – Sol must have made it.

'What's that?' Louise asked from behind him.

Johnny turned around to see a stubby white spaceship unleash a barrage of fire that disintegrated two of the krun ships. The other three scattered. Only one was heading for the Piccadilly. 'Sorry guys,' Johnny shouted as he deliberately started the shuttle spinning in a downward spiral towards Neptune, through the rings, just trusting to luck. A blast of green light passed them very close on one side and Johnny pulled upwards, narrowly missing a rock twice the Piccadilly's size as the shuttle's engines whined horribly. Again the fighter overshot. Scanning the surrounding space told Johnny that only two krun ships now survived: one emerging from the rings, still right behind; the other heading away from the planet and out into space. The white spaceship was speeding towards the Piccadilly head-on while the krun fighter was right on Johnny's tail. A familiar voice sounded inside Johnny's head and he swung the Piccadilly away to the left, just as a beam of white light came from the larger craft. The fighter disappeared in a blinding cloud of light and gas and Johnny breathed another sigh of relief.

He heard the voice again, this time coming out of the Piccadilly's speakers. 'This is Imperial Frigate Cheybora – do you require assistance?'

'I think you've just given it,' said Johnny. 'Thanks guys.'

Back on the Spirit of London, Johnny left Bentley and Rusty with his dad and Louise in sickbay and sprinted straight down the corridor to the lifts. He ran out onto the dinodeck, only to find it deserted except for the figure of Alf, supporting Clara on top of the rock near the centre. It made no sense at all, but Sol's drones were already stripping away the vegetation and carrying it off, restoring the deck to a five-a-side football pitch. They couldn't *all* be dead . . . could they? It had looked to be going so well from that brief flash he'd seen back on Nereid. A moment earlier Johnny had been so happy, but now . . . He walked slowly over to where the other two were sitting.

'What happened?' Johnny asked. 'What went wrong?'

Clara looked up, saw Johnny's face and started to cry.

'Ptery? Donna?' Johnny asked again. He knew it was too dangerous and he should never have asked them to go.

'They're . . . they're fine,' Clara replied, between sobs.

'Then why are you crying?' Johnny asked.

''Cos I'm so happy, stupid.'

Girls certainly behaved oddly at times. 'Then where are they all?' Johnny asked.

'They don't want to come back, Johnny,' Clara replied. 'I think they love it there – it's perfect for them.'

'It's what?'

'It's perfect – you should see it. They seem at home.'

'What about the krun?'

They're all gone. I'll show you.' Clara closed her eyes, steadied her breathing and stretched out her hands.

Light flooded into the dinodeck. Johnny shaded his eyes with his hands and stared – it was coming from an artificial sun, placed at the very centre of an enormous inside-out world. Johnny looked across at Clara whose eyes were shut, but then to Alf who nodded, so he stepped through the archway and into the insides of Triton. He was standing on springy turf. The gravity felt strong – not like Earth, but he was much heavier than on Nereid. The crust must be very thick or very dense, or probably both. There were some low-lying black buildings scattered around, with the same metallic doors that he'd seen on Nereid, but mostly the world looked as though it consisted of parkland, with strange grasses and giant trees straining upwards towards the central sun. No doubt about it – this was a miracle of engineering. A few of the dinosaurs were nearby, gathered around something on the ground. Johnny was pretty sure they knew not to hurt him by now, and walked slowly forward to take a closer look.

One of them, about three metres tall and standing on two legs, raised its horn-crested head towards Johnny as he approached and then bowed. Black blood was dripping from its tooth-filled jaws. Johnny looked down to whatever it was the dinosaurs were clustered around, and saw them tearing chunks out of a deflated and very dead krun soldier. As he looked, he saw there were other krun, strewn on the ground all across the landscape. He walked away from the dinosaurs and examined a few of the bodies. Clearly some had met a savage end at the claws and teeth of some very hungry dinosaurs, but on the whole he couldn't actually see much wrong with them. They just seemed to have . . . well, died. Maybe it was simply fright? A hissing noise coming from above distracted him. Johnny turned his face upwards and was sprayed by beautifully warm, very fine raindrops, as though someone had turned a sprinkler on. They were falling from the artificial sun at the centre of the globe. Johnny laughed out loud. Someone *had* turned a sprinkler on – it was an automated climate control system and the perfect habitat for the dinosaurs.

The next moment the sun and rain were blotted out as Ptery swooped down to meet him. The leather-winged creature reached out his black-blood-spattered talons and plucked Johnny off the ground.

'Hi, Ptery,' Johnny shouted above him.

'We fight well,' screeched Ptery, wheeling around in excitement to be sure Johnny could see the destruction they'd caused.

They flew for about five minutes, Ptery determined to show off the new vista the dinosaurs had won in battle. Nearby was the most built-up area Johnny could see – a mini spaceport. Already Sol's drones had got to work and were replanting the vegetation from the dinodeck to cover it over with a little piece of prehistoric Earth. They crossed a stream, which ran into a small lake, and then they flew away from the buildings altogether and over some purple grassland. A little herd of dinosaurs had already discovered this mini savannah and were grazing below. Johnny watched his and Ptery's combined shadow grow bigger then smaller as it raced above the little undulations in the surface.

Then their silhouette was lost as the winged dinosaur reached the edge of a forest of gigantic trees, with leaves like giant water-lily pads open wide, collecting the rainwater. Soon Ptery was rapidly beating his wings to slow himself down and he dropped Johnny into the uppermost branches of the very tallest tree. Instead of bark and foliage he landed noisily on top of metal and plastic sheets that looked like they'd somehow found their way from the spaceport. Ptery settled down next to him and then there was the sound of more beating wings. Donna landed beside them, carrying a large sheet of metal in her claws. She moved it a little way along the branches, turned her crested head onto one side to look at it from a different angle and then straightened up, apparently satisfied. Johnny understood.

'It's a nest,' he said. 'You're building a nest.'

'This home now,' said Donna. 'We win it.'

'You sure did,' Johnny replied. 'I love it.'

'You keep promise,' said Ptery, looking across at Donna and then back to Johnny. 'Much thank you.'

Johnny looked at the pair of unlikely friends and stretched out a hand onto each of their bony faces.

'We bond now,' said Ptery. 'We kin. You need us – we help.'

'Thank you,' said Johnny. He knew it was his turn to bow.

'Hello, Johnny,' came Sol's voice in his ear. 'I have a Captain Valdour requesting permission to come aboard.'

Johnny straightened, raised his wristcom to his mouth and said, 'Tell him, permission granted. I'm on my way.' He held both dinosaurs for a final time as their eyes met, before saying, 'I've got to go to my home now. Ptery, can you fly me back to where you found me?'

✡ ✡ ✡
✡ ✡

Johnny and Clara arrived in the shuttle bay just in time to see a pock-marked craft settle between the Piccadilly and the

Bakerloo. It looked very businesslike and not at all as frivolous as the gleaming bus and taxi on either side. A door opened upwards with a hydraulic hiss and out stepped a man with a scarred brown face and a patch covering his right eye.

'Captain Mackintosh,' he said, clicking his heels together and saluting Johnny.

'Captain Valdour,' said Johnny, trying to copy the salute but getting halfway through it with his wrong hand before he realized and changed. Clara put her hand to her mouth but managed not to laugh.

'Congratulations, Johnny,' said Valdour, ignoring any lapse in protocol. 'You have an impressive ship. I only wish I had time to inspect her properly.'

'You've got to come and see the bridge,' said Johnny. 'It's awesome.'

Valdour shook his head. 'While we stand here talking, the Andromedans advance. Nymac is encircling a nearby system. If we are to stop him I must return to the front at once.'

'How did you know to come?' Clara asked.

'I do not pretend to understand it,' Valdour replied. 'I am a simple soldier. Yesterday I saw you both being carried away to the Imperial Palace – indeed I planned to await your return.'

'I remember,' said Johnny.

'Then today, I received a direct Imperial order to go at full speed to the eighth planet of the Sol system, fight any krun, collect Chancellor Gronack and provide you with a new shield generator.'

'You're taking Gronack? Great,' said Johnny.

'Who is also, so I believe, on Melania,' said Valdour. 'I am to keep it incommunicado for at least the next twenty-one days.'

Clara smiled at Johnny and said, 'Can you believe we're getting rid of that windbag?'

'In all my years I have never felt so tempted to refuse an

order,' said Valdour, smiling too. The look didn't suit his battered face. 'Having just rid myself of the Dauphin, it does seem a poor reward to have another phasmeer forced upon me.'

'I'm sorry,' said Johnny, even though he most definitely wasn't. 'Sol – can you tell Chancellor Gronack to come to the shuttle bay straightaway? Tell it it's going home.'

'Chancellor Gronack is not aboard, Johnny,' Sol replied.

'What do you mean "not aboard"? Where is it this time?'

'I do not have that information. The Chancellor disembarked 27 hours, 18 minutes and 28.18284 seconds ago.'

'What? How?' Johnny asked.

'It took the shuttle Jubilee – destination was unknown.'

Johnny had assumed the Jubilee was waiting for them in the taxi rank outside the London Gherkin. He knew Gronack was unhappy but surely even it wouldn't have taken a shuttle craft to try to return to Melania.

'It seems,' said Valdour, 'that it is my lucky day. If I am able I will return to collect my cargo soon – should you have the misfortune to locate it. There is, though, one more thing.' Valdour turned, walked over to his shuttle craft and reached inside the door. He returned a moment later holding a pulsing crystalline sphere. 'Here,' he said to Johnny. 'The Emperor must value you greatly to give you this.' Gently he placed the shield generator down on the floor in front of Johnny and Clara.

'Thanks,' said Johnny. 'Thanks for everything.'

'Until next time,' said Valdour, saluting again and nodding to Clara.

Johnny saluted back, properly this time and, as Valdour clicked his heels together and climbed back into his shuttle craft, Clara shouted, 'Be careful.'

Johnny turned to his sister and said, 'Come on – he's being a bit weird, but I want you to meet Dad.'

13 ✧ ✦

THE BATTERY ✧ ✦

'Now that's better isn't it?' asked Clara, turning her father's head so he was looking into the mirror facing him. The horror of the last eleven years was plainly etched across his face, but after a couple of hours of forceful scrubbing and grooming, finished off by a severe haircut, Michael Mackintosh looked nearly human again. Even so, Johnny made a mental note never to let Clara cut his hair. Their dad sat on a chair in his new clothes, a plain white top and trousers. He was in front of the mirror that ran along one wall of Johnny's quarters. Clara put the scissors down and came to sit next to Bentley and Johnny on the bed that folded down into the middle of the room. They watched from behind in silence as their grey-haired father turned his head one way then the other, stuck his tongue out at his reflection and then reached his right index finger forward until it met the left index finger of his mirror image. He quickly drew back.

'Don't think I don't know what's going on,' he said to the well-groomed figure in front of him.

'Dad – nothing's going on,' said Johnny from the bed.

His father leant forward so he was almost nose to nose with his reflection, and said, 'You don't think so, do you? You don't think they're here? You don't think I know they're watching?'

'No one's watching,' said Johnny. 'It's just us.'

'I'll show you who's watching,' said his dad, who got to his feet, grabbed hold of the back of the chair and whipped it round in the air so it crashed into the mirror with surprising force. It bounced off across the room, narrowly missing Clara, who ducked just in time. The mirrors on the Spirit of London were pretty much unbreakable, but that didn't stop Michael Mackintosh pointing towards it as though he'd just exposed a secret viewing room behind, saying, 'Who's that then? Nobody watching us, eh? Think you could fool me?'

Johnny got to his feet and walked over to his dad, trying to pat him on the arm. 'Stop it, Dad. It's me and this is Clara. She's your daughter. Mum must have been pregnant when you were arrested.'

'I don't have a daughter. Get off me. Get off. I told you not to touch. Get off.'

'OK,' said Johnny, holding up both his hands while his dad backed away into the corner of the room, slid down the wall and brought his knees up to his chest. He was holding onto his ankles and started to rock to and fro.

'It's not fair,' said Clara. 'At least he knows who you are – even if he thinks you're not real. I'm going to check on Louise.' She got up and walked, head bowed, out of the door.

'I'll come too,' shouted Johnny. Right now there wasn't much point staying. He took a last look at his father, turned away and had almost followed Clara out of the room when a voice called him back.

'Johnny – don't go. Don't leave me here.' Michael Mackintosh was sobbing and shaking uncontrollably in the corner.

'Dad?'

'If you go they'll come back. Please don't let them come back. I might . . . I might not see you again.'

Johnny ran back to the tearful figure, sat down on the floor next to him and hugged him. 'Dad – no one's coming for you. You're safe now. We're going to get Mum and we'll be together again.'

'I miss her so much, Johnny,' said his father. Together they held each other and rocked backwards and forwards for a long time.

⚴   ⚴   ⚴
⚴   ⚴

Johnny decided that getting his two new passengers into the gel pods and trying to explain about folding space would be way too much hassle. Besides, a conventional flight would give Sol some time to install the replacement shield generator. The door to sickbay swished open and he walked through to hear Alf saying, '. . . if you are quite finished.'

Louise was lying on one of the beds with Rusty curled contentedly at her feet, while Alf monitored an instrument panel next to her. As Johnny entered she sat up, turned to him, and said, 'Bit of a temper your robot, hasn't he? Nice piece of kit though.'

'I *am* listening in case you were unaware of this,' said Alf. 'Master Johnny – I must protest at this treatment. This human insists on calling me a simple robot and asking me what *stuff* I am programmed for. Please tell her I am an artificial life form, I am trying to perform a complex medical procedure and she is proving very distracting.'

'All right threepio. Don't blow a fuse,' said Louise. 'It's only a few stitches.'

'I think she heard, Alf,' said Johnny, trying hard not to laugh. 'How's it going?'

'As I have been saying to your . . . your friend, it is not simply a few stitches, though I hate to imagine what she means by that. I am repairing severe damage to her internal organs, which may take several days and some considerable skill to heal. If I am not constantly interrupted.'

'OK, metal man – I can take a hint,' said Louise. She lay back down on the bed.

'Thank you,' said Alf, who sounded at the end of his tether.

'Where's Bentley?' Louise asked. It was clearly very hard for her to lie still and do nothing.

'Left him with my dad,' Johnny replied. 'He needed the company. You seen Clara?'

'Yeah. She was in here earlier – seemed a bit down.'

'What do you mean?' Johnny sat down on the edge of Louise's bed.

'Come on – I thought you were pretty bright. If I had that nutter down there – no offence but I spent a day with him – as my father I'd be upset.'

'That's not fair.'

Louise sat up again, making Rusty whine, while Alf threw his hands up in despair. She looked at Johnny and said, 'Listen – I can see he's been through a lot, but all he talked about was his Nicky, little Johnny and Mary. Never mentioned anything about Clara once. How d'ya think that makes her feel?'

'He'll get better. He's started already. It's just . . . it's just he's never seen her before.'

'And I thought my family was weird. You lot take the biscuit. What are you going to do about it?'

'It's not my fault.' Johnny knew he'd got a lot of things wrong over the past few days but he didn't see how he could be blamed for this.

'I'm not saying it is, but you've got to talk to her, Johnny. She's only got you – you've got your dad . . . and Bentley.' Louise sighed as she lay back on the bed as though this was all the most obvious thing in the world.

'Thank goodness for that,' muttered Alf in the background

Johnny thought for a moment. 'When we get home we're going to get her mum. We won't be weird – we'll be a proper family.'

'Great – but make sure you tell her.' Louise raised her head and looked straight into Johnny's eyes. 'OK?'

'OK,' said Johnny.

He stood up and was about to leave when Louise called after him.

'And Johnny?' He stopped, standing in the open doorway.

'Thanks for coming back. If you hadn't . . .'

'No worries,' said Johnny. He turned away and ran down the corridor before Louise could burst into tears. As he reached the antigrav lifts he asked, 'Sol – where's Clara?'

'Clara is in the strategy room on deck 14.'

'Deck 14,' said Johnny as he stepped into mid-air and began flying downwards. He stopped moving, hovered in front of the Level 14 corridor and then stepped forwards onto solid ground. His mind was definitely made up – the Chancellor could wait. It was its own fault it had gone off. Tomorrow they'd fold their way straight into St Catharine's and bring Mum back to sickbay. Between them Sol and Alf would make her better in no time. The door to the strategy room opened. Clara was on the very far side of the force-field table, staring out of the windows into space. She didn't turn round, but said, 'I can see your stars,' pointing to Cassiopeia below them to the right. 'They're so much brighter here.'

'There's no atmosphere to block them out,' Johnny replied, as he walked across to join his sister. 'Look at that white band. That's the Milky Way, the galaxy. Sometimes it's like I can hear it whispering my name.'

Clara nodded. 'Where's Melania?' she asked.

Johnny pointed to the spot. 'Weird isn't it? We're there as well as here. I spoke to Bram this morning just as we arrived.'

'I thought it was you!' said Clara. 'That head floating by the fire.'

'I told him to give us sticky toffee pudding.'

Clara giggled and Johnny smiled. He was pleased she was laughing. 'You know what we're going to do when we get back?

We'll get Mum straightaway – just like the Diaquant said. Then everything will start being loads better.'

'Promise?'

'Cross my heart.'

'I tried to make a start,' said Clara, pointing to the near-invisible planning table in the middle of the room, 'but Sol couldn't find it. I must have got the hospital name wrong.'

'Let's take a look,' said Johnny, turning away from the gigantic window to face the table. 'Hi, Sol.'

'Hello, Johnny,' replied the ship.

'Can you give me a projection of St Catharine's Hospital for the Criminally Insane? Same as you did for the Proteus Institute.'

'From this distance I have to rely on Earth records I have been adding to my database. As I told Clara, there is no mention of such an institution anywhere.'

'But that's crazy,' said Johnny. 'It's in Sussex – right by Wittonbury station.'

'This is the area around Wittonbury,' Sol replied, and the see-through table changed to show a high-resolution satellite photograph. 'If you can identify the structure I will create a projection.'

Johnny climbed the stairs to the mezzanine platform over-looking the table to give himself a better view. He spotted the train line and followed it south with a laser pointer embedded in his wristcom, until he eventually reached the station itself. 'Sol – give me a two mile radius around there, will you?' The image changed and the little town appeared in much greater detail. Johnny had no trouble recognizing some of the buildings surrounding the station. He had no difficulty at all identifying the route he'd taken many times out of the station to St Catharine's. It was just that St Catharine's wasn't there in the photographs. The path led to a collection of green fields. 'I don't get it,' he said. 'Why can't we see it?'

'I cannot guarantee the reliability of images from your planet's satellites, Johnny.'

'Maybe it's like a military thing,' said Clara. 'And they don't show it in the pictures.'

'The images do not appear to have been tampered with,' said Sol. 'My resources are fully occupied integrating the new shield generator. Once we are safely back on Earth I will make the problem a priority.'

Clara looked crestfallen. She was about to say something but Johnny put his finger to his lips and shook his head. As innocently as he could he asked Sol, 'Can you get a message to Kovac? I'm sure he'll find the hospital in no time.'

'It is highly unlikely that such a box of silicon and transistors will find St Catharine's before I do,' Sol replied. 'I shall map the area and perform any necessary searches myself before we reach Earth orbit.'

'I'm sure you will, Sol,' said Johnny grinning at Clara. They walked out of the door and made their way down the corridor.

'I don't think she likes Kovac,' said Clara as they stepped into the lifts.

'The feeling's mutual,' Johnny replied. They reached the door to his quarters, which swished open. Bentley barked a hello from next to their dad, who was crouched in the corner turning Johnny's battered games console over and over in his hands. 'Want to say goodnight?' Johnny asked.

Clara stood in the doorway staring at her father for a few seconds. 'No – I think I'll leave it tonight,' she said, turning away down the corridor as the door closed silently.

Johnny walked across to the corner of the room. 'I'll take that, Dad,' he said, lifting the handheld from out of his father's hands and pocketing it inside his tunic.

'That was my son's,' said Michael Mackintosh, staring up at Johnny full of anger.

'Dad – it's me. It's Johnny.'

'What have you done with him? He was here earlier. I won't let you hurt my family.' Bentley placed his paws on top of his head and whimpered softly. Johnny wished he knew the right thing to say. 'I won't let you hurt my kids,' said his dad, but the strength had gone out of his voice. He curled himself up into a little ball on the floor.

At Johnny's request the bed folded out of the invisible join in the wall. He picked the duvet and a pillow from it, lifted his dad's head off the floor and slid the pillow underneath, before gently covering him with the quilt. There didn't seem anything else to be done for now, so he went and lay down on the bed, said, 'Lights off,' and was immediately plunged into darkness. 'Sol – wake me up when we're thirty minutes away or you've got a fix on St Catharine's. Or on the Jubilee for that matter.'

'Of course, Johnny,' replied the ship.

'Night, Dad,' said Johnny, but there was no response. He lay wide awake with his eyes open, getting increasingly used to the darkness in the room, wondering what the next day would have in store. Bentley curled up at the foot of the bed and was soon snoring. Johnny could tell his dad was asleep from the regular rise and fall of the duvet on the floor and the steady breathing from the corner. He wished he, too, could get to sleep. He wished it even more, as his father began muttering away to himself and Johnny spent the night listening to his dad's nightmares and imagining the terrible things the krun must have done to him over the past decade.

☆　☆　☆
☆　☆

It was a gloriously crisp morning. The commuters, all looking the same in their dark suits and ties and shiny black shoes, were busy funnelling through the entrance to the London Gherkin, which was framed against a clear blue sky. As Clara prepared for the fold, Johnny studied her face, wondering how Alf had known when to give the signal before. He'd told Sol not to disturb Alf, who was still looking after Louise in sickbay. Instead, he'd decided to come in the shuttle with Clara. Besides, he'd been dying to do it ever since Clara had told him about the last time. Breaking orbit like that and coming down from the jet black of space all the way through the clouds, while invisible, had been awesome. He was about to say how great it was for probably the hundredth time, when he noticed the expression on Clara's face change. It was as though she was somewhere else now – the same look Johnny had seen that first time on Cheybora, when Valdour had kept her out of the gel pods. He knew she was ready. Raising the wristcom to his mouth, he said, 'Now, Sol.'

Johnny looked up. There'd been no sound and nothing to see, but he could feel it was the Spirit of London now towering magnificently above him. Of course the workers who, a moment before, were walking through the giant M and W entrance into the Gherkin had no idea they were instead now stepping straight into hyperspace – into a little pocket of the universe that hadn't existed a second earlier. He stood up and helped Clara to her feet. She smiled at him, wobbled for a moment but then found her balance and they joined the crowds of people walking across the paving and towards the giant spaceship. Before they'd taken more than half a dozen steps a familiar voice squeaked inside Johnny's ear.

'Johnny . . . Clara . . . help me.' It was the Chancellor.

'What's happened?' Johnny asked, raising his wristcom to his mouth as he and Clara stared at each other.

'They're coming . . . help me.'

'Who's coming? . . . Where are you? . . . Gronack?' Johnny's questions were met with silence. 'Sol,' he continued. 'Where was that message from?'

'Computing . . . approximately 743.5925 metres from here

on a bearing of 141.42 degrees. The street name is Tower Bridge Road.'

'Come on,' said Clara. 'That's just down here. You can see Tower Bridge from Sol.'

She started running and Johnny soon caught her, speeding downhill towards the Thames past the startled workers. Sol guided them as they sprinted through the streets, Johnny now ahead of Clara, hoping to reach the Chancellor before it was too late. Soon a square turret connected to giant, light blue suspension cables came into view that marked one side of the famous bridge.

'How much further, Sol?' Johnny asked as he looked ahead for some sign of the phasmeer.

'You are 161.8033 metres from the source of the Chancellor's last transmission,' Sol replied.

Johnny stopped allowing Clara, breathing heavily, to catch him up. There was a problem: the bridge had been raised for a high-masted sailing boat to pass underneath and the Chancellor must be on the other side. The traffic and pedestrians had had to stop, making the pavement very busy. As well as commuters there was a streetsweeper in green overalls clearing up litter from the night before, loads of camera-carrying tourists come to view the impressive scene and some workmen in hard hats and yellow bibs.

Painfully slowly the boat cleared the bridge, sailing upstream. A bell sounded, lights flashed and the raised central portion of the bridge began to lower. Johnny and Clara were swept forward by the crowd, eager to cross to the other side. Surrounded by so many people jostling, someone's umbrella jabbed Johnny right in the leg. He kept glancing round to check Clara was still close by, and peering ahead for any sign of the Chancellor or the Jubilee. They were surrounded by workmen now, and he and Clara had to stop because the streetsweeper pushed his cart right in front of them. It was only then that he noticed his leg was actually really sore. Not that he had time to worry about that now – he'd sort it out in sickbay once they got back to the Spirit of London. But he was also struggling to focus. The traffic was moving again. Coming the other way was a black London taxi. Johnny squinted to see if he could recognize the Jubilee's trademark camouflage, but as he looked one cab blurred into two and then four. He turned to the side to get round the cart and bumped into the streetsweeper, holding onto the man's overalls to try to stay on his feet. Sol was talking to him through his earpiece, but he couldn't seem to understand what she was saying. And where was Clara? And why was he being lowered to the pavement?

'I've called an ambulance,' shouted the sweeper, sounding very far away. 'It'll be here in a moment.'

'No,' said Johnny, trying to get to his feet. He could hear sirens, and felt a firm hand pressed on his chest holding him down. He couldn't focus on anything now. He was being carried. He tried to fight, but his arms and legs seemed to be working several seconds behind what his head was telling them to do. He heard doors being slammed shut, and someone saying that they were both inside. He was dimly aware of Clara lying on a stretcher on what must be the other side of the ambulance, of hearing more sirens and of Sol's voice asking him what was happening. Someone was putting a mask over Johnny's face.

'Deep breaths now – it's oxygen. You took quite a turn.'

Johnny breathed and his lungs seemed to empty of any air that had been there – it certainly wasn't oxygen. He tried to take off the mask, but it was being held firmly to his face by a hand at the end of a green sleeve. His arms and legs were strapped down. The sirens were the only thing filling his brain. His eyes were far too heavy to keep open.

☆　☆　☆
☆　☆

'You're sure about the results?' It was a woman speaking in a flat drawling voice – American, thought Johnny, but not at all like Miss Harutunian.

A man replied. 'There's no doubt . . . none at all. With both children. No. No doubt at all.'

'But you still have no idea what the other half is?'

'Impossible to say. We can only test for a few others. No. Not anything we've seen before.'

Johnny knew better than to open his eyes, but something about that second voice sounded familiar. Very slowly he tried moving his arms and his legs, but they were still fixed to the stretcher he was lying on.

'What have I been telling you?' squeaked a voice that was definitely familiar. 'These infants kidnapped me from the galactic capital. I've given you what we agreed. Release me and I assure you that your cooperation will not go unrewarded.'

'Can you be more specific about the nature of those rewards . . . Chancellor, did you say it was?' asked the woman.

'Chancellor Gronack . . . Chief emissary between the office of Its Highness The Regent and His Divine Imperial Majesty, Emperor Bram Khari.'

'And the rewards?' prompted the woman.

'Naturally diplomatic protocols do not allow for an exchange of technology with an inferior species such as yourselves,' said Gronack. 'However, I am sure payment can be made to your government in whatever mineral resources are deemed valuable on this planet.'

'You say there is a spaceship,' asked the woman.

'Of course there is a spaceship – how else can I travel home? Besides, you couldn't possibly be given that,' said the Chancellor. 'Imagine the disparity on this world if one government possessed such technology while others did not.'

'Imagine indeed,' said the woman. 'But I agree with you that governments cannot be trusted. That's why I and my colleagues are above such niceties. We will take your ship, Chancellor, but I assure you it will be in good hands.'

'There is clearly a misunderstanding,' squeaked Gronack. 'Regardless of governments, as a representative of the Imperial Court, I insist you carry out my wishes.'

'Actually,' said the woman, 'I believe it is you who misunderstands. You are in no position to make demands. Take him away.'

'Him? Him? I have never been so insulted in all my life.'

'Ah it's a female, yes, a female,' said the other voice.'

'I most certainly am not. My gender is not sullied by such primitive distinctions . . . take your hands off me. We had a deal.'

'Oh and do something to shut it up, will you,' said the woman, as Chancellor Gronack was led away out of the room.

Johnny risked opening an eye to see what was happening. He was lying inside a cage close to some sleek steel bars running from floor to ceiling, separating him from the remainder of a large rectangular room. On the other side of the bars stood a tall balding man in a white coat and a slim woman with shoulder-length black hair in a navy blue jacket and skirt, wearing very high heels. Both of them were standing with their backs to him, in front of a portable table, watching two security guards escort the Chancellor through a thick metal door in the far corner. The man in the white coat turned around. Johnny half closed his eye again, but then opened both of them in surprise. Standing in front of him was Dr Carrington from St Catharine's.

'I do believe this one is awake . . . yes, awake now,' said Dr Carrington.

'Hello, Johnny,' said the woman turning round, walking across until she was right next to the cage where she knelt down, her face close to Johnny's, and smiled at him. Johnny thought he'd never seen such a cold smile anywhere. 'I'd like to ask you a few questions.'

'Where's Clara?' said Johnny.

'Clara is right behind you,' said the woman, still smiling. 'As you can see, she is perfectly safe and will remain so as long as we receive your full cooperation.'

Johnny turned his head and saw Clara, lying apparently unconscious, on an identical stretcher beside him. Behind her, metal shutters covered what he assumed were three windows along one wall, giving no clue whether it was day or night outside. As he looked at his sister he heard a door swing open behind him and the clicking of the woman's heels as she walked into the cage. Johnny turned back to see the American standing beside his stretcher. 'If you hurt her,' he said.

'Johnny . . . dear,' said the woman, patting him on the stomach. 'I'm here to help.'

'What do you want?'

'There's no need to be aggressive. I'm your friend, Johnny,' said the woman. 'Call me Bobbi. I'm on your side, but I'd like you to help me. I just need a few answers.'

Johnny wondered what on earth he was about to be asked. Did they know where the Spirit of London was? It didn't sound as though Gronack had told them that. What about his mum? With Dr Carrington here in the room what did that mean for her? And why couldn't he hear Alf or Sol in his ear? They must be looking for him. He mustn't give anything away.

'Can you remember what you did on the 23rd April?' asked Bobbi.

'What? Er . . . That's my birthday,' said Johnny, puzzled.

'Of course it is. Busy opening presents were you? Out with friends having fun? You didn't do anything bad like trying to hack into the guidance system of a group of radio telescopes?'

'Oh that,' said Johnny, almost relieved, but instantly kicking himself.

'So you admit it? You attempted to seize control of the Very Large Array – a collection of radio telescopes in New Mexico.'

'Well yeah – I didn't do any harm.'

Bobbi was walking around Johnny's stretcher and he strained to lift his neck to follow her. She stopped by his sister's stretcher and stood with her back to him, stroking Clara's hair. 'That's not really for you to say, is it now, Johnny? And it's not the first time either, according to our scientists.'

'Whose scientists? Where am I?'

'Why you're in America, of course,' said Bobbi, turning round and showing off a straight set of the whitest teeth Johnny had ever seen.

'We can't be. I wasn't out that long.'

Bobbi raised a pencil-thin black eyebrow. 'Believe me, Johnny. You *are* in America, I'm your only friend here and now I'd like you to tell me about those telescopes.'

'It was nothing – just a little subroutine. It couldn't affect them at all.'

'So why did you do it?'

'It was . . . .' There didn't seem to be anything gained by lying. 'It was just a SETI thing.'

'SETI?'

'The search for extra-terrestrial intelligence – signals from space.'

'Ah . . . extra-terrestrials. We're making progress. Tell me why a supposed thirteen-year-old boy is so interested?'

'Look – I answered your question. I said I did it. I'm not saying any more till you untie me.'

The woman smiled at him. 'I've got something to show you,' she said, moving to the end of the stretcher, holding onto the metal handles either side of his feet, and wheeling him out into

319

the main room beyond the cage and towards the table. She picked up a coloured printout and held it out in front of her. 'Do you know what this is, Johnny?'

Johnny looked at the piece of paper. It reminded him of some graphs he'd seen on Kovac's monitor what seemed forever ago, but he wasn't going to give Bobbi the satisfaction of telling her.

'No, Johnny? I'll tell you what it is. Something we call a DNA test. Do you know what DNA is?'

'Of course I do.'

'Yours is very interesting – and your sister's for that matter. Do you know why?'

'I'm sure you can't wait to tell me.'

'Johnny . . . dear – I can't help you if you won't help yourself. You see, I know what you are . . . or rather, this test tells me what you're not.'

Johnny tried to look defiant, but he was worried. He couldn't help thinking of the journalist he'd met in the alley, going home from the park that day. He'd said, 'I know what you are' too. What were they talking about? Johnny bit his lip and asked, 'So what am I?'

'Oh you can do better than that, Johnny,' said the woman. 'You break into some of the world's most advanced computer systems. You search for signals from outer space. As we just saw with that jumped-up stick insect, you keep some very strange company. You might pretend to be a thirteen year old from somewhere called . . . Castle Dudbury New Town, but we both know that can't possibly be true, can it?

'What do you mean?'

'What I mean is that this little piece of paper proves you're not human.' The American woman was holding the sheet right in front of Johnny's face.

'That's stupid,' he said. 'How can it prove that?' Johnny looked across to Dr Carrington who was refusing to make eye contact with him. Instead, the doctor was looking down at a syringe he was holding.

'Stupid is it?' Bobbi continued. 'This is Dr Carrington – one of the world's experts on xenobiology.' As Johnny glared at him, Dr Carrington played nervously with the syringe. 'That's right, Johnny. A xenobiologist,' continued the American. 'His test shows you're not human.'

'Well, partly human to be entirely correct. Partly, yes.'

'How?' Johnny asked, genuinely puzzled. 'How can it show that?'

The doctor stepped forward. 'Our DNA is made up of four nucleotides or base pairs, yes four, all fitted together into a double helix.'

'Adenine, cytosine, guanine and thymine,' said Johnny, who'd learnt this for his own test. 'A, C, G, T . . . so what?'

'So look at the chart,' said the woman.

Johnny peered forward as far as he could while strapped to the stretcher – it was much the same as he'd seen at Halader House. There were the different sequences of letters he'd seen before. 'It would help if you untied me,' he said.

'Oh I don't think so,' said Bobbi. 'Who knows what you're capable of with your alien DNA.'

'But what alien DNA?' Johnny asked. 'There isn't anything.'

'Exactly. You have gaps,' Bobbi said.

Johnny looked to the doctor for an explanation.

'We can only test for human – for terrestrial base pairs. The gaps must come from something else. Yes . . . something non-terrestrial. Not from this world, Jonathan.'

'Oh,' was all Johnny said. Of course he'd met aliens – could they have contaminated him? Yet even before, when he'd taken the test himself, he'd still had the gaps. Had the krun been experimenting on him in the past, like those poor people he'd seen in the tanks? That could be it – it would explain why they

321

were so interested in him now. His father had probably found out, which was why he'd been taken.

'Very convincing, little Mr Surprised,' said Bobbi. 'It's time to get down to business. Where do your people really come from? How many of you are there here?'

Back inside the cage, Clara spluttered, as though about to wake up. The doctor moved quickly across towards her. Johnny turned his head to watch as Dr Carrington placed his pneumatic syringe on her exposed neck and air hissed out. For a second, Johnny thought he saw a look of surprise in Clara's eyes as she lifted her head, but then she fell back onto the stretcher, sound asleep.

'What are you doing, Carrington?' asked the woman. 'I need to question her.'

'Too much of a risk having them both conscious at once. A risk, yes.'

'Hmmm. I suppose you're right. Next time ask before you act. I'm the one in charge here.'

'Sorry ma'am,' said the doctor, looking back down at his hands. 'Won't happen again, no . . . sorry.'

'Make sure it doesn't,' said the woman, before turning back to Johnny. 'We've been monitoring you for some time. Then our unlikely informant arrived and forced our hand. One way or another, we will find out more. You know our races could cooperate. I am authorized to propose a deal.'

'What kind of a deal?' Johnny asked.

Your life . . . your lives,' she said looking beyond Johnny to Clara, 'in exchange for information. Where you're from, how many there are of you. I want your ship, of course, and all your technology.'

'I don't have a ship,' Johnny replied, desperately concentrating on his face not turning red.

'If that's really true I don't give much for your chances. I'd say it's the dissection table for you, or perhaps her,' said Bobbi, smiling across to Clara again. 'Just like your associate . . . Chancellor Gronack.'

'You wouldn't,' said Johnny. 'You can't,' he shouted, struggling against the straps holding him down.

'I can and, believe me, I will,' said the woman. 'But I am not ungenerous. I'll give you the night to think about it. And before you get any ideas, we analysed your communications device.' She walked back to the table and held up two wristcoms that must have been taken from Johnny and Clara. 'We've calibrated a special field around this building to ensure they are inoperative. Carrington,' she said, turning to the doctor. 'I think about eight hours should do it. Would you mind?'

'Eight hours, yes of course, eight.'

'And then you should lock him in the cage – just to be sure.'

Doctor Carrington walked over and placed the syringe against Johnny's neck. There was a hiss. Johnny fought to stay awake, but it felt as though he was disappearing under water. The gleaming silver of the cage bars began to fuzz together as he was wheeled through them and came to rest. Dr Carrington was fiddling with Johnny's right arm. As a reflex Johnny tried to move it away and almost did before the doctor grabbed it. The straps had been undone. For a moment it felt like breaking the surface of the water back to consciousness. He stared, wide eyed, but Dr Carrington shook his head slightly and slipped something into Johnny's pocket. Then he felt himself going under again, drowning in darkness. The last thing he heard was the door to the cage clanking shut.

☆ ☆ ☆
☆ ☆

It was freezing cold and very uncomfortable. Johnny tried to focus in the faint red glow of the emergency lighting. The outlines of metal bars reminded him where he was. The even sound of breathing beside him suggested Clara was asleep. He tried to sit up – the straps were still holding him, but much tighter on his left side than his right. And when he lifted his right arm the bonds slid smoothly away. He was free. He sat up, undid the straps on his left arm and rubbed both his wrists. Then he turned his attention to the restraints on his legs. Once they were removed, he slid off the stretcher as quietly as he could and onto the floor.

'Clara, wake up,' Johnny hissed in her ear. There was no reaction – her steady breathing continued exactly as before. He tried again, tapping her lightly on the cheek, but still nothing happened so he got to work on undoing the straps that were fixing her onto the stretcher. Once she was free he tried lifting her up, but she simply flopped back down as she was before. With Clara sedated, getting out of wherever they were would be a lot more difficult. He looked around the room. By now his eyes were used to the dim red light. Johnny walked over to the corner of the cage and put his hands onto the bars of the door. It swung smoothly open as he touched it, with Johnny almost falling forward in surprise. It couldn't have been locked properly when Dr Carrington and that Bobbi woman had left.

He walked silently across the room to the table and picked up one of the wristcoms. Raising it to his mouth he whispered 'Sol,' but before he could say anything else he clutched the side of his face due to an ear-splitting whistling. He wasn't going to try that again in a hurry, but he strapped the device to his wrist anyway, and slipped the other one into his pocket.

Also on the table were a couple of half-drunk cups of what smelled like coffee, the printouts of the DNA tests, Johnny's games console and a file marked 'TOP SECRET – HIGHLY CONFIDENTIAL.' He opened it up – there were pages headed with the names of several radio telescopes, each with times and dates on them, and maps, with circular areas shaded, a few showing the part of southern England that contained Castle Dudbury, some of Canada and other places too. There were also names and photographs of people – David Barnes, Jonas Faltskog and others – none of whom he recognized – except he did find one picture of him walking Bentley in the park.

Another page had portions of the script he'd written to track the telescopes, with annotations in different-coloured ink. After a few moments Johnny stopped reading the comments about his programming style and put the file down. He was wasting time – this wasn't telling him anything he needed now. He picked up the games console and was about to pocket it when he had a thought. He turned it on, switched it over to his old mobile phone mode and waited while it searched for a network signal. Coughing from outside the door distracted him. Johnny froze, holding his breath and staring at the door. It didn't open. He exhaled and looked down at the handheld. He had just one bar. Again looking nervously over to the door, Johnny held the device up to his mouth and whispered 'Kovac – are you there?'

'I might as well not be for all the attention I get,' came an irritated reply.

'Kovac – can you triangulate my position? I think I'm in America.'

'I see – yes I suppose you are aren't you?'

'What does that mean? Where am I exactly?'

'You're in Grosvenor Square, in what I believe is termed London's West end.'

'But you said I was in America.'

'You appear to be inside the American Embassy. Technically it is part of the United States of America.'

'Oh . . .' said Johnny. 'Look – we need help. Can you contact Sol – tell her where I am? We need rescuing.'

'Pass on a message. You need rescuing.'

'Yes, but hurry. It's really important,' said Johnny, looking anxiously across at the door which could open at any moment.

'I'm in the middle of determining the amount of dark energy in the universe to deduce if it will collapse or expand for ever. But you want me to stop to pass on a message.'

'Kovac,' hissed Johnny. 'The universe will still be here tomorrow. We might not be.'

'If that organic energy-matrix supercomputer is so clever, why do you need me to tell it what to do?'

'Kovac – just do it will you? Get Sol to send Alf in one of the shuttles.'

'Very well – it's done,' said Kovac, huffily. 'But she doesn't like me and I have to say the feeling is most definitely reciprocated.'

'Thank you,' said Johnny. He turned away from the table and slipped the console inside his tunic. Oddly, something else was already in there. Johnny pulled it out – it looked like a little map. He unfolded it to reveal the floorplan of an immense building, titled 24–32 Grosvenor Square. Various features had been marked using a highlighting pen. There was writing coming through from the other side of the paper. Johnny turned it over, spread it out on the table and began to read.

Dear Jonathan

I have just heard that you and your sister have been captured together and taken to the US embassy in Grosvenor Square. Do not be fooled. There is nothing 'official' about the organization holding you. You are where you are because it is convenient, away from prying eyes and these people are extremely well connected. I do not know what they intend to do with you, but they are not bound by the normal rule of law and it is unlikely to be pleasant. I have been summoned to perform some tests on you.

On this plan I have marked the area of the embassy where they are likely to detain you, as well as a route out of the building should that be necessary. Having witnessed your sister's escape from me at the Proteus Institute, I suspect you can simply disappear to where you need to go – a hitherto unforeseen development.

You must believe me that in most difficult circumstances I have always sought to do my best for you and your family. When I discovered your mother's pregnancy while in her comatose state, I was able to deliver Clara successfully and persuaded the krun she required a human upbringing. I have tried to keep you both alive and safe from those who would use you. I worked tirelessly at the Proteus Institute to prevent experiments on your sister and monitor and guide her progress. The group that has captured you are particularly dangerous. I believe the destiny of humankind may be in your hands and you would fulfil that better away from them.

Your friend

Peter Carrington

Stunned, Johnny picked up the plans and went over to try to wake Clara again. He shook her several times but, despite a few groans there was no sign of consciousness. According to his wristcom it was 2.55 in the morning. Johnny spread the plan out on his vacated stretcher and tried to get his bearings. A room marked 'holding area', on the third floor was highlighted. Its shape matched the one he was in. Johnny noticed that towards the end of the corridor was another marked 'operating theatre' and he shuddered, but tried to put that out of his mind. A route labelled 'AC' was marked leading away from the corner of the holding area opposite the door. On the plans it looked as though it would eventually take them beyond the main building, into a little park outside. But there was no door to be seen, just a blank wall. And it was uncomfortable standing there as he was smack underneath a vent, blasting him with cold air. Johnny placed his hand on the wall at what he was sure was the right spot, but nothing happened. He looked upwards so his face felt the full effect of the air conditioning and wondered if there was any way he could turn it off. And then he realized that *was* their escape route. Remove the grille and the pipes would carry him and Clara all the way out of the building. Even better, they were so wide that if he collapsed the legs on Clara's stretcher he'd be able to push her along in front of him. He grabbed a chair from beside the table, placed it underneath the vent and started work on the screws. The freezing cold air numbed his fingers, but nothing was going to stop him and, once he'd prised the first one out, the other three followed easily. Johnny removed the grille covering the broad vent and pushed it inside. If he could he'd replace it behind them once they were through.

He ran over to the cage, rubbing his hands together to warm them up again, and wheeled Clara's stretcher so it was under the vent. The hard part would be lifting her up, but he'd had enough practice carrying her before in the much stronger gravity of Melania and he knew he could do it.

But something about sneaking away wasn't right. Johnny might find the Chancellor annoying but he didn't want it dissected. It was Gronack's fault they were all being held prisoner, but he knew he couldn't leave it behind. First he had to try to rescue the Chancellor and then they could all escape together.

Johnny wheeled Clara over to the table. He took the top secret file and placed it underneath her trolley, and then he

328

pushed his sister to the far corner of the room. There was a keypad beside the big metal door and Johnny placed his hand over it. He was getting better at this and could feel the combination. Silently he unlocked the door, opened it just a fraction and froze – there was a soldier sitting in a chair facing the doorway. The man didn't move. For a few seconds Johnny stood with the door ajar watching the regular rise and fall of the man's chest and decided he was asleep. So Johnny opened the door fully – it creaked loudly but the marine didn't react. Very quietly Johnny wheeled Clara's trolley past the slumped soldier before going back to close the door. Every noise he made, his footsteps, breathing and heartbeat, seemed to be magnified in the cavernous corridor, wider than Barnard Way, and when the door creaked shut he was sure the soldier would wake. But the man just coughed again in his sleep before repositioning himself and Johnny tiptoed back to Clara's stretcher.

He made his way along past pieces of office equipment, referring to the plan a couple of times to check the names and numbers on doors to be sure he was going the right way. Coming to an alcove he stopped and tried one last attempt to revive Clara, when a whirring noise distracted him. They were right next to a lift shaft and someone was heading for their floor. Looking round desperately for cover Johnny wheeled the trolley behind a large photocopier in the corridor and crouched down out of sight. There was an electronic chime and the doors swished open.

A woman said 'After you, Carrington,' and out stepped the doctor followed by Bobbi, both of them walking up the corridor towards Johnny. He was done for. Dr Carrington reached the copier first, his eyes met Johnny's and he stopped stock-still in his tracks.

Bobbi crashed into the back of him. 'What the?' said the startled woman.

'So sorry, Colonel Hartman . . . so sorry, yes,' said Dr

Carrington, who turned to face the American, standing to block her view of Johnny. 'I do believe I left some equipment in your office. Would you object if we went to get it now? Equipment . . .'

'Very well,' said Bobbi, 'but be quick about it.' She turned and started walking the other way down the corridor with the doctor. 'I want to be in position well before they wake up,' she said as they returned to the lift and the doors closed behind them.

Johnny ran down the corridor pushing Clara's trolley in front of him until they were nearly at the end. He slowed and started checking the signs on doors, stopping at one on the left marked 'theatre' where, all being well, he should find Chancellor Gronack.

Again Johnny put his hand on the keypad and this time tutted – the combination was the same as before. He turned the handle and pushed the heavy door very slightly ajar. A sliver of light fell onto the figure of the phasmeer, standing in the middle of the room. Gronack turned to see where the light was coming from and squeaked, 'Johnny – in here. Help me.'

'Hang on,' said Johnny. He used Clara's trolley to hold the door open as he pushed her through and followed into the room. The door closed behind him and the lights came on, all of them focused on an operating table surrounded by a mixture of medical equipment and video cameras. In front of the table, strewn across the floor, were the dead bodies of several people, some in white coats and others in uniforms. So that was why they'd not met any soldiers in the corridor. 'How did you . . .' asked Johnny, open-mouthed. The Chancellor didn't answer. Instead a voice from behind said, 'It didn't. We dropped by to help.' He whirled around to see Stevens smiling, standing beside two other suited krun, each with their weapons pointed at Johnny. Instinctively he raised his hands. Stevens stepped forward and inspected Clara's unconscious body. Satisfied she wasn't about to wake up, he walked over to where Gronack was standing, robes flashing yellow and blue, in front of a giant window. The phasmeer was shaking with laughter.

Stevens nodded to the spindly alien and turned to face Johnny. 'Well, well, well,' he said. 'Caught defenceless – you know I really would like to kill you after all the trouble you've caused. I still may, but the Andromedans have offered a very high price for you. I'm sure we'll double it if we throw in the girl.'

'Quite inexplicable really,' squeaked Gronack. 'They're worthless Terrans and killing them would be a pleasure, but orders are orders.'

'Orders? Whose orders?' Johnny asked.

'The Andromedans of course,' said Gronack. 'You will find it pays to be on the winning side.' Gronack's robes flushed purple with pride. 'As soon as I discovered it I gave them Khari's spaceship plantation. When I present them with you two meddling upstarts . . .'

'How could you? I came here to save you,' said Johnny.

'So I see. I always knew your misplaced hero complex would get you into trouble. Life on your ship was a risk I'm no longer prepared to take.'

'But Bram trusted you,' said Johnny, who could feel his face going red. 'How could you betray him? He even sent a ship for you – just yesterday. You could've been going back to Melania.'

'You think everything is so black and white, you silly little boy,' squeaked Gronack. Its robes started pulsing all the colours of the rainbow. 'You see there's more to this galaxy than that. I am a phasmeer, a born diplomat – we understand every shade, every nuance.'

'Enough . . . Chancellor,' said Stevens. He walked towards Johnny and Clara, when an alarm went off in the corridor outside. Bangs and shouting were coming closer too. Perhaps Bobbi had finally reached the holding area, found them missing and set it off.

'Whatever now?' asked Gronack.

'I'll deal with it,' said Stevens, who strode purposefully towards the door. A moment later there was an almighty crash and the krun's body flew back past Johnny, straight into the Chancellor, knocking it to the floor. Into the room came what looked like a London taxi that placed itself between Johnny and Clara and the other krun, shielding them from the energy blasts as the aliens opened fire. The doors flew open.

'Brilliant, Alf,' shouted Johnny as he lifted Clara off the stretcher and flung her onto the back seat of the Bakerloo. Only it wasn't Alf. It was his father, whose green eyes blazed back at him, with Bentley next to him coiled to spring from the front seat if needed. 'Dad?' said Johnny, disbelieving.

'Get in, son,' shouted Michael Mackintosh as the green ray from a krun weapon flew just over Johnny's left shoulder.

He dived onto the back seat next to Clara. Through the open door he heard Gronack scream, 'Stop them,' and the craft jerked forwards. They passed the prone Chancellor, smashed the operating table out of the way and continued on, shattering the glass of the window on the far side of the room and flying out into the square. The shuttle dropped alarmingly, almost decapitating a statue of a man in uniform with his hands on his hips, before soaring upwards again and over the trees.

'Sorry 'bout that,' said Johnny's dad, blinking hard over and over again. 'Not quite got the hang of these controls.'

'You did brilliantly, Dad,' said Johnny. 'You saved us.'

'That's my job.'

'But where's Alf – my friend with the bowler hat?'

'Your android? He'd stopped working. He was on the sickbay floor.'

How stupid – Johnny realized he hadn't warned Alf about the fold. He must still have been working on Louise when it happened.

'I left the girl there to see what she could do,' continued Johnny's dad. 'The ship said you needed help. We should get back.'

'No, Dad – we've got to go and get Mum – straightaway.'

'Mary? You know where she is?'

'I think so,' said Johnny, who climbed into the front seat beside Bentley and reached out with his thoughts to the Bakerloo, taking over the controls. Instantly the ride became smoother. 'Watch out for this – it's a bit freaky till you get used to it,' and he turned on the shields. They flew disembodied over Big Ben with an invisible Bentley barking very loudly, picked up speed and within a couple of minutes they'd left the sprawl of south London behind and were setting down beside Wittonbury station. It was beginning to get light. The sedative was wearing off and Clara seemed slightly more awake, at least enough to wrap her arms around her father's neck as he picked her up out of the shuttle and carried her. Johnny and Bentley led the way, retracing the short route between the station to St Catharine's Hospital for the Criminally Insane. Though as Johnny drew nearer, he couldn't escape the feeling of disappointment in the pit of his stomach. He kept on walking but he could see it was pointless. They crossed the footbridge that had always been just before the main gate, only Sol's projections in the strategy room had been correct – instead of the hospital there were only fields. Johnny slumped down onto the top of the grassy bank next to the little brook.

Clara opened her eyes and smiled. 'Dad?' she said, as though she daren't really believe it.

'Oh, so my little princess is awake is she?' said her father. 'I hope that means I can put you down now.'

'OK, I guess,' said Clara.

Michael Mackintosh kissed her tenderly on the forehead and lowered her gently to the ground.

Clara stared at the brook and then towards Johnny, smiling. 'Remind you of anything?' she asked.

'What do you mean?'

'It's like the waterfall on Melania. Can't you see it's running uphill?'

When Johnny looked properly, he saw his sister was absolutely right. All the times he'd come here he'd never noticed.

'There's an opening here. In fact, it's right here,' she said, pointing, and as Johnny watched, the end of Clara's arm vanished into nothingness. 'Well, come on.'

Johnny got to his feet and followed Clara through the invisible gateway with Bentley and his dad, re-emerging into the familiar entrance of St Catharine's. Yet though the outline of the building was the same, what surrounded it was like nothing Johnny had ever seen. There was no Sussex countryside in the distance – there was nothing in the distance at all. There wasn't even any sky. In its place swirled a pink, purple and black vortex of nothingness. Bolts of lightning flashed continuously in the background, with peels of thunder to accompany them. Having crossed through the fold, Michael Mackintosh passed out. Johnny and Clara revived him and helped him back to his feet, each supporting him underneath one arm. He looked around for a moment, muttering, 'This is an evil place,' before they all hurried across the grounds, past the giant incinerator tower and towards the main entrance to the building. As they approached, Johnny shouted above the thunder. 'Bentley – find Mum.' They followed as the Old English sheepdog scampered around the corner of the building and came to a stop outside a window halfway along, wagging his tail enthusiastically.

Inside, lit up by the lightning, was Johnny's mum, exactly as she always looked, hooked up to a plethora of machines. Together Johnny and his dad were able to prise the window open, lift Clara and Bentley through and then climb inside.

Instinctively, Johnny and Clara hung back as their father walked across the room to his wife's bedside. 'What have they done to you, Mary?' he said. He bent over her face, stroked her limp blonde hair, kissed her tenderly on the lips and began shaking with tears. He turned to Johnny and Clara and beckoned them forward, so they each took hold of one of their mother's hands while he stroked her forehead and hair. Bentley came forward too, standing with his front paws on the end of the bed, his head at an angle as he whimpered quietly.

'Dad – they'll be here any minute,' said Johnny. 'We need to get Mum back to the Spirit of London. Sol can make her better . . . I'm sure.'

Michael Mackintosh turned towards Johnny, the tears still running down his cheeks and shook his head. 'Can't you feel it, son? Your mother's not meant to be here any more. She's in limbo – they're just using her, using her shell as a giant battery to power this place. And while they do that there's a part of her still trapped . . . imprisoned in this body.'

'Dad, you don't know what you're saying. We're taking her back to the ship.' Johnny spoke slowly, worried that his dad had stopped thinking straight again.

'I have to release her. I'm turning these machines off.'

'No you can't,' said Johnny. 'We need her back.'

'I wish there was another way,' said Michael Mackintosh.

'Stop!' shouted Johnny as his father walked over to the series of plugs on the wall. 'What about Clara? She needs a mum. She's never even met her.'

'It's OK, Johnny,' said Clara, staring across at her brother, eyes bulging with tears. 'Dad's right. And I have met her – don't you remember? This is what she asked us to do.'

Clara was clearly going mad too. Maybe their dad's condition was contagious. 'I won't let you,' shouted Johnny, as the door burst open and into the room came half a dozen krun, headed again by Stevens whose weapon was pointed firmly at Johnny's dad. Calmly the alien said, 'I would listen to your son if I were you, Mr Mackintosh. Move away from those switches.'

Unperturbed, Michael Mackintosh started pulling all the plugs from out of their sockets on the wall.

'You cannot seriously believe that turning off a few plugs has any real physical effect in this place,' Stevens continued. Johnny could see that only a few of the pieces of equipment were still showing anything on their displays.

'The machines aren't important,' replied Johnny's dad. 'It's the act of turning them off that matters. It means my wife can move on with my blessing. Ask yourself why it's getting dark outside. Why's everything going quiet?'

It was true – the thunder and lightning had slowed almost to a stop. Stevens looked quickly to the window and back. 'I ordered you to stop,' he said, but now there was a note of panic in his voice.

With the noise from outside almost gone, everyone could hear when the heartbeat monitor at the bedside started to emit a single continuous beep – for a few seconds it was the only sound in the room. Johnny's dad unplugged the very last piece of equipment and said, 'Go ahead – shoot. You can't hurt me any more.'

'Maybe not,' said Stevens, 'but I can hurt them.' He turned the weapon towards Clara, squeezed the trigger and fired.

'No!' shouted Michael Mackintosh, who flung himself forward into the path of the green beam. For a moment his body was suspended, brilliantly illuminated in mid-air, but then it slumped down lifeless on top of his wife. Bentley leapt up and fastened his jaws onto Stevens's throat. Everyone in the room seemed transfixed as krun and dog, both covered in blood, rolled across the floor. Stevens pushed Bentley off him and hissed the command, 'Kill them' to the other krun, before

336

wrapping his hands around the sheepdog's neck. The spell broken, the men in suits pointed their weapons at the two children. Johnny couldn't help shutting his eyes. He heard a body fall to the ground – they must have shot Clara first. Then there was another, and then several more.

He opened his eyes. Clara was standing nearby . . . they were still alive. It was very dark now, but he could just make out the bodies of all the krun, slumped on the floor, twitching very occasionally.

'We're almost cut off,' said Clara.

'What do you mean?' Johnny knew the words had come from his mouth, but it was as though someone else had spoken them. This couldn't be real. His mum and dad couldn't be dead. Not now.

'The krun can't function without the link to their queen. It's like what happened on Triton when they all stopped working.' Clara's voice sounded strangely flat.

'Good,' said Johnny. He'd never hated anything more than he hated the krun now.

'No it's not good. It's like at the football match – the Klein fold – when I trapped them in a pocket of hyperspace with no way out.' Johnny heard the words but they didn't sink in. Clara carried on. 'The power source keeping the gateway open from the inside isn't there any more. It's going to close. If we're going to get out we have to go now.' Though she said it, Clara didn't move.

Johnny didn't want to go anywhere either. It was as though they were both paralysed. But he also didn't want to look at the two bodies on the bed next to him. Instead he focused on the outlines of the krun, who were hardly moving at all now. He walked across to where Stevens lay and kicked his body off the bloodstained Bentley. He held the sheepdog in his hands and Bentley opened his eyes, before rolling his huge tongue across

Johnny's face. Johnny smiled weakly at the dog, lifting the grey and white hair out of Bentley's eyes.

'Look out,' screamed Clara. Stevens had forced himself up from the pool of blood he was lying in and, though shaking, tried to point his gun at Johnny. The alien fired wildly and Johnny ducked just in time as one of the energy bolts grazed his and Bentley's heads. Clara jumped on top of Stevens and grabbed his hair, forcing him to drop the weapon before passing out on the floor.

'He's still breathing,' she said. 'Something's keeping the link open – but only just or they'd all be awake. It's like a door that can't shut properly.'

'It's the tower,' said Johnny. 'The one in the grounds – I think it's a transmitter. It's got to be.' He didn't know how, but he knew he was right. Finally he made himself look at the bodies of his two parents slumped on the hospital bed. If it weren't for the odd ways his arms and legs were pointing, his dad might have been asleep. And even now, with the life-support machines switched off, his mum looked just as she'd looked for almost all his life. He walked forward and put a hand onto each of them. 'I don't want to leave them,' he said. 'Not now – not when we're together for the first time.'

'He saved me,' said Clara, from across the bed. She placed her head against her father's back and put her arms around him. 'I didn't think he even knew who I was, but he saved me.'

'That's what dads do. He said it was his job.'

'We can't let it be for nothing. We should get out while we can.' For the first time Clara seemed energized. She lifted herself off her father and walked around the bed to Johnny.

'What if they're not . . . dead,' said Johnny. 'What if Dad's just been knocked out?' He took hold of both arms and started shaking his father, trying to revive him. If he could just get all of them back to the Spirit of London it could still be OK. Clara put her arms around Johnny's waist, gently trying to pull him away, but he didn't care. He wasn't moving. Even if they were dead, he couldn't just leave them here on their own – leave their bodies in this dark, vile nothingness. Only it wasn't dark anymore. A soft white light was coming from behind. Johnny turned around to see a tall young woman, dressed all in silver, with shining silver eyes and long blonde hair that seemed to glow all on its own. It was the Diaquant.

'You came back,' said Clara, and the Diaquant stepped forward, took Johnny's sister in her arms, and held her tightly.

'It's all right, Johnny, my love,' said the glowing figure. 'He's with me now.' The Diaquant touched the lifeless hand of Michael Mackintosh. It was as though she was reaching inside him and, as she pulled, a shining white hand emerged from his body, not flesh and bone, but glowing with energy. Then came an arm, and then the rest of a shimmering version of the man Johnny remembered as his father, but as he'd looked years ago – dark-haired, fresh-faced and handsome.

The new Michael Macintosh glanced at his lifeless corpse on the bed, before he turned to meet the gaze of the Diaquant. 'Mary,' he said, and he hugged the beautiful woman before him, and the whole room filled with light and warmth.

Johnny looked first at the shining figures – engulfed in their light even Clara seemed to be glowing – and then back to his mother's body on the bed. And seeing his mum's face, he was reminded of another. She looked just the same as the Diaquant, aged and frail, after he'd first taken her from the tower on Atlantis. And finally he understood. The Diaquant he'd rescued from Atlantis. The one who'd sent them through time to the present day. It was her. She *was* his mother. She was the reason for everything. While he'd thought she was comatose in her hospital bed, she'd been watching over him all along. He turned away from the bed. 'Mum,' he said simply. He walked forward and joined the other three members of his family in an embrace.

'Listen to me, my children,' said the Diaquant. 'You must return to your world before the gateway closes.'

'But you're coming with us, aren't you?' asked Johnny. 'Both of you.'

The Diaquant stroked his hair tenderly while shaking her head. 'No, my love. From here on your father and I must take a separate path. There are different adventures ahead for all of us.'

'Will we see you again?' Clara asked.

'I hope so, my sweet,' said the Diaquant, smiling, but Johnny couldn't help thinking the smile looked forced. 'But now you must go. I've slowed time for you to reach the tower, but even so you must be quick. Johnny – it will be for you to supply the power to the gateway. Clara – you will have to prise it open and find your way back. When you're on the other side, always remember you did this together.'

'Goodbye, son,' said Johnny's dad, squeezing him tightly for one last time. 'Goodbye, princess,' he said, hugging Clara.

'Now go,' said the Diaquant, 'and don't look back.'

Released from their parents' grip, Johnny and Clara made for the door, together with Bentley, who seemed to understand that now was the time to leave. Clara followed Bentley through the door, but Johnny turned to take one last look at his parents. His mother, the Diaquant, had collapsed into his father's arms and was weeping uncontrollably.

'Johnny . . . come on,' said Clara, grabbing him and pulling him away into the corridor. They ran hand in hand as Bentley led the way towards the main entrance. Everywhere lay bodies of the krun, twitching very occasionally, that they had to jump over.

Out of the main doors, in almost total darkness, Johnny

sprinted towards the incinerator tower. Bentley and Clara ran on towards the empty cabin on the edge of the grounds – the edge of the void – while Johnny felt for a door, found one, opened it and stepped inside. The tower was hollow, but its inner walls glowed faintly red – it was made of Atlantean orichalcum. Johnny stood at its foot and stretched out both arms so they just reached to either side. As he touched the red walls, there was a crackle of electricity through his fingers. The tower hummed with a background rhythm – like the strange music he'd heard before in the grounds of the Imperial Palace. Johnny added a simple melody. A line of blue sparks spread from both his hands until it encircled him. Johnny raised his head and looked upwards, willing the song to move in that direction. Slowly, the circle of blue sparks began to rise above him, while another one formed in its place between his hands. Again, it rose up the column. He could feel the music beginning to flow through him, the exhilaration, as though this was what he'd been born to do. Another pulse of energy left his fingertips and rose up, then another.

'C'mon Johnny – it's open,' shouted Clara in the distance, but Johnny didn't want to leave. Not just yet. Not when he could do this. The pulses were almost continuous now, lighting up the insides of the tower with a brilliant blue glow. The music was becoming ever faster and more complex. Clara shouted again. 'Quickly, Johnny – they're coming.'

Bentley entered through the open doorway and grabbed Johnny's foot, tugging at it for him to move. The spell was broken. Johnny took his hands away from the walls, and realized his fingers and palms were badly burnt. Energy bolts were flying across the grounds outside. Johnny followed Bentley back out of the door, to see hundreds of krun running towards them across the field, firing their weapons.

He sped towards where Clara was – to where he could now see beyond the void to the little stone footbridge. A bolt from the krun almost hit him, causing him to do a forward roll on the lawn before getting to his feet and carrying on. He and Bentley reached Clara, sitting cross-legged on the ground in front of the opening. Johnny picked her up, despite the waves of pain that surged through his burnt hands, and carried his sister through to the other side. Bentley turned and barked defiantly at the advancing krun. Johnny couldn't go on any more and dropped Clara down on the grassy bank by the side of the bridge. He looked back – the entrance was beginning to close.

'Bentley,' he called weakly, and the dog turned and leapt through the air as space itself folded shut around him. The ball of grey and white landed clumsily on the bank and couldn't stop himself rolling straight down into the little brook below. The water was flowing the right way now. Johnny turned. The gateway had closed. There were no more krun – just the rolling green and yellow fields of the Sussex countryside.

Clara put her arms around him. There were hot tears pouring down both their faces – Johnny didn't know whether they were hers or his. 'It's not fair,' he heard himself saying. 'I thought we could be a proper family, all together. Now we're so alone.'

Clara pulled herself away and looked at him through fiercely gleaming, teary blue and silver eyes. 'We're not alone,' she said. 'We'll never be alone. We've got each other,' and she hugged him and he hugged her and they sat together in each other's arms on the grassy bank.

Finally, after it seemed hours had passed, Johnny pulled himself away, got to his feet and asked, 'Remember what Mum said to us? We've got our own adventures ahead. We should go home.' And together, two blond children and a bedraggled Old English sheepdog walked back towards Wittonbury station and climbed into the black London taxi that was waiting.

Acknowledgements

It's impossible to write in isolation. From the earliest of ages I devoured book after book and it is inevitable that some of what I read will have resurfaced onto the pages of Johnny Mackintosh. Into the mix, I have tried to sprinkle traces of the science I learnt later, to make Johnny's universe as plausible as I could while still fitting the story. The greatest of all scientists, Isaac Newton, once wrote, 'If I have seen further it is by standing on the shoulders of giants.' So to all those authors who gave me a much needed leg up, I offer my heartfelt thanks. Sadly, I was wearing neither glasses nor contacts that day, so my vision will have fallen well short of those I admire most.

My friends and family have been a never-ending source of inspiration and support. Many have read draft after draft, helping nudge the story in the right direction and encouraging me to keep writing when the distractions that repeatedly stop me completing anything threatened to overwhelm me. Special mentions must go to Craig, Donna, Stacy and, especially, to Jane. And, if Craig hadn't started writing his own books, the competitive monster within me would have lain dormant and Johnny would never have even begun his adventures.

Finally, a book is nothing without a publisher behind it and I am privileged to have had the backing of the very best. Having witnessed the support they have given me, it is no surprise that Quercus has quickly established itself as a player to be reckoned with and there could be no better home from which to launch the Johnny Mackintosh stories. In children's editorial, Suzy Jenvey's belief in the book and my writing humbled me from the outset. When she moved on, I was privileged to have Roisin Heycock and Parul Bavishi take up the reins, improving the book and steering it to publication with immense skill and sensitivity. At their instigation, Mandy Norman created the magnificent cover design. Lucie Ewin of Rook Books devised the beautiful text design and managed the whole project superbly, as well as indulging all my (ridiculous) whims. Christine Kloet, the copy-editor, showed me what a clumsy job I have made of other people's manuscripts over the years – I'm thankful to her for honing my prose and removing several embarrassing errors that would otherwise have slipped through, and I'm grateful to Paul Lee the proofreader who found still more. Anthony Cheetham, who I thought would have far more important things to do with his time, has been an unstinting champion of Johnny Mackintosh throughout, while Mark Smith has been the most capable, helpful and approachable of CEOs.

Of course I have omitted countless names here. So many people work on a book nowadays that I cannot list everyone. And, at the time of writing, some crucial jobs have not even begun, so I am yet to encounter those involved. To all, I crave their indulgence and offer my thanks. My final mention, however, must be for Wayne Davies. Few people, can be so fortunate as to have a friend found a publishing house that later becomes the stable for their own books. I would like to think that, without Quercus, Johnny Mackintosh would have taken off elsewhere, but away from Wayne and Mark's company the experience for me, as author, would have paled in comparison.